Stone Bride

Stone Bride

Book One
in *The Great Land Fantasy Series*

D.P. Benjamin

ELEVATION PRESS

Stone Bride
By D.P. Benjamin

Copyright © 2022 by Donald Paul Benjamin

For more information, please see *About the Author* at the close of this book and visit benjaminauthor.com

Cover painting by Pete Denzin.
Cover design, interior design, and formatting by Donna Marie Benjamin.

All characters and events in this novel, other than those clearly in the public domain, are fictitious and any resemblance to real persons, living or dead, is purely coincidental.

All rights reserved. No part of this publication may be reproduced, distributed, or transmitted in any form or by any means, including photocopying, recording, or other electronic or mechanical methods, without the prior written permission of the publisher, except in the case of brief quotations embodied in critical reviews and certain other noncommercial uses permitted by copyright law. For permission requests, write to the publisher, addressed "Attention: Permission Coordinator," at the address below:

Elevation Press
P.O. Box 603
Cedaredge, CO 81413

Ordering information: Quantity sales. Special discounts are available on quantity purchases by book clubs, corporations, associations, and others. For details, contact the publisher at the address above.

ISBN 978-0-932624-10-9

1. Main category—[Fantasy] 2. Other categories—[Epic Fantasy]—[Paranormal Romance]

ELEVATION PRESS

© 2022
Elevation Press
Cedaredge, Colorado
www.elevation-press-books.com

For information on services offered by Elevation Press, please see the final page of this book.

Acknowledgments

Stone Bride is my first fantasy novel—the first of many, I hope. This book was first published to coincide with the occasion of my birthday and, I have to say, the years have passed by at an implausible pace. And yet, here I am: seven years past seventy and still—as Leonard Cohen once remarked—just a kid with a crazy dream.

Those who follow my work as a mystery novelist will recall that I have a habit of basing my strong female characters on my dearly-departed sister, Ann Benjamin, who died in 1942 as a stillborn infant.

My mother was devastated by the loss.

When pregnant, she'd created a scrapbook composed of magazine clippings. The book was filled with images of mothers and babies, visiting a duck pond; engrossed in story time; playing house; and taking walks. She kept that scrapbook for decades, lovingly stored in our family cedar-chest, until my brother's wife gave birth to a baby girl. On that happy day, my mother retrieved her precious scrapbook and eventually shared it with Pamela Carol Benjamin, her new granddaughter.

Ann's death also apparently inspired my mother, a registered nurse, to ask to be assigned to the local hospital's "preemie ward." She never spoke directly of her reasons for taking on the heart-wrenching task of working with premature babies. I like to believe that caring for such at-risk infants—celebrating those who lived and mourning those who didn't—helped my mother cope with her own loss and, perhaps, made her feel somehow connected to her dead daughter.

I never knew my sister, who died three years before I was born. But I like to think Ann would have grown up to embody my mother's most endearing traits: her sense of fun and humor; her commitment to fair-play and justice; her insatiable curiosity; and her tireless work ethic. To keep the memory of my mother and my sister alive, I continue to base my heroes on the two most important females in my life: my mother, Carol Ruth, and my sister, Ann.

Their spirits endure in the women of *Stone Bride*.

Speaking of significant influences, for over half a century my dear friends, Pete and Colleen Denzin, have encouraged me to pursue my artistic endeavors and dreams of authorship. I am particularly indebted to Pete whose inspiring artwork appears on the Stone Bride cover. Other more recent acquaintances have also contributed to this novel. Prior to publication, I rely on "beta readers" to review early manuscripts. The concept originated with the computer industry which relies on beta users to test and refine new products and software. My intrepid first-look readers greatly improve the story with their valuable insights and suggestions. I'd be, quite frankly, lost without them. I gratefully acknowledge the fine work of readers Lon Helmick, Wendy Olson, Donna Marie Benjamin, Ann Boelter, Stacy Malmgren, and Mckenzie Moore.

In closing, I must thank my dear wife, Donna Marie, for her unflagging good humor, her patient support, and unparalleled expertise in formatting my novels and designing compelling book covers. She is the joy of my life and an unbending source of moral support who, every day, gives me the invaluable gift of time to write. I am truly blessed.

For a list of future titles in *The Great Land Fantasy Series,* please see the closing pages of this book.

Donald Paul Benjamin/June 8, 2022

**For my dearly-departed mother
and my angelic sister.**

*"So long as men can breathe, or eyes can see,
So long lives this, and this gives life to thee."*
—Wm. Shakespeare

Prologue

Princess Ann of Middlemount is about to die.

The war is lost. The usurpers have made it abundantly clear that no hint of the old kingdom will be allowed to linger. The last of the Middlemount rulers must be exterminated. The final vestige of the Wolfkind race must disappear. In an hour, the Princess will be executed—burned first, then chopped to pieces. She is to be obliterated and efficiently erased as if she never existed. Each gruesome step is required to kill a Wolfkind, and the completion of that deadly process seems inevitable.

The Princess allows herself a fleeting smile.

During the final days of the war, she'd unwittingly aided the usurpers in their quest to purge all memory of her kind. She herself had pulled down the family statues, dismantled the immense iron horses and riders, and cast the broken bits into the furnaces of war. It had been a futile attempt to repel the invaders—this last-ditch scavenging of iron—a desperate effort to forge more weapons to defend the Middlemount castle.

The Princess thinks then of the little iron garden angel—the image of a human girl in prayer which she'd cherished when she was a cub. How she'd loved that inanimate statue, spending hours sitting on a garden bench beside the imaginary girl—telling stories, sharing secrets. And yet, by her own command, it too had been condemned to the furnace.

Recalling her folly, Ann's thoughts betray her. *What a fool I've been! What an arrogant fool! Arrogant to believe in the supremacy of my powers. Instead, my own idiotic faults and deadly errors lost the war, caused the death of my mate, led to my capture, and doomed me to this place of final judgment.*

Cursing her folly, Ann voices her rage in a prolonged rumbling growl. The captive's piercing snarl silences the crowd which had been gathering all morning, filling the town square to witness her end. Pricking her ears, she listens closely and hears the multitude judging her—the vanquished soldier. She wonders what they make of their captured Wolfkind Princess. Few have seen her face. She probably appears smaller without her plumed helmet, but she imagines her tall and solid body, still clad in armor, must impress them. She will yet appear strong, still formidable.

Formidable, but doomed.

Ann hears the whispers of the crowd. She is their former Princess now, a fading hero, who in the space of three tumultuous weeks, has been deposed, captured, and declared a dangerous rebel by the usurpers—the treacherous Fishals. Without warning, advancing armies had swept in from the north. Aided by magic, traitorous intrigues, and daunting weapons, the merciless force had outflanked, overwhelmed, and destroyed the Middlemount rulers—all but her.

Now her fickle subjects have come to see the last Princess of the deposed realm lashed to the Maypole, buried to the waist in firewood, awaiting her fate. An ordinary being might despair as she waited there, pinioned to that metal pole like a pig for roasting.

Like a pig, Ann tells herself.

Held fast by sturdy ropes, she is bound so tightly that coarse fibers penetrate the knee and elbow joints of her body armor and press cold metal against her hide. The Princess smiles again. The metal of her armor will not be cold much longer.

She moves her head—with effort for her neck is tightly bound with the same thick ropes which encompass her body. She strains and glances to either side. Cauldrons of fat are burning in the courtyard below, three cauldrons to the left and three to the right. Above the flames, dark smoke rises to smudge the clear blue sky.

Stone Bride

An ordinary being might despair.

Four tall men stand at each cauldron. One man holds an axe, the other three hold stout wooden torches, the upper tips slathered with a thick nodule of grease—like giant matches, as yet unlit. When the order is given, men will swirl their torches in the cauldrons, then rush forward to ignite the tinder-dry pyre and spark a terrible bonfire that will roast the Princess alive in her own armor. When the fire dies down, the axmen will extract the Princess' burnt body from the smoldering armor and hack her corpse to pieces.

It will be a very thorough execution.

That thought should give an ordinary being pause, might cause a coward to scream for mercy, and might even inspire the condemned to pray. Princess Ann of Middlemount is certainly condemned, but she is neither ordinary nor a coward. And she'd already said prayers. One might say she had exhausted them.

She'd prayed the moment she awoke in the grip of the foul potion which rendered her helpless—the witch's doing no doubt. Prayed as she lay paralyzed while they bound her with ropes and chains. Prayed while they propped her up in a hay wagon and paraded her through narrow streets to the town square. She'd prayed when they removed the chains but left the ropes in place. Prayed as they struggled to bear the bulk of her up crude stairs and onto the platform. Moreover, she'd prayed while they pinned her against the Maypole and coiled more ropes around her armored body.

Ann had prayed silently to El. Each prayer was answered, and each answer was *no*. Could she return to the past to undo her mistakes? *No.* Could her strength be restored so she could break free to kill her enemies? *No.* Could she restore her kingdom by magic? *No.*

She'd continued to pray when they piled kindling and branches around her, laughing as they did so. She'd prayed as they encircled her lower torso with thatch and wood, making jokes about roasted pheasant and the results of the meeting between flesh and flame. She'd prayed silently, not wishing her captors to hear and think her weak. She had prayed to seek vengeance, prayed to alter her fate.

Each time the answer was *no*.

The Princess remembers these setbacks as her tormentors weave their web of wood. At last, they finish their noxious work and she is alone on the platform. A wave of gloom washes over her and she closes her eyes to fashion one final prayer which is interrupted when El speaks to her in the voice of the mind.

I have told you no. Why do you persist? Have you learned nothing from your errors? It is unbecoming to question your fate. Cease your lamentations, lamb. Be still and listen.

And so, the Princess prays that she can be still enough and wise enough to listen to her deity and that prayer is answered yes. Brimming with hope, Ann looks upward and communes with the sky, sending thoughts aloft, her creator's voice responding for the Princess' ears alone.

This life which you seek to prolong is already an old dream.

El loves to speak in riddles, she told herself.

Discipline your mind, El cautioned her. *You must bid this life farewell. Another life awaits you.*

"In Velyn? With Destin?" she asked aloud.

Be still and listen.

"Yes, my El."

It is not your time for Velyn. As for your mate, only have faith, child, and your lost love may yet be your love again. But now is not the moment for matters of the flesh. Your time is short, so listen.

"Yes, my El."

The flames of today will not reach you. To escape you must call to me three times. Each time the tower clock strikes a quarter-hour, you must call to me with your most strident howl. Send me one, then another, then one more. Hearing your third cry, I will send my storm and you will fly from this place. You will no longer be Middlemount. That kingdom must be born anew. You will still be my Princess and you shall have the memories and the thinking of my Princess and—after a fashion—her power. You will retain vestiges of Wolfkind, but you will be much changed. And listen well, my child—when you next awake—you must forsake the name of Middlemount. You must take another name, a new surname.

"What name, my El?"

A name of your choice. A name to chart your new life—to fulfill our new dream. You must choose a new name and choose wisely.

"How shall I choose?"

The choice will become clear to you. I leave you now, but I am with you always. When next we meet, I will come to you in disguise. I will say to you 'the wolf dies' and you must say to me 'the lamb is born.' Repeat what I have said.

"The wolf dies, the lamb is born."

Remember all I say and have faith and prepare for your salvation.

The Princess sighs as the voice of El fades and the smoke of the cauldrons reaches her nostrils. Her faith is about to be tested—sorely tested. Within seconds, the clock strikes the quarter hour and she gives voice to her first howl.

Far above the town square, housed in his sanctum, her foe, the Lord Mayor N'dependee, hears that strident call. Hears it and wonders. The mayor has been clever. He's taken precautions to nullify the vanquished Princess. The rumors describing her Wolfkind powers were undoubtedly exaggerated, but the mayor is taking no chances.

The mayor is shrewd but only as a politician. There are boundaries to his cleverness and, in staging this hasty public execution, the Lord Mayor has been careful in some things, but careless in others. Truly, he had subdued the Princess with a powerful potion. He'd kept the last of the Middlemounts imprisoned in her own armor and apart from the ground to remove the sting of her lethal power. He'd bound the Princess securely. But he'd failed to blindfold her, or gag her, or stop her ears. These were grave errors, for—though denied motion and the magic of her connection to the earth—the Princess retained her other senses. The Lord Mayor has been lax in failing to fetter the throat, the eyes, and ears of his intended victim.

In fairness, it is the Lord Mayor's first execution, so he might be forgiven for overlooking certain details. In the main, it must be said that N'dependee has gotten much of it right. Using the Maypole was an inspired idea since, in all the town, it stands alone as the only remnant of metal which had not been melted down to forge sword and shield. Moreover, the pole is strategic, occupying as it does the very center of the town square. Everyone knew the Maypole. Everyone knew its location. Thus, it was a small matter to inform the population of the site of the execution and issue an explicit edict demanding their attendance.

The echo of Ann's plaintive cry fades. In the following hush, the sound of the tower's clockworks can be heard, grinding their way toward the next quarter hour. That unrelenting sound fills the ears of those in the square and the crowd turns their collective faces toward the clock which squats like an indifferent Sphinx above the high windows of the town hall. The Princess follows their gaze and understands what the townspeople see there.

Framed in the window, is the person of the Lord Mayor N'dependee—may his name live in infamy. Scathing nicknames for the mayor had been secretly circulating for decades and his recent treachery has spawned a new crop. Fresh insults are surfacing now, though as private thoughts only. The Princess hears the condescending names swirling in the unspoken thoughts of the crowd. Some call the mayor *golden traitor*. Others label him *lapdog of the usurpers*. The boldest use the ever-popular diminutive *biscuit*—a tag which is rumored to send the mayor into an apoplectic rage.

And yet, despite the subtext of insults running through the minds of the crowd this morning, Ann watches with scorn as the assembled masses face the tower window to grin and touch their caps. In response to the crowd's outward display of fealty, she observes the mayor nodding regally in return. Clad in ostentatious robes of office and wearing a ridiculously flamboyant chain of authority, the overweight bureaucrat is striving to project a serene self-assurance. It is a false confidence, for—even at a distance—Ann's remarkable Wolfkind vision perceives a drop of perspiration on N'dependee's troubled brow.

The Lord Mayor is nervous and impatient. Time passes much too slowly. But he has strict instructions not to burn the captive Princess until the chimes sound noon. It is now a quarter past eleven-of-the-clock. An eternity seems to linger as the mayor waits for the chimes to measure the passing moments.

When at last the clock strikes half-past, Ann howls a second time, spawning a cascade of visceral echoes which vibrate the cobblestones of the square and penetrate the venerable chinks of the ancient town walls. While the crowd grows uneasy and the Lord Mayor sweats, the Princess remains in full possession of her senses. She can call upon her deity, she can see and anticipate her executioners, and she can hear the voices—even the thoughts—of all around her.

Unaware of his captive's residual powers, the Lord Mayor surveys the crowd, hoping this compelled assembly of fickle citizens won't abruptly change allegiances and devolve into an unruly mob. The cautious bureaucrat had favored a less conspicuous execution, but the witch had insisted a crowd be on hand to witness the performance. The Lord Mayor shudders as he recalls his recent, and wholly unnerving, encounter with the witch.

"Why must I do these things?" the Lord Mayor had asked the witch.

"Because I wish it," Ahoo had answered. "The subject is closed."

What could the mayor do but comply? The witch was fond of ending her arguments with "the subject is closed." Ahoo was also fond of turning those who dared utter a retort into insects which she threatened to grind into the cobblestones with the toe of her iron boots. The fact that she made such threats, but never followed through, did little to lessen the feelings of intimidation which gripped her listeners. It was rumored that Ahoo was an old-world witch and therefore could not kill. On the other hand, there were other, equally saliant rumors that she used her powers to enlist others to do the killing. Better to play it safe and say nothing once the witch had closed the subject.

Ahoo had come. Ahoo had spoken and that, the mayor had decided, was that. The witch had directed the Lord Mayor to employ carpenters with orders to erect a raised platform around the pole. The purpose of this precaution was to separate the Princess from the earth, which was her ally, and to position the victim on top to provide spectators with an unobstructed view of the proceedings. The mayor had also been ordered to recruit strong men to lash the Princess to the pole and he'd been obliged to compel the Dung people—who had no love for the Princess—to heap thatch, kindling, and a final layer of wrist-sized branches upon the execution pyre. If N'dependee did his part, Ann would be precisely where the witch wanted the Princess: above the ground, on prominent display, and embedded in a waist-high cocoon of wood from which there was no escape. The final details of the execution the witch left to N'dependee. Surely the fool could manage the fire and the chopping. Even the lowliest farmwife could manage such a recipe.

Having recalled the witch's instructions, the Lord Mayor returns his attention to the present, unaware that Ann continues to probe his mind. The Princess watches the traitor smile and hears him comment to his chancellor that, "All is well. Our captive appears ready for consumption, like a spoonful of chocolate atop a rounded wooden tart."

The chancellor shudders with disgust as the clock strikes the final quarter before noon. The squeamish bureaucrat feels ill and might have been on the verge of raising a belated objection to the execution had Princess Ann not suddenly silenced him with a third and most powerful blood-curdling howl. The Lord Mayor sneers as echoes of the captive Wolfkind's most recent cry reach his ears.

"That makes three," the mayor crows. "Thrice does the wretched creature lament her end. Hear her plaintive wailing."

"Perhaps," the chancellor ventures, "she has slipped into madness." Then the nervous man adds in a seemingly unnecessary whisper, for they are alone in the tower. "Slipped wholly into madness—like her father."

"Very like," agrees the mayor in a whispered reply.

Why whisper?

Why give credence to the Princess' legendary powers? The two collaborators are thirty yards away and two stories above the square. So far removed that even a Princess rumored to have the enhanced senses of the animals would be hard-pressed to hear their conversation. If her powers are as strong as the people claim, how had the usurpers managed to defeat the vaunted

Wolfkind warrior? How had the Lord Mayor—with the witch Ahoo's help—managed to truss her up like a sacrificial beast?

To believe the Princess possesses the hearing and sight of a hovering hawk, that she draws power from the earth which allows her to move gigantic boulders, that she can read thoughts—it was nonsense!

And yet, Ann of Middlemount hears their thoughts and, what is more, she uses her own thoughts to infect the collaborators with a message which they feel in their very bones.

I'm coming back, her unspoken message conveys the icy promise.

The vibration of this oath courses like a sudden chill through the frightened bureaucrats and N'dependee—though it is not yet noon—shouts, "Torches!"

But it is too late.

A massive whirlwind descends from the cloudless sky—a cosmic gale which flings the torchbearers and axmen aside, upends the flaming cauldrons, and ignites the wood. The startled crowd flees as the Princess' wooden cocoon explodes, sending smoldering thatch, smoking kindling, and blazing branches arcing outward like the whirling arms of a demented pinwheel. Flames scatter in every direction until the burning debris strikes the far walls and splinters to dust.

The wind slackens and absolute silence reigns in the empty courtyard until the chimes strike noon. From the tower, the mayor and the chancellor bear witness as the end unfolds like a waking dream. On the twelfth stroke, the sky darkens and a cascade of rain pummels the courtyard. Piercing thunder shakes the town to its very foundations and a blinding flash of lightning hammers the Maypole. The prisoner shudders, then pitches forward, bursting the ropes. With a crash, the heavy Wolfkind armor sprawls noisily upon the cobblestones—a crumpled pile of metal and utterly empty.

Chapter 1

Awakening

Magic and religion often mingle, and both require an arduous mixture of conjuring and faith.

The power which El invoked to rescue the condemned Wolfkind from her ordeal had greatly sapped the strength of the deity. Thus, El was at rest and recuperating when the liberated Princess was whisked away and delivered to her new life.

The next morning and miles away, uncertain that her appearance would be sufficiently changed to deceive others, Ann arose from her bed of straw. Stubbing her toe on an obstacle, she reached down to discover her discarded shield. When the soldiers had seized her, the Middlemount shield must have been kicked under the straw and forgotten. Or perhaps one of the more enterprising villains had hidden it there, hoping to retrieve and sell it later.

Regardless of how the shield came to be there, its presence confirmed that the Princess had been returned to the scene of her ignoble capture. The familiar shield was as she last recalled it, caked with the mud and blood of battle, the Middlemount crest just barely visible in a dented upper corner. Hopeful that other vestiges of her armaments were likewise concealed, she pawed through the straw.

No sword, she thought. *No battle-axe, of course. Not even a trifling dagger. Not one single offensive weapon. Only the shield, nothing more.*

Taking up the lone souvenir of her downfall, she used her naked forearm to burnish a viewing spot on the pitted surface of the mud-caked shield. Her smooth, pink arm and the shining face which smiled back at her in the dim light certainly looked unfamiliar. To be certain, she picked up the shield and walked out of the dark stable and into the sunlight.

It was apparently El's will that she should be lifted from the town square, transformed, and transported here to this unremarkable rural hovel—to the very spot where she'd been betrayed and apprehended only three days past.

It was early, not yet eight-of-the-clock, and not yet warm enough to stand naked for long in the crisp morning air. But Ann persisted until she'd gazed at her reflection in the shield from every angle, turning her bald head this way and that, marveling at her flattened face, even tilting the makeshift mirror downward to study her new, hairless torso. She smiled upon seeing her unusually smooth and firm breasts and her thinner but still strong arms and legs. But she frowned at the shock of her smallish feet.

Somehow, through El's intervention, she had been converted from a sturdy Wolfkind to a somewhat ordinary human female—albeit one who was, top to bottom, as hairless as a skinned rabbit. If ever the opportunity arose, she would have to ask her deity why her new identity lacked the luxurious curly locks she'd observed on other humans. For the moment, she continued to study her reflection until a peculiar thought crept into her smooth, naked head.

I wonder, thought the last Princess of Middlemount. *Suppose the little garden angel—my imaginary playmate—had been real and had grown to womanhood. Might she have taken this form? Have I become that person? Certainly, I am no angel—as I understand the human vision of such creatures. And yet—*

A chill ran through her as she simultaneously savored the thought of personifying her fanciful angel while also mourning the loss of her former Wolfkind self. She had died—what else could one call it but "died?" Yesterday she'd been a sturdy specimen of vigorous Wolfkind, a Princess of the animal-folk, heir to the Middlemount kingdom, and wearing the heavy armor of her forebearers. Then—in El's fantastic flash of weather—she'd been robbed of her armor and reborn in a rural stable: taller than before but clearly less massive.

And yet, she thought, *such ridiculous appendages!*

She thrust the tall shield onto the hard-packed earth, standing it on edge, and looked again at her seemingly inadequate feet.

"I see you have become already a typical woman—obsessed with her appearance."

Ann flinched and involuntarily pushed her knees together and covered her crotch with one pink hairless hand and strove to obscure her breasts with her other hand and forearm. She felt a rush of blood surging up her neck to redden her face.

"And modest as well! Excellent! I am most pleased with the result of my turbulent deliverance!"

"Will you show yourself?" shouted Ann. She was angry but also confused. She recognized the voice and yet—

I am here, Majesty, the thought reached her.

Ann scanned the farmyard but could see only the rustic stable, a primitive corral, a substantial tree, and a stone well—nothing alive except a fat donkey tied to the outer railing of the corral.

"Surely not—" Ann laughed.

Look up, my Princess!

Reluctantly, Ann released one hand from her crotch and shaded her eyes to look up into the bright sky. A coal black raven floated on the morning air.

"Of course," Ann said. "You were always fond of looking down on others."

"Only too true," said Migral as he landed, in the form of a raven, on the crossbeam of the water-well and set about preening.

"And I see your vanity has survived intact," added Ann. "You vainly groom yourself *and* take credit for El's storm."

"El may be our deity, but I still control the clouds. And this," said Migral plucking an uncooperative feather, "is not vanity." He shook his dark head and the feather floated away. "My preening is merely instinctive. I act as the raven because I must not appear unlike my brethren. I must blend in, be nothing but another ebony bird in a nameless flock."

"And where is your sheltering flock now, my conspicuous friend?"

"Where-away on the wing, I fancy. I'll join them soon enough, just as you yourself must now join your new race."

"If my memory serves—and it has been given quite a jolt by my escape from the pyre—these humans you and El are so keen on having me join do not go about in public without their—shall we call it—their armor."

"You ought not to call that abomination upon which the golden traitor most recently pinioned you a 'pyre.' It gives N'dependee's treachery too elegant a name. Pyres are constructed to honor the dead. You, if you will recall, were about to be put to the flames while still alive."

"I *stand* corrected," said Ann as she stood erect and placed her newly-formed hands on her well-rounded hips. The Princess grinned as she realized her conversation with her old comrade had so diminished her instinctive human embarrassment that she no longer felt compelled to conceal her nakedness.

"Better and better. You are exhibiting human pride now with your proud stance. Very convincing. And your 'I stand corrected' comment. Very droll. It might pass for what humans call a sense of humor. You'll do. Yes, I believe you'll do. As for your 'armor,' there'll be nothing so grand for you in this life. You and I are no longer soldiers, my friend. I am a sky acrobat and spawner of storms and messenger to our deity, and you have become a peasant—albeit an incredibly powerful peasant with—shall we say—potential."

Potential? Ann thought as though she'd never heard the word.

"Yes," said Migral, smoothly intercepting his comrade's thought. "But quickly now, they are coming! Move with all speed! Dispose of the shield—into the well! No time to return to the stable to clothe yourself—drop the bucket in after the shield, haul up water, and pretend to bathe! Swiftly now or you'll find yourself back in the fire and our hopes burning with it!" Voicing a final entreaty to hurry, which devolved into a plaintive caw, the raven Migral took wing.

Pleased to find that her lightning reflexes remained intact, Ann rapidly scooped up the shield and, though reluctant to part with it, she raised this final token of Middlemount and flung it down the well. Following the discarded shield with the wooden bucket and its appended rope, she swiftly cranked the windlass to retrieve water. It was a matter of moments from Migral's warning until Ann was no longer alone. But her reactions had been rapid—so swift that she repeated the motion of retrieving water and doused herself a second time before a troop of riders topped the hill behind the stable and galloped swiftly toward her.

"Wretched peasant!" shouted the nearest rider, an officer no doubt, for the broad-shouldered woman wore the golden sash and violet plume of leadership. "Stand fast!"

The riders were clad in Fishal uniforms and carried the fearsome firesticks which had overcome the Middlemount defenders. Ann could see the wooden stocks of long muskets jutting from their saddle scabbards. A half dozen of the riders also wore shorter powder weapons in holsters mounted on belts around their waists. With such weapons and larger devices, the Fishals had over-matched the swords and arrows of Middlemount. Muskets, pistols, and cannon—the Princess and her warriors had learned a new vocabulary of war, but learned it too late.

There were fourteen riders in all, each astride a tall, burgundy-colored horse—a congregation of sturdy stallions which Ann recognized as Middlemount stock. Seeing the pilfered animals kindled her anger and her pink face involuntarily ignited to a conspicuous shade of crimson—an emotional response which the officer misinterpreted.

"Stifle your shyness, peasant, your nakedness is nothing to us. Nothing we have not seen before, eh men? Naked as a jay-bird and bald as an egg to boot—what won't these peasants do to muddle their appearance? What purpose to shave one's head? A religious sacrifice no doubt—blind, superstitious fools." For a moment Ann and the troop stared at one another. Then the officer said in a matter-of-fact tone which suggested she was bored with the situation, "Seize the wench."

Two soldiers dismounted, laughing heartily as the other horsemen guffawed and the officer grinned. The men strode menacingly forward. They were at least as tall as Ann and muscular. Each seized an arm as they herded their captive forward. It was all the former Princess could do to resist her rising urge to wrest free from their grip, kill them both by smashing their grinning heads together, and then savage the officer and slash through the other troops. It would only take a matter of seconds to slay these men, but a harsh raven call sounding from above caused Ann to suppress her fury.

Instead, the erstwhile Wolfkind quelled her anger and allowed herself to be manhandled as she was forced to her knees on the ground before the officer and her prancing horse. Then, as the officer prattled on, Ann decided to test the scope of her new human senses. As Wolfkind, she had been able to hear the thoughts of others.

Is that ability still mine? she wondered.

Focusing on the officer's golden sash of leadership, Ann ignored the stout woman's spoken words. She pushed beyond them, seeking to reach her enemy's thoughts. But she found it impossible to simultaneously listen to the woman's chatter while also accessing her unspoken thoughts.

"I'll ask again," the officer said aloud. "Have you seen a Wolfkind or any of the upright animal-folk here about?"

The speaker's plume proclaimed her a major and, though she could not reach the woman's thoughts, Ann sensed the pompous Fishal was new to command. For, though her outward talk was bold, the officer's nervous mannerisms suggested she masked an inner terror. Ann's ability to achieve this insight seemed to have uncovered a unique human vulnerability—a flaw of using bluster to disguise fear—a flaw which the Princess was willing to explore.

"Well, speak up, wench! Or shall I have my corporal loosen your tongue by discharging his pistol into your leg?"

Mindful of her new role as subservient, Ann lowered her eyes and spoke softly.

"Please, your worship, I have seen none of the creatures you seek."

The major stirred in her saddle and Ann realized the Fishal officer would judge her articulate response to be too well-spoken for a peasant.

Ah, Ann decided, *time for some playacting.*

"Tis a'fear my lard what makes me talk'a so," Ann mumbled, hoping to mimic a rustic accent. "I shakes and kinnot find me words when I thinks of the wolf and such a beast be so near about as your worship sez."

Hearing the diction of the countryside, the major chortled causing Ann to involuntarily raise her head. In her enemy's rotund face, the Princess detected a cavalcade of emotions—not only fear, but also anger and jealousy.

This unlovely woman is threatened by my looks, thought Ann.

Raising her whip, the officer seemed poised to strike the captive before her. Only Ann's dramatic show of cringing stayed the woman's hand.

"See how the bitch ducks without she has even received the blow? What a pack of cowardly dunces we have conquered! Release her and let's away or—" The major paused and tapped the whip handle against her teeth while a sardonic smile animated her features. "Better still—toss her down yonder well as a lesson in Fishal justice."

The riders roared their approval as the two men dragged Ann to the well and cast her in, throwing the bucket after her for good measure. The odious Fishals roared even louder to hear echoes as the falling woman collided with the stone walls on her way down and they cheered when a tremendous splash sounded at the bottom of the well. In falling, Ann had scraped an arm, but was otherwise unhurt as she floated in the cool water and listened to the riders above.

"Odd that she did not cry out," said the major.

"Too stupid or too frightened to scream no doubt, sir," observed her corporal.

"No doubt," agreed the major. "Come, Mika, seize that donkey! And, Seaton, I feel a draft! Let us have a fire!"

"Yes, sir!"

Ann heard the donkey braying vociferously—apparently resisting being taken. When she could no longer hear the departing horses, the Princess took an expansive breath and submerged beneath the icy water, hoping she could retrieve the shield. This desperate swim might be a fool's errand, for she had no firm idea of the thing's utility in the new life which awaited her. And yet, she sought it because it was a connection with her past—the only connection so far as she knew and, perhaps, the last.

With powerful strokes, she swam deep, emerging from the well shaft into what appeared to be the underwater expanse of a bottomless aquifer. The subterranean current was strong and it was all she could do to reverse her swim lest she be swept to oblivion. Like the war, the shield was lost—swept away by a powerful force, a leaf in the grip of a cascading stream.

Disheartened and in need of air, she abandoned her search, returned to the shaft, and kicked upward. Surfacing to find the bucket floating languidly, she was tempted to take advantage of the rope, but decided to test her strength by using her bare hands to climb, inch-by-inch out of the well.

Above, she found the donkey still there and the small stable aflame. The burning roof and walls collapsed as the Princess sat on the ground kneading mud into a gash in her arm. Migral reappeared and perched again on the crossbeam of the water-well watching the injured woman.

"You can leave that, you know," said Migral.

"I know."

"It will heal instantly."

"I understand, but it feels good, the cool soil on my flesh."

"Quite a sensation without the intervening fur is it not?"

"Quite so."

"This encounter with the Fishals, very inconvenient."

"For you or for me? I am the one who was cast down the well, you know."

"Yes, but leaving that aside, this propensity of the usurpers to put things to the torch means that I shall have to busy myself finding you a new set of clothing. Thanks to their detestable passion for fire, your intended outfit is now turned to ashes. It will prove a damnable nuisance to gather things using only beak and feet."

"As for feet, my own seem wholly lacking," Ann said as she wriggled her toes and frowned. "How, I wonder, can I achieve anything approaching dexterity and speed using so woeful a platform? As for clothing, I'll find coverings for myself. It should be a simple matter given these handy devices," she laughed as she flexed her thumbs. "Much more useful than my old paws. I wonder how, as Wolfkind, I ever held sword or bow. These extra joints are most useful—made my climb out almost enjoyable."

"Your affinity for your new body does you credit. But have you noticed that your old—"

"My old powers—so far as I can tell—have somewhat changed," said Ann. "My ability to hear thoughts seems reduced. You and I can exchange the voice of the mind, but I'm unable to probe the heads of mere humans. So, yes, I have noticed limitations. It is with you as well?"

"It is," sighed Migral. "My dying prayer for the gift of flight was answered, but I was obliged to sacrifice other abilities to make it so." The downward tilt of the raven's head suggested to Ann one of the sensual things her friend must have forsaken to soar through the heavens.

"My condolences," she said with feeling.

"No matter," the bird responded. "As you will soon discover, lovemaking outside the wolf skin is vastly overrated. Now to more important matters. El has given you a task. Have you chosen your surname?"

In truth, Ann had forgotten to attend to this matter.

"Is it so important after all, this second name?"

"Your choice is vital to your new identity and our cause. Choose carefully, the proper surname can open doors for you—doors which will remain closed should you choose unwisely."

"And how—?" But Ann spoke too late, for the capricious bird was already aloft and a mere speck in the open sky. Flight and speed were daunting gifts. She hoped Migral found them worth the sacrifice. Ann gazed for a moment more at the empty blueness above. The day was advancing. She must choose a name and she must find clothing and she was uncertain how to begin either task.

"May I assist?"

The voice behind Ann was deep but surprisingly melodic. So melodic that, when she turned to behold the man, she was sufficiently awestruck that she failed to cover herself. Instead, she stood gaping with her new hairless arms hanging useless at her sides.

Chapter 2

The Man with Flaxen Hair

Much later in her human existence, the former Wolfkind would come to learn that poets are considered stale if they write that a man "kindles a fire." Writers of verse are also denounced as trite should they pen a line declaring that a female human, when first she sees her beloved, hears heavenly music.

Yet, standing there naked in the mud with the smoke of the destroyed stable still tingeing her nostrils, Ann did in fact perceive a patina of diffused light surrounding the man who stood before her. Moreover, she heard, as if cascading over her like a magical waterfall, the angelic music of a lyre.

She felt and saw and heard these things even though, as a newly-minted human, she had yet to experience any romantic notion of angels or halos—much less could she appreciate fine music or recognize the melody of a lyre. The Wolfkind had their own cherubs of course, a worthy pantheon of warrior spirits. The Wolfkind had music as well, although it relied heavily on unaccompanied guttural chanting and an occasional drum.

Regardless of her limited experience, Ann felt this new set of incredibly abstract—and therefore decidedly human—concepts as keenly as though angels and music had been native aspects of her Wolfkind nature. As an unschooled whelp, she had pretended her garden angel was real and entertained the juvenile fantasy of an imaginary playmate. However, she had never accepted—on an intellectual or even a spiritual level—the notion of actual angels or angelic behaviors.

Such notions were foolish. And yet, here she was mooning over this stranger like an infatuated adolescent. It was as if these decidedly new, and damnably enticing, romantic sensations had been with her always, had been ingrained in her before her lupine eyes were open, and had been imprinted upon her unblemished brain while she and her siblings competed with one another in their mother's womb.

"You are—" she started to say "beautiful," but she felt a sudden inexplicable pain in her side which drove her to her knees.

"You're hurt," he dropped the reins of his pony and knelt beside her. "I—"

The pony whinnied and pressed forward to nudge the man, compelling him to turn to meet the animal's gaze.

"Of course," he nodded. Unknotting the saddle strings, he unfurled a blanket and spread it gently over the stricken woman. "Is there a wound?"

"My side," Ann managed to say. It hurt to breathe. "No wound. No blood. Just a searing pain as if—" Then, realizing she'd failed to alter her speech, she added, "Me innards, sir, tis burnin' but you ought not bend down to—to the likes'a me."

"Nonsense," he said helping her to her feet. "You're hurt. Come with me." He guided her—blanket and all—to the shade of the broad tree and eased her to the ground again. "I'll fetch water." He rushed toward the well and, as he worked the windlass, a raven alighted on the crossbeam and seemed to consider him. He could hear the bird's impudent thoughts as he looked up and addressed the creature. "Oh, never you mind. I'm not so helpless as you think. You'll see."

The raven stared at the handsome man's flowing blonde hair, the smooth texture of his skin, and the lean but muscular arm which reached for the rope and unhooked the sloshing bucket. Although his beak made it impossible to discern a smirk, the bird's skepticism was apparent.

"Shoo!" the man commanded.

Migral flapped briefly up, but quickly reestablished himself on the crossbeam to watch as the stranger dipped a ladle in the bucket and carried the water back to the tree.

"Drink," he ordered as he knelt beside Ann. "Again. Now lie back and I shall see to your injuries." He examined her side but could see no evidence of a wound. He reached beneath the blanket, placed a hand on each of her feet, and said, "No need for alarm. Just tell me if anything hurts."

He began to work his hands up her legs spawning sensations which Ann feared she'd left behind with the end of her Wolfkind life. She writhed with a growing stir of pleasure, and he misinterpreted her reaction.

"Sorry," he stopped.

"No. It's a'right, sir, the pain she's gone apart now."

"But—"

"Truly, sir. Not for you to bother. I'm a'right as rain, see?" She stood quickly up, struck her head on a low branch, and sat heavily down again.

As right as rain, but fairly stupid, he thought, and—catching his unspoken assessment—Ann grinned up at him. Her ability to read minds seemed to be returning. He knelt again beside her, and she held his gaze. His eyes were bright green like a summer meadow and flecked with grains of gold that seemed to—

Can we stop this game, my Princess? He seemed to say, though his lips failed to move.

Princess? How could this man know? she asked herself.

His question confounded her. Her mind reeling, Ann felt like she was trapped again inside her armor, tied to the Maypole in the town square, feeling the shock and heat of the lightning as she evaporated. The stranger's unspoken question was unexpected, perhaps dangerous. Her instincts counseled caution, but she could not master her surprise or contain her curiosity.

"You seem to know who and what I am," she said, "and, furthermore, I can hear your thoughts."

"I hear your thoughts as well. And yet, do you not know me?" he seemed distressed.

Ann looked into the man's eyes, then followed the tracks of two tears as they slid down his cheeks and splashed into the shadows beneath the tree. The droplets seemed to linger there on a blade of grass until a ray of sunshine reached them, whereupon they shone with internal radiance like discarded jewels.

"Did you not see the glow?" he asked without looking up. "I am told such a glow is something to which women respond. Of course, I am much changed but—did you not hear the music, my love?"

The Princess felt a stirring. "Destin? My lost mate! Is it you? Is it possible?" Flinging the blanket aside, she crawled toward him, embraced him, and nuzzled his neck.

"Old habits die hard, eh?" He pulled away and stood over her. "You're no longer Wolfkind, my love. Nor am I. Destin is gone. I am called Seth now. Well, anyway, this is me now, your old mate made new, 'for better or worse,' as the humans say. So, let's see how you look."

He stepped back, crossed his arms, and struck an appraising pose to admire her new physique. *Not bad,* he thought, *those breasts of yours will take some getting used to. But never mind, my love, I've been schooled in ways to—*

A raucous caw interrupted their reunion.

"Time enough for that," laughed Seth. "Migral is correct. Your nakedness is interesting but far too conspicuous. Let us find for you some clothing lest more travelers pass this way. You would never know we were in the country with all this alarming traffic of horsemen and ravens and ponies."

They set off—Seth on his pony and Ann riding the previously uncooperative, but now surprisingly docile, donkey. Both were silent but continued to trade thoughts until Ann suddenly spoke.

"I understand now! My powers have changed. I have lost the ability to probe the thoughts of some but have retained it with others—with you and with Migral, for instance. It seems to be a way of sorting out the gifted from the ordinary—a method of discerning magic from mortal. So, tell me, is your pony also your familiar?" she asked. "Does she speak out loud or through the mind? She seems to share your thoughts."

"My Daffodil is merely a clever animal. She is loyal and smart but otherwise unmagical." Seth laughed and patted his mount. "Sometimes a pony is just a pony."

They had traveled three miles and were nearing a village when they discovered an untended clothesline where Ann helped herself to a shirt and pair of trousers.

"It seems wrong to take these things," she told Seth as she donned the shirt and pulled on the trousers. "We must leave something in exchange."

When they returned to the country road Seth could not stop smiling.

What, he thought, *will the owner of the missing clothing think when she finds a fat donkey tethered to her clothesline?*

Wondering if Ann had the same thought, Seth looked down from his pony and regarded his barefoot mate as she stumbled along the rocky road. He had insisted she ride while he walked alongside, but Ann was equally insistent that Wolfkind customs be observed.

"Ride as my mate walks?" she scoffed. "Nonsense!"

After another hour, they came upon a traveling peddler-woman and Seth entered into negotiations until they came away with a pair of rough socks and passable shoes. Ann looked doubtfully at the shoes and hobbled along the road trying to get used to wearing them.

"Tell me again what you exchanged for these torturous devices," she frowned as she struggled to master the shoes and stumbled over yet another stone.

"It is called a kiss," Seth smiled. "And I have found it opens many doors."

"Opens doors—" Ann repeated. Then, reminded of her surname task, she fell to musing. El had admonished her to choose wisely. Migral, the deity's messenger, had cautioned the vanquished Princess that a wrong choice would mean that doors would be closed to her. What doors? And where?

"I have it," Ann announced after they'd traveled without speaking for a time.

"What, my love?"

"My new surname."

They walked several more paces in silence.

"Well? Are you practicing your fledgling human's notion of suspense? Or are you planning to tell me your choice?"

In answer, Ann leaned down without missing a stride despite her new shoes, picked up a pebble, and cast it purposefully aside. It landed where she aimed it, in the middle of a placid stream flowing near the road. Where it entered the water, a halo of concentric ripples lingered for a moment on the surface before the current whisked them away.

"I am your bride who is challenged to walk along this rocky road," she observed.

"I see, my love," said Seth, his voice suggesting he *did not* see.

"Therefore," she began.

"Therefore—?" he prompted.

"Therefore, my new name shall be *Stone Bride*," she grinned.

"Hmm," said Seth. "Perhaps this choice of yours and your watery throw means that it is time for us to make some waves, Mrs. Stone Bride." He nodded courteously in her direction. "And by human custom, that makes me Mr. Stone Bride. Seth Stone Bride—it is a fair name. Now what about your war name—are you changing that too?"

"I'm keeping Ann."

"Unwise perhaps," Seth frowned. "But it's a common enough name, so I doubt anyone will notice. Just take care not to forget yourself by adding the title 'Princess' for good measure."

"No fear of that," she assured him. "It'll be plain ordinary everyday Ann Stone Bride for now—perhaps forever."

"Forever is a long time," he frowned.

Not as long as never, she thought. She meant to conceal the thought, but it slipped free, so she continued in the voice of the mind. *In the battle, when you fell, I feared I would never see you again, my love, not until I perished also, and never on this side of Velyn.*

Receiving this thought, Seth blushed at Ann's sentiment—such a tender emotion—so unlike her former gruff Wolfkind self.

Ann watched the crimson flush across her mate's fair skin and found it a becoming reaction.

"The sun is setting," Seth said regaining his composure. "It will be dark soon and you'll find it chilly without your insulating fur. Not only that, but this road is dangerous at night. The woods ahead are, so they tell me, filled with brigands and cut-throats."

Ann was about to say that she feared no bandit when she heard the first arrow whistling through the shadows of the waning daylight.

Chapter 3

The Brigand

The Princess had yet to test the breadth of her powers and it is well that the peril she faced was a mild one.

It was a simple matter for Ann to step aside, snatch the arrow in midflight, and snap it asunder. She did the same with the second arrow. And the next. And the next.

"By my breath!" The shout from beyond the dark trees was more exasperated than angry. "What must one do? How is one to make an honest living?"

Another arrow emerged from the forest. With a casual flick of her wrist, Ann swatted the feathered missile as if it were no more substantial than a troublesome insect.

"That does it! I surrender!" A discarded bow clattered to the forest floor, immediately followed by an empty quiver. "You may pass."

Seth moved his pony closer to examine the weapons. He tried to stifle a laugh, but the brigand—as yet unseen—seemed to sense his derision.

"Am I to be mocked as well as defeated? Pass I say. Pass on and leave me my pride at least." His last remark came from a constricted throat.

The brigand's tone evoked such pathos in Seth that he regretted his unkindness. "I'm sorry," he said with as much sincerity as he could manage, for he was still bemused by this inept bandit. "However—as for passing—we respectively decline. We don't intend to venture farther into such a dangerous forest with the dark coming on."

"Now that is indeed a sensible statement," the brigand confirmed, his voice wafting through the darkening trees. "It is dangerous here. So dangerous that I often think to myself that I ought not to linger here after sunset."

"Well," declared Seth, "you have certainly chosen a strange profession for one so squeamish—if you'll pardon my saying so—and—oh my!"

The bandit suddenly appeared, his arms and legs churning the air, as the flailing man flew headfirst out of the trees to tumble among his discarded weapons. While Seth and the hidden man had been conversing, Ann had moved rapidly and unobserved behind the ambusher. Grabbing the unprepared man by the scruff of the neck, she had gleefully tossed the rascal into the clearing. So sudden had been this turn of fortune that the startled man had no opportunity to cry out. He lay in an abject heap—his face pressed to the ground—and seemed to be weeping.

Without a second thought, Seth dismounted and rushed forward to kneel beside the defeated bandit. For her part, Ann emerged from the forest, admiring her closed fists, and flexing her thumbs which had proven so useful in grasping and throwing the man.

"You needn't have been so rough with this little fellow," Seth chastised the Princess. "He surrendered. He said we could pass."

"And what do you suppose he intended to do with this?" Ann asked as she spread her fingers to reveal a small, sheathed dirk which she extracted to expose a wicked looking blade. "This is yours I presume," she confronted the man.

Seth suddenly stood up and assumed a defensive stance, "Why you little weasel! You would have lured us into the forest and waylaid us with your hidden knife?"

"Please, mister, it ain't mine!" protested the man.

"How did I manage to find it in your pocket, I wonder?" asked Ann.

"Please, these ain't my pockets neither," said the man as he rolled over on his back and struggled with his over-sized jacket as if it were an animal that held him in its unwelcome embrace. "What I mean is—"

"What you mean is," said Ann as she re-sheathed the blade and passed it to Seth, "you stole the jacket you're wearing."

"'Xactly so, that's the honest truth. I took it from—an individual who was—indisposed alongside a ditch which I happened to be in and—" His voice trailed off as he struggled to his feet with the look of a man who was already in a deep hole and had decided to cease digging.

"Are you capable of telling the truth?" asked Ann, curious what the man would say.

"Me mum said not," the brigand sniffed.

"Your mother?" asked Seth.

"Yes, sir, Velyn rest her."

"She's dead?" asked Seth.

"Oh no, mister, she's alright I reckon, just tired."

Seth and Ann exchanged a glance, unable to decide what to do next.

"I should go," suggested the man.

"I think that would be best," agreed Seth.

The man started to gather up his things. "I had a hat," he looked hopefully at Ann who shrugged. "I don't suppose you'd let me collect me arrows—no, no, never mind that—I'll—I'll get some others, shall I?" He turned and disappeared into the darkening forest muttering, "I had a hat."

Ann looked at Seth and the two burst out laughing. It felt good to laugh. Laughter caused her supple human skin to tingle, and she found it was much easier to prolong a smile without a snout and fierce jaws to contend with.

Seth embraced Ann and, rather than remounting, he took the reins of his pony and he and his mate walked side-by-side. Retracing their steps, they followed the road back as it curved away from the forest. An hour ago, they had passed an inn and, as they left the forest behind, Ann suddenly realized she was very tired and very hungry. Seth must be equally fatigued. It was time to sample some human hospitality.

"Indeed," agreed Seth as he intercepted her thought.

So, they walked together in the darkness toward the glow of lantern light which streamed from the outline of a distant window.

Chapter 4

Bluebell Inn

When the New Chronicles are written, the scribe assigned to set down the tale of Seth and Ann's night together at the Bluebell Inn will be obliged to invent a more robust name for the establishment. The Princess of Middlemount—with her name and her former being already fading from memory—was becoming a woman, but she had by no means left behind her aggressive heritage. As for Seth, he was becoming a man and beginning to embrace a human maleness which was contrary to his Wolfkind nature. And for either mate to admit that they spent their second honeymoon in an establishment called 'The Bluebell' would seem to make for a feeble tale.

Suffice it to say, the Bluebell Inn was not accustomed to receiving visitors. The inn was, to put it plainly, an establishment that catered exclusively by reservation to matronly women whose husbands sent them into the country for "the cure." Which is to say that the ladies who ended up residing at the Bluebell were there—for as long as it would take—for one reason and one reason only, which was to rekindle their extinguished desires. Their mission might have been a noble one had it not been for the fact that the inn offered no logical path to success.

In truth, the occupants had been diagnosed as hysterics and sent away to wither and die.

Unaware that the inn was populated by a bevy of timid women, Ann strode forth and rapped sharply on the blue painted door of the inn. There was no answer. The blue taffeta curtains on either side of the indigo lintel fluttered once, then twice, but the door remained shut.

"Let me try," said Seth. "You're a frightful apparition on a moonlit night." He pushed Ann aside and handed her the reins. "Put Daffodil in the stable. I'll handle things here. Go on. Go!"

Ann lingered a second more, then obeyed, and Seth turned to tap lightly on the window. "Good evening, good people," he said cheerily. "Sorry to disturb you but my wife and I—and our pony—need lodging for the night and your sign—" He looked up at the shingle swinging in the cooling night breeze to make certain. "Your sign says 'Gasthaus' and—well there doesn't seem to be anything else nearby and, it being our first night together, I—"

The door opened a crack.

"What wants thee?"

"A room is all. For the night. We can pay," said Seth as sweetly as he could manage, though his patience was wearing thin. Like Ann, he too was tired and hungry, and he longed to lie down in a warm bed with his rediscovered mate. He listened through the crack as anxious words were exchanged inside. He could hear several voices—women's voices—and not so young.

"They can pay."

"But the man?"

"He's handsome—I say let him in and let's have a look at him by lantern light!"

"You old pervert! I'd lose my charter!"

"It's only for the night and they have a pony. People with ponies are usually well-behaved."

"Nonsense! Where did you hear such a thing?"

"From my 'gram! Ah, they're leaving!"

Seth had had enough. He was turning from the entrance, intent on sleeping in the stable, when the door flung open, and light spilled into the night.

"Come in, sir. Sorry to have kept you waiting. This old door, she sticks sometimes. Did you say you had a payment—that is, a wife?"

"Yes," smiled Seth. "I have both. I'll fetch her."

"And the money?"

"Of course."

By the time Seth and Ann assembled in the living room of the inn and endured the questions and scrutiny of a dozen middle-aged womenfolk, they were truly exhausted. So exhausted was the nodding pair that they forgot to ask for a meal and allowed a wizened humpbacked woman to lead them to their room. They followed her up the stairs like sleepwalking children and stumbled inside where they fell into the bed and instantly slept.

That night in the living room Seth, who was new to money, had placed far too many coins into the wrinkled, out-stretched hand of the humpbacked woman, who had presented herself as proprietress and headmistress. So uncommonly generous had he been that, when he and Ann awoke, he realized they were completely without cash of any kind.

"Being a penniless peasant is far from pleasant," cooed Seth. Though they were bankrupt, he was feeling sated by his mate's early morning lovemaking, so he was waxing poetic. "What else rhymes with 'pleasant' I wonder?" He spoke to Ann's naked back as he traced circles on her peerless skin with his smooth pink fingers.

"Pheasant," she growled back. "And I wish I had some. I'm starving."

"Too starving to try the trice-accomplished lovemaking we shared at dawn?" he asked.

"Definitely too starving for such vigorous exercise, my dear," she laughed. Pulling away, she slipped out of bed and began dressing. "So, my amorous mate, no more pleasuring until we have eaten. Using what for money, I have no idea."

"A kiss?" Seth suggested.

"I doubt your kiss will carry much weight with these doleful females," she laughed. "On the other hand, you might try going downstairs naked and asking for a biscuit or two. That would certainly get their attention."

A knock at the hallway door made Ann leap back into bed and burrow her half-naked torso under the covers.

Human modesty again—what a nuisance!

"May we come in?" said a sing-song voice.

"A moment please—" Seth pleaded. He quickly rose to dress and threw Ann her pantaloons.

"Of course, sir," came a contrite voice from beyond the closed door. "Sorry to disturb you lovebirds, but we've brought thy breakfast."

"Come in!!" Seth and Ann shouted in unison.

The door burst open as three ladies entered. The first two strained to carry trays which brimmed with sausages, toast, muffins, fruit, scones, and flapjacks. The third carried a jug of milk in one hand and a steaming pot of tea in the other. Seth was about to close the door when more women shouted from the hallway.

"Make way!"

"Coming through."

A fourth woman entered—a stout woman—bearing a table in her strong arms and two chairs somehow balanced on her head. This acrobat was followed by a fifth woman who bore a fantastic spray of flowers and a handsome vase. The women bustled about, laying out the breakfast, and then exited as suddenly as they had come.

"Heavens," panted Seth.

"How much money did you give them, my sweet?"

"All of it, I'm afraid."

"Honest folk after all," said Ann with a tone akin to reverence. "Folk who seem intent on giving us our money's worth. I have been too long among schemers and politicians to realize how honest gentlefolk behave. Shall we?"

After the meal, Seth rang the little bell which had been left on a silver tray for the purpose of summoning the women to clear away. The same five appeared instantly and whisked everything—crumbs and all, though there were very few crumbs—away and gently closed the door behind them.

But of course, they left the flowers.

Chapter 5

A Miraculous Cure

Delicious food and passionate love are two basic needs. Best not ask your lover to choose between them.

Their hunger satisfied and once again alone, the ardor with which the reunited mates rekindled their coupling made the inn's fragile bed shake and rattled the windows of their upstairs room. Many songs and at least one lengthy play would eventually be written in an effort to capture the compass of their enthusiastic wrangling, but these would fall short of the mark. Suffice it to say that the couple was good and truly satiated by ten-of-the-clock.

Seth was first to rise and descend the inn's stairway humming merrily to himself. He crossed the courtyard and entered the stables. As he stood in the straw brushing Daffodil, he was joined by Pawstel, the humpbacked, bespectacled proprietress who had ushered them upstairs the night before.

"Must thee be away?" the old woman asked anxiously.

"Yes. I'm afraid so," said Seth. "We cannot tarry."

"Ah," said Pawstel, with a sigh that betrayed her disappointment. "Thee'll be wanting thy change money then."

"If it's not too much trouble."

Pawstel counted out the coins, thought for a moment, then counted out several more. She looked up to see Seth studying her. "It's not the money, sir.

We don't begrudge the loss of money. It's just that—" The old woman sniffed and buried her gray head in her apron.

"What is it, dear-heart," Seth asked. "Have we offended you?"

"No—no." The woman sighed and seemed to struggle to master her emotions. "Thou misunderstand me. Thou hast given us so much more than the money. Thy presence here—the love thy brought us—and the pleasures too. Thy passionate wrangling echoed through our dreary sterile abode. Thou rattled the windows—literally rattled them. And never have we felt such warmth. The fire of your love! The heavenly zeal of it!" She stopped for a breath and felt her heart. She seemed intent on holding the organ in place—bidding it to remain still as though she feared it might leap from her breast. "To put it bluntly, we are cured, one and all. The others are packing now to return to their waiting husbands, to pounce upon them and rekindle the flames of their lost ardor—and I—I am going to paint this inn red from top to bottom and perhaps change the name—what does thou think?"

Without awaiting an answer, she shouted to one of her companions and the woman trundled across the courtyard bearing an armload of goods. As the woman hurried away, Pawstel continued, her voice and manner projecting a growing sense of resolve.

"Take these cloaks and warm blankets for your journey," she insisted. "And likewise these water skins. Heartfelt gifts from myself and the others. Those fortunate females are off on their own blessed journeys while I shall labor here to set aside three rooms for future recovering sisters while reserving the other twelve exclusively for newlyweds. In that way, we old ones may continue to bask in the glorious sunshine of young love!"

"Your praise astonishes me," Seth blushed. "My mate and I are but simple folk—"

"Not so," whispered Pawstel as she motioned the befuddled man forward. "I know thy secret. I am blessed—some say cursed—with vivid dreams which reveal much. Much," she added with emphasis.

"I—" Seth began.

"Fear not," Pawstel interrupted. "Trust this dreamer to keep secret the presence of our much-changed Princess. I know not the reasons. Only that you two must by all means remain undetected. I will not fail you."

Pawstel was still proclaiming her new gospel of rediscovered passion when Ann lumbered downstairs, out the front door, and across the inn's courtyard. The still-sleepy Princess hardly recognized the place, filled as it was with luggage-laden ox wagons. Among the wagons the former residents of Bluebell Inn hugged one another and bade goodbye and petted the oxen and flirted with the teamsters.

After she'd endured the grateful embraces of Pawstel and watched the old woman scamper away to greet a wagonload of painters, Ann scratched her head. The painters seemed also bewildered by the old woman's passion. The men stood dumbfounded on the inn's front doorstep with brushes and ladders and quizzical looks on their ruddy mustached faces.

"What has happened here?" Ann asked as she arrived at the stables.

In answer, Seth kissed her gently on the cheek. "Love, Mrs. Stone Bride. Love has happened here. This little blue box of blue women has been bitten by the venom of galloping infectious love! And, moreover, a prescient dream has—"

Before Seth could reveal Pawstel's insights, their hostess rapidly reappeared.

"I nearly forgot," the breathless woman said. "In the dream—but never mind. Wait here while I fetch something for thee. Wait here while I bring—well thou shalt see. Think of it as a wedding present." She rushed away from the bewildered pair, ducked with astounding agility into the next stall, and returned leading a tall stallion with flowing mane and a handsome coat as vibrant as warm wine.

"A Middlemount steed—but—how—?" Ann gasped.

Before Pawstel could answer, the energetic woman bade them farewell and rushed back to the bustling courtyard.

"She knows," Seth confided.

"Knows?" Ann asked.

"A dream revealed to her your true identity," Seth explained.

"If we are known," Ann declared, "we must leave at once!"

"Pawstel seems to share your urgency for she has your horse saddled and ready," said Seth. "It will take but a moment for me to saddle the pony."

As Seth hurried his preparations, Ann heard someone enter the stable from behind. Wheeling around, she crouched in a defensive stance, expecting to see a Fishal trooper with pistol drawn, come to claim what the usurper would insist was a stolen horse. Instead, a diminutive figure emerged from the shadows.

"The wolf dies," said the little man as he doffed his hat and Ann recognized the brigand from the evening before.

"The lamb is born," smiled Ann as she and Seth bowed low.

"My El," they spoke in unison and breathless astonishment.

"My children," smiled El the brigand. "If you are quite rested and otherwise sated, it is time to begin."

Chapter 6
Trio

It is written that wonderous things come in threes. Three acorns encircle the fallen crest of Middlemount. Those appealing to El, place three wreaths on water. Two travelers on a journey lay claim to a duet. Three creatures bound in the same direction may constitute a quest.

The three set off at once, though where they were bound Ann and Seth were uncertain. Their deity bade them follow and so they followed. It was a curious beginning. Both the Princess and her mate were pious believers. In their former life, their Wolfkind household had held not one, not two, but three altars dedicated to the deity El. The chief-most altar, the one in the alcove directly outside their bed chamber, held a portrait of El as the Prophet Pentum, a whiskered old man. This was the popular image of the deity, one which graced every house and hovel in the Middlemount kingdom.

Never in their wildest imaginings had either of them pictured El as a diminutive bandit. Let alone had they dreamt that they would one day accompany their deity on a journey.

And what is this journey? Where and to what end are we bound? These thoughts danced through their minds.

But neither Seth nor the Princess could find voice to question the deity and so they rode on while El, as the brigand, remarked reverently on all he saw: the beauty of rolling hills, the majesty of a certain tree, the crystalline blueness of the sky, the ethereal whiteness of a cloud. It was as if the deity was seeing these earthly wonders for the first time—though Ann detected something in his manner which suggested he was seeing them for perhaps the last.

With Seth on his pony and Ann and El riding double on the wine-colored stallion, the trio traveled ten miles through the forest without encountering the rumored bandits. At the far end of the trees, they reached the base of the Northern Range. There at the foot of Windlass Peak, they dismounted, freed the horses to seek their own footing, and climbed upward, following the animals.

El did not lead but rather trusted in the horses and—though they had no notion of the reason for the climb—the two new humans did not question their divine leader. Ascending, they left behind leafy woodlands and entered the realm of sturdy, soaring ponderosa pines. Recalling her early schooling, Ann paused and pressed her nose against the rough bark.

"Vanilla," she pronounced. "Though the aroma is less intense than I remember."

"Indeed," Seth agreed as his gaze took in the increasingly rugged panorama. "Our senses have diminished. My vision, for example, leaves much to be desired. And breathing has become a challenge."

"Best save our breath then," his mate suggested and the pair continued in silence.

After an hour of steady climbing, the trees thinned and the haunting call of a boreal owl convinced Ann they'd entered the realm of spruce and fir. Reaching up to pluck a handful of needles and finding them soft against the skin of her new human fingers, she surmised they must be fir. Ahead she caught a glimpse of higher ground and guessed their path would take them into the sparse landscape of alpine tundra as their demanding journey carried them still higher.

"Up and over," she decided. Above the tree line, the way was arduous with much struggling over loose rocks and unstable soil.

"Is it my imagination," asked Ann when she and Seth stopped to rest. "Or does El seem frail to you?"

Seth looked back at the deity, who was lagging far behind. "Truly he might have chosen a more vigorous form," he observed.

"It is not merely his size in this form," Ann frowned. "It is his essence. I sense his spirit is fading."

"An odd choice of words," her mate responded. "But hush, he is nigh. Will you rest a while, Majesty?"

"We are nearly there, lamb," said El. The look of concern on Seth's face compelled the deity to add, "This body may appear tired, but it will muddle through. For my part, I am unused to the challenges of terrestrial climbing—go on you two—follow the animals. I shall join you presently and at my own pace."

"As you wish," said Ann and she nodded to Seth to follow, though she sensed her mate desired to remain with their deity. When they'd climbed far enough to mask the voices of the mind and were, therefore, also beyond the range of normal hearing, she touched Seth's arm and spoke gravely. "You heard it, did you not, the weariness in his voice?"

"Yes," said Seth looking far back at the small form following them. "Truly his spirit *is* flagging. What can we do?"

"Whatever he asks of us," said Ann. "Let us climb on since that is his wish."

So, the Princess and Seth, led ever upward by Daffodil and the stallion, obeyed their deity and ascended.

Two hours later, at the close of an exhausting climb, humans and animals reached the apex of the first of several steep mountainsides. There they stood obediently and waited for their deity. Reunited, the three stepped single file along a narrow deer path. Here the way, though still treacherous, was more level and El kept pace as he joined the others.

Step by challenging step, the climbers rose steadily until they left the narrow pathway and reached the pinnacle of Windlass Peak. The wind buffeting the peak was fierce until they passed through a narrow opening and emerged into a calmer region. There they came upon a craggy outcropping with a large and perfectly circular depression in its center. The depression was filled with rounded stones—some as large as a lawn bowler's ball, others smaller and egg-shaped, and still others holed like carnival donuts. Looking upward, Ann could see a ledge above.

"A waterfall formed this basin," she frowned. "But now the rocks are barren. Cascading waters once carved this circular cauldron and these stones were worn smooth and shaped by its power. Too bad it is the dry season."

"Drink here," said El and where he touched the naked rock, a wrist-sized flow of spring water spiraled forth and cool refreshing liquid began filling the basin. The grateful humans drank lustily. Then Ann moved the horses to the far side of the basin where she allowed them to drink while she submerged and filled the sealed skins of eight travel bladders to capture water for their anticipated journey. As the coursing water covered the stones, Seth reached in and plucked out a holed one. He placed three fingers through the center, curved them around the rim, and held the stone toward Ann.

"A contract," he said and grinned broadly.

"That, my love, is a foolish ritual," frowned Ann. She'd been frowning much since they left The Bluebell. As El grew weaker, she too seemed to feel her powers ebbing, or at least changing, and she wondered if her passionate morning of lovemaking might be the cause.

"Lord El," called Seth to the deity's brigand-form. The little man had moved apart from the couple and stood near the far edge of the crag. He seemed to be staring back in the direction from which they had come. He seemed not to hear. "Lord El," Seth repeated, "can a human man not demand a public Tell-Town and compel his would-be wife to pledge a lover's contract before witnesses?"

"This is so," said El abstractly, his attention still focused elsewhere.

"I am not your would-be wife," protested Ann. "We are life-mates already—wed as you will recall on our knees before the mulberry tree at the solstice by custom and blood."

"That was a Wolfkind ceremony performed in an old dream to which we can never return," Seth said, his firm voice betraying his rising passion. "As a human I demand a Tell-Town—a public declaration of our intentions and I name this stone as our token. Will you not grasp this hole with me and pledge your love before these witnesses?" He made an overly extravagant gesture in the direction of El and the horses.

"Before the divine one and these animals?" Ann scoffed. "I grant that El is a competent witness, for he sees all. But I'll not pledge my troth in the presence of these animals. And to what end do you waggle this wretched stone in my direction? Do you not know the nature of a holed-stone contract?"

"It binds us," Seth declared, his lip protruding in a lover's pout. "Do you not wish to be bound to me?"

"El?" Ann appealed to her deity. But the divine one seemed not to hear—seemed lost in thought—so Ann was compelled to plead her own case. "My love, it pains me to say that you have misunderstood this foolish human ceremony. This pledge is not what it seems. The custom is that humans seal a business contract between buyer and seller by shaking hands through a holed-stone. That is the custom. But when a man and woman pledge by grasping such a stone—well you must know that their pledge is not forever."

"I know this," he said.

"You know and yet you agree to a Tell-Town—to a marriage lasting a year and a day?"

"Yes."

"And you understand that at the close of that year and a day, either you or I can return to this spot and reject the stone and undo our bond?" she asked.

"Is there any danger that you will return and do so?"

"No, my love. You are my mate for life—whatever dream we live in," said Ann. "In a year and a day, I will be at your side. Not here on this wretched cliff seeking to reject that miserable stone."

"Neither do I intend to return hither," he declared. "So let us make this bargain that neither of us intends to break. What is the harm?"

"The harm? The harm is—"

"Smoke," said Seth, suddenly looking past the shoulder of his incredulous mate. Ann turned and followed his gaze to see that Seth and El were staring southward—their eyes fixed on a thread of smoke rising in the distance. They joined El at the cliff and all three watched the smoke rising far below and beyond the far edge of the distant forest.

"The Bluebell?" Seth asked.

"I fear so," said Ann. Then she turned abruptly, strode to her mount, and tested the firmness of the bridle, saddle, and cinch—preparing the stallion's tack for a precipitous descent down the mountain and a hard ride back through the forest. She kept her head down, intent on her preparations, pretending she did not see El approaching. When the little man stood before her, Ann spoke.

"You have come to tell me I will be too late." She did not look up.

"Yes," said her deity.

"The woman Pawstel is already dead?"

"Yes."

"And the others?"

"Safely fled by the grace of your and Seth's love."

"You're going to tell me it was the woman's time," she looked then directly at her deity.

"Yes. Even now she is being received with honor into Velyn."

"With honor?" Ann could not hold her temper. "What good is—?"

"Only look now, child. Look over my shoulder and see how that woman's willing sacrifice has aided us in our quest," El stepped aside and Ann looked beyond her deity.

"More smoke."

"Yes."

"A second fire—farther south."

"Yes."

"That is what you were watching for."

"Yes."

"You were watching for a sign that Pawstel kept our secret—that she deliberately sent the searching Fishals south—sent them in the wrong direction."

"Yes."

"A life ended to save us?" Ann's tone was accusing.

"A life reborn in paradise," corrected El. "And so that her sacrifice is not wasted, you must now continue north and, by the grace of her courage, struggle through these mountains, turn toward the sunset, then descend and cross the river to reach the Western Sea before full moon. Come, lamb! Collect your husband!"

When Seth and Ann mounted their animals, El did not take Ann's hand to ride behind the Princess.

"I must leave you now for a time. You shall have hard days ahead to cross these immense mountains. Have a care as you journey. Beyond this crag, the slopes will become ever more daunting and, with weather approaching, you will not want to tempt the lightning. Make haste, but do not stray from the trail. You are creatures of the lowlands and this alpine region can be unforgiving. Mark now what I say. The mountains will test you, but this trial is merely a preamble to the crux of your journey. The trail ahead will seem endless and, often, impossibly narrow. But, if you make good time, you will—within two days—reach an oasis where you can take refuge until morning. Regrettably, this may prove to be your only restful night. Beyond that point, you will need to travel steadily with only brief sleeps to reach the farther side from which you can glimpse the distant sea."

El paused, pleased to see Seth had produced a scrap of parchment and a charcoal stub. He nodded at the enterprising man who was using a saddlebag as an improvised table to sketch a crude map. The deity and his resourceful follower exchanged a brief smile.

"In time, you will become aware of a massive waterfall—the sound of the cataract will reach your questing ears long before you discover it. The descend will prove challenging, but—"

El paused again, apparently losing his train of thought before returning to his description.

"In any event," he continued as before, although his tone seemed to lack confidence, "at its base you should find a steeply descending river which I seem to recall is bordered by a broad game trail unless it runs beside a wagon road. Follow the waterway until its wild cascades are tamed by a wider channel which courses, as I remember it, through a verdant valley or it might be a desert—my memory is hazy. Owing to your ordeal in the mountains, you will be tempted to rest there, but do not yield to that urge. You must continue to follow the westward flowing river until it approaches the sea. There you must cross-over to reach the shore and beach beyond. The horse knows the way."

El patted the stallion.

"Migral will meet you at the estuary. I go to prepare the ship for our crossing and to attend to other matters. You have a far journey and mere days to reach the sea. We must be on the water before the moon begins to wane. Go with my blessing and do not delay!"

"I—" Ann began to protest, but her deity dissolved and drifted away—a fading mist—no more substantial than the distant southern smoke.

Chapter 7

Mountains

Mountaineering is an uphill struggle. Why we climb is a mystery and, halfway up, we long to turn back. But what mortal can resist the view from the top?

Beyond the holed-stone pool, there was a trail—of sorts. It soon devolved into a slender and steadily rising track, more suited to a nimble Dall sheep or an acrobatic stone ram. Yet the mountains must be crossed. Breathing raggedly, feeling light-headed, the travelers paused repeatedly, then pressed on until exhaustion compelled a halt. Climbing into the teeth of a biting alpine wind, Ann and Seth had struggled no more than five miles when darkness overtook them and they spent a restless night clinging to a barren and inhospitable slope.

Arising stiff and cold with nothing to eat but hard bread and a portion of dried fruit, Ann and her mate stumbled upward, alternately leading and riding their mounts. At noon on the second day, they reached the apex of a challenging peak where they momentarily glimpsed a view of the distant sea. Then the trail descended and they found themselves in a dark realm of overarching pines which obscured the sun. Among the crowding trees, the buzzing of stinging insects troubled riders and mounts alike.

"Oh, for a shield of fur and more durable hide," the recently-made man complained.

"Oh, for a squadron of bats to carve a path through this curtain of pestilent creatures," the novice woman grumbled.

Emerging from the shadows, they ascended to another viewpoint—only to once again travel downward into a tree-lined and pest-infested darkness. Twelve more times, they trundled up and down until they began to believe they were covering the same ground over and over again, caught in a never-ending cycle of repeating ascents and descents which seemed to lead nowhere.

"Treading water—" Ann suggested, her laboring lungs unable to complete her thought.

"Swimming against the tide," Seth finished the analogy.

At last, the travelers passed above the trees and reached an expanse of blue-shaded mountains. Extending across the base of this rugged, snow-capped range was a fundamentally level escarpment, one edge of which was blocked by a wall of dark rock.

For several minutes, the Princess and her mate paused to take in the view of distant peaks before considering the nearer wall. Crisscrossed with rose-colored veins, the otherwise unremarkable rock seemed to be held in place by a web of meandering red ribbons. The dusky rock formed a stark background for a patchwork of crimson veins, speckled at random intervals, with brilliant ingots of silver and gold.

"Inspiration for a poet," suggested Seth.

"Or a hard-rock miner," mused his more practical mate who was busy testing the weight of the water skins. "We are low. What of your supply?"

"Low also," Seth frowned. "Enough water for the horses, little enough for we riders."

"Let's allow our mounts to cool down and walk them on this level ground while we can," Ruth decided.

Several weary steps onto the multi-colored escarpment and the ears of both horses pricked up as their heads swiveled skyward. Seconds later, the riders also heard the sound as, high above, a flock of passing sandhill cranes trumpeted their haunting calls.

"Far from home," Seth noted as he strained to catch a glimpse of the lofty birds—clearly heard, but, as yet, unseen.

I know the feeling, sighed Ann. "There!" She pointed to the barely visible flock.

As the soaring cranes broadcast a final echoing cry, the pair turned their attention to terrestrial matters. They walked in silence, suppressing their thoughts, content to be on the flat and thankful for a respite from the undulating tedium of their meandering journey.

Too soon, the wide escarpment shrank and they were obliged, once again, to mount-up and press their horses onto a constricted track. At times, the ever-tightening artery was scarcely wide enough for horse and rider. Soon, the narrowing trail was reduced to a shelf with a towering wall of rock on one margin and a precipitous drop on the other.

Hours passed and, just when it seemed the steadily thinning track must disappear entirely, the rock wall appeared to melt away. Suddenly freed from the restraining pathway, the horses galloped into a broad meadow of belly-high grass and spent wildflowers. Each blade of grass and flower was past its prime, casting the meadow in a mixture of flaxen and golden hues.

Both riders reigned-in their enthusiastic mounts and sat for a moment taking in the sight while Daffodil and the wine-colored stallion took advantage of the halt to sample the faded fruits of the sprawling pasture.

"A *heah-strate,*" said Seth.

"You and your folk-talk," Ann teased. "Though I have to agree this rural park could be labeled a *high-street* especially when compared to the slender footpaths we've survived this day." She turned in her saddle to glance back. "From here, that razor-thin entrance we left behind is nearly invisible."

Following his mate's gaze, Seth seemed to agree as he added, "The way in is indeed indiscernible and I'll wager we'll likewise find the way out to be no wider than a shallow rabbit-dent of a pathway which leads to and from a peasant's privy."

"Such a way with words," Ann laughed. "This alpine meadow must be the oasis El foretold. We are meant to rest here, surely. Stopping overnight will be a welcome respite from our rocky journey. As for how to proceed in the morning, neither your map nor El's directions touch on our exit which may—as you suggest—be as indistinct as was our entry. See how we are ringed by sheer walls? We'll have a time locating the way out, though it will likely be somewhere in the opposite wall."

"Most likely," Seth said. "And as for staying the night—" He glanced skyward and wetted a finger to sample the wind. "Do I sense a change in the weather?"

The Princess sniffed the air, searching for fragments of her Wolfkind instincts. "Smells of rain despite the lack of clouds. If my memory serves, things change rapidly at this altitude."

With the eye of a military commander evaluating a tenting site, Ann scanned the meadow.

"A stand of aspen trees to our left," she decided. "No other cover. There will be windfall limbs for a fire. And—" She cocked her head.

"I hear it too," said Seth. "Running water. Allowing for echoes in this vast cauldron, I'd say there's a spring or rivulet somewhere to the west—among the trees I'll wager—which would account for their greenness in this otherwise dry expanse. Soon it will be dark. Dare we give these animals their heads? My guess is they'll scout out the water."

"Let's point their noses west and see what comes," said Ann. "I think we could do no better."

Though logic suggested the robust stallion would be the perfect pathfinder, it was Daffodil who took the lead. The pony seemed to know the way to water and the stallion fell in behind. For a furlong, the animals walked in sunshine until a rising breeze caused cloud shadows to race across the open meadow. As if hastened by the breeze, the horses broke into a trot, quickening their pace while wallowing through a veritable ocean of chest-high golden grasses and forlorn flower stalks. Achieving a canter, the animals were about to stretch into a gallop when the sky darkened. Instantly, a deafening peal of thunder caused, first the pony, then the stallion, to wheel in opposite directions, shy back, and collide—unseating both riders.

Gaining their feet beneath a thickening blanket of murky clouds, Ann and Seth set out to retrieve the horses which, despite the thunder-shock and to their credit, hadn't strayed far. Bridles in hand, the Princess and her mate had seconds to mount again and scramble for cover before a torrent of rain turned their idyllic oasis into a miserable maelstrom of mud and moisture.

The target of their desperate flight was the distant stand of trees. The narrow-leafed canopies might offer cold comfort. But occupying the spot was preferable to being soaked to the skin, not to mention the hazard of remaining in an exposed field to risk a lightning strike.

Arriving among the trees, the two storm-tossed refugees dismounted, unsaddled their horses, and used handfuls of dry grass to rub the animals down. Employing cloaks supplied by the ladies of the Bluebell Inn, Seth blanketed the stallion and Daffodil while Ann fashioned rope hobbles to gently constrain the weary animals. Seemingly unfazed by the storm, both mounts lowered their heads and drank contentedly from a bubbling spring which Daffodil's keen nose had detected.

Moments later, the rain ceased as abruptly as it had begun, although thunder still grumbled and inky clouds continued to obscure the sky. Discharges of sheet lightning flickered overhead, but these dispersed flashes were far less troubling than the fearsome forked variety which failed to materialize. Gradually, the chaos subsided as the brief alpine storm, so typical of transitory mountain weather, gave way to a gently descending twilight.

Feeling safe beneath the trees, Ann and Seth gathered handfuls of tinder and an armload of dry wood while also searching beneath the sheltering canopies for a shard of quartz or jasper. Seth had appropriated El's blade—or rather the steel knife confiscated from the masquerading brigand. As veterans of many a soldiers' bivouac, both he and the Princess had the knack of striking steel and stone to coax sparks in order to ignite tinder and kindle a campfire. As they huddled together to block an occasional wind from interfering with their efforts to spark a blaze, the pair locked eyes.

"Like old times," Seth suggested.

"Don't remind me," Ann replied. "Camping for sport is one thing. But I prefer a roof and hearth to an open fire and life on the run."

"A pampered princess," Seth joked.

"This will prove a chilly night if you and I don't share a blanket," she chided.

"A fair warning," he decided. "I'll curb my tongue."

"So, my garrulous mate pledges to stifle his sardonic remarks?" Her tone was dubious as she added, "I shan't hold my breath. And speaking of breath, lean closer, love, and use that unique body of yours to block the breeze."

Three more collisions of stone and steel were required to spark a fire. As the flames grew, the nearby horses reacted to the aroma of smoke by flaring their nostrils and nickering their tacit approval.

"A feral beast might object to our flames," Ann observed. "But a domesticated animal will have learnt that a rider who builds a fire at sunset is settling in for the night—signaling, for an insightful horse, an end to further service."

"Would that we could confirm their internal musings by intercepting their equine thoughts," Seth suggested.

"An impractical notion, for would not our heads explode if we could hear the thoughts of every creature hereabouts?" Ann replied. "But attend to the fire, my love. More fuel if you please."

Hmm, Seth sent this thought to his mate.

What's amiss? the Princess responded in the voice of the mind.

These lengths of wrist-sized wood—

What? Ann prompted.

In the dim light, Seth mused, *I took these to be ordinary limbs. Yet, in truth, they appear to be a collection of bones—*

Danger, Princess!

Your thought, Seth? the Princess ventured.

Not I, he assured her.

Danger!

As the echoes of that urgent thought died on the freshening breeze, an explosion of twigs and leaves rained down from above. In that same instant, a gray streak rocketed overhead as a high-leaping wolf suddenly appeared and sank its teeth into a writhing mass of coils. Unbalanced but relentless, a gigantic serpent deflected the attack as it wriggled fully from the treed canopy. Spiraling to the ground, it rose again, intent on assaulting the horses. The huge venomous head reared back, its fangs bared, its wicked tongue measuring its prey. For an instant, the reptile commanded the scene, its massive mid-body thicker than the neighboring aspen trunks, its hexadic skull and muscular neck splintering lower limbs as it poised to strike. Then the threat was overwhelmed in a frenzy of snarling fur as a trailing wolfpack engulfed and destroyed the appalling creature.

Throughout the snake's assault and the wolves' counterattack, Ann and Seth remained motionless—frozen, not so much in fear, as with astonished surprise. The horses too seemed dumbfounded and immobile. Surely, had it not been for the unexpected actions of a platoon of lupine saviors, all four creatures would have perished.

Ann was first to awaken from her stupor and, though she thought communication unlikely, she knelt to minister to the nearest wolf—the creature, as clearly as the Princess could recall, which had led the attack and now seemed injured.

"Are you hurt?" she asked.

My pride only, the wolf responded in the voice of the mind as she—for it was a female—got shakily to her feet.

You are conversant in the voice of the mind? Ann asked.

Forgive my impertinence, but the obvious was seldom so succinctly stated, the wolf answered.

"A well-spoken wolf indeed," Seth observed. "Can you also understand our primitive speech?"

I can.

"Yet you do not speak aloud?"

That, I submit, would be against Nature. Almost as unnatural as Wolfkind assimilating into the ranks of those with opposing thumbs. Without enlarging on this thought, the she-wolf grew silent as the full pack arrived and assembled in ragged order behind her, each animal fresh from its kill and licking its still-bloodied chops.

Surrounded by the new arrivals, Ann and her mate automatically crouched into defensive positions with Seth brandishing his purloined knife.

Pardon my pack-mates, the she-wolf said. *Their instincts remain primitive and your warrior stances prove that you yourselves are not far removed from that realm.*

"You seem to know us," said Ann aloud. Her vigilance was ebbing, yet she continued to monitor the nearby pack with a wary eye. "By virtue of our exchange of thoughts, we pronounce you a magical being. But we know little else."

I sincerely regret—, the she-wolf began, then paused to glance, with animalistic subtlety, over her shoulder in the direction of the slaughtered snake. *I sincerely regret that the resolution of our recent crisis did not allow an opportunity for proper introductions. We have met, Princess, though I suspect you have forgotten the encounter. You will know me as Erato Gnomon—the muse of the sundial.*

"The Timekeeper," Seth interjected.

If you like, Erato responded, the tone of her thought suggesting she didn't care for that particular nickname.

"Forgive my impetuous mate," Ann explained.

His recent transformation appears to have preserved his so-called wit. The clear-thinking wolf made this suggestion without altering her non-committal lupine expression to summon the wry smile which would ordinarily accompany such a cutting remark.

"Indeed," Ann said and, despite their circumstances, she couldn't avoid gracing the wolf with a complementary grin. "If his wit were cut in twain," she added, "my adroit mate would yet be a—"

"Half-wit," Seth guessed. "Truly, ladies, in this contest of clever phrases, I am out of my league. Therefore, I'll retire from this battle of wits and hold my peace."

"A rare occurrence by half," Ann whispered to the bemused wolf.

"I heard that," retorted Seth as he pocketed his knife and raised his sword hand to assure the pack he was unarmed.

Holding the wolves' full attention, Seth furrowed his brow and lowered his hand. When his hand was shoulder high, he pushed it forward and held it in a locked position—palm toward the wolfpack and fingers pointing skyward. His nonverbal gesture seemed to resonate with the feral beasts as each wolf sat back on its haunches, then dropped to its elbows and looked expectantly up. To his delight, the entire pack assumed a universal pose of obedience as if the wolves were domestic dogs reacting to their master's command to sit and stay.

As Seth strode triumphantly away, presumably to see to the horses, the females—woman and wolf—watched him go. When he was beyond hearing or thinking range, Erato reached out to Ann in the voice of the mind.

That one believes he commands my pack.

Whereas— Ann prompted.

Lean closer, she told her human counterpart.

Ann obeyed.

Notice, please, the disposition of my ears, Erato confided.

A delicate flick of the she-wolf's left ear produced in the pack a low rumbling growl. A similar mild movement of her right ear jerked the savage cohort to its feet and a cessation of that riffle sent them back to their facsimile position as obedient show dogs.

Impressive, Ann thought.

All in a day's work, Seth agreed as he belatedly drew within range of the voice of the mind and intercepted what he took to be a belated compliment praising the perfection of his triumph over the pack.

The Princess sought Erato's eye and hoped she conveyed, in that furtive glance, the Wolfkind to Alpha-Wolf equivalent of a silent plea to "let this be our little secret."

After sunset, darkness shrouded the sprawling meadow and obscured the immensity of the vast rock-walled cauldron. Around the glow of a campfire—in keeping with custom—traditional tales were warmly exchanged. Ann and Seth sat side-by-side swathed in their Bluebell cloaks. As for the animals, the fireside occasion was tolerated by the horses, shunned by the pack in general, but attended—even relished—by Erato. While the horses bedded down and wolves kept vigil just beyond the pool of campfire light, the pack's lucid leader seemed to enjoy keeping company with the newly-minted humans. When the old stories of disembodied spirits, mysterious one-armed bell-ringers, and avenging headless horsemen had been told, Ann and Seth took a leap of faith.

"May we share what we understand regarding our transformations from Wolfkind to human?" Ann asked.

The wolf nodded her assent.

Ann told of her escape from the town square and Seth told a similar story of battlefield survival—though he could not recall many details.

"I hoped I would ascend to Velyn," Seth confided. "Instead, I somehow returned to this world without knowing the means of my salvation."

We can only know what we know, Erato reasoned.

"Amen," Ann added aloud as she caught the wolf's eye and suggested a change of topic. "And you may also wish to hear what little we know of the deity's desire to enlist our aid in reaching the sea."

As you wish, Erato agreed. *Then, in fairness, I will entertain your questions.*

"A generous offer," Ann suggested.

Quid pro quo, said the wolf.

It did indeed take but little time to share what was known of El's plans. The travelers were instructed to cross the mountains, locate a waterfall, then follow and cross a river in order to reach the Western Sea. There was also mention of a ship.

"We know little else," said Ann.

"Except that we were meant to sleep at this oasis," Seth said. He produced his crude map, spread it on the ground, and pulled a burning branch from the fire—then thought better of using it to provide light. "I hope the flames do not trouble you," he told the wolf.

Kind of you to mention it, Erato thought, *but fire and I are old friends. Heat and light are two sides of a single coin.*

"Hmm," said Seth and his tone suggested puzzlement. Kneeling to study his map, he was joined by the others who sat beside him. "We were told to rest here and avoid the temptation to linger in a meadow farther on. Why, I wonder, were we not warned about the snake? Unless—"

A full minute passed while the three creatures sat in silence.

"El did not seem himself," Ann theorized. "He seemed to lack energy and focus—curious flaws for an omnipotent one. Recall how he lagged behind as we climbed—how his human forms lacked divine traits. Perhaps he was unaware of the reptile—no, that seems unlikely—what is more plausible is that he simply mixed up the stopping places, confusing the deadly place with the tempting one."

"A grave error," Seth complained. "An omission which nearly consigned us to an early grave."

And yet it was an error, surely, Erato suggested. *Be not so quick to judge our deity. There may yet be a further reason for El's apparent failure to warn you.*

"What reason?" Seth wondered aloud.

Perhaps, my rash young comrade, he merely wanted the three of us to meet. A dramatic meeting, I admit. But our El is known—is he not—for a certain flair? And now, children, the hour grows late. You need rest and I must return to my pack. Therefore, your questions please and then—though I have thoroughly enjoyed the companionship of intellectual beings—I must bid you adieu.

"I have a question," said Seth, "if you will not think me impolite."

Perish the thought, the wolf assured the man.

"Very well—here is my inquiry—a moment please—" Seth began as he rose to search through a nearby pile of branches. "And here are my exhibits." He held aloft a bleached bone in each hand. "Clutched tightly in my left fist—unless I have totally forgotten my academy classes in comparative anatomy and physiology—is a humerus—an arm bone. In my right is a leg bone—a femur as I recall."

Your question? Erato prompted.

"My question is this," Seth continued—ignoring his mate's frowning efforts to forestall his interrogation. "Since you imply that you enjoy our intellectual companionship, how does it happen that you have—apparently and for some time—allowed our resident aspen serpent to feast upon an untold number of human visitors?"

A fair question deserving a fair answer, the she-wolf's thoughts came rapidly and without bitterness. *Humans, you must know, are the sworn enemies of the wolf. For millennia, humans have hounded—literally hounded using fierce dogs—and hunted and poisoned and trapped and maimed and killed my sisters and brothers. They have broken our bodies, scalped and coveted our pelts—even dressed their wretched bodies in our purloined fur, while leaving our flesh to rot. My own parents—my untamed father and my cultured mother—were dispatched in an unholy wolf-drive. I still dream of the terror—which my siblings and I barely escaped. A dreadful afternoon when our pack was jolted from our siesta as human women and children roused us to the point of frantic madness with banging pots and blaring trumpets. Feral families forced into the open and herded into deadly glades where men in trees waited to fling nets in order to club to death the captured prey. The adults were slaughtered, the pups allowed to live, but only so they too could one day be harassed and likewise harvested. Is it any wonder that we allowed the snake to devour the random human traveler?*

And, moreover, was it not the treachery of humans which so recently upended Middlemount and vanquished the Wolfkind? Our deity must have a jaundiced sense of humor to have rescued a race he claims to love so dearly and recast them, as he has surely done with you two, in human form. I may be struck with lightning on a clear day for saying so, but from where I stand, I'm beginning to wonder if my El is playing—as they say in human gambling halls—with a fulsome deck. As for the deadly snake, that unholy creature has long ruled the aspen grove, poaching unsuspecting travelers and unlucky fauna for decades—possibly centuries. Even the grasses and flowering flora seem cowed by the odious creature's overshadowing dominion—hench the perpetual autumn pallor which persists regardless of the season.

"I cannot deny that humans have treated wolves shamefully," Seth agreed. "And, though Wolfkind have lived for centuries in peace with most humans, I can assure you my mate and I feel no kinship with the odious Fishals. Nor do we love the humans of Middlemount who collaborated to provoke the invasion, nor those who continue to support the invaders. We did not choose these human forms and, in fact, we daily struggle to compensate for these unfamiliar shells. It is probable that El formed us thus to supply we two with inconspicuous disguises."

"That is my view also," said Ann who, though she may have originally been opposed to her mate's candid questioning, seemed now willing to take up his cause. "So, it would seem that we share with you a common enemy."

"Leaving humanity aside—and I have to say that 'aside' is a good place for them," mused Seth, "I must reiterate that it does indeed seem odd that El did not warn us of the extremely huge and decidedly deadly hazard populating this so-called oasis."

"He advised us to avoid tarrying" Ann recalled. "Knowing his riddles, that may have passed for a warning."

"I'm satisfied that he mixed up his meadows," Seth suggested. "He did warn us not to be tempted to linger, but that caution seemed to apply to the lower pasture, not the upper one."

"As we said earlier—" Ann began, but hesitated before continuing. "Even giving our deity the benefit of the doubt, we did notice a—what shall we call it—a fraying of attention—gaps in his speech and memory—as if—"

"Can a deity—like other lesser angels—lose a step over time?" Seth asked. "Can a god age, grow frail, and—"

A deity cannot die, surely— Erato let that thought hang in the air.

The vague hissing and mild pops of the crackling fire seemed to amplify and fill the night. So distressing was the notion of El's mortality and so ominous the implications of such thinking that the storytellers grew quiet. As the seconds-long silence stretched into anxious minutes, each creature contemplated the weight of their discourse until the pensive spell was broken by the tumble of a single fiery log.

Reduced to glowing coals, the wayward log crashed into the flames with an audible crack, its unexpected fall sending a shower of embers skittering up to spangle the night sky. The unholy eruption of noise and sparks startled worldly-wise wolf and newly-formed humans alike and sent the fireside trio scrambling.

When decorum had been restored and the party reassembled around, albeit farther from, the firepit, the curious Princess posed what seemed to her to be an obvious question.

"Why, when the snake—?" Ann began, but Erato's thought interrupted. *Aggro—his name was Aggro.*

"Very well," Ann conceded. "Since Aggro has been feeding off travelers for centuries at a time and since your pack had strong reasons not to intervene to save those unfortunates—"

"What, pray tell," Seth gave voice to his own burning question, "what compunction compelled you to come to our aid?"

"My mate puts it succinctly," Ann agreed. "You despise humans and yet you and your pack came to our rescue, choosing to deliver us from certain death and safeguard our human form. Therefore, why—? Ah—"

You have anticipated your own answer, Erato guessed.

"Indeed," Ann agreed. "From the moment of our arrival, you sensed that we were not as we seemed."

"What a dunce I am!" Seth exclaimed. "Feel free to contradict me," he jested.

"Proceed, dunce," Ann laughed.

"The incident with the serpent was merely a case of wolf-kind helping Wolfkind," Seth suggested, using his ghastly exhibits to gesture broadly in an effort to emphasize his points. "You may not follow my statement, but pretend you can visualize my use of both 'kinds' and distinguish, while also connecting, the two species."

I can see your argument as clearly as I perceive the white-bleached bones of our common enemy in your human-like hands, Erato declared. *As for the catalyst for our assistance—* Erato began then paused and asked without the least hint of condescension. *Dost thou know the meaning of catalyst?*

"Motivation," said Ann.

"Stimulus—nay reason," said Seth.

Excellent. To continue, then, the catalyst or reason for our help was—naturally—our kinship. Even before you related this night your tale of transformation and resurrection, I sensed—from the moment you entered our realm—that you were once, and in many ways, still remain denizens of the noble Wolfkind race. The moment the pair of you squeezed through that infernal crack in the southern wall, I said to myself—for who else had I to share the thought— Oh, fie—

Erato paused.

I have—how do the humans put it? Lost the thread of my thoughts. Ah yes, I have it. The moment you appeared astride your disparate mounts, I told myself this: 'That which was presumed lost has been found.' I said as much to myself. And so, in answer to Seth's fervent inquiry, we wolves did as we always do—as we always will do—we did for our kit and kin—we did for our kind—in this case, our Wolfkind. When the storm drove you thence—or thirst—or whatever the cause—we, that is I, could not allow the snake to exercise dominion over you. The reptiles once ruled this dream, but not today!

"And we have yet to properly thank you," said Ann. "Moreover, we have shamefully neglected to acknowledge and honor your part and the courage of our dear cousins." Having rendered this sincere Mea culpa, Ann knelt before the she-wolf then, with sincere tears of contrition clouding her eyes, the Princess reached up to embrace the flustered animal.

Not so, Erato protested. *Not so, great Princess. You should not pay me homage. Go to! Go to, child. Regain your feet or at least sit down. You break my heart, good soul. Arise, fair one, and leave me my dignity at least. Forsooth. Go to, I say! Arise!*

"I'll curtail my present praise," said Ann. "But carry it here—always here," she touched her heart.

Forsooth, came Erato's final, but decidedly irresolute, rebuke.

"My mate steals my thunder," said Seth whose attempt at strong words faded while his subdued tone betrayed his own emotion. "And my gratitude will reside here as well," he touched his own heart.

The honor is mine, their host closed both keen eyes, lowered her sleek muzzle, and bowed her powerful neck. *Now I must add more regarding your earlier question,* she continued. *Regarding why, over the years, we have not intervened to check Aggro's appetite for visitors. We have little love for ordinary humans. But, in my memory, only a handful of strangers have penetrated this far into the mountains. A very few attempt the ascent. Only a fraction of those survive to pass beyond the first range. Those which are not disheartened by the vanishing trail, perish over its unforgiving edge. An infinitesimal percentage of wayfarers discover one end of the crack which leads to this meadow. A scintilla of that much-diminished herd finds the way through and the head of a pin holds more rain than the droplets of upright beings which stumble herein. Do I make my meaning clear?*

"Not much passes this way," Ann ventured.

Precisely.

"And our brother and sister wolves know well enough to steer clear of the mother—or rather the father—of all serpents," added Seth.

Naturally.

"Which," Ann suggested, "makes for one extremely ill-tempered, not to mention hungry, slinking ambassador of death."

Well put.

"Which part," Ann wondered aloud. "The slinking-part or the ambassador-part?"

The Death-part.

The nighttime thunder which accompanied this thought may have been coincidental. Then again, it may have been prescient.

"Ah," said Ann. "I presume we are talking *Death* with a capital *D*."

Capital-D Death, Erato confirmed.

"The snake—Aggro—represents an instrument of Death?" speculated Seth unable to mask the tremulous warble which unbalanced his voice.

One of many ills which the Blessed Chronicles maintain the Dark Lord is prepared to unleash upon the World as we know it. May it not come to pass.

"May it not come to pass," Seth repeated the sentiment, intoning the fervent incantation which every Middlemount denizen from an early age recites before committing the soul to rest. It is the prayer of every human, Wolfkind, or wolf—this shared desire to forestall the ravages of Death. It is the hope of every conscious and sentient being; the hope even of rocks and plants and water and the very air.

"May it never come to pass," parroted Ann.

Amen, concluded the unlikely trio sharing the night and the campfire. It was a thought expressed in unison with the living world—a thought in solidarity to sustain and continue in perpetuity that world's current—and only known—dream.

Chapter 8

Waterfall

Gravity is one of this dream's unerring laws. At first, within the friendly confines of a gently sloping channel, gravity coaxes water downward and the flow trickles blithefully along with unhurried dignity, seeking the sea. The upstream conversation among rock, sand, and water is polite and civil and languid. But downstream can be heard a growing vibration—not unlike the labored breathing of a sleeping giant. As the angle of descent increases, that rhythmic breath becomes an audible rumble. Farther on, rumbling gives way to a steadily rising pulse, as insistent as a drumroll, as urgent as the unbridled rhythm of pouring rain. Soon, conversation is reduced to shouting. Ahead is a visceral roar, punctuated with irregular booms, more reminiscent of aerial thunder than anything experienced here below. A surge of speed and the riverbed dissolves as rushing water meets empty air and dives, in the grip of gravity, over a sudden cliff and into an unthinkable abyss.

Without Erato's aid, the travelers would have been long in searching for the exit from the harrowing stop-over which Seth labeled "Aggro's Retreat" on his primitive parchment map. The way in had amounted to a barely discernable crease in the living rock and the way out appeared narrower still.

"I don't believe we'll fit in there with our clothes on," Seth quipped.

Absolutely no interest in seeing a bare-naked human, Erato assured her guests. *Zero,* the she-wolf added emphatically.

"Take a deep breath," Ann instructed her doubting mate. "And think about something small—"

"Nothing springs to mind," Seth interrupted. "And I have no intention of emptying my pockets. I need our knife and I have a great fondness for our holed-stone."

"I've asked you kindly to drop that foolish custom," Ann chided.

If you two are commencing an argument, Erato cautioned, *I also have no interest in enduring the cacophony of that particular human foible.*

"To pursue a credible argument," Ann noted, "both parties must be prepared to introduce elements of logic, plausible examples, statistics, and—where appropriate—apt quotations from learned sources. If this were a proper debate, I doubt the proposition that a pony and said pony's fair-haired rider cannot fit into a perfectly passable corridor will carry the day."

"You were always best at making a case," Seth admitted. "Whereas I excel at games and contests of speed."

"Shall we race?" Ann cried as she urged her stallion into the opening. "I am off!"

"A foul!" shouted Seth as he started to follow, only to immediately check Daffodil, then turn the pony and canter back to address the wolf. "I bid you good morning, mistress," he smiled, doffed his hat, and wheeled back to pursue his charging mate. "A palpable foul!" he yelled as he galloped toward the rockface and, though the crack he entered was indeed a subtle opening, it seemed to swallow horse and rider.

A man and woman alone, Erato sighed. *As brave and as foolish as unweaned children. May El protect and guide them.*

"Did you perceive our benefactor's final thoughts?" Ann asked when Seth emerged on the far side of the cauldron exit.

"Muddled by the rocks," said Seth. "A prayer to El, I think."

"Not a bad idea," Ann mused as the two riders aligned their horses and trotted abreast. "What better way to commence this portion of our journey than suspending our haste to invoke El's blessing?"

"I can pray while riding," Seth assured his mate. "And my horseback prayer will include an inquiry regarding our near disaster among the aspens. In any event, we'll see our deity soon and, with luck, I can satisfy my curiosity in person."

"Luck is a fickle companion," Ann declared. "In truth, I will go no further without a morning prayer. Stand fast, my love, and join me in silent reflection."

"As you wish."

Reaching a crossroads, the two travelers reined-in their mounts and paused to pray. Eyes closed and head bowed, each entered that elegant realm of the mind set aside for spiritual reflection.

For her part, Ann was grateful for fine weather and a change of scenery. She silently sang El's praises and prayed to still be singing when evening fell.

Less pious in his meditation, Seth began with a desire to seek an explanation of the snake incident. But he had sufficient humility to curb his selfish urges by seeking El's blessing upon his mate, their journey, and Migral's departed soul.

Moments later, Seth ended his prayers with a spoken, "Amen."

When he didn't hear Ann's corresponding conclusion, he opened both eyes and found himself alone at the crossroads. Spying his mate as she veered off the main trail, he called after her.

"Where away, my love?"

Without changing direction, Ann shouted back.

"My stallion prefers a westward track," she declared. "Maintaining our former morning line would carry us to the Northern Sea. We are surely bound for the western ocean. To reach that grand destination, we must pass by way of what I am given to understand is a substantial fall of water. And to find said waterfall, I surmise we must follow yonder stream. Do you disagree?"

Hearing no response, she turned in her saddle in time to catch a glimpse of Seth and his prancing pony as they rocketed past.

"Catch us if you can," he crowed.

The westward trail was broad and flat and the two riders raced briskly through open country. Then they slowed their mounts and proceeded at a more practical pace, following a gradual incline of rolling hills and the downstream flow of an ever-widening waterway. Water was plentiful as were bushes teeming with berries and uncultivated orchards resplendent with firm apples and succulent pears. Briefly dismounting to replenish their supplies, Ann and Seth refilled water skins and stuffed saddlebags until all containers overflowed with abundance. As they continued on, deer stood motionless, watching the travelers ride past. Here and there, at discreet distances, they glimpsed an occasional fox and other woodland creatures.

It was a land of plenty and yet entirely devoid, so far as their descent could discern, of people.

"Odd this place," Seth commented.

"My definition of odd has, of late, been ever-expanding," said his mate.

"Indeed," Seth agreed. "Enough changes of fortune to *make an odd king seem tame.*" He broke off his comment and, had it not been impractical and possibly fatal, would have bitten his tongue. He'd been careless to let slip that old Middlemount folk saying which touched on the madness of the late king.

The two rode in silence for a time until Ann spoke.

"You mustn't feel compelled to restrain your remarks," she assured her mate. "My father was indeed odd, though drink made him more-so. But having a sire who, literally, howled at the moon is water over the dam. We cannot choose our family—only our friends."

"And our mates," Seth observed.

"And our track," Ann added as she studied the ground. "The once-plain trail has merged into the landscape. Another course correction seems in order." She glanced back at the now-distant mountains. "Keeping those peaks over our shoulder seems our best path. Last night's overcast sky yielded no stars to calculate our way."

"And our outstanding session of daybreak passion meant we missed also the morning stars," Seth declared.

"Did you not see stars, my love?" Ann chided. "But peace—" She reined in her mount and resisted Seth's efforts to pull alongside to steal a midday kiss. "Listen. Do you not hear it?"

"Our elusive waterfall?" Seth guessed. "But surely this timid ground is much too tame to hold a hidden cataract."

"Ride with me and see," Ann proposed as she urged the wine-colored stallion forward.

By degrees and over the course of two hours, a constant drumming reached their ears. Steadily, the noise amplified and the very air grew crisper and more humid while a freshening breeze arrived to pull them onward. With each westward step, their senses were further overwhelmed by a resonant booming which saturated the hearing and tingled the skin. Feeling and almost tasting the tumbling water, they hastened forward, longing to see it.

Within a league, the riders topped a hillock and beheld the lower reaches of the energetic stream they'd been following. Far below, that single waterway converged with a dozen others to form a multi-pronged confluence which, in turn, spawned a roaring river. Looking downstream, their eyes were drawn to a huge outcropping of granite which, though submerged, was clearly visible in the crystal-clear current of the free-running river. Glistening beneath the noonday sun, the underwater outcropping extended horizontally for a deceptive distance before abruptly truncating to form the brink of a sharp-edged cliff.

"Behold the crest," said Seth.

"The top of the bottom," Ann said as she and her mate exchanged a delighted grin.

Unlike its several tributaries, which meandered through streambeds lined with yielding pebbles, the rampant river raced unimpeded over a solid pavement of granite. Unable to resist the influence of a primeval aqueduct, the unchecked torrent had nowhere else to go. Commanded by gravity, the raging river was compelled to accelerate and rush pell-mell toward what the two riders guessed must be a sheer vertical drop.

"A breathtaking vista," the Princess sighed. "A glimpse of Velyn."

"A slice of heaven," Seth agreed.

Even from afar, the topmost edge of the as-yet-unseen waterfall was evident. As if designed to tantalize the viewer, the broad crest of the anticipated marvel was marked by a translucent mist which dominated the near horizon. The mist was fine-spun and might have been invisible to the distant viewer had not an oblique angle of mid-afternoon sunbeams illuminated the haze to ignite a vast cluster of incandescent rainbows.

"El's lamplights," Ann invoked a well-remembered image from her days as a cub listening with rapt attention to her mother's recitations of the Blessed Chronicles.

"Some human thinkers," Seth noted, "claim they can reproduce the sacred lamplights at will using an angular piece of glass—"

"A piece of glass and a vivid imagination," the Princess suggested. "I pray that the influence of our newly-adopted human shells will not likewise mold our thinking to the extent that we question and abandon our faith."

"My faith, which was never so firm as yours, once hung by the merest of threads. And, lately, that tether has dwindled to a spider's gossamer filament—owing to our inconvenient encounter with the snake."

"Once more you quibble over the snake. Sounding a single note," Ann chided, "does not a symphony make."

"So long as we're quoting from the Chronicles," said Seth as he pointedly omitted the use of the more reverent term Blessed Chronicles, "allow me to add the maxim: *Make haste while the sun is shining.*"

"The correct phrase is to *make hay*," she corrected. "However, I discern your meaning. Let us descend in haste, the better to behold for ourselves the wondrous facets of yonder waterfall."

Discovering a game trail, Ann and Seth guided their mounts down an otherwise unmanageable slope. Negotiating a series of hairpin turns, horses and riders zig-zagged from their lofty viewpoint toward a marshy meadow at the base of the hillock. The trail proved to be a surprisingly broad shelf of hard-packed clay bearing the indentations of a sizeable herd of hooved animals.

"What do you make of these abundant tracks?" Ann asked her mate who, in his former life as Wolfkind warrior, had gained a reputation as a skilled and ardent tracker.

Taking up the challenge, Seth halted Daffodil, dismounted, and knelt to examine the marks.

"A variety of cattle I should imagine," he said, sounding thoughtful. "A cloven hoof to be sure, but much larger than an ordinary cow or bull. Too broad for deer or elk, yet undoubtedly a quadruped. Four-footed and stout-bodied with a stride—" Seth crouched lower, turned his head until his cheek nearly touched the ground, and stretched out his arm—lining up a single set of hoof-prints. "Hmm."

"Is that a scientific term?" the Princess laughed.

"Just a small one," her mate continued. "I say *hmm* by way of astonishment, for this animal's ample stride exceeds the margins of my out-stretched arm—my extra-long human fingers touching the far print and the near print coming even with the center of my puny human chest. Making the size of this stride to be—let us say—thirty-six of what my former mathematics teacher used to call 'inches' or roughly equivalent to old Professor Taw's idea of a so-called yard-stick."

"Ciphering was never my long suit," Ann frowned.

"The stride of whichever beast made these marks," said Seth as he remounted. "Is about half my height. Therefore, let us hope we don't meet one, let alone a herd of these beasts. And let us hope these mega-cows are not supplied with antlers or horns, since our horses would be hard-pressed to outrun them."

An hour more was required to reach a vantage point where the vastness of the falls could be appreciated.

"I judge us to be well beyond the cascade," said Seth. "And yet the air remains saturated, drenching the ground, and soaking us as if we were caught in a downpour."

"A neat trick," Ann said as she studied the clear-blue sky. "Not a cloud to be seen."

"And dry times ahead," Seth noted.

With their backs to the waterfall and the Western Sea now fully visible along the far horizon, the two travelers paused their mounts on a grassy hillside and surveyed the bleak landscape which lay between the falls and the ocean. A sizeable river flowed westward from the base of the cataract, but the waterway seemed to represent the only glimmer of life in a barren expanse of muted earth and scruffy bushes.

"Map-makers label this wasteland the High Western Plains," Seth reminded his mate.

"Western and plain to be sure," Ann scoffed. "But not so high, I fear. And bisected, so near as I can see, by a roiling ribbon of mud."

"That soiled ribbon will be The River Smedlarge, the headwaters of which emerge cold and crystal-clear from the base of our precipitating waterfall, then churn westward, to carve an unholy trench through the plains, fomenting a muddy flow which carries an agitated ooze of red-brown muck to the sea." Seth seemed proud of his colorful recitation.

"That lecture neatly summarizes the path before us," the Princess sighed. "Have we water enough for the journey?"

"The skins dangling from Daffodil are yet brimming," Seth noted although, to make certain of his diagnosis, he tapped each vessel, seeking the telltale sound of fullness. "And as for yours—" he raised an eyebrow.

"Both nearly empty from watering the horses," Ann frowned. "And a hard journey to retrace our steps to reach unclouded water and fill the skins again."

"Fear not, fair maiden," said Seth as he dismounted. "I have a plan. Your bridle please."

Leading the way downhill to a small meadow which contained a single elm tree, Seth bade his mate dismount, set both horses to grazing, and divulged his plan. It took but a little convincing for Ann to agree to join her mate in stripping naked to wring, from their mist-drenched garments, a surprisingly ample supply of fresh water. When both horses were watered and the last skin filled to overflowing, each traveler wrung a final mouthful of moisture from the sodden sleeves of their Bluebell cloaks, then stood for a moment in the sunshine examining one another.

"Now what?" Ann asked, then hastily added, "And don't you dare suggest aloud those notions your thoughts betray."

To make love in the open, Seth proposed in the voice of the mind. *Does that not stir memories?*

It stirs them a'right, Ann admitted. *But we were warned not to linger, lest we miss the moon.*

That for the moon, Seth thought as he snapped his fingers and took two giant steps to embrace his mate.

Such ardent strides, she laughed as she welcomed his encircling arms. *A pace to rival the wide-stepping hooves of our mysterious bovines.*

"A man must conquer great distances to satisfy his mate," Seth declared.

"Less talking please," Ann cooed as she took the hand of her amorous mate and guided him toward the sheltering elm. Arriving there, and locating a dry spot under the broad canopy, she kissed Seth soundly and, with a loving gesture, bade him lie beside her on the soft, virgin grass.

"A nest for two—" he began, but she pressed her finger to his lips.

"Less talking," she repeated as they entwined beneath the last standing tree, and upon the last remaining tuff of green foliage, they were likely to encounter for some time.

After an hour of bliss and another twenty minutes of restful cuddling, the loving pair had reluctantly agreed to continue their journey when the horses, which were grazing nearby, stirred and snickered. Clearly agitated with ears pinned back and tails swishing, the shuffling mounts shook heads and pawed the earth. By the time the two riders emerged from beneath their trysting tree and rushed to the horses, both animals were circling and snorting.

Attempting to calm Daffodil, Seth held the pony's head and minded her prancing hooves, not wishing to have his bare feet trampled. Thus, he was standing naked beside his mount with his feet spread far apart when he felt the ground tremble. Glancing toward Ann, who had taken up a similar stance beside the stallion, Seth could tell from his mate's puzzled expression that she felt it too. Instinctively, the nude man reached for his pantaloons.

"No time for modesty," Ann shouted. "Mount up!"

Seth seemed not to hear as a vibrating rumble assaulted their ears and the meadow vanished in a cloaking swirl of grit and thunder.

"To horse!" Ann yelled.

In seconds, both riders were in the saddle, deeply confused and entirely naked, as their mounts wheeled in the dust, gained a modicum of equine balance, and—with little urging—rushed off in a mad dash. Neither horses nor riders knew precisely where they were bound. The only thing motivating all four creatures was an instinctive notion that survival depended on keeping well ahead of an onrushing cacophony of earth-shaking turmoil and billowing dust.

It was horse sense which saved them.

Though mad with fear, Daffodil's keen sense of preservation spotted high ground and the pony made a bee-line for a nearby knoll. The stallion followed and, safely above the dust, horses and riders watched as an enormous stampede of gigantic shaggy animals flooded past on either side.

"Bison!" Seth bellowed to be heard over the thundering din.

"What?" Ann yelled back, then immediately switched to the voice of the mind. *What did you say?*

I remember now, Seth responded with an urgent thought. *The heavy hoofmarks, the overreaching stride. Clues which should have pointed me in the direction of bison. I'd only seen drawings of course—and I dismissed them. Couldn't be anything that big and that ugly, I told myself. The real thing is something to behold!*

This is what comes of neglecting your studies, Ann chided. *Will this unholy parade never end?*

A glance in all directions suggested it would be a long wait. The passing herd occupied every point of the compass and, to make matters worse, the initial stampede began to die down as the once-frantic mass slowed to an unhurried stroll.

"Could these ambling monsters move any slower?" Ann asked.

"At least the dust is reduced," Seth observed.

"Thank El for small favors," Ann grumbled.

"Speaking of El," Seth complained. "Here's another fine mess he neglected to mention."

"He told us not to linger," Ann noted.

"Tell that to the bison multitude which seem intent on dawdling," Seth said.

Within sight of the Western Sea, but unable to advance, the two travelers shrugged, unpacked their dusty garments, dislodged a layer of grit, and dressed. They unsaddled their mounts and checked their provisions as bison milled around the hillock. Within an hour, the herd diminished and, after a trailing procession of calves and a handful of stragglers came and went, it seemed safe to continue.

"Luckily, the lumbering beasts are migrating in a direction which won't further impede us," said Seth as he prepared his pony for the final stage of their journey.

"Unless they take a notion to turn around," Ann frowned.

Seth mounted his pony and scanned the horizon.

"Yonder dust cloud suggests they are tending east and we are westward bound," he said.

"Let's away," said Ann as she swung into the saddle. "We and our mounts are dusty as a country road but rested, which is well since we have ground and time to gain."

"We follow the river?" Seth suggested.

"The river," the Princess confirmed.

Chapter 9

The River Smedlarge

The River Smedlarge is a robust waterway. From the base of a gigantic waterfall, it flows out over the western plains of Middlemount. By the time it reaches willow-lined banks which lead to the sea, it is a muddy expanse which stretches wide and deep. It is a formidable obstacle and one which causes many timid souls to abandon their journey.

Having followed the river for some distance, the Princess was scratching her head, pleased to feel the stirrings of growth on her scalp and regretting that she did not quiz El about his decision to resurrect her as a conspicuously bald female human. She was also scratching for a third reason, because she was truly puzzled.

She'd been diligently searching the riverbank upstream for an hour and yet she could not find a logical crossing. Seth, she knew, was conducting his own search downstream. It was growing dark, and the stallion refused to enter the broad river. Ann tried another likely spot to ford the current, but again the horse balked. So, Ann gave the animal its head and the stallion galloped a half-mile upstream before stopping to bow his majestic neck and drink. As the stallion slaked his thirst, Ann studied the near bank, then looked across the river. She could see there, on the far side, the remnants of a crossing structure.

Two stumps shoulder-width apart were visible just beneath the mottled surface of the river. Visible also were the sodden remains of a broken rope trailing on the downstream side of the farthest stump, its free end undulating in the water like a tethered serpent. She studied the bank next to her and found two more stumps, positioned exactly opposite the ones on the farther bank. A rope ferry had once operated here, a crossing device with a pair of stout ropes extending across the river. The ropes had been secured to sizeable poles which once stood where the submerged stumps now lay. Ann had seen such a structure before.

One rope would have been tied off as high as one could comfortably reach and the other tied parallel to the first only lower—just high enough to touch one's buttocks. Someone standing in an open boat could cross the river, hand over hand, using sheer muscle to keep the boat steady in the current and between the two ropes. If a boatman drifted downstream, the lower rope would catch him and push him back toward the pull-rope as he worked across the river. A strong rider astride a strong horse could make similar use of the ropes.

It would be a fine place to cross if the poles had still been standing and the ropes in place. But, without the aid of sturdy poles and supporting ropes, this spot might as easily prove to be a deep water crossing as a shallow one. Ann thought for a moment and decided that the odds favored it to be shallow—if only because many who tried to cross here would have fallen in once or twice before they managed to get across such a swift and wide river. Only a skilled and a very strong person could manage the crossing without a dunking. Ann was making mental notes on her chances of fording the river without a rope and congratulating herself upon the logic of her observations when Seth addressed her from the far bank.

"Hello, pilgrim," he shouted. "Pray tell, do you intend lingering there all day?"

"How—?" Ann began, but before she could finish her question, the stallion—possibly chagrined at seeing that the short-legged pony had already crossed—jumped from the bank and plunged into the river. Then, with reckless abandon, the animal half-swam, half-stumbled toward the far side dragging its startled rider through the powerful current. When horse and rider arrived on the far bank, Ann was soaked to the skin.

"That was a pretty picture, I must say," Seth laughed as Ann dismounted and hopped on one foot while she emptied river water from first one shoe then the other. "Did you not see the bridge?" he asked.

Ann looked farther downstream as Seth regaled her with peals of laughter. Looking closely, the soaked Princess could barely detect the outline of an arch spanning the river. She had to stoop down to see it. When she stood erect, it was barely detectable against the background of the surrounding plain. When she mounted, it seemed to disappear altogether.

"Pays to be short. Is this not so, Daffodil?" Seth asked. "The problem, my love, is that you and your lofty mount are far too high in the air to see yonder cleverly concealed bridge. If only you and—your animal—had been less grand—you and—" He paused and examined the two wet creatures with an amused look on his face. "Madam, pray tell, what in the world *is* the name of your steed?"

Ann laughed. "He came without a name, but I think I shall call him Grand-Dive in honor of his love for aquatic acrobatics and in memory of this highly embarrassing occasion, the details of which I pray you will not divulge ever in this life or the next."

"Or the next," added Migral as he landed on a nearby branch. "I heard you praying—calling 'pray tell' this and 'pray you' that. You shall wear me out with your praying. I have other things to do you know."

"You realize I wasn't actually summoning you," said Ann—even though she was heartily glad to see their old friend.

"Nor I," said Seth. "We were merely making conversation."

"And bathing apparently," said Migral, turning his black feathered head this way and that to observe Ann's dripping countenance. "Very efficient: to launder your clothing and shoes while also cleansing your body. I marvel at your ingenuity."

"Are you arrived to aid us or mock us? You were expected to meet us at the estuary and, unless my eyes deceive me again," Ann glanced once more at the river and its illusive bridge, "we are yet miles from that landmark." The Princess seemed to enjoy pointing out flaws in her deity's divine planning.

"I will have you know that, within a stone's throw of where we stand palavering," Migral spoke indignantly, "The Mighty River Smedlarge is heavily seasoned with the brine of the salty sea. I wonder you did not taste it with your dunking."

"Would you care to learn how far I can throw a stone?" asked Ann as she pretended to search for a handy missile to hurl at the raven.

"Fair enough. No need for violence. This way, if you please, to the estuary. Let us race the moon!" And, so saying, Migral took wing with the two travelers following at a gallop.

Chapter 10

A Tell-town

Wolfkind are excellent riders and proud of their prowess on horseback. Sturdy wine-colored horses, several hands higher than ordinary mounts, are specially bred to carry a stout Wolfkind warrior. The Princess had yet to test her abilities as an inexperienced human equestrian and the broad path which led beside the river seemed an excellent track for experimentation.

Ann gave her stallion free rein, steadied herself in the saddle, and bobbed in rhythm with the galloping horse. Instead of watching the path, she looked up into the sky and strove to keep Migral in sight. The summer day was drifting languidly toward night, so there seemed little reason to hurry. The moon was unlikely to appear nor the ocean liable to vanish before they reached the coast.

Behind her, Daffodil's delicate hooves clopped on the hard-packed thoroughfare and the music of Seth's lyrical voice encouraged the small horse to keep up with the soaring raven and speeding stallion.

"Good girl," Seth cooed to Daffodil. "My pretty pony. You are the wind, my darling. We will overtake the coming night, you and I."

The River Smedlarge continued to flow beside the path, though it was broader now and slowing to a leisurely crawl as it drew nearer the sea. Its brown churning depths had grown brackish while the banks bore a white mantle of saline—influences of the tide merging with fresh water. Ann glanced at the river and realized that Grand-Dive was easily outpacing the sluggish flow. She thought then of the random pebble she'd tossed into the brook on the far side of the mountains—an act which reinforced her recently chosen surname.

For all the fuss that El and Migral had raised regarding the name, she seemed so far to have little use for it. How was a name meant to open doors? Not many doors in the forest or the mountains or even here on the broad plains. Soon they would be on a ship, another unlikely place to encounter many doors. Thinking of doors made her remember The Bluebell. The last person whom they had compelled to open her door had paid a terrible price. Ann would think twice before knocking on another.

Ann Stone Bride, she thought to herself. *And my Seth tells me that the human custom requires mates to share a surname—Seth Stone Bride,* she thought.

Yes, he answered her in the voice of the mind.

"Mr. Stone Bride, do you still possess the holed-stone from Windlass Peak?" she shouted to her trailing mate.

"Aye," he said aloud, wondering that his impractical mate did not use the voice of the mind.

"Throw it to me." Without interrupting Grand-Dive's galloping pace, she turned in the saddle to look back at Seth and the pony.

"You jest."

"Indeed, I do not," said Ann and she grinned broadly. "Throw it or speak of it no more."

Seth reached into the pony's saddlebag and brought forth the stone. He balanced it in his hand wondering if he possessed sufficient skill to aim it forward. "Let us stop and I'll hand it instead."

"No time," said Ann, pointing skyward. "The night star is nigh."

"Very well. If you promise to at least try to catch it."

"I will do better than that. I *shall* catch it—never fear." She pulled her feet from the stirrups, held onto the pommel, swung her right leg over Grand-Dive's head and her left over the horse's rump until she'd pivoted completely around and was facing backwards on the charging stallion.

"Now you're just showing off," Seth scolded, but he nevertheless seemed thrilled to witness such a daring trick.

"It is, I am told, a very human tendency—this showing off—but enough of that, my love. Throw it." She motioned for him to cast the stone.

The path curved left. Seth waited until both horses were running true again. Then he spurred his pony forward to lessen the distance and flung the stone. Ann reached up, almost casually, and snared it in one hand.

Is this the stone which your mettlesome fingers entwined? She grinned as she addressed her mate in the voice of the mind.

The very stone, he smiled back.

So, I entwine it, thus. She threaded two fingers into the hole and grasped the stone. *And thus, do I pledge you a Tell-Town in the presence of these witnesses: this true path, these passing willows, this sluggish sea-bound stream and,* she looked aloft, *yond pesky raven as well as the night star and the coming darkness and,* she looked back at her husband to complete her inventory, *your handsome self, your prancing pony, and—*

"A horse's ass!" called Migral aloud as he swooped down from the darkening sky. "What are you two playing at? Do you not see the barricade?"

The raven's warning came too late. Lost in the rapture of Ann's sentiment, Seth had eyes only for his bride, and captivated by her own speech and facing her husband, Ann too had failed to watch ahead.

As they rounded the bend, a broad obstacle barred the way. The barricade was made of four thick logs, newly cut and hidden just beyond the arc of the blind curve. It was an intentional trap and well-laid.

The pony skidded to a stop while Grand-Dive continued at a gallop. The stallion cleared the first hurdle, but his jump unseated his rider. Then the stallion's back hooves grazed the next obstruction, causing the horse to roll heavily down and crash noisily between the next two barriers.

Unseen assailants seized Daffodil's bridle and Seth was pulled from his pony, overwhelmed by superior numbers, tied, and gagged. The pony was mad with terror, but invisible hands held Daffodil's bridle. Ann tried to rise to aid Seth, but unseen hands constrained her. She sought to summon her power but, as she lay there face up gasping to catch her breath, she felt a trickle of blood oozing from her forehead and sliding down her cheek.

In falling, she had tumbled awkwardly and collided headfirst with one of the logs and the blow had rendered her nearly senseless. The injury made her weak and blurred her vision. Her final muddled thought before blackness overcame her sight was an odd one.

The horizontal obstructions surrounding me and upon which I have so roundly cracked my head are much too thick and far too uniform in size to have been harvested from the thin willows nearby.

Her head was throbbing. She ought to have been thinking of Seth, but her damaged skull caused her to fixate on the barricade.

"These cannot be willows, they must needs be stout trees cut in the mountains and floated down the river," she said aloud.

"Ha, not so, wench," said an unseen voice. "Quickly! Bind her before her strength returns."

Ann felt rough ropes being forced over and around her body. The ropes were wet and, as they tightened, she abruptly realized the source of the sodden restraints and the four broad obstacles.

"The rope ferry," the Princess guessed aloud, her mind still caught in the grip of her injury. "You cut it down."

"Quite right," said the voice. "Now let us see what treasure you hold in your clenched fingers."

"My husband?" the Princess asked.

"Enough! Gag this talkative harlot! And force her hand open!"

Ann felt a sodden rope being forced between her teeth and invisible hands grappling with her closed fist. She tried to resist. But her head began to throb as she felt her strength ebbing.

"Hurry, fools! And someone gather stones to drive away that damned raven! Schawk! How the bothersome creature dives and shrieks!"

The Princess heard Migral's frantic cries. She could see nothing. She felt unseen hands trying to lift her until she was summarily dropped.

"Leave the cuss! She's much too heavy to carry," shouted a voice.

"We'll be punished if we don't take prisoners," said another voice.

"Take the man then and the horses! Let's away!"

Unable to see, Ann heard no more, but she definitely smelled an unpleasant odor. As she lost consciousness, her clenched fist relaxed, and the holed-stone fell from her grasp.

As the stone lay on the path, an unseen foot stumbled into it. Uttering an oath, the owner of that invisible toe reached down to grasp the offending object and hurled the stone over the pathway into the passing river where it instantly sank, never to be seen again.

Chapter 11

A Cave

A Wolfkind is unused to losing consciousness. It would take a tremendous blow, a concussive force much stronger than a mere fall from a horse, to knock a thick-skulled Wolfkind senseless.

The Princess' human form might be attractive in a way and its smooth nakedness made it a useful device for lovemaking, but it was far less sturdy than her previous vessel. Ann would have to take more care in this life, and she intended to do so, if only she could awaken. She seemed to float just outside the realm of waking. Her thoughts were jumbled but, thinking of her missing mate, she forced herself by degrees to return to the world. When at last she opened her eyes, her sight had returned, but she was supine between the logs and still tightly bound.

Migral had done what he could to free Ann, but it was well that the Princess awakened because it would have taken the bird a week to peck through the sturdy ropes.

With her strength returned, the Princess shed the ropes with a single shrug and leapt upright, intent on giving chase. "Which way?" she shouted.

"Southward," Migral answered.

"How long?"

"An hour. But never fear, I trailed them to their cave."

Ann recalled the odor which filled her nostrils before she swooned. "Dung people?" she asked. As she questioned the bird, the Princess snatched two willow branches, broke them off to make sharp points, and carried them south, running at full speed with the raven flying close beside her.

"They are surely Dungs," agreed Migral. "Though I never knew the foul creatures to be invisible."

"Bewitched, no doubt," the Princess decided.

"No doubt," the raven agreed.

"Haste then! If Ahoo is behind this ambush, we must rescue Seth! I have their scent now! Fly ahead and do what you can to help him!" As the raven rose, Ann called after the speeding bird, "How far?"

"Four leagues! I have called my flock—you'll see them circling!"

Ann put her head down then and ran like the wind—a driving gale and faster—for she would not lose her love again. As she ran, dusk descended. After a league, she topped a hill and saw the circling ravens. She redoubled her speed and rapidly covered the remaining ground.

In moments, she reached a pile of boulders above which the birds formed a lofty arc. The ravens were high and nearly indiscernible in the darkening sky, but their caustic calls were unmistakable. On the ground, a circle of small fires ringed a clearing. The fires were clustered in front of the boulders and provided enough light for Ann to detect a dark opening between the largest rocks. As she surveyed the scene, formulating a plan, Migral landed on her shoulder.

"There is the cave of which I spoke," the bird reported. "Your Seth is inside and unharmed—as best I can determine—unharmed but caged."

"Caged?" Ann growled. She cast her willow spears aside as her anger rose and might have rushed pell-mell into the clearing had Migral not dug his talons into her tense shoulder.

"Remember these Dung people cannot be seen, which makes them dangerous out of proportion to their diminutive size. But now that darkness has fallen, we can use the shadows to our advantage. Be guided by me in this. I will bring a storm to extinguish those fires and herd our foes away from the cave."

The Princess was tempted to ask why Migral hadn't employed his magic to rescue them at the barricade, but she remembered that her own powers seemed to ebb and flow. It must be the same with the raven. Even while she considered these things, her strength seemed much diminished as if her energetic run to the cave had tired her. Being tired was a new sensation. Given her diminished state, she decided to conform to Migral's suggestion, although she couldn't resist voicing an observation. "You will find invisible creatures difficult to herd."

"Leave that to me. The Dungs are a sheepish and skittish lot and fog is my ally. Encased in fog, even the invisible breeze is seen to stir. Once my fog descends, the Dungs cannot hide. When I detect them, I will bring wind and sleet and hail to drive them that way." Migral pointed his wing eastward. "While you—" the bird pointed in the opposite direction. "You sidle that way toward the cave."

"Sidle, you say?"

"Yes, *sidle*. Go around and do not enter the clearing."

"But—"

"Look closely, Princess, nearer the fires. What do you see?"

Ann looked and saw that the spaces between the fires were pockmarked with wide indentations in the ground—each indentation covered with loose branches.

"Tiger pits," she sneered.

"Yes, tiger pits—traps that will work as well to snare a former Wolfkind or new human. Tumble in and the Dungs will cast wood and stones and fire upon you until that pit becomes your grave."

"I understand," said Ann. "I will sidle. Only let us hurry."

"My part commences," said Migral as he took to the air.

A breeze rose instantly and gathered strength while clouds obscured the stars and extinguished the moon. Ann remembered the wind which had heralded the beginning of her salvation from the town square—was that three days ago, or four, or more? It seemed an age since she'd escaped from her armor.

Where is that metallic heirloom now? she wondered. *In a museum? Unlikely.*

Her thoughts were meandering. Perhaps she was still feeling the effects of the blow to her skull. She shook her head and willed herself to stay focused.

The rising wind was followed by a thick swirling fog which blanketed the fires, surmounted the boulders, and reached high into the darkened sky. No sooner were the fires muffled, than hail and sleet slashed out of the west. In the deluge, Ann could discern the movement of frantic shapes as the otherwise unseen Dungs darted through the fog while the storm drove them relentlessly eastward. The Dungs ran wildly to escape the sudden weather. They abandoned the clearing and fled toward a precipice where many were forced to cling to a narrow ledge, unable to go farther, unable to return.

When the storm was howling at full tilt, Ann slipped along the edge of the clearing. She was nearing the cave entrance when an invisible body collided with her. Apparently, an individual had eluded the storm and returned to seek shelter in the cave. She seized the apparition and brought her clenched fist down hard upon what she imagined to be the creature's head. It smelled of Dung and she knocked it senseless. Twice more she encountered careening bodies seeking to shelter in the cave and twice more she left the specter unconscious. At last, she reached the cave mouth and darted in.

Inside the cave, the roaring of the storm was left behind and Ann was enveloped in darkness. Water seemed to be dripping somewhere, though echoes made it difficult to determine its exact direction. Migral had said Seth was inside a cage.

Where might a cage be? she wondered. *Dung people are inherently lazy and would be reluctant to build a cage let alone, once built, drag it very far. So, the cage must be near the entrance.*

She reached out with her thoughts but received no reply. Something was interfering with the voice of the mind—perhaps the echoes—unless—

The Princess froze in place as the terrifying thought that Seth might be dead flickered through her head—a dreadful notion which pierced her mind like a white-hot poker.

"Seth!" she shouted as echoes washed over her.

"Here, love!"

The cage was not far. Ann reached it in seven steps and her hands encountered the thick metal bars. She grasped them tightly, intending to peel them apart, when she felt the ground tremble.

"The cave!" Migral's voice echoed from the entrance. "The pile is collapsing! This way! This—" The bird's voice was lost in a rumble of crashing boulders.

Chapter 12

The Invisible Shepherd

The distance between life and death is narrow. One moment a being is erect and feeling power; the next she is prostrate and gasping for air. Seconds pass, and the constricted interval between existence and oblivion evaporates.

Choking dust filled the cave. All vision was lost. All hearing was muffled by the noise of the collapse and a ringing sensation which echoed in her ears. The Princess felt the weight of soil and solid rock upon her back. With effort, she turned her head and tried to breathe.

The earth—a source of Wolfkind power—pressed upon her, but she seemed unable to draw strength from it. Instead, it was crushing the life from her. Ann tried not to imagine what it was doing to her mate. She could neither hear Seth, nor sense him. She could not reach him. She could not move. They would die here together if he was not already dead. Her ribs ached. She closed her eyes against the pain. There would be time yet for one more prayer. She prayed that her mate's suffering would be brief, that she would see him in Velyn.

"Arise, lamb. It is not your time."

The voice of El filled her ears.

"Arise—there is yet much to be done."

Ann flexed her muscles and felt the crushing boulders shudder. She pressed her palms against the ground, then extended her arms and forced her upper torso free as rocks and soil rolled off her back like beads of water. She stood erect, used a finger to dislodge a mouthful of dirt and pebbles, and was relieved to see that the cage was untouched.

Sitting cross-legged inside the enclosure, Seth gazed bemusedly in her direction. "Did you enjoy your nap?" he smiled.

In answer, Ann parted the metal bars, swept her love into her arms, and held him tightly, forcing her strength to moderate to avoid crushing the startled man.

"My goodness how you carry on," said Seth, but he did not resist her passionate embrace. She held him for several moments more before she kissed his neck and led him out. When they were clear of the cage, she surveyed the damage. The cave itself remained intact. Only a small portion of the ceiling and one wall had fallen—enough to bury her and block the entrance.

"What caused this landslide?" asked Ann.

"The storm I think," Seth speculated.

"And Migral?" asked Ann.

"Outside I think."

"El?"

"Unseen, as usual."

"The horses?"

Seth frowned. He had no answer.

"We will find them," Ann assured him. "Stand aside, my love, while I clear away this rubble." She broke two bars from the cage and used them to carve an exit through the wall of rocks and boulders which blocked the entrance.

"Such a lady," Seth said, "to open a door for a gentleman."

Ann smiled—here was a door at last—and she redoubled her digging until she broke through. The refreshing night air rushed over them as, breathing deeply, they emerged from the cave. She was tempted to drop the bars, but a sense of caution compelled her to retain them as weapons. The fog still lingered, but the storm had passed, leaving in its powerful wake only a mild breeze.

"My captors?" Seth asked.

"I knocked some senseless and Migral drove the rest toward the precipice. They might return but—"

Seth called out as something nudged him from behind. "Oh! I found my pony," he announced. "Or rather she has found me," he added as he grasped Daffodil's reins.

"Migral!" Ann called, but she heard only the night wind. Her ears were still ringing from the noise of the cave-in, but she strained to listen. At last, she detected a noise. Rushing to the spot, she located Grand-Dive. Her noble stallion was confined behind a high fence of rough brush, and he whinnied enthusiastically as Ann pulled the obstruction apart. Grand-Dive had scratches on his chest and haunches, but the horse was otherwise unharmed.

"The heroic Grand-Dive struggled against the Dungs," said Seth as he and Daffodil joined Ann at the make-shift corral. "As for myself, I find that my once-virile Wolfkind powers have entirely deserted me. By rights, I should have never been taken by any human force, let alone a handful of undernourished Dungs. By rights, *it is I* who should have crushed the iron bars of my captive's cage and *rescued you* from the rocks, my love. Meantime, your valiant steed functioned in my stead. The fearless horse fought them with his hooves and kicks and cracked a few heads I'm sure—a brave boy, indeed!"

Daffodil seemed to agree as the pony nuzzled the stallion. The two touched noses.

"A love-match," grinned Ann.

But the fond reunion was soon shattered as Daffodil pulled back and rose up—her hooves chopping the air. She lurched and pulled the reins from Seth's hand and twirled and bucked toward the clearing.

"Whoa! Easy!" shouted Seth as he rushed after the frantic pony.

"Stay back, my love, lest you fall into a tiger pit!" said Ann as she threw the broken bars aside and sprang into action.

Placing herself between the pony and Seth, she stood her ground as Daffodil wheeled back, galloped toward them, and reared again. Her hooves grazed the Princess' shoulder. Ducking the blow, Ann reached up and grappled with the saddle and came away, her arms flexing as she seemed to struggle with the empty air. She threw the invisible adversary to the ground and landed on top of the creature. Holding the unseen being with one hand, the Princess reached for a rock and held the weapon aloft.

"Trying to escape no doubt," she raised the rock higher. "I will send this creature below! It will be a busy day at the gates of Callus!"

"Don't kill it!" shouted Seth. "The Dungs were forced to serve the witch! Stay your hand. Please!" He rushed forward and grabbed Ann's arm.

"Forced? How?" asked Ann. She kept the invisible creature pinioned, but yielded to Seth's touch and lowered the rock.

"Ahoo holds their children captive. The woman who locked me in the cage confessed this to me. This creature here may be one of the females and should be spared on that account alone. And in any event, we must pity these enslaved creatures and lessen our harm to them."

"Hmm," said Ann as she set the rock aside. She reached down and ran both hands over the seemingly empty ground. "This one is a male, or I am very much mistaken." She reached higher until she found the creature's neck and applied pressure. "Speak, weasel, how came your foul tribe to assault us?"

"Mercy, Great Princess," the unseen figure coughed.

"This one knows me," growled Ann. "We have no choice now. He must die."

"Mercy! Spare me!"

"Spare you? For what reason? Come, wretch, speak or die!"

"Will Your Imperial Majesty please remove her royal knee from off my chest? And her regal fingers from about my throat? Else I cannot draw breath to answer thee."

"He is well-spoken for a Dung," said Seth.

"Please you, sir, I am no Dung."

"But the others—"

"Yes, sir, that's right enough. Them others is Dungs. But not I. I'm their herder you see—a shepherd by trade. It was a job, see. Just a job—no offense intended."

"No offense? I'm offended by anyone who does the witch's dirty work. She is your employer I presume," said Ann.

"Aye. Though I dare not speak her name."

"And you were stealing the pony to ride away. To warn your mistress, yes?" asked Ann.

"Not so, great Princess," said the shepherd. "I could see the battle was lost and—" he lowered his voice as if in shame, "I sought only to save myself."

There was silence as the unseen man breathed raggedly. He sounded defeated and frightened.

"Do you have a name, fellow?" asked Seth.

"Esau."

"A surname?" demanded Seth.

"Please, sir, don't make me shame my family further."

"No need to press him, love," said Ann as she stood and released the man. "If he is a shepherd of these parts, it will be Esau Downsea I reckon."

"You know me, Majesty?" the man's voice was thick with emotion.

"Only your people. An honest folk I once believed."

Ann heard the man moan, then felt a shape groveling before her and grasping her ankles. "Mercy on my people, Majesty! Spare them! Spare my people!"

"Get up!" ordered Ann. "Middlemounts do not kill for vengeance. Now show yourself if you can. Show yourself, I say!"

"Sadly, Majesty, I cannot. The spell—it—"

"It is a curse," prompted Seth.

"Yes, sir."

"Poor man," said Seth.

"Pity me not. I took this loathsome job for the lowest of reasons. For profit. Much good may the coins do me now."

Silence again.

Thinking the man gone and regretting she hadn't questioned him further, Ann turned to see to her stallion.

"Please, Your Worship," said a voice softly at the Princess' elbow. The unseen man had followed Ann and now seemed to wish to speak in confidence.

"Still here?"

"Yes, Majesty. I've done wrong. I know I have offended. Therefore, I wish—I wish to offer my services."

Ann scoffed. "And of what use would the likes of you be to my service?"

"The likes of me, Princess? One which cannot be seen? What could I not do?"

Chapter 13

The Death of Migral

The song of Velyn is an ancient ritual. It is a way of focusing grief and honoring those who have left this dream to join another. Singing that primordial song and rending cloth as a symbol of mourning, these are how the Wolfkind grieve.

It was Seth who found the raven. The fragile body had been crushed beneath a falling boulder. Only the lifeless wing was visible.

"Shall I lift the stone?" asked Ann.

"I couldn't bear to see—" said Seth.

"I will add other stones then and make this his tomb," said Ann. Her heart was heavy, and she sought a task to hide her grief. Fighting back tears, she rolled two more boulders into place so that a triad of touching stones marked the spot. Then, as was the custom, she drove three willow branches into the ground and intertwined them into a cornice, securing them in place with a strip of cloth torn from her sleeve.

"A place in Velyn," said Ann. She tore a strip from her tunic and tied it to the branches as a further banner of grief.

"As we speak of him, his soul ascends there," said Seth, completing the ritual benediction and adding a shred from his sleeve.

"Amen," said the unseen Esau and then he added apologetically. "I am naked and have no cloth to add, but I can sing if I may."

Ann inclined her head in assent.

"Nowie, Nowie, Nowie," sang Esau and his voice filled the dark clearing. "Lord El almighty. Peace, we pray on all our land. Peace, we pray thy mercy."

"Thank you," said Ann. "A beautiful voice."

"It comes of singing the sheep to rest," said Esau. "I ought to have stayed in the seaside meadows. I ought never to have—"

"We do this, or we do that—either way leads to regret," the voice of El filled their minds. Even the horses stirred.

"Migral is dead," Ann said.

"He has joined our dream," answered El.

"You might have saved him," Ann sighed.

"I was needed elsewhere. I was busy freeing the Dung children from their captivity."

"Praise El!" Unseen voices shouted from every corner of the clearing.

"The witch's curse is lifted, my lambs," said El.

A score of Dungs popped into sight—clusters of naked males and females—and all fell to their knees and gazed toward the sky.

"Go and sin no more," said El. "I forgive you as I hope you will likewise forgive my former slights and neglect of your people."

One by one, the Dungs rose, looked apologetically at Ann and Seth, begged forgiveness and shuffled off. The redeemed Dungs departed—bowing to the Princess and her mate and continuing to praise their deity. When the celebrants were gone, Ann and Seth looked toward the spot where they'd last heard the sound of Esau's voice, but they saw nothing. Then they heard the man speak.

"I understand, my El," Esau remained invisible and spoke in a barely perceptible voice which was heavy with emotion. "I am yours to command as you wish."

"Is Esau not to be restored to his former self?" asked Ann.

"His skill of invisibility is yet needed," said El. "He will be restored by-and-by in this life or the next. He has made his peace and I have secured his pledge to serve us even unto death. Now, lambs, we must hold a council for there is much I would impart. Gather at the precipice while I prepare Esau for his journey. Go, my lambs. I will take form myself and join you there anon."

Ann and Seth were exhausted and when the pair did not immediately move toward the precipice, El amended his instructions.

"Forgive me, lambs. You need food and rest and your horses also. I will provide these things."

"But the tide and what of the moon—?" asked Ann. She was weary, but unwilling to abandon their journey—although in truth the Princess knew not where they were bound or to what purpose.

"For your sakes, I will alter the sea and stay the moon until you are fit to journey farther. Sleep now while I suspend the world. There will be time enough to continue our quest when you wake. Sleep, my lambs, and dream of better days."

Chapter 14

Recitation

When paired Wolfkind slumber, the two vigilant mates sleep back-to-back, facing opposite—ready to repel attacks from either direction—ready to fight. It is an instinctive ritual and not liable to change even in those whose Wolfkind bodies have been replaced by less durable human skin.

Opening her eyes, Ann felt the warmth of Seth's body lying next to hers. She lay perfectly still—not wishing to wake him—their backs touching in the way of Wolfkind. She closed her eyes again and listened to the soft rhythm of his breathing. She could hear the horses breathing too—up on the ground above—though not so softly. The sound was unique, though not unpleasant, an earthy sound of audible snuffles vibrating lips and distinctive puffs escaping equine noses. Freed of saddles and livery the horses stood on the ground above, beside the pit, side-by-side, and nose to tail, eyes closed but ears erect, and legs locked—poised to flee. The sound they made was not quite a human snore and not quite a whinny.

The Princess smiled. She knew that—like all slumbering animals—Daffodil and Grand-Drive were balancing upon the thin line which separates the bestial and the sentient. Asleep and dreaming, the horses inhabited that slender border between the animal and the human—the delicate boundary which separates primordial instinct from the abstractions that plague humanity.

The animal is content to survive, living from moment to moment, while humans are besieged by opposing thoughts of the past, present, and future.

This, Ann realized, was the threefold yoke that humanity must bear in exchange for its precious self-awareness. It was an oppressive yoke which the Wolfkind avoided. With a dual existence, one in the animal world and the other nearly human, the Wolfkind were exempt from the dilemma that plagues the fully human.

The fully human are simultaneously haunted, burdened, and plagued. They are haunted by memories of the past, burdened with present demands, and plagued by their inability to control the future. To be human is to perpetually juggle the contending thoughts of what one should have done with what one is doing and what the unseen future may hold.

"Three balls in the air," said Ann aloud. "Is it any wonder that humans go mad?"

"Hmm," Seth answered in his sleep.

The Princess sighed. Before today she'd lived for twenty-seven years—a venerable age for her kind. Straddling the razor's edge as an upright animal, she'd lived as a Wolfkind with one hind paw in the animal world and the other in the world of the near humans. Now—through strife—she had landed squarely in the midst of humanity. She had become human with the burden of the three dilemmas but was as yet a poor juggler.

"Sleep, my love," cooed Ann as she eased from his side. "I will juggle for us both and attend on my own to our deity's Council of the Precipice."

"Hmm."

The Princess rose and tiptoed through the scattered plates, apple cores, pheasant bones, and empty chalices. Their evening meal had been a bountiful feast and the wine which Ann had avoided throughout her Wolfkind life had last night tasted uncommonly sweet.

She and Seth had spent a cozy night in one of the tiger pits—a sizeable, and once deadly, hole in the ground which El had refurbished for their use. The deity's renovation had been neatly done. The lethal pointed spears had been pulled up, four reversed and pounded into the ground to form bed posts, another dozen laid on end to form a bed frame, and thatch meant to hide the pit was winnowed into a soft mattress on which El bade his lambs lie down. The remaining spears had been fashioned into a ladder—a convenience they'd used last night to climb down into their cozy hole where they ate and drank and slept.

In providing succor, El had been as good as his word, for the Princess felt rested and ready to resume the journey. It had not escaped her notice that the deity had dubbed this rambling journey a "quest."

If this be a quest, she told herself, *then so be it. I shall follow—whatever it is and wherever it might lead.*

Having made this irrevocable pledge, she reached the ladder and climbed.

Stars were dissolving in the morning sky as Ann emerged from the tiger pit. Returning to the world above, she found the horses awake and, like any good soldier, she saw to her animals before seeking out El. Only when the pony and the stallion were properly fed and watered did the Princess proceed to the precipice to commune with her deity.

"Good morning," El greeted her in the ordinary robes of an old man with a short gray beard and flowing white hair. He had manifested himself in the familiar form of the Prophet Pentum. Taking on the likeness which adorned household shrines throughout the kingdom, he was the very image of popular icons which the Fishals were taking great pains to confiscate and shatter and burn.

Ann bowed to her deity.

El-as-Pentum was sitting on a rocky ledge, and he nodded toward his Princess, but did not invite her to sit. "You slept well I trust," he said. If the deity had grown impatient waiting for his lambs to arrive, his tone did not suggest annoyance. But the Princess remained standing, just in case.

"I have come alone," said Ann.

"As I knew you would."

"You saw the future?" Ann asked.

"The future is a dream which none can see—not even me. It was not the future which guided my conjecture but your past. Because of what happened to you in the past at the water-well, I knew you would come alone to speak with me. You have come alone because you have something to say to me that you do not wish your mate to hear."

"You know what I long to ask?"

"Yes."

"About the pain in my side?" she ventured.

"Yes."

"I have explored my body."

"A very human trait," El smiled.

"So, I am told. And you will not be surprised to hear me say that I am missing a rib—just here," Ann said as she probed her right side with her fingers.

"You are correct, lamb. And I am not surprised."

"Am I also right in thinking that the missing rib has to do with Destin—with Seth?" Ann paused. Would she ever get used to her mate's new name?

"But for your absent rib, he would not be with us," El said.

"Was there no other way to—save him?" asked the Princess.

"You will recall how he fell," said El.

Ann wished she could purge that image from her mind.

A month ago, she and her mate were cloaked in armor standing back-to-back, fighting the enemy at close quarters. The invading Fishals secured a hill, formed a line, and used fearsome weapons to fire a withering volley down into the melee, felling both friend and foe. The musketeers reloaded and fired again until the fog of their spent powder cloaked the battlefield, and it appeared the day was lost. But before the Fishals could reload a third time, the Middlemounts rushed uphill through the smoke. Overwhelmed by the counterattack, the enemy was reduced to using their miraculous muskets as clubs while the Wolfkind warriors savaged their ranks with sword and axe.

"This way," Destin had shouted, "a breech!" Her mate turned then and rushed toward a gap in the Fishal line. Ann followed. Mounting a hillock, she saw him running ahead of her, up a narrow valley, and directly toward a line of cannon concealed in the trees. She howled a warning. Destin heard her cry and, seeing the cannon ahead, he turned to wave her back just as the massive guns fired. The valley erupted and Destin disappeared in a confusion of shot and flames. Though Ann was beyond the reach of the cannon shot, a roiling shock wave knocked her senseless, and she remembered nothing until Migral found her. Migral was still a massive Wolfkind in those days before his own death and transformation to raven. The faithful warrior easily lifted the Princess in his strong arms and carried her to safety. In the aftermath of the battle, a band of Wolfkind skirmishers searched the valley and returned with nothing but Destin's chainmail glove—mangled and bloody.

Immersed in the grip of this memory, Ann stood in silence.

"That valley was a cauldron of fire and horrible mutilation," said El. "The destructive bane of every Wolfkind—the self-same ruin that N'dependee sought to inflict on you. In the terrible twinkling of an eye, Destin of Middlemount was gone—body and soul—beyond all hope of resurrection. Which is why—."

"Which is why he had to be created anew and from a piece of myself," Ann deduced.

"Yes."

"Does he know?" she asked.

"He believes he was pulled by me from the carnage just prior to the instant of death."

"Like my miracle in the town square?" she surmised.

"Very like," El confirmed.

"This is a terrible secret to keep from one's mate," Ann frowned.

"Yes."

"And yet he is Destin is he not?"

"In every way which matters, he is your mate."

"And he is Wolfkind?"

"As much as yourself—he is part of you," said El.

"And his memories—?"

"Destin's essence was floating short of its union with Velyn," El recalled. "And I bent down to ask the dew of his ethereal soul if it would take this one last journey with us."

"And his answer?" Ann asked.

"He said 'yes' on condition that his manifestation retains no knowledge of his violent death."

"It is settled then?" she asked.

"Yes."

"To tell him would break faith with his soul," said the Princess.

"Yes. And, as for why all this is so, I point you toward the Chronicles. I know you have memorized the scrolls and I am confident you can recite the creation story—I have heard you do so at your coming-of-age ceremony—and in your native Woolish no less."

"That was years ago," said Ann. "I was a cub then. Do you listen to all such recitations?"

"Every single one," El confirmed. "And every naming ceremony. And every mating ceremony. And every prayer for the departed. And so on."

"Must be boring," Ann suggested.

"Not in the least. And, today, if you recount the story, the telling will ease the distress you feel regarding the need to keep this secret. Reciting the scrolls will cleanse your soul. Therefore, let me hear the story please," El requested.

Ann seemed to hesitate, then steeled her resolve. She squared her shoulders, raised her chin, and rolled up both sleeves. She would do as her deity asked. The Princess would become a cub again and recite the scrolls. She placed one hand behind her back. She raised her free hand and prepared to make the ritual gestures that every Wolfkind whelp memorizes as their rite of passage, the hand motions which, for millennia, have been used to convey the creation story.

The Princess glanced at her smooth, naked forearm. At age thirteen—when she last recited the story from beginning to end—she'd worn the ceremonial nestafil.

If I were to don that sacred armband now, she thought, I would wrap it tightly in place around my forearm and the contrast of the dark leather strips against the pinkness of this new flesh would form a startling image. It would look like a pair of serpents winding around my arm.

El intercepted her thought and marveled at his Princess' memory. Then he gently bade Ann to begin.

The Princess cleared her throat, struck the classic recitation pose, and swept her arm from left to right pantomiming the opening of a curtain—the traditional introduction to a classic tale.

"In the beginning, El looked upon what he had made and pronounced it good," said Ann in a stentorian voice as she warmed to her task. "And the mountains and the air and the waters he filled with beasts and birds and fishes. And this was good. And El strung the stars on bowstrings and hung them into the darkness and he hung likewise the moon. And he polished the sun and set it in the morning sky. And this was good. But El felt suddenly lonely."

Ann glanced at El and saw that the old man had shed a single tear which he wiped away with his sleeve. She smiled and continued.

"And so, El formed the idea that he would make creatures in his image. El knelt in the dust to form his great creations. El fashioned the dust and made Woman reflecting his human side and set Woman in a room of flowers. And El made Wolfkind reflecting his animal side and set Wolfkind in a room of mud. And El rested."

El sighed audibly and Ann looked up to see if the divine one was listening. Indeed, the old man seemed transfixed with rapture as he nodded for the Princess to continue.

"On the third day, El went down to visit his creations. And he found Woman sitting in a corner of the beautiful room crying and pouting.

'What is the matter, my lamb?' asked El.

'There is so little to do here,' complained Woman.

'What of these beautiful flowers?' asked El.

'Why should I care for them, for their aroma, or their colors, or their delicate petals? I crave the smell of meat roasting on fire. I crave the color red, not green. I detest these weak things! I desire iron—bring me swords and arrows!'"

"El closed the garden door and left peevish Woman among the flowers. And El was sad. And so, before opening the next door, he stopped outside the mud room and looked through a knothole. Inside, he saw Wolfkind laughing and jumping and diving as the cavorting creature seemed to play joyfully in the mud. And El looked away and shook his head. His Woman had been a disappointment—a complainer, a disdainer of beauty, aggressive and warlike. And now his Wolfkind appeared a failure also, for it seemed that his second creation had gone completely mad.

"In a rage, El flung open the mud room door and shouted at Wolfkind: 'Foolish creature, what possesses you to behave so? Why do you dance and cavort in this room of useless mud?'

"Wolfkind was afraid and fell to his knees, 'Great Majesty,' Wolfkind said with sincere humility, 'forgive my exuberance, but I felt compelled to search.'

'To search?' asked his deity.

'Yes, Master,' answered Wolfkind. 'With all this lovely mud in here, I imagined that, if I searched thoroughly enough, there must also be flowers.'"

Chapter 15

Creation

A Wolfkind, though bulky, can move swiftly and silently. These stealthy traits run deep and are unlikely to fade no matter what form the creatures may take.

Seth's laughter and applause took the Princess by surprise. In the throes of her recitation, she'd failed to notice her mate approach.

"Well remembered!" he laughed. "May I join you?"

"Good morning, lamb." El greeted Seth with a nod.

"Good morning, lord." When El was silent, Seth asked again. "May I take up the tale?"

"Of course. What could be more fitting?" said El.

"I perform better when my audience is seated and attending to my recitation," he stared critically at Ann.

"Beg pardon," she joined El on the rocky ledge. The rough shelf of stone they shared would have to substitute for theatrical seating in this primitive open-air arena.

"You too," Seth addressed this comment to the nearby trees.

Ann leapt to her feet, prepared for battle. "Who is there?" she challenged the shadows.

"Be calm," said El. "It is only our invisible shepherd in his new guise. Come out now. Don't be afraid."

"I look foolish," said a small voice—too near the tree roots to be a man.

"Nonsense. Come out and join us. You are among friends here." El said and his soothing tone seemed to coax the creature forward. "That's it. Good boy. Come."

After a moment more of hesitation, Ann saw a glistening nose appear near the base of the tree trunks. Then a white snout and two keen eyes and two alert ears became visible. A stout neck came next, a firm chest, two forepaws, muscular shoulders, all wrapped in a crisp coat of black and white fur, until—by stages—a handsome border collie emerged from the shadows.

"Esau—why you're beautiful," cried Seth and he took a step, seeking to pet the dog. But the shepherd—apparently doubting Seth's intentions—turned, flashed his handsome tail, and skittered back into the shadows.

"Too soon, I'm afraid," El decided. "I suspect if we give him time, he'll come out again. So, Seth, let us hear your recitation if you please."

Ann sat back down and Seth—as his mate had done—stood erect with one hand behind his back and the other free to gesture. Recalling his youth, he began with a broad sweeping gesture, pantomiming the opening of a new scene.

"At last," said Seth, "there dawned a day when Woman came to El with a further complaint.

'I am weary of tending the garden,' said Woman. 'I need a help-meet that I may have some leisure to hunt and fish and ride and make war.' And El tapped Woman on the forehead—"

"Checking for the brain no doubt," interjected Seth in an exaggerated stage whisper before he resumed the strict text of his recitation.

"Not amused," Ann growled.

"—and Woman slept. And while Woman slept El pulled from her side a rib and, from that rib, he fashioned Man. Not only to help Woman, but to make Woman complete and moderate her baser tendencies."

Seth executed a flourishing curtsey as El applauded his recitation. Basking in his deity's adulation, he didn't seem to notice his mate's reaction. Ann failed to applaud. Instead, she looked pensive.

"Thank you, thank you," Seth laughed. "And I do not forget the balcony!" He crowed in the direction of the sky. "But I have not yet finished. As you will recall, Man and Woman were made for one another, but Wolfkind did not yet have a mate."

Seth resumed his recitation position and he noted with satisfaction that Esau had left the shadows. The dog edged warily closer until he sat at El's feet, whereupon the deity rewarded the creature by scratching behind his ears. Another flourish and Seth rekindled his tale with one attentive eye on his mate.

"And it came to pass that El went to Wolfkind and asked if he was lonely. Wolfkind told El that he slept yet felt tired; that he drank but remained thirsty; and that when he ate, he hungered still. And El knew the cure for this emptiness. 'I will make you a wife,' said El."

Pausing, Seth beamed at El and his deity acknowledged his smile with a nod.

"And Wolfkind answered, 'Better you should make me a mate. Make me a friend as strong and as clever and as carefree as I—an equal partner—not a piece of myself, but a separate creation just as you have created me.' And so, El did not take Wolfkind's rib. Instead, he knelt again in the dust and took up the earth and molded it—as he had molded the first Wolfkind—into a distinct creation—a unique being—strong and clever and carefree and wise and beautiful and kind."

"I don't recall those last details," Ann frowned.

"That is what we humans call 'poetic license.' If I have embellished, I do apologize. I am but a fountain of truth which—"

"Woof!" Esau sounded a warning bark and vanished.

The others too sensed danger and all three were on their feet in defensive stances, but they reacted too late. In a heartbeat, the witch was among them—and horses, humans, and deity-incarnate were instantly turned to stone.

Chapter 16

Witch

An old-world witch is a being who treads a fine line between the mortal and the magical. Such a witch emerges when a mortal is woefully abused, desperately lonely, and devoid of hope. Wretched and disheartened, she calls upon any power which will heed her cries. Since Death is ever-present and always listening, it is unsurprising when a distressed child is seduced by the honeyed promises of that dark angel. Even so was Ahoo formed when a forlorn girl forged a bond with and became the handmaiden, though not the instrument, of Death.

Ahoo's triumphant laughter echoed in the morning air as she twirled with delight and danced among the stone statues which had once been flesh.

"Good morning, my lady, my man, my precious horses, and you doddering old fool," she mocked each statue in turn, saving her most blasphemous venom for El.

She was boastful, yet cautious, being careful not to speak possessively of El. The last time she and the deity had done battle, the witch had made the tactical error of saying "my El" and that slip of the tongue violated the delicate balance between good and evil.

On that day, her powers evaporated, and she barely escaped with her life. To say "my El" would be to acknowledge belief and to believe in El would be fatal for an old-world witch. She would not make that mistake again. She would address him as mortal, take his name in vain, patronize and chastise him, as one might disrespect an aging parent.

So, she danced circles around the old man.

"Fool! Hypocrite! Imaginary insect!" she shouted.

She stood nose to nose with the deity's statute and grinned and spat. She couldn't kill him of course—assuming he could be killed. In fact, as an old-world witch, she couldn't harm a fly. Her inability to personally murder, kill, slay, assassinate, slaughter, or exterminate any other being was a nuisance to be sure. But it was a limitation she had consistently managed to overcome. Unlike El, her pious and sanctimonious opponent, she could not invoke faith to persuade others to obey her. But she could coerce them to do her bidding by appealing to their vices.

"Nowie, Nowie, Nowie," she mocked the deity and danced. Dancing, she thought of the creative ways in which she had wielded her power short of committing homicide and recalled the delicious obedience she had reaped.

Money was a prime motivator and the promise of wealth combined with a promise of power was an even more effective inducement to compel others to do her dirty work. Take the Lord Mayor N'dependee, for example.

Thinking of the officious mayor she grinned—someday she would indeed *take* that man. For the present he was banished. By-and-by she would carry his punishment farther.

In recruiting N'dependee and that weak-willed bureaucrat's toadying chancellor, it had been an incredibly simple matter to turn them from minor public officials into willing executioners. Too bad the golden traitor was such a bungler. But no worries, it was all right now. It had taken a few extra days to sort things out—less than a week actually—and that sorting had required her to take matters into her own hands—but her scheme was once again on schedule.

There would be no quest. There would be nothing to interfere with her master's wishes.

It was well that she took matters into her hands. The Fishals—who had proven efficient tools in military matters—had been useless detectives. The soldiers had been maddeningly incapable of locating the missing Princess. Torturing and killing women, burning houses, the Fishals had their uses, but they were poor trackers. What would have happened had the witch not surmised from Fishal field reports and her own insights into the scrolls and the deity's thinking, that the Middlemount survivor had been reshaped into a human? And what would have transpired if she hadn't had the sense to round up the Dungs—kidnap their children, curse the men and women into invisibility, and scatter them throughout the country to block the roads? What then? If she hadn't done those things, the search for the Princess would still be headed in the wrong direction and the quest would be advancing.

As it was, she herself had nearly missed the directional clue. In fact, she might never have known to look this way if the old fool El hadn't stopped time—

Ahoo paused her dancing.

Why had the old man done that? Why did he stop time? Wouldn't he know she would take notice? Wouldn't he realize she would track the stoppage?

She left El's statue and sat down on the ground, hitching up her skirts. She hadn't danced so vigorously in a while and her iron boots made dancing all the more tiring. The witch hated to sweat. She glanced up at the warm cloudless sky and furrowed her brow until clouds formed to dilute the sun's heat.

"Weather!" she scoffed as the sky clouded over.

Controlling weather was child's play. Even the lowliest wizard or the most-inept conjurer could manipulate the skies. It was boring. She flicked a finger and sent lightning careening off the nearby boulders. It was then that she noticed the grave.

Standing, the witch walked to the clearing and stared at the three boulders and the willow cornice—a Wolfkind ritual. She grinned. This burial site confirmed what she'd hoped. It confirmed that one of the statues she'd created was a Wolfkind in disguise. But which one? Not El surely, so it must be the man or the woman.

A few days ago, in the deserted town square the witch had used the toe of her iron boot to push up the visor on the Princess' vacant armor and she'd pondered the Wolfkind's irritating disappearance. El had intervened to thwart the execution, of that there could be no doubt. She needed information and N'dependee was worse than useless. All the man could do was babble about dead wolves and newborn sheep.

Bah! A waste of space!

The witch had left the town behind that day and walked beyond the walls until she reached the shadow of the smoldering castle. She needed to think. In a matter of days, the castle had fallen. The Middlemounts had been easily subdued and exterminated—all save the Princess. When the Middlemount defenses had crumbled, she imagined that El must have abandoned his chosen people, the wolf-breeds. The war she had fomented had been so easily won that she assumed El had decided to sit this one out.

It would not be the first time the deity had failed his people.

In the early years, El had abandoned the Dungs to their fate—why do the foolish creatures still revere him? It is that damnable faith at work again, no doubt.

The witch made a promise to herself. She would see to it that the unlucky Dungs were exterminated, starting with their children who were languishing in the vanquished castle's deepest dungeon. Regardless of the deity's motives, the incident of Ann's botched execution made it clear that El was still in the picture. Probably he was still helping the fugitive Princess. The divine one had whisked the doomed Wolfkind to safety and altered her appearance. Ahoo had suspected all these things days ago when she stood alone, gazing at the smoking parapets of Middlemount Castle.

Now, as she paused in the clearing contemplating the Wolfkind grave, she was certain of everything. Interrupting her thoughts, the witch glanced back toward the precipice. The statues there seemed lifelike. She could almost imagine them moving, as one might imagine the eyes of a dead portrait following one around a room. These statues were not dead, of course. She could not kill them even if she wanted to—and she passionately, fervently, sincerely, and earnestly desired to kill the creatures encased in her magical stone cocoons, especially since one of them must be Wolfkind—but which one? It would be just like El to engender the fugitive female as a man—and yet the missing Princess had to be the woman.

"Schawk!" Ahoo cursed aloud. "I would kill them both."

But desire was not action. If she harmed any living thing, her power would be ripped from her bosom and she would be doomed to fall forever in the direction of Callus, falling but never reaching it, never returning home.

Thinking of her bosom, she removed her cloak and unbuttoned her blouse.

Ah—much better.

Despite her conjured clouds, it remained a hot day. She longed to drop her skirt and strip off her pantaloons—but decided against the struggle of fitting the troublesome garment over her iron boots.

Oh, how I wish I could remove these wretched boots!

Her step-father had locked the vexatious boots to her naked feet as a way to keep the girl from fleeing her chores. A pious man, he declared that she bore the mark of the beast and regularly beat her with nettles trying to erase the birthmark from her shoulder. One day, he found her levitating above her bed and imprisoned her in the boots to keep her from escaping. He told her the boots were her twelfth birthday present and he laughed heartily as the girl wept. She had cursed him for his cruelty—had lain in her bed and wished he would be consumed by fire. She'd heard the screams that night but, thinking it was the screeching of an owl, she'd only pulled the covers over her head. So, it was a surprise in the morning when she was awakened and ushered out of her room by two matrons. The silent women led her down the hallway, shielded her from turning toward her step-father's room, and rushed her downstairs into a waiting carriage.

Ahoo could smell the smoke as they drove away. When they arrived at the workhouse, the matrons unlocked her iron boots and cast them into the millstream and tried to force the girl to wear normal shoes. But she defied them and went barefoot, and they beat her every day until at last she escaped and fled to the seaside. Sitting alone in an abandoned fisherman's shack, she used the sharp edges of clamshells to shear her locks away until her hair was bobbed short like a boy's.

She hoped that by disguising her sex she would be less likely to be molested. But her luck was dreadful. One night while she roamed through alleyways in search of food, a press-gang set upon her, knocked her senseless, popped her in a gunnysack, and bundled her aboard a grain ship bound for the Southern Sea.

Shanghaied and put to work in the galley, she was forced to strip, and her disguise proved inadequate. Her shirt and trousers were taken away. She was given a shift to wear. Then they locked her in the brig while the sailors drew lots to see which among them—and in what order—would have the brutish pleasure of raping the virgin girl. Frightened but defiant, she cursed the entire crew and wished for them the same fire which she had called upon her step-father. That night she listened for hours until the screams above decks ceased. Then she slept peacefully.

The wretched sailors did not die. But the burning left them hideously scarred from head-to-toe including their loins from which—if they were extremely lucky—they could manage no more than an occasional trickle of urine. Carnal pleasure became the furthest thing from their tortured minds as, one by one, the stricken men jumped overboard and consigned their wretched souls to the deep. In their agony, they seemed to have entirely forgotten their prisoner. How she survived in the brig without food and water, she could not call to mind.

She only recalled that when she had grown weak from hunger and thirst, she seemed to enter a kind of trance which allowed her to suspend between the physical world of her locked cell and the unbridled world of her fertile mind. During this time of suspension, she pulled a single nail from the floorboards and used it to carve symbols and runes upon the wooden walls—imitating images she'd seen in her dreams. She prayed intermittently to a variety of divinities and, when none of the traditional deities answered, she turned to darker sources and thereby began, by degrees, to enhance her shadowy magic.

Ahoo embraced her budding enchantments despite their limitations. In truth there was only one limitation which mattered. In exchange for being endowed with a plethora of magic, the girl was obliged by dark spirits to accept one condition. It was the limitation of an old-world witch. She was forbidden to kill. This condition was invoked by an unlikely source, by Death himself, who loved to bargain.

Death responded to the girl's cries for help by adopting her as his earthly daughter, an honor which carried with it the self-same limitation which governed his own existence. Through a bargain struck before time with the deity, Death is allowed to rule the dead, but he must wait for other forces to create his subjects—the dead are his domain but not his handiwork.

As with the sailors, the fire which Ahoo had wished upon her step-father did not kill him. Even then, when she cursed that cruel man, Death was grooming her and, even then, she was incapable of killing. Her step-father lived, although he spent the remainder of his life in torment. His blackened flesh somehow clinging to his bones, he suffered constantly.

On the night her step-father chose to end his agony, Ahoo was locked in the brig and in a trance and dreaming. Having cursed the sailors, she remained a prisoner in the bowels of a ghost ship which plied the Southern Sea without a living soul—save her—onboard. Leagues away, her wretched step-father filled his pockets with stones and threw himself into The River Smedlarge. He tumbled in the rushing water, cursing his daughter, and was carried to the sea where he drowned.

At the moment of her step-father's death, his daughter felt a burning pain in her feet as the hated boots returned and her flesh melted into the iron. Now the boots were part of her. It was that simple. She could no more remove them than she could pull off her hand. The boots were a curse but also a blessing in disguise—a combination of factors which Ahoo would come to realize characterized most of life's experience. On that fateful night, she cursed her boots, but found them nevertheless useful for, without them, she would never have been able to use her metallic feet as battering rams to break through the stout door of the confining brig. In a flurry of furious activity, she screamed, kicked down the door, stumbled to the upper deck, and escaped from her floating prison.

All this—her twelfth birthday, the cursed boots, her imprisonment, her step-father's death, her escape from the ship—happened a decade ago although the girl seemed not to have grown older. Every night, just before she fell asleep, she saw in her mind the saga of her sad life, her suffering in the workhouse, her ordeal at sea, her step-father's self-inflicted death, and his vengeance made manifest by the return of the iron boots. It was a recurring image which reminded her why she hated the world and why her growing powers would forever be used against it.

Ahoo left off musing about her past and stood in the clearing in the presence of her statues, relishing the joy of her power and feeling mischievous. She returned to the boulders, examining the grave. Curious, she waved both hands toward the assembled rocks and they rolled apart.

A bird?

The witch would never understand these Wolfkind rituals. She leaned closer to examine the raven and was squatting in the dust when she noticed a handful of leaves in motion. The leaves swirled, then left the ground and seemed to float away—a strange sequence, for there was no wind. Standing, she turned to watch them go, and was knocked off her feet. Landing on her back, she wrestled with an unseen assailant. Then she heard ferocious growling and felt teeth sink into her shoulder.

She screamed in pain and her mind emptied. The pain pulsated through her. She was unable to remember a single spell or utter a saving incantation as her shoulder bled and unseen hands dragged her toward an open pit. She was thrown in and stones rained down on her. Ahoo could feel her strength ebbing and her powers weakening as stone after stone crashed into her body. At last, the witch recalled a single spell—one from her girlhood—which allowed her to do the only thing which her besieged self could manage. She would fly as she had sought to fly from her step-father's abuse. She would escape this trap just as she had soared away from the ghost ship. She could not fight so she would flee—if she could. The boots would not hold her, if only she could gather the strength to rise.

The beleaguered witch was losing consciousness, but she concentrated all her remaining energy on thoughts of escape until at last she felt herself rising from the pit. Her limp body continued upward, leaving the earth behind as she willed herself to elude her tormentors. Higher and higher she rose until the invisible forms of Esau and the Dungs who ringed the pit saw her disappear into the upper limits of the sky.

Chapter 17

Sheep on Water

A witch's laughter is a monstrous thing. It is exempt from the laws of Nature. It can pierce the earth, fly to all points of the compass, and trouble the souls of multitudes. Thus, does foul mirth travel far and thus does it reach especially those in whom an enchantment lingers.

When Ahoo had succeeded in turning her foes to statues, her triumphant laughter had been exceedingly intense. So potent that it had reached the ears of the Dungs who were a full league away and trudging home. The chilling laughter was accompanied by the return of the witch's curse of invisibility and the Dungs had wailed as they watched one another and their own naked flesh melt away again into nothingness.

The wretched creatures fell down in despair and wept, and they might be weeping still had one Dung woman not struggled to her feet and shouted.

"Are we sheep on water?" she bellowed, "Are we afraid to move for fear of rocking the boat of our meaningless existence? For fear of drowning? The witch has returned! Our children are once again in danger! What good are your tears? Shall we lay here forever in the ditch while our children are again enslaved? I say, 'no!' I say we return to assist our deity! I say we fight!" She picked up a stone and brandished it. "Who is with me?"

"Why should we fight for El?" asked a young man.

"Fool!" shouted the woman. "Only El can release this curse from us. El freed our children and now we must protect them. I place my faith in El. Stay here and grovel if you wish. I go to fight!" She turned and her footprints made a single path in the dust as she headed back the way they had come. For a moment, only a lone trail could be seen, then one-by-one other footprints appeared until the road was enveloped in imprints and dust as the Dungs took up the march of their lives.

While the Dungs hastened back toward the clearing, the dog Esau had remained hidden. He'd sensed the witch's arrival and had restored his invisibility before she was upon them. Bolting unseen into the trees, he'd cowered there while the witch danced around the statues and spat and swore. He'd watched as she paused and seemed lost in thought. Crawling farther into the underbrush, he'd been curious but striving to remain hidden, when she suddenly turned and walked toward Migral's grave.

"Coward. Coward. Coward." Esau cursed himself over and over again under his breath. He looked at Seth—his visage frozen, encased in stone. He might be dead, this man who had been kind. He looked at the hardened image of El, his deity, who had heard his confession and given him a path to redemption. He beheld the unmoving Princess who might have killed him but had stayed her hand. He even looked fondly upon the horses with whom—because he was now also an animal—he felt a sudden kinship.

Move your miserable bones! he thought.

His thoughts might yet command his limbs. He had pledged to serve El and the others—horses and all—unto death and now at the first sign of crisis he'd fled from danger. He gathered his courage and crawled toward the witch, watching her through narrowed eyes as she turned her back to examine the grave. The dog crawled still closer, his invisible lips curling back to reveal his glistening hidden canines, his unseen ears pinned back, his transparent paws flexing as he crept farther into the clearing. He was inches away when the ground seemed to come alive with the twirling of leaves. The witch turned and he propelled himself like a lightning bolt. As she fell back his teeth closed on her shoulder and he locked his jaws in a death hold—expecting all the while to be obliterated by her magic.

Yet he seemed to be winning. No time to contemplate why. He simply growled and held on for dear life. Just when he was losing strength, just as his jaws began to give out, he felt the struggling witch being lifted. He had enough sense to let go and jump clear as she was cast into the pit followed by a barrage of stones.

The Dungs had returned. They'd distracted the witch with pulsating leaves. Now stones were seen to levitate off the ground then fly downward into the pit, but that seeming miracle had to be the invisible folk picking up and throwing the missiles. It seemed a day for the meek—he included—to rise up. The stone throwers could not see him of course, no more than he could see them. If the Dungs wondered why the lone witch had been writhing on the ground with blood spurting from her shoulder, they had apparently not bothered to question the anomaly, being content instead to seize and stone her.

Lest a stray stone strike him, Esau moved back until he was well clear of the melee. From that safe distance, he watched as stone after stone sailed into the pit. Sitting there, he rolled his tongue around and tried to vomit the foul taste of the witch from his canine mouth. It was a rancid sensation and he wondered if the irritation was there to stay. His uncompromising bite had drawn blood from the bitch. At this thought he involuntarily laughed—or rather barked. Given his recent entry into the canine world, the word "bitch" had taken on a whole new meaning, and he felt an unwelcome stirring.

Could such a bitch ever be in heat?

Still clinging to a vestige of his human urges, Esau had to admit that—under other circumstances—mingling with that firm female body might not have been entirely unpleasant. He shook his head and tried to force the image from his mind and, seeking relief, sought again to vomit, but achieved only a dry retch.

What am I thinking?

The witch's beauty was probably nothing more than a spell she'd cast on the eyes of others. Based on his childhood storybooks, a witch was supposed to be an unlovely hag with a craggy nose, hollow eyes, spindly fingers, foul hair, warts, and shrunken breasts. Ahoo was none of these, in fact—

Esau fell to musing—perhaps fantasizing—about the witch's incongruous appearance—her angelic face, her compact but pleasing shape, and the lush ringlets of her sleek coal-black hair. Thusly transported, he failed to notice that the Dungs had ceased their attack. Still invisible, the dog moved closer just in time to witness Ahoo ascending from the pit—her apparent beauty still intact though marred by wounds and blood. Her clothing was in tatters, her eyes were closed, and she seemed unconscious. Her body—and looking up Esau could see it was indeed a fine body—continued to drift upward until it gathered height and disappeared.

The instant the witch's body flew from sight, Esau heard shouts. Turning from the pit, he ran back toward the precipice. With each advancing step the sprinting dog became more visible until he had fully materialized a few feet from the others. Seth and Ann and El lay on the ground, each returned to flesh, and each surrounded by shards of shattered stone. The dog was overjoyed to see them, and he rushed from one prone form to the other, barking and licking at hands and faces.

"A timely rescue," grinned El as he embraced and praised the dog. "We are restored and likewise, the horses!"

"Others deserve more acclaim," whispered Esau. With a diffident posture which suggested humility, the newly-created dog drew his master's attention to the crowd of Dungs whose bodies had been rendered visible again. Restored by the witch's dramatic departure and moving hesitantly, the reconstituted Dungs approached. When they had drawn near the precipice, they formed a semi-circle and knelt before El.

"We have failed, holy one," sobbed the woman who had delivered her people from the dusty road of despair. "We were unable to kill the witch."

"Nothing like it, child," said El as he touched her bowed head. "Rise up and stand before me as my brave warriors—as my friends. Rise up, all of you."

The Dungs stood uneasily before their deity. They were silent, awaiting, it seemed, instructions.

"I saw it all," said El. "We were imprisoned in stone, but our sight and senses remained. It was a pleasure, I can tell you, to watch the witch writhing and rolling in the dust and to see her cast into the pit—how appropriate. Yes, I was disappointed, but not entirely surprised, to see Ahoo ascend—she must have conjured just enough magic to flee. And as for her escape—that cannot be helped. You have freed us, and you have done well to defeat her."

"Is she defeated?" asked Seth.

"Where will she go?" asked Ann.

"She will continue ascending," said El looking upward.

"All the way to Velyn? That seems a strange reward for her treachery," scoffed the Princess.

"Not so far as heaven," said El. "She will, I foresee, rise until she reaches the rivers of the sky. And those lofty streams of wind will carry her—" He wetted a finger and held it aloft. "West as I reckon it."

Everyone turned and looked toward the ocean.

"And we'll be following on," sighed Ann.

"Unavoidable," said El. "Our path lies that way also, carried by the same prevailing winds."

Ironic, said the dog philosopher in the voice of the mind.

Yes, my boy, agreed El as he patted the collie.

"And what of us?" asked the brave Dung woman.

"What is your name, lamb?"

"I am called Roseland, lord."

"Roseland? You are well met." El placed a hand on the woman's shoulder as he addressed her comrades. "Hear me, brave ones. The time of Dung has ended. I was wrong to abandon your forefathers. You must forgive me. I was young and impetuous then. Even a deity must grow and change and admit fault. A deity is after all not—" El paused and seemed lost in thought for a moment until he recovered himself. "But I am prattling, forgive me. Now, my lambs, from this day forth you shall no longer walk with head bowed, burdened with a foul odor, shunned by your brethren, doomed to lowly labor. You and your children and all your future generations shall journey across the sea to a new land, where you will dwell forever in joy and peace. Send runners back to gather your children and all the rest of your folk and return to follow The River Smedlarge to the sea. I will send ships to carry you to freedom."

The Dungs cheered, then talked excitedly and quickly delegated runners. Those enthusiastic messengers might have set off at once had El not stayed them for a benediction.

"My blessings and love abide with you always. You arrived here as slaves. You leave this place as freemen and freewomen. Soon you will return to the sea as pioneers—embarking upon lives of great adventure and fulfillment. Leave behind your woes. Leave behind your fears. Cast off the name of 'Dung' and go forth now as a new race to be called henceforth the Dreamers."

The Dungs raised a clamor of thanksgiving. The newly-ordained Dreamers slapped one another on the back and roared with joy as the chosen runners set off to collect their people. Those who remained turned to Roseland seeking leadership and she proved equal to the challenge.

"You three, gather firewood," she commanded pointing around the circle. "You five, cut willow limbs and strip the bark to make slings. You four, gather stones for the slings, then all of you comb the forest for game. We'll need pheasants and rabbits to roast for tonight's supper. The rest of you join me to search for our clothing."

"No need to search," said Esau bounding forth.

"A talking beast!" shouted Roseland and she and the others picked up stones to slay what they must have perceived to be a latent aspect of the witch's magic.

"Stay your attack!" shouted El moving to protect the dog. "This is my faithful hound—he is an arm of your deity—injure him not for he has ways," El linked eyes with the dog willing him to remain silent. "He has ways of ferreting out your garments. You know how resourceful dogs can be and you will be amazed if you allow him to lead you. He will discover what has been concealed as easily as if he himself had hidden the lost items. Therefore, follow this noble dog and you will discover your lost clothing."

Esau bounded off and Roseland and the others gave chase, laughing like excited children embarking on a vacation outing. Ann watched the parade pass and then she motioned El to move closer. When the old man was near, Ann whispered.

"That dog damn-well knows where the clothes are hidden, for I have no doubt that Esau, their former shepherd, was the author of their concealment."

"Best the Dreamers remain unaware of his true identity don't you think?"

"Thy will be done," smiled Ann.

Chapter 18

A Witch Descends

The Western Sea is a broad expanse, and its deep blue waters touch not only the shores of Middlemount, but also the beaches of Redhackle Isle and the far realm of Memora. For centuries, the Western Sea has both isolated and protected these disparate lands. Now, with the war of the Fishals widening, those who have given little thought to geography or politics are about to be drawn into a world in conflict.

Far across the Western Sea, the residents of Redhackle Isle were mending nets when one of the islanders looked aloft and gave a shout. Soon many locals had gathered on the sandy beach, all staring into the sky.

"A bird surely," said one man.

"But falling? Have you ever seen a bird fall thus?"

"A pelican. I have seen pelicans plunge so from out the sky."

"To a purpose only—and in pursuit of a smelt perhaps—but never from such a height."

"But it is a bird surely. What else can it be? May-be it will break off its fall at the last minute and glide away unharmed."

"The time for that maneuver is running short. See it speed! How long before it reaches the water?"

The crowd had not long to wait because ten seconds later the plummeting body of Ahoo the witch splashed into the sea. Immediately, men took to their boats and rowed furiously toward the point of impact, heedless of the shouts of women who remained on shore and pleaded with them to return. The women watched apprehensively as the boats converged on the spot. For several minutes, the boats bobbed in place before starting back.

"They have likely found nothing," said Ewslet the wife of Gigwar, the chief fisherman. "A wasted effort, the fools."

Ewslet was about to return home to start the supper fire when men in the nearest of the returning boats began shouting toward the shore. She returned to stand with a gaggle of women who had advanced as far as the edge of the surf.

"What did they say?" yelled Ewslet, for the wind was now blowing ashore in a furious gale and voices—even those as close as the woman next to her—were swallowed up.

"They are shouting for us to fetch the doctor."

"I'll go!" shouted Meage, whom all knew to be fleet of foot.

Running with rugged resolve, the breathless woman reached the doctor's hut. She pounded on the door until the doctor—who had been napping—responded.

"Doctor! Doctor! You are needed at the beach! An emergency!" she declared and ran off before he could ask the nature of the emergency.

The last time he'd been called to the beach on short notice it was to examine a mermaid. A mermaid? The so-called mermaid turned out to be the carved torso of a woman—a ship's wooden masthead, washed ashore decades after a collision with the island's deadly reefs. The doctor shook his head. So superstitious, these island folk. He grabbed his medical box, fitted the strap over his shoulder, and put on his hat and coat. It would probably rain. He turned up his collar and looked at his watch. He would miss his supper.

At the beach it seemed as if the entire village was gathered in a tight circle. The wind had died down and it was eerily calm. The crowd was hunched over, apparently looking down at something on the sand.

Another mermaid, the doctor sighed.

"Make way," someone said. "Make a hole for the doctor."

The crowd parted and the doctor could see, lying there on the sand, a woman's torso—not wooden this time. A tangle of seaweed was wrapped about the hips of the naked woman—the work of the island women, no doubt, for a similar wrap covered the woman's breasts. Unlikely that she had been pulled from the water with her private parts so discretely obscured.

"Stand back, please," said the doctor as he removed his jacket, knelt, and rolled up his sleeves. "This woman needs air."

"Likely she'll die unless we put her back in the water," suggested a male bystander

"This is no mermaid," said the doctor. "She's got legs like you and me."

"I've seen your legs—and hers is finer!" quipped another man.

"Shush, fools! Don't lust after the dead!" said an irate woman.

The doctor looked up. "Has anyone rolled her?"

Silence.

"My sainted trousers!" exclaimed the doctor. "And you call yourselves seamen? Give me a hand." With assistance, the doctor rolled the woman sideways and expelled a quantity of seawater. Then they rolled her back again. The doctor felt for a pulse and leaned down to detect breathing.

"This woman is alive but only barely. Has anyone a blanket?"

The oldest woman in the crowd stepped forward and offered her shawl.

"That's a start," said the doctor. "Anyone else?"

Three more shawls were volunteered, then the doctor began wrapping his patient snuggly until he reached her ankles.

"Hello, what's this?" he wondered aloud.

Briefly fingering the iron boots, he felt for laces and finding none, he instructed the fishermen to bring a plank in order to carry the woman to the nearest shelter.

"Bring her hither," said Ewslet. "Our hut is nearest." She looked directly at her husband who was in the process of opening his mouth, apparently to raise objection. "She'll go into our house, Gigwar, that is settled. Now run ahead, husband, and clear the kitchen table and start some water boiling."

"And put a kettle on, dear Giggie," joked one of the men, but as Ewslet passed the comic, she cuffed him with such a tremendous blow that he was knocked off his feet. After that, no other voice was raised to mock Gigwar Wingford.

With six fishermen toting the plank, the doctor walking alongside, and the remaining crowd trailing behind, the procession wound up the seawall stairway, down a narrow lane, up another short flight of stairs, and into the Wingford's stilted hut. At the doorway, the doctor paused and addressed the crowd which seemed poised to ascend the staircase.

"Now, we'll not all fit inside. I'm sure you can see that," the doctor spoke gently, as if addressing children. "Go on about your business. We're enough here without you. Go on now. Go home. I'll send a boy around with news if there's anything to report."

"I kin report that she's a looker, doc!" shouted one of the departing ne'er do wells.

"Save some for the rest of us," added another dirty-minded sailor.

"For shame, you heathens," shouted an angry female.

"Go home and soak your heads," suggested another woman.

"Aww!" bawled the bachelors. "Applesauce!"

The married men were silent, perhaps knowing all too well what their wives would say and do if they joined in the catcalls. The single men clapped one another on their backs and lit pipes and took pulls on chewing tobacco as they clomped down the lane in the direction of the tavern. The married men watched them go, dolefully, and turned to follow their wives to home and hearth.

The plank carriers deposited the patient on the family's kitchen table and were sent away—all but the youngest whom the doctor enlisted as a runner. The lad—the only village male the doctor knew who had a sensible head on his shoulders—was dispatched to the surgery to bring back a list of necessaries—bandages and liniment and a bag of medicinal roots.

"Don't delay, Vestil, and don't be pulled away from your errand by those seeking gossip. Quickly now—this woman is not yet out of danger and your speed may be the only thing which saves her!"

The boy was off like a shot and the doctor turned to Mrs. Wingford.

"Have you a tub, my good woman?"

Ewslet beamed at the doctor. For all her bluster, she loved good manners, and the doctor was a charmer.

"Of course," she cooed. "Gig!" she snapped her fingers. "Fetch the claw-foot and be quick about it!"

Gigwar grumbled quietly as he trundled into the far room and returned lugging an enormous copper bathtub which he deposited on the kitchen floor with a resounding bang.

"Well?" Ewslet demanded.

Her husband blinked.

"Do you think this tub is going to fill itself? Hop to it! Boil and bring the water! Must I think of everything?" Then she turned to the doctor with a more lilting tone, "Now, how can I help?"

"Hold her head please," instructed the doctor and he forced his patient's clenched jaws open while he ladled foul-smelling syrup into her mouth. She gagged and turned her head and vomited noisily as she regurgitated a mouthful of bile and sea water. "Mind your feet," said the doctor as vomit and brine spewed forth and splattered Ewlet's shoes and stockings.

"Much more inside her do you think?" the disgruntled housewife asked the doctor as she looked down and frowned at the sight of her fouled floor and sopping feet.

"I think that's done it. Wipe her mouth if you please."

Ewslet had a towel in her hand, but it was an heirloom, her mother's favorite, passed down from her granny. She considered the towel and glanced doubtfully at the spittle oozing from the patient's mouth.

"If you please," repeated the doctor.

"Of course," Ewslet winced as she dabbed weakly at the dribbling mouth with an uninspired motion.

"Not as easy as it looks, eh?" smiled the doctor. "Not so simple this doctoring and nursing?"

"Hmm," responded Ewslet. She was apparently beginning to regret volunteering her home to serve as a waystation for naked women who fell from the sky.

"Shall I see to the water?" the unhappy woman asked.

"I have every confidence that Gigwar can boil and carry water," the doctor said. "We only have need of a modest bath to warm and cleanse her. Her temperature is much diminished and it will be good to soak away the brine."

"Did they tell you she fell?" she asked the doctor.

"Fell in do you mean?"

"You might say that. She came out of the sky."

The doctor seemed not to hear her.

"I said out of—" Ewslet started to repeat her statement.

"This mark on her shoulder," he interrupted, leaning closer. "Could you bring the lantern please?"

Ewslet fetched the lantern, but seemed hesitant to approach.

"Closer please. Hold it just there. Ah," said the doctor, as he eased the patient's shoulder up and glanced beneath. "Look you here on the back. Does the mark mean anything to you? Some sort of local symbol perhaps?"

"I know it not," said Ewslet and she was about to replace the lantern when the doctor stayed her hand.

"A moment," he said. His tone was casual but also clinical. He was apparently not finished with his examination. He took the lantern from Ewslet and held it high in one hand while he pulled the uppermost shawl down to study the clavicle. He inhaled sharply. Despite his role as a detached observer of human anatomy, the shoulder's perfection caused him to raise an eyebrow. His critical eye took in the smoothness of the skin, its apparent firmness—then he looked closer. "Hmm," he said. "Have a look and tell me what you see."

Ewslet looked sidelong at the front of the woman's shoulder, recalling perhaps a time when her own now middle-aged torso might have competed with its firm and perfect loveliness. Her tone was noncommittal. Then she looked closer and sounded incredulous. "Bite mark."

"Yes. A deep bite. And not from a shark, but from a canine I would venture—unless my medical training has been totally wasted."

"A canine?"

"A wolf perhaps—or a dog."

"A dog? What dog could have bitten her like that up in the sky?" asked Ewslet as she leaned in for a closer look. Her curiosity was apparently piqued as she joined the doctor in staring at the injury.

"What indeed?" asked the doctor. "And what do you make of these boots?" He covered the woman's shoulder and lifted the lower shawl.

"They look uncomfortable," observed Ewslet.

"No doubt of that," said the doctor. "Aside from being composed of well-rusted iron, they appear to be bonded to her." He took a reflex hammer from his pocket and tapped on one of the boots. "As I feared—it sounds hollow—I doubt if she has anything inside these heavy boots but her bones."

"How—?"

"How indeed?" asked the doctor and his inner thoughts repeated the question.

Then, for a moment, the two mortals stood in the kitchen, staring at the mystery lying on the table before them. And they might have remained in that position all night had the mysterious woman not altered the situation by opening her eyes.

Chapter 19

The Lost Day

For the Dungs to accept their new mantle as Dreamers took but little time. In less than two hours, a downtrodden race had faced its enemy and been rewarded with a new station in life. Not only that, but they had been rewarded by no less a benefactor than their own blessed deity, who lifted them up and spoke to them in a familiar form and touched their minds and hearts. The literature of the Dungs nee Dreamers began that day long ago with the first chapter being scribbled by the matriarch Roseland. Using a crude quill pen upon a scrap of parchment, she sat in the dust and wrote while her people sang and roasted rabbits on their rekindled campfires.

As the Dreamers prepared supper, El excused himself and left the clearing. He told the others he needed time to meditate. It was an excuse, but hardly a lie, because he truly had much to meditate about. The day was ending. The quest had stalled. In fact, it had very nearly come to an appalling end. He'd been foolish but also fortunate. A deity ought not to rely on luck. So, he would meditate and strive for clarity.

El saw now that it had been a mistake to stop time while his lambs rested, he saw that now. His compassion as a doting parent had nearly unraveled the quest. He'd been wrong to let his sympathy for his lambs interrupt the urgency of their journey. He was a deity after all. He could have ordered the exhausted group to travel on—to reach the sea and board the ship as planned by full moon.

He could have ordered them to march on and they would have obeyed. Stopping time had been an error. Stopping time had brought the witch. The stoppage would go unnoticed by mortals, but of course the witch had noticed. Why had he done it? What was the truth behind his action—what was the truth?

The truth was simple. The truth was that he himself was tired and the decision to rest had been intended as much for him as for the others. A deity ought not to tire. A tired deity made mistakes and a slumbering deity was as good as none at all. For ages, philosophers have suspected that many of the world's ills occurred while deities slept. The philosophers got much wrong, but those learned souls had been right about the inattention of sleeping divinities. El vowed that he would not sleep again, not until the quest was ended.

And it would soon be over—one way or another.

After one moment more of regret, El ceased to chastise himself and turned his thoughts to another more pressing matter. His immediate problem was how to explain the quest to the Princess and her mate? He might as well try explaining it to the horses or the rocks on which he sat or the air he breathed.

Am I still breathing? he asked himself.

El put his hand before his face and tried to exhale through his mouth and nostrils.

Nothing.

He tried to draw a breath.

Again, nothing.

How long before the others discovered that their deity was a walking corpse? A dying deity whose powers were ebbing, a dying deity who dreaded his demise, and who dreaded even more the question that he knew his lambs longed to ask him and would inevitably have to ask. As they embarked on this quest, how long before someone asked the obvious questions?

In his presence his creatures would be diffident, demure, and hesitant, but they were no fools. How long before someone would take courage and ask the sovereign of their fathers, the ruler of all things known and unknown, the almighty king of this world and the next, the questions which El dreaded to answer?

The questioning could be diplomatic: "Heavenly father, is there some particular reason why you are having us climb over mountains and ford rivers and ride horses and sail in ships to reach our destination (wherever that may be)? Could you not simply whisk us there and be done with this wearisome journeying?"

Or the questions might be more direct: "Why, in your hallowed name, is this so-called quest necessary? Why, in Velyn's name did you not warn us to avoid the snake and buffalo? Why should such obstacles bar our way when thou hast but to furrow thy holy brow to stay the moon? Tell us please what the hell you are playing at and, by the way, if it's not too much trouble, please tell us where the hell we are going."

Given Ann's frowning countenance and Seth's inquisitive glances, El feared that the questioning would probably take the latter form—without the "pleases."

How long after El tried to explain the quest would the living listen to anything a corpse had to say? A talking dead man would be a novelty, nothing more. How long before his lambs pulled down his images and took axes to his icons and destroyed the altars they had so lovingly erected in his name?

And how long after that will the world dissolve?

Madness lay in that direction. El would not go there. Not yet at any rate. His strength was ebbing, his powers were flickering. He had only his spirit left and that was eroding daily.

El felt the need for prayer, but to whom could he pray? Here was a puzzle for the philosophers. To whom did a deity pray for guidance? Let alone a dying one? It was a dilemma.

The anxious deity lowered his weary head and, appealing to the universe, whispered an earnest prayer.

Moments later, El heard a noise on the path. He'd sought out this isolated grotto deep in the trees in order to be alone. He looked up, intending to order the intruders away, and saw Esau padding down the path toward him. The dog stopped before his deity, sat on his haunches, and tilted his head inquisitively.

"You have found that which was lost," El smiled and he motioned the animal forward.

"Excuse me for imposing on your solitude," said Esau.

Was it El's imagination or had the dog grown more eloquent with each passing hour since his conversion from invisible shepherd to collie?

I have in truth grown wiser, answered Esau in the language of the mind.

Sorry, El's thoughts conveyed his apology. *I did not mean to suggest that you were ignorant before.*

Oh, but I was ignorant, Esau admitted. *Until I donned this animal existence, I knew only the human way, and that incompletely. Now I have come also to know the way of an animal and my thinking has expanded into something more wonderful, but also more frightening.*

The unlikely pair was silent for a time. A breeze stirred and the melodic trill of a meadowlark gently enriched the quiet.

What frightens you, lamb? El asked.
I am frightened by sensing the thoughts of others—hearing those thoughts as though they were spoken—of being inside another—of having them inside me.
Yes, that can be alarming, the deity agreed.
El?
Yes, my child.

For some moments, the dog was silent until his poignant thought conveyed his concern.

I know, Esau said.
What do you know, my child?

I know that you are—disappearing, El.

Esau conveyed this thought, hesitated, then continued.

I sense it. I had to tell you. Perhaps I am incorrect in this, the dog suggested.
No, child, you are correct.
How can this be? Esau asked.

El sighed, then spoke openly. "Sit here beside me and I will try to explain. I will practice by talking aloud with you since there will soon come a time when I must tell the others. You will keep my secret for now?"

"As you wish, my El," said Esau aloud.

"Sit then and hear my tale," said El. "I may have trouble finding the words. It is not a memorized recitation like the remembered speeches of Ann or Seth and their practiced repetitions of the scrolls. I have not rehearsed and so, starting now, I will test my story and measure my words. And dog?"

"Yes, my El?"

"You must interrupt me if I do a poor job of explaining. Do you promise?" El insisted.

"I promise," the dog said.

"Good," said El. "And I must tell you that I am convinced you were once a dog in a previous life. Yes, I'm certain of it because you are so loyal a creature now."

"You flatter me, El."

"I speak only the truth—so far at any rate. Let us begin."

Chapter 20

The Tale of El, the Swan, and the Cup of Death

The tradition of reciting the scriptures aloud is as old as the unseen world. It is El's favorite pastime, whether he himself is reciting, or listening as his lambs convey their prayers and formal recitations. The stories are his rapture and his creatures—be they human or animal or something in between—delight also in the telling.

Esau lay down and rested his head upon his paws and looked expectantly up at his deity. El smiled at the dog and began his tale, speaking softly lest his words be overheard by others.

"You may not know the tale of El and the Swan," he told the dog. "It is in the Old Tribune—a book which has fallen from favor. The tale goes thusly: when I was young and my creations were just beginning to explore their wondrous new world, I would delight in taking various forms so as to move across the earth and visit my creatures undetected. You see, I thought my creatures would behave differently in the presence of their deity and I wanted to observe and learn about them in their natural state. Does that make sense?"

"Yes, my El."

"Good," said El. "Over time, I took the forms of man and Wolfkind, bat and shark, mouse and bear, gnat and eagle and many other creatures besides.

And one day I descended to earth as a swan and glided upon the surface of a mirrored lake in the western district known as Memora."

"The land of lakes," said Esau.

"Exactly," said El. "In Memora there dwelled a clan of humans who were wondrously skilled in the making of pottery. From the bottom of the lakes, they dredged marvelous clay which they molded, then baked into sturdy bowls and vases and goblets and cups. It was their cups of which they were most proud and justifiably so, for it was said that water drunk from a Memorian cup tasted sweeter than a father's kiss."

Esau whimpered and stirred. His eyes were closed. He seemed to be asleep.

"Are you attending to my story, dog?"

"Only too well, my lord," said Esau opening his eyes. "Just now when you described a father's kiss, I cried because I never knew my father and will never taste such joy."

El knelt beside the dog and leaned down to gently kiss the top of Esau's head. Then the deity returned to his seat and resumed his tale and did so in a more forceful voice for he suspected that the dog had indeed fallen asleep.

"On that day on which I swam as a swan, it so happened that a spurned lover came rushing to the lake and threw with all his might a Memorian cup into the deepest waters. He was soon followed by the maiden herself, who fell upon her knees and pled with him to return her mother's sacred cup which the knave had stolen in a fit of anger. He spoke harshly to her saying, 'To punish thy indifference to my suit, I have cast thy precious cup away. You shall see it nevermore.' With that heartless proclamation, he left the maiden weeping beside the lake. I heard and saw all that had happened, and I changed to my human form. Swimming to the shore, I appeared to the maiden, who recognized me and bowed low."

'Rise up, my child. I will retrieve your cup,' I promised. 'I will likewise punish your detractor.'

'For the cup's return, I thank you,' said the maiden. 'But spare my suitor. His action was but the foolish ire of a spurned youth.'

'As you wish,' said I, marveling at the maiden's compassion. 'Wait upon me here and I shall bring your cup.'

"Relishing the power of my human form, I swam to the very center of the lake and dove downward. The lake was indeed deep. And I was some while in reaching the bottom when at last I spied the cup. As I hovered above the muddy lakebed, I reached down to grasp the errant vessel when I felt the cold grip of Death upon my wrist."

'Thou art in my domain now,' said Death. 'And as thou art in mortal form, so shall I claim thee.'

'Ah,' said I, 'you have caught me it is true but, as I am on an errand of mercy, you cannot claim me.'

'Schawk,' said Death uttering an oath. 'Thou ought not to joust with one such as me who knows his scripture. To speak of mercy to me is a hollow argument. Mercy is nothing to me, I do not subscribe to it. Even so I cannot, of course, kill thee, but I can force thee to watch as I orchestrate my grand intention. I will compel thee to watch as I extinguish the world.'

"It was then, tightly gripped by Death, that I listened in horror to that angel's dark plan to link up the thousand lakes of Memora. To these he would join the waters of every other land and also connect the vast oceans. To earth's accumulated waters he would add a punishing rain and thereby flood every corner of the world and allow the waters to destroy all life."

'Hadst thou been aloft in thy palace of clouds, thou might have prevented this,' Death scoffed. "But I have thee trapped here. Thus, I shall proceed. Watch now as the world thou made washes away.'

'Many will die in this foul venture of yours,' said I as I sought to plead for the world.

'Yes, and the dead will increase my dominion. This is my intent,' said Death.

'Would it not be more a prize to spare the world and kill me instead?' I asked.

"Hearing this unexpected question, Death—who was about to raise his scepter to summon the destructive waters—paused in the midst of his evil intent and gazed upon me."

'Thou wouldst deliver thyself into my hands and submit to die?'
'I will if you will spare the world.'
'Thou propose a bargain?'
'Yes.'
'Thy life in exchange for the world to live?'
'Yes.'

'But wait—' said Death as he sensed a flaw. 'If I accept thy bargain then I wish still to require that thy creatures continue to die *in their time.* And I will also require that their mortal remains come to me *as before* while their souls—which are useless to me—fly up or down according to their merits.'

'That is our old agreement. And I will honor it and also add a new bargain that my life is forfeit in exchange for the world's exemption from its immediate mass destruction.'

'When do I claim my prize? When can I have thy death?' Death asked.
'At a time of your choosing.'
'Must I choose now?' Death wondered.
'As you wish,' I said.

"Death considered when he might best claim the prize of my life. And then Death, not satisfied with my demise alone, devised a plan to not only end my life but increase my suffering. Death knew that, of all the deity's creatures, I loved the Wolfkind best and then the humans. Death smiled as he realized how to sweeten his vengeance."

'I know that thou dost love the Wolfkind best,' he smiled. 'Therefore, thou shalt begin to die when the Wolfkind are vanquished by humans. And your death shall be final when the last Wolfkind perishes. Thus, as I pull thee from the world, thou shalt see it left in the undeserved hands of humanity. Swear on this cup which I shall retain here as symbol of our bargain. So long as this durable cup holds the wine of my vengeance, that long shall your death be mine for the taking. Swear and we have a bargain.'"

El paused in his story.

"You may not know this," he told the dog. "But the Old Tribune ends exactly there with the outcome of the bargain undocumented. That was my doing I'm afraid. Scholars have argued for millennia over the meaning of that unresolved ending. And their conclusion—an erroneous one which I have allowed to stand—was—well my clever lamb, can you guess?" El looked to the dog as Esau sat up alertly and seemed to be pondering.

"Ah," said Esau. "The scholars have made an intellectual mistake. They have assumed that the past and the present are infallible predictors of the future. They have assumed that El—your holy self—will live forever. They have come to this erroneous conclusion thusly: They believe that Death's bargain must not have been struck because the world exists and was therefore *not lost in a flood*. Ergo, inasmuch as there was no flood, it must also follow that the Wolfkind (who have reigned for all of history) will continue to reign forever. In short, because the world exists, there was no flood. It follows then, that the bargain was proposed, but never sworn. And, because the Wolfkind rule now, they must continue to rule forever. And therefore, neither the world nor El will ever die."

"You have summarized the scholars' thinking precisely," said El, his fulsome tone reflecting parental pride in the dog's insightful deductions.

"But their logic is flawed," Esau concluded.

"Even so. And here is the truth of it: I forbade the outcome of the bargain to be written down because I did not wish to unnecessarily distress future readers and worshipers who might fixate on the fragility of the world. And yet, in fact, the bargain *was made,* and made with all its clauses. I was young when I agreed to it but felt it necessary because, by agreeing, I exempted the world from immediate destruction. But this exemption may not, as I had hoped, last forever. In that moment long ago, in the grip of Death, I reasoned that the Wolfkind were a strong and noble race and the likelihood of their being overthrown by humans seemed to me exceedingly remote. Therefore, the bargain seemed to me a safe one. I might have tried to dicker with Death there at the bottom of Deep Lake, but I feared that, if I sought to amend the bargain, he might lose patience and doom the world to instant destruction. And so, I made the bargain and trusted to luck."

"Luck which ran out," said the dog. "Luck which dissolved a month ago when the Fischals and their invincible weapons poured across the Middlemount borders."

"Yes. The Fischals came and they came with Death's handmaiden, the witch Ahoo, in their vanguard. It was a disastrous invasion which I had not foreseen."

An interval of silence embraced the grotto as deity and dog sat in the lengthening shadows.

"And here we are," El sighed. "Death is on the verge of claiming his bargain. The Middlemounts are over-thrown, the Wolfkind race hangs in the balance, I am dying, and, though the world may yet be spared its flood, this dream is nevertheless pushed to the brink of destruction. Unless the bargain is altered, I will disappear. Death and war will reign, and the world will lose its peace and its soul. All this will come to pass unless our measures succeed. The question now is how to reveal all which I have told you to the others and still rely upon them to follow their failed deity on his dubious quest."

"That has already been accomplished, lord." Ann stepped out of the shadows and onto the path followed by Seth and the horses and the Dreamers. At Esau's request, the others had followed and remained hidden while they linked minds with the dog. The link was strong with Ann and Seth by virtue of their magical origins and less strong but potent enough with the Dreamers by virtue of their recent enchantment by the witch. In this way, all that had been said and thought between dog and deity had also been understood by the rest. Even the horses seemed poised for action.

Ann spoke for them all when she asked, "So now, old man, our holy corpse, don't you think it's time that we continued this most urgent quest?"

Chapter 21

The Quest

A great weight can be lifted when one imparts a secret fear to others. To hold an anxiety in, to allow it to fester and boil inside, is to magnify it beyond its dimensions. As El's mortality increases, so do his burdens. To whom can a deity turn when the yoke of humanity encumbers him? Can a quest succeed when the deity in whose name the journey is attempted becomes himself a cumbersome, dragging anchor?

Once El had revealed the tale behind his quest, it was a small matter to explain what he hoped to accomplish. Seeing the war lost and the Wolfkind about to be obliterated, the deity feared that Death's bargain was coming due. Therefore, El envisioned a quest to thwart and reverse the coming doom. "Our quest is deceptively simple," the deity explained. "We must journey to Deep Lake and break the bargain by confronting Death and destroying the Memorian cup. Time is fleeting, but I have extended our chances by keeping alive the last vestiges of Wolfkind heritage. The Fishals and their foul allies have destroyed much but not yet the entirety of that proud race."

To this end, El had gathered three beings who possess Wolfkind blood: Ann and her mate and Migral, their military comrade. Owing to Ahoo's treachery and an accident of altered weather, Migral was lost at the cave, but the conversion of Esau from human shepherd to canine had replenished their ranks.

The eavesdroppers were assembled in the grotto as El took a seat and explained how the dog was created.

"Last night—while the moon halted in the sky and as Ann and Seth slept in a modified tiger pit, I reached in and retrieved one of the goblets from which they had drunk their evening wine. These former Wolfkinds being unused to spirits, they slept soundly as I used my holy finger to collect moisture left behind where their lips had touched the goblet's rim. From that spittle I created an elixir which I bade Esau drink. To manifest our repentant shepherd as a true Wolfkind would have attracted unwelcome attention, so I opted for the next most intelligent creature I could imagine. Thus, I created this resourceful border collie who is part dog, part Wolfkind, and part human. And so far, the transformed Esau has exceeded my wildest expectations. As for the Dreamers they too have proven valuable allies."

El paused and looked up at the assemblage.

"My lambs, here is the truth of it: Due to errors and miscalculations on my part, I am with you in this form whatever comes. My powers have ebbed so that I could not leave this body if I wished it—and I do not wish it. As to why I cannot whisk this party across the sea or perform other miracles, my abilities have much diminished and they continue to fade. Due to distractions, I erred in failing to warn my mountaineers of risks which—owing to their lingering warrior abilities—they nevertheless overcame. I have had flashes of my old skills—as when I freed the Dungs and transformed one of the tiger pits and brought forth this noble dog—but now I can do little else. Because my strength is disappearing, it does this old man good to behold this company. And make no mistake about it—El the deity is now an old man. Much of me—my breath, my beating heart—is already dead. The rest is becoming mortal and dying by stages. Forgive me, lambs, for my procrastination has put not only myself but all of you and all the world in jeopardy—"

El hesitated, glanced skyward, and breathed a heavy sigh before continuing.

"I have even put Velyn at risk. Though I once commanded time, I recognize I have misjudged and badly managed these recent months. Distracted by Death, I allowed things to spiral out of hand. Believing in my own infallibility, I failed to comprehend how rapidly I am fading. It is well you understand the kernel of our quest. And so, come, we must not linger here. Though we journey all night, we must speed toward the sea."

Setting out at once, they reached the coast and found the waiting ship. Though they hastened, they were nearly too late. For, as they boarded, the old man, who had once been El the powerful, the all-seeing and all-knowing, had to be carried on a litter. Ann walked beside the prostrate deity, then she returned to give Roseland final instructions regarding the horses.

"They are a pair," Ann told the woman.

"I understand," smiled Roseland.

"There will be a fine colt by-and-by," Ann said as she rubbed the pony's nose.

"Have you a preferred name for the coming foal?"

"Call her or him Dreamer, will you do that?" Ann asked.

"That I will. And the one after that?" asked Roseland.

"If a female, please you to call it Ann," the Princess requested.

"Of course."

"If a male," Ann added. "Bestow the name Destin."

"Not Seth?"

"It is an old story," Ann sighed.

The two women exchanged a glance.

"As you wish, mistress," said Roseland. "And what of the one after that?"

"I think, by then, you will have earned the privilege of naming the succeeding foals," Ann smiled.

"Will you be coming back this way, mistress?"

"That is uncertain," the Princess admitted.

"This quest? Will it restore the peace?" Roseland asked.

"We hope it shall. That is our hope."

"You will be our hope then," said Roseland and, hesitating to hug so great a personage as she perceived Ann to be, she offered her hand.

Ann took the woman's small hand, encircled it with both of hers, and held it warmly.

"Well met," the Princess told the courageous woman. "And may El's blessing guide and protect you."

"We'll not fail you, mistress," said Roseland with emotion.

Left behind at the estuary as the ship weighed anchor, Roseland secured Daffodil and Grand-Dive among a stand of willows. Then she joined the others as they armed themselves with slings and rocks and clubs. The Dreamers intended to await the arrival of their families, but the intrepid creatures had also volunteered to form themselves into a rear guard. With their backs to the sea, they vowed to thwart any pursuit, though doing so meant their lives.

No one doubted that the Fishals would be coming.

Surely Ahoo had alerted the soldiers before she attacked the fugitives. That morning her magic had allowed her to fly swiftly over the mountains and fall upon El and the others quickly, but Fishal men and horses and their cumbersome weapons would be slower to arrive. The army would have to cross the mountains. Then they would be forced to search for the hidden bridge—which seemed likely to elude them—or ford the river and either tactic would cause further delay. But inevitably, however long it took, the Fishal juggernaut would reach the beach where the Dreamers waited.

As the good ship *Catspaw*—under the able command of Commodore Alphonse Dell—sailed westward, two figures stood in the stern of the sturdy three-masted ship watching the coming darkness envelop the Middlemount horizon.

"Those little people you left behind are doomed, you know," stated Dell as he and Seth gazed toward the vanishing shore. "The Western Sea is a battleground and the ships they have been promised may not arrive in time to rescue them."

"They have continued to surprise us," Seth answered. "I have no doubt that they'll give a strong account of themselves."

"Hmm," said the commodore. He seemed unconvinced. "In any event, they are on their own as are we. We know but little of the old man's plan. It falls to you and your missus to convey his wishes."

"I will confer with her this very night," promised Seth. He might then have told the commodore that the *old man* who'd commissioned *Catspaw* to pick up her mysterious passengers, and who even now lay unconscious below decks, was indeed the lord of Velyn.

Yet clearly, Seth thought, *El meant to keep his identity secret from the commodore. But circumstances are rapidly changing. Now that El is fading, I might yet reveal that my "missus" is a royal Princess, but I'll not divulge that secret without first conferring with said missus.*

"The old man seems to believe that you have Wolfkind blood. Do you also possess Wolfkind powers?" the commodore interrupted his passenger's thoughts.

"After a fashion," Seth replied.

The commodore looked dubious. "I am no diplomat, so pardon me for asking, but you seem to me an ordinary man—would it be too much to request a demonstration? After all, we are sailing into dangerous waters and the lives of my men may depend upon your unproven skills."

Seth and the commodore stood in *Catspaw's* stern, directly beneath the rear-most spanker sail. In answer to the commodore's request, Seth took a few steps forward, turned toward the mainsails, took a deep breath, and blew. The sails billowed lustily. First the main course nearest the deck bowed out, then topsails, topgallant, royal, and skysail followed suit all the way up the mast.

Whereupon, the ship, which had been lumbering along under a light wind and upon a docile sea, leapt instantly forward. The lookout in the crow's nest lost his cap and shouted with alarm. The sailing master, who owing to the placid sea had been allowing the cabin boy a turn at the helm, was spurred into action. The master pushed the frightened lad aside, wrested the wheel back, and nearly dislocated both arms trying to steer while the ship bucked like a wild pony and surged forward with the sudden momentum of a cannon shot.

The burst of speed was brief, and the ship quickly regained her equilibrium, but the commodore seemed impressed.

"Well played, my man," Dell smiled as he touched his hat. "Forgive my saying so, but I wonder what might have been the outcome if the Wolfkind had formed a timely alliance with our forces. Consider that we took pains to marshal our defenses by mastering the use of gunpowder, shot, and cannonade and were thus more prepared to face the forces of evil—"

The commodore paused, measuring the man before him and measuring also his words.

"Well, only this," Dell continued. "I wonder if the tragic outcome of the Middlemount skirmish might have turned out different."

"Those ways are gone now, I suppose," said Seth. "Trampled by a pitiless hoard of more-progressive warriors."

"I fear you are correct," said the commodore. "Though I take no pleasure in it. A sad end to a noble race. And now, on that somber note, I must take my leave," the nautical officer touched his hat again and excused himself to attend to his vessel.

"Show off," chided Ann who had watched this male pissing contest from afar.

"You ought to know that women are not allowed on deck," cautioned Seth.

"And how would you and the commodore like it if I went to the front—what do you call it?"

"The bow," Seth smiled.

"Well, how would it be if I strolled to the other end of this ship—to what you call the bow? And once there, how would you and the commodore like it if I turned around and blew the sails in the other direction?"

"Point taken. And, as for my showing off, that little stunt exhausted me. I fear my Wolfkind powers ebbing. I doubt if I could duplicate tonight's extravagance, even if I wanted to."

Ann raised an eyebrow.

"Which I don't," Seth hastily added. "In the meantime, I'll make certain the commodore understands that we are primary mates. Surely, as a sailing man, he will understand the concept of a first mate."

"First and only, I trust."

"You may count on it, my love," Seth assured her.

He put his arm around Ann and they both looked back toward the distant shore—a dark horizon on a darkening sea.

"Will we ever see our land again?" he asked as he laid his head against her shoulder.

"Only time will tell," she answered. "At present we have work to do. We must care for El by turns. Moreover, Esau and I must join you in studying the commodore's charts and the intelligence reports arriving from Memora. Redundancy of knowledge is a military virtue—a maxim from our school days which I'm certain you will recall."

"Our old master used to call it carrying the flag," Seth smiled.

"Yes—if the regimental flag goes down, the next soldier picks it up and continues forward."

"And so on," he interjected.

"And so on," Ann agreed.

"And our flag is?" he asked.

"Wolfkind blood—we must carry it forward, preferably while it's still coursing through the living veins of one of the three of us."

"Morbid," he observed.

"Reality, my love," said Ann. "Either you or I or the dog must live to reach Deep Lake. We must face Death, retrieve the cup, and destroy it."

"Our quest," Seth said, acknowledging the plan which had been imparted to them by El before the old man lost consciousness. "Unaware of the weight of our mission, my pride tempted me to voice my displeasure over our encounters with Aggro and the nameless bison herd. Now those adventures seem small potatoes. I will hold my peace."

"Indeed," said Ann. She looked eastward as night arrived and the Western Sea seemed to melt into the darkness. "The moon is late," she frowned.

"An omen?" he asked.

Chapter 22

As a Thunderbolt

Middlemount royalty, along with other Wolfkind warriors, are schooled in the art and practice of classical war with an emphasis upon personal combat. The instructors are steeped in oral history and liable to enliven their lectures and demonstrations with pithy quotations and maxims, whether or not their pupils attend to their words. Sooner, or possibly later, a Wolfkind teetering upon the edge of tactical ruin or faced with an impossible obstacle or some other military conundrum, will recall his masters' words—recall them, and smile.

As *Catspaw* plied the dark sea, Ann sat in the small cabin she shared with her mate and recalled the words of her old master. She grinned at the memory.

"Obscure your plans in a cloak of darkness," the classic warrior told his students. "Then strike, and strike swiftly as a thunderbolt."

Wesletter of Middlemount had reigned as Wolfkind champion for three decades running. General Wesletter had dispatched no fewer than twenty-seven foes in single combat. A dozen of those matches had decided the kingdom's fate. His prowess had decisively settled protracted battles which would otherwise have dragged on for years. Wesletter's specialty was striding onto a field of honor, bowing to his rival, and then ending a stalemate in seconds by dispatching an opponent's champion with as few as two decisive blows.

"Any Wolfkind or man—if there be such a man—who brags that he has felled a worthy adversary—mark you I say a *worthy* adversary—and claims to have done so with a single blow is a liar, or drunk, or both." The idea was one of the old warrior's favorite themes.

Ann remembered that Wesletter was himself quite drunk the night she last heard the old warrior utter those words. It was the night of graduation when Migral and that noble warrior's fellows—along with twelve females including her—had completed the last of their trials and had been initiated into a higher order. She was not drinking, she remembered. Drink had been the undoing of her father and she would have nothing to do with spirits. Instead, she focused on the solemnity of the event.

Destin was at the celebration too. Not as a graduate, because he was still a raw recruit. Young Destin was envious of the graduates and more than that, he was instantly smitten with Ann of Middlemount. Before that night, he had seen the heir to the Wolfkind throne only twice and both times she had seemed to him the very model of pomposity, a pretentious ass in fact. But seeing her at the ceremony, hearing her reverently speak the class charge, seeing her affection for Wesletter, and her deference to her classmates, he fell instantly in love.

The Princess and the other graduates were joining the pack within the pack—The Circle of Canis—a fierce and intelligent cadre of Wolfkind who were destined for higher things. Ann was becoming elite, in a way untouchable, but all her young admirer could think of on that graduation night long ago was what it would be like to touch her. He was two years behind the Princess' graduating class and, in time, would make his own mark. But that night he was a vulnerable schoolboy with an impossible crush on a Princess of the realm.

Onboard *Catspaw,* Ann sat at the table in their cramped ship's cabin. She should have been studying the charts, but she'd allowed her mind to stray. Trying to focus, she heard Seth, who'd been napping, stir and rise from the uncomfortable shelf which passed for a bed on this seagoing vessel. Though unspoken, her thoughts had undoubtedly reached her mate.

"You were in my thoughts," she said when he stood beside her and placed a hand on her shoulder.

"Yes, love, I noticed," said Seth as he leaned down to kiss her neck, then ran his fingers gently through the silky strands of his mate's emerging coiffure.

"It's growing by leaps and bounds," she purred. "Soon I will have enough to be plaiting my hair and braiding it."

"I've grown accustomed to it," Seth assured her. "And accustomed also, to the thoughts emerging from that short-cropped head of yours. I have to say, I like your hair short, but if longer pleases you, then it also pleases me."

"Life was simpler in the past," Ann sighed. "As Wolfkind, there was no question of short hair or long—my covering was what it was: pleasingly soft where softness was required and wiry where that rougher mode served. Tell me, my impetuous mate, do you even recall how I wore my locks—such as they were—on the occasion of my graduation?"

"I remember it well—" Seth began, but paused ever so slightly, striving—Ann suspected—to recall exactly how his Princess looked at that long-ago ceremony. "In ribbons?" he ventured.

"Well-remembered, love," Ann congratulated him.

"That was a glorious night, that graduation long ago," Seth recalled, "but not so glorious as the following year when you returned to teach a bevy of raw recruits the finer points of wrestling."

Thinking of that day, Ann felt a pleasant tingling. "Is that what you call it? Wrestling? And what male logic made you think I would agree to a private tutorial?"

He leaned farther over to kiss her cheek. "The look in your eyes caused me to believe you would be a willing teacher."

She turned in place and sought his lips. Standing, she allowed him to lead her to the cramped bench where the two paused, then decided instead to try the hammock. After a hilarious series of experimental positions, they at last found a rhythm and joined until their pleasure was mutually spent. Lying together, entwined in the hammock, they slept and swayed with the rocking of the ship.

After a time, Ann allowed her thoughts to drift once again to her graduation day. Convinced that Seth was truly sleeping, she closed her eyes and remembered.

She'd been born a princess but was still required to prove her merit and prowess. She was still required to demonstrate her potential. Potential? A few days ago, Migral had labeled Ann a "peasant with potential." So little time had passed since her friend—who had all too briefly manifested himself as a raven—had spoken those words. So little time since Migral had died at the cave. So little time and yet so much had happened.

Unable to sleep, she pushed her thoughts aside and left her love slumbering. It was time to take her turn at El's bedside. Carrying one of the charts and a sheaf of parchments, Ann left the cabin and had to ask directions to find the stairwell on the unfamiliar vessel. Using a candle lantern to light the way, she journeyed deep into the bowels of *Catspaw*. Esau was there, taking his turn, and the dog yawned and stretched as the Princess descended the final rungs of the coil ladder.

"Any change?" she asked.

"No change," said the dog.

For twenty-four hours, they'd been taking turns—the Princess, Seth, and the dog—reading aloud to the old man, who may or may not be able to hear them and studying the quest's order of battle. They'd made El as comfortable as possible in the cramped warship. Even so, it was dark and dank below decks and Ann wondered—and not for the first time—whether it might not be better to take El topside and lash him to the mast and let him die on his feet. At least the air would be fresher there.

El coughed and Ann reached to feel his forehead. The fever seemed less, but El remained unconscious. That morning the commodore had announced at breakfast that they would reach Redhackle Isle at dusk. Rather than risk deadly reefs in the dark, they would lay offshore and wait until morning to take on supplies there. After a brief stop at the island, if the wind was fair, the ship would take another day to complete the final leg of the sea journey to

Memora. From the coast it would take half a day—perhaps more—on horseback to reach Deep Lake.

In all, that meant nearly three more days to the lake—to Ann it seemed an eternity.

Intelligence had reached them, carried by ships which fled the fighting to the west, and those encounters confirmed that Ectrican pirates were sacking towns along the Memorian coast. The opportunistic mercenaries, whose ships and swords were available to the highest bidder, had been paid in gold to serve as allies to the treacherous Fishals. The pirates had arrived by sea in a vast armada. The attackers had laid waste to Stove Point—the harbor which was *Catspaw's* destination. Then the bastards had marched inland, killing, looting, and burning as they went—until they reached Deep Lake, where they encamped on the shoreline and formed a strong defensive barrier. Clearly, their presence was intended to discourage any attempt to approach, let alone reach Deep Lake.

The crude sketches which informants had managed to smuggle out of the interior were just that—sketchy. The rudimentary diagrams suggested the pirates, who were most dangerous at sea but still a formidable land force, were aligned with a contingent of Fishals soldiers. Together, the detestable alliance encircled the lake with two battalions. Even given the fluctuating definitions of "battalion," that meant at least two thousand men.

Under the "old man's" original plan, the commodore was instructed to surprise the enemy, who would not be expecting a sea-borne attack. *Catspaw* would slip into the harbor at Stove Point under cover of darkness, then bombard the pirate ships and coast at first light. The plan was to pin down and kill as many pirates as possible while Ann and her party—reinforced by a platoon of ship's marines—stole ashore to begin a forced march to the lake.

But that plan would have to be altered because, by the time *Catspaw* arrived at Stove Point, there would be virtually no one there to shoot at. *Catspaw* gunners could certainly sink any pirate ships in the harbor and annihilate their skeleton crews. But as near as Ann could make it out, the invaders had abandoned the harbor and concentrated most of their force inland around the lake. Clearly, Ahoo would have deployed them there—her intimate contact with Death making her abundantly aware of the importance of safeguarding the cup until the end.

The end, Ann thought.

She looked up from her plans and schematics. If El died, truly and wholly died, before they reached the lake and acquired the cup, then their quest would be for nothing. Even if they somehow managed to destroy the cup and prevent the flood, of what use would a saved world be without its deity?

Already the Princess had been informed that the world's creatures were beginning to lose their faith. True or not, the rumors were spreading like wildfire. It was claimed that prayers were being neglected. Crops were failing. Babies were dying. The paint on iconic images was seen to fade and blister. A statue of El in the far north had unaccountably crumbled on its own. Doubt was giving way to despair, and such despair was the gateway to panic.

The world was approaching a tipping point.

The fugitives needed more time, but that resource was in short supply. Ann put her papers aside and stood up to stretch. She was beginning to think in circles. She needed air. She ought not to leave the old man alone, but Seth was due at any moment to relieve her. With luck, Ann could leave now, and she would probably pass her love in the stairwell coming down. So, she donned a wool cap—a gift from the commodore—and put on a pea jacket—also borrowed from Commodore Dell. She and her dying deity were far below decks in the bulkhead, directly below the stern and aft of the main gangway. It was a place considered safest in case they came under attack at sea. Ann had buttoned up her jacket and was just turning to climb up and begin the arduous trek to the sea deck when El spoke.

"Take me with you," El pleaded. His voice was weak, but there was enough of the old spirit in it to suggest he was up to the journey.

Chapter 23

Redhackle Isle

A hospital is a poor place to recover from illness. The anemic light, the stifling cleanliness, the cloying odors of a medicinal setting are abhorrent to good health. An infirmary, no matter how cheerful it is dressed up to be, is the antithesis of wellness, let alone the dank dark bowels of a ship of war. An open cemetery with its rolling grounds and sweeping skies is a far better place for the sick.

Ann was guiding El topside when they met Seth coming down. He exchanged a worried glance with his mate but, when El insisted, Seth relented and helped carry the old man up.

Moments later, El was relishing the sea air as the ship neared Redhackle Isle. It was cold on deck, but the fresh air seemed to do the old man good. He was sufficiently alert to take an active interest in the progress of the quest. To everyone's surprise, the invalid asked to be given a telescope to scan the primitive harbor. Commodore Dell and Ann stood beside El at the ship's railing while Seth went below to look for something to assuage El's stated desire to eat. Which was strange, for he was under the impression that the deity required no literal sustenance.

"We are far away yet. But I see a wharf and a small village," El frowned. "Are you certain of supplies there?"

The commodore seemed irritated by the question, but he apparently decided to humor the old man. "Pardon my bluntness, but when we saw the war was going badly, we thought it best to prepare by stockpiling supplies at this way-station."

"Quite right," agreed Ann. "A wise choice."

"Your grace is kind," Commodore Dell was trying to make amends. He hadn't realized when he questioned his guests' fitness for battle at the start of this voyage that Ann might be an incarnation of the last Princess of Middlemount. Such was the rumor circulating among the crew. The commodore had his doubts, but he'd apparently decided to take no chances.

Ann guessed the commodore's intentions and spoke magnanimously, "I thank you for your courtesy, but we are equals—you and I—and less than equals at present since you rule this ship. I am indebted to you for your service to our quest and I am, for the present, yours to command."

The commodore appeared uncertain.

"Well at any rate, let us at least be friends," Ann extended her hand, and the commodore shook it heartily.

"Well met," the commodore beamed.

"Well met," responded Ann.

Observing this congenial exchange, the crew of *Catspaw* breathed a collective sigh of relief. They'd heard rumors regarding Ann's importance. Having hauled their share of royalty in the past, the sailors had previously begrudged the way their commodore was slighted by his privileged passengers. As she clasped hands with the commodore, Ann sensed this change in the crew's demeanor, and she congratulated herself for having correctly interpreted human behavior without the luxury of actually being able to hear their thoughts.

Egotism, El spoke to her in the voice of the mind, *your human traits—good and bad—are multiplying and improving daily. It will be a wonder if there is a drop of Wolfkind blood left in your veins by the time we reach Memora.*

She met his thoughts with her own.

Truly my former powers seem to have been somewhat altered. But some things are intact. Would you care to hear me howl?

Ann sent this mischievous thought to El and looked to see his reaction. But the old man had abandoned the railing and retreated to a position some distance away on the deck. Looking frail, the fading deity leaned against the mast while Seth helped him eat. Hearing his Princess' thoughts and digesting her plan to howl, the old man nearly choked on the porridge Seth was spooning into his hungry mouth.

"Take care," Seth said. "Clearly, lord, you are out of practice."

"Yes, my child," agreed El. "It has been a long while since I last ate a meal or had need of one. Over time, I grew used to dining on praise and prayers. With luck, I shall feast again on such victuals."

"The moon was late again last night," Seth observed. He was trying to sound casual, but in truth he'd been fretting over that omen since their first night on the water. Now, even as El seemed to be losing strength, he sought his deity's reassurance.

It takes less of my waning energy to reach you this way, said El as he sent his thoughts to Seth. *If you do not mind, let us communicate without speaking. It will also ensure that we are not overheard.*

Obscure your plans in a cloak of darkness, thought Seth.

And strike swiftly as a thunderbolt, El completed the notion.

That military maxim is the source of my worry, my El, Seth thought. Then he hesitated before plowing on. *Here, I fear, is the truth of it: We are hardly concealed here on this ship bobbing in the middle of the ocean. And as for striking swiftly, there are yet days ahead of us by sea and land and our halting pace belies the name of swift. Pardon me for saying so, for I know it was your plan to come by sea, but I feel that we are, at present, as vulnerable as the proverbial sitting duck.*

You speak plainly, child, and your passion is commendable. Retain that passion and hone it. It will be needed when we reach Memora. And be assured that my own strength is returning. I too will be ready when the time arises.

Forgive me, El. I never doubted you. But the moon—

The moon is doing the best it can under the circumstances. It is not used to being interrupted—not even by a deity. It will regain its lunar schedule by-and-by. Meantime, it is not the heavens which concern me. There is something about this island which likes me not.

It seems a poor habitation, frowned Seth.

More than that, even at this distance I sense a patina of magic. I cannot see it clearly. It is like a glaze upon an unfired clay pot—seemingly transparent—but when subjected to heat—

What do you see? What magic? Seth asked.

It is unclear, but I can guess, said El

Ahoo? Is it the witch? Seth wondered.

It seems inconceivable, El declared. *And yet there is a chance that she has landed somewhere in our path.*

Why not in the sea? That tiny island is the smaller target, said Seth.

I doubt, given the condition she was in when last we saw her, that she was aiming one way or the other, the deity's thought seemed to hover in the humid air.

What are you two thinking about? Ann questioned as she rushed toward them.

We are debating whether or not the witch might have landed on this island, answered Seth.

"Why not ask her yourself?" Ann suggested. Her eyes were fixed on the distant shore and, following her gaze westward, they found Redhackle Isle engulfed in an inferno.

Chapter 24

A Reunion

A ship leaving land is said to "sink" the terra firma it leaves behind. A ship approaching an as yet unseen shore is said to have the land "rising" to meet it. An ocean vessel should not be visible to someone standing on a distant beach until it is within a league—some three miles—whereas rising land, if it is high enough, can be detected by an approaching ship as far away as four leagues. For this reason, all lands bordering the sea claim as their territory the so-called twelve-mile limit.

Though subject to the twelve-mile notion, the unarmed denizens of Redhackle Isle were in no position to contest their territory. The visible portion of Redhackle—much like its unassuming occupants—lies low in the Western Sea. But the isle holds invisible terrors, for it is surrounded by subterranean mountains which rise up from the seafloor and manifest themselves as jagged reefs. Because the island is both seen and unseen, it ought to be approached with reverence and caution, particularly if it is afire.

Catspaw sailed landward until the ship reached the outer banks of the smoldering isle just before sunset. Not wishing to chance the reefs in the dying light, Commodore Dell dropped anchor and looked through his telescope. He could see boats floating in the small harbor, blackened, and still smoldering. The main body of flames had subsided, but the air was filled with thick gray smoke.

"Our supplies are gone, I reckon, and there was not much else to burn," said the commodore. "Nothing but a few houses and boats. The island's small forest was felled years ago to build the town. No trees left now, just stumps."

"What do—or rather did they burn for cooking fires and for heat?" asked Ann.

"Shit," said the commodore.

"I beg your pardon."

"My apologies," Dell blushed. "I meant to say they burn manure. Two things Redhackle Isle has in abundance are fish and sheep. And, besides wool, the main thing that sheep produce is manure. The animals may not have survived. But, at one time, there were more sheep than people. And, as for the people, I don't see a soul. Can we be certain this so-called witch of yours is the source of this destruction?"

"Reasonably certain," answered Ann.

"She loves fire," added El and he gave Esau a stern look because he sensed the dog was about to say something. Urgently, he spoke to the collie in the voice of the mind.

Better we should not throw a talking dog into the mix just now.

As you wish, lord, Esau obeyed with his thoughts and lay down on the deck with his head between his paws.

"Your dog seems quite intelligent," said the commodore.

"Just so," said El with obvious pride. "Tell me, how long do you imagine it takes this dog to drive a herd of sheep unassisted for five miles over rocky ground, across a narrow bridge, and into their corral?"

"How long?" asked the commodore.

"Six hours, but in that time, he is also busy with quill and paper writing a sonnet."

The commodore laughed and returned to his telescope. "Ah, I see movement—this may be your witch coming now."

One large boat had apparently remained unburned, for it was plying forth from the harbor with its bow pointed toward *Catspaw*. The commodore counted eight men rowing with several other figures seeming to lie in the keel between the rowers. And in the bow stood a woman, the sea breeze blowing her dark locks in a swirl that alternately revealed and obscured her face. Even at a distance, he could tell it was a pretty face.

"A beauty it seems," said the commodore as he relinquished the telescope.

"Until you get to know her better," said Ann. She trained the telescope on the witch who seemed to sense her gaze for Ahoo looked directly into the lens. There was something in that look—was it fear or determination or something else? "I'd suggest firing a warning shot. Then, if they don't heave-to, we'll have to risk sinking the boat. The rowers and the others may or may not be her men, but we can't wait for them to overhaul us to sort them out."

Ordinarily the commodore would bristle at someone presuming to give orders on his ship. He glanced side-long at the remarkable woman standing at his side. Ann was tall and well-proportioned with a healthy complexion and well-shaped but clearly strong arms. Her face was smooth and unblemished. She wore a sailor's watch cap on her short-cropped-nearly-bald head, a white tunic, ordinary trousers, and practical boots. Her voice was firm and husky. If not for her ample breasts, she might have been mistaken for a man. For all that, she was clearly a fine woman who loved her husband Seth, even though he was two heads shorter than her. Nevertheless, the commodore had decided, Seth was also a fine fellow—a hardy sort, not only handsome but also wiry. They were indeed a well-matched pair and both, in their own way, commanded respect.

The commodore cleared his throat and hesitated only a second before implementing Ann's suggestion. The witch's boat was still advancing, and he shouted commands as *Catspaw* swung round to bring her starboard side parallel to the island. When the ship was suitably positioned for a proper broadside, he gave orders to aim the cannon.

"Range?" cried the master gunner.

"I make it half a league!" shouted the lookout.

"Less than two miles," said Ann. "Within our range surely."

The commodore smiled, a remarkable woman indeed.

Moments later, the ship shuddered as a single shot roared forth. Ann saw the splash, a well-laid warning shot. Close enough to drench the witch and the rowers.

"Still on course, sir!" the lookout shouted.

"Fire at—" the commodore bellowed. Then he abruptly shouted, "Belay that order!"

Ahoo was waving a white flag.

"Can we trust a flag of truce?" asked Seth as he joined them on the quarterdeck.

"Commodore?" asked Ann.

"We'll train every powder gun we possess on the woman. If she so much as winks, we'll pulverize her."

"Don't let her come too close," Ann warned. "Remember, she's a magical being."

"Luckily, I don't believe in magic," the commodore smiled. The boat was nearer now. Dell raised a speaking trumpet. "Close enough!" he shouted through the trumpet. "Ship oars or we'll fire!"

The men ceased rowing, but kept their oars in the water as momentum carried the boat closer. So near did the craft approach that those onboard could see several other forms huddled in the drifting vessel.

"Please!" Ahoo shouted back. Even without the aid of a trumpet, her voice reached them clearly as she added, "I don't know your sea-talk, sir. Do you wish us to stop or continue? And please don't shoot at us again."

"A trick," hissed Ann.

"Something is amiss," said El. "Help me to the railing."

Seth rushed to the old man, helped the deity to his feet, trundled him forward, and steadied him against the starboard side facing the bobbing boat. El asked for the speaking trumpet and the commodore passed it over.

"Good evening, young lady," said El. "May we be of assistance?"

"We have had a fire," said the witch, pointing unnecessarily toward the smoking island.

"As we see," said El. Ann cleared her throat and would have spoken. But El raised a hand to silence her and—trusting her deity—Ann in turn signaled the commodore to stand down.

"We'd best give them room," whispered Ann.

The commodore nodded and motioned for the crew to move away from the railing. For an instant, a handful of curious sailors lingered until the boatswain and Esau joined forces to push the onlookers back to the port side. The huge boatswain used both his rank and his substantial bulk to discourage the onlookers, while Esau deftly employed his herding instincts, until at last the sailors gave way and the rail was clear.

What's afoot? Ann asked El in the voice of the mind.

What's the foul witch up to? Seth asked.

Steady, we are in uncharted waters, came El's terse reply.

"How can we help?" El asked the witch again.

"As you can see, we have injured aboard and more on shore in need of assistance," said Ahoo, with a tone of such sincerity that even Ann was persuaded something was different. "We have brought the most badly wounded. We are hoping you have a surgeon onboard."

"That we do," said the commodore. "But do you not have the services of the island doctor?"

"Our doctor is among our injured, sir—and grievously so—I pray you, please, can we get these people aboard? We have injured men and women and children. In the name of my El we beg for mercy."

"We will assist you!" cried El, setting the speaking trumpet aside and continuing in a voice filled with passion and power. "We will assist you, my child! Have your men row hither!"

The deity was energized by hearing the witch invoke the name of "my El" in her plea for assistance—so inspired that his pale cheeks grew suddenly rosy, and his voice thundered across the waves.

The commodore stared at the old man who seemed to have instantly increased in stature and authority. Being no fool, he recognized that he indeed had a deity onboard. Accordingly, in obedience to this divine being, the commodore issued a command to his boatswain, and the boatswain, in obedience to his commodore, bellowed orders to the crew. The obedient crew responded with a rush and soon netting was draped over the railing to assist the able-bodied in climbing up the side and the starboard boatswain's chair was made ready to hoist the more seriously injured aboard.

Esau was inspired by this flurry of activity and the eager dog positioned himself near the starboard railing as the refugees were helped onboard. Thus, he was intently watching each new face when the witch climbed over the railing. Seeing her, he instantly crouched and growled, but almost immediately raised his ears and wagged his tail. The dog was confused by his mixed reactions, but nevertheless he inched forward to sniff at and ultimately lick the witch's proffered hand.

"What a handsome fellow you are," she cooed as she leaned down to pat the dog.

Somehow Ahoo seemed, if not harmless, at least much changed. She was clad in ordinary pantaloons and a plain shirt, but it was not merely her rough clothing which caught the dog's attention. She seemed not to be the same woman Esau had attacked a few days ago. Nevertheless, the dog remained cautious and gave her a wide berth when she straightened up and walked across the deck. The crew also stepped aside to let the young woman pass, although their reactions seemed to reflect more deference to her beauty than an overabundance of caution. To them, she seemed nothing more or less than an attractive female and, if any gave credence to the rumor that she was also a witch, it didn't stop them from saluting her as she glided by and wishing her a good evening.

After the witch passed among them, the sailors immediately returned to their duties. *Catspaw* had seen its share of sea rescues and soon the crew had the island boat unloaded and the injured safely on deck. The ship's surgeon walked from patient to patient, trailed by the cabin boy who either gave the injured a drink or abstained from offering the ladle according to the surgeon's instructions. The surgeon paused ever so briefly to examine his colleague, the island doctor. He felt for a pulse and shook his head.

"No water," he told the boy. "Hear me now. This man is gravely ill. See that he's moved to my cabin."

The boy handed over the water bucket and ran for help as the surgeon moved on.

The riggers, the carpenters, and even the powder monkeys all joined in the effort to minister to the wounded, and each seemed to know his particular job. Some sailors shredded sailcloth into bandages, some slathered oil on burns, others used water buckets and sponges to clean open wounds, and still others splinted limbs. Seth also ministered to the injured and Esau helped by lying next to and, thereby distracting, the weeping children. It grew dark and torches and wax candles were lit. These welcome illuminations were placed in metal sconces surrounding the main deck so that the ship glowed brightly from stem to stern.

As *Catspaw* became a floating hospital, El and Ann approached Ahoo and ushered the witch aside, away from prying eyes and out of earshot. As magical beings, they had endeavored, but failed, to question her less conspicuously with the voice of the mind. But she did not seem to hear their thoughts and they were unable to perceive hers.

For his part, the commodore followed the three of them and stood nearby, a few paces away, his cutlass drawn and a pair of pistols in his belt. Ann gave him a grateful nod, but made it clear with gestures that it would be better if he stayed where he was for the time being.

"Do you know who I am?" El asked the witch.

"I have seen your image, yes," said Ahoo in a voice so timid that Ann and El exchanged a puzzled glance. "You are my El. I ought not to speak to you directly, lord, for I am well behind in my prayers. But thank you for answering my most recent one. Thank you, a thousand times over, my El!" The witch fell then upon her knees and wrapped her arms around El's ankles.

I cannot hear her thoughts, said El in the voice of the mind.

Nor I, Ann replied. *Can we presume as well that she hears us not?*

Difficult to be certain, and yet the voice of the mind is a two-way lane— I have never known it otherwise, thought El. The deity grew silent. Then, seemingly bewildered by Ahoo's worshipful attention, he reached down to help the witch off her knees.

"Child, child," said El. "Your devotion does you credit, but please help us understand what is happening here. You seem to recognize me. Do you know this lady?" El placed a hand on Ann's shoulder.

"No, lord."

"Another question for you then and please think carefully before you answer," said El.

The witch remained standing, but she looked down and did not meet the deity's gaze.

El reached forward and gently lifted her chin until their eyes met. "My question is this: Do you know who *you* are?"

"Yes, lord."

A moment of silence stretched between them before she continued.

"I am the old-world witch Ahoo of the North—a miserable sinner and tardy repentant and one unworthy to stand in your presence." She was on her knees again, this time pressing her forehead to the wooden deck in a posture of abject veneration.

I am at a loss. Ann sent her puzzled thoughts to El. *Can this be the same creature that tried to burn me and lately turned us to stone and danced and spat in our faces and desecrated the grave of our fallen comrade? Who paraded about wantonly, was battered by stones, and ascended?*

These are the very questions I have asked myself, responded El.

And what answers have you deduced?

This girl is undoubtedly Ahoo, but as for whether she is the same creature—

"Lord, I ask a boon," said Ahoo without rising.

Here we go, thought Ann.

"What do you wish, child?" El asked.

"I know that you and this lady must feel it is important to question me, but I ask that I be released from this interview so that I might minister to my injured friends. If it be thy will—please release me."

"Granted and go with my blessing."

Ahoo did not speak. Instead, she stood and bowed several times before she turned and ran across the quarterdeck intending to hurry down the stairs to the main deck. Her iron boots made a terrible racket as she ran. Commodore Dell stepped forward and seemed ready to impede her. But El motioned him to let her pass and the commodore stepped back. Ann and El followed the departing witch and joined the commodore on the edge of the quarterdeck. The three of them stood at the railing and stared below as the surgeon and sailors, and now the witch, ministered to their patients.

Seth was down there too and Ahoo was kneeling nearby bandaging the arm of a village woman whose smudged face suggested she'd narrowly escaped the fire. Seth pointed at the witch and then he looked up toward his mate with a puzzled expression. Ann held her palm up signaling—signaling what?

What are we doing? Seth reached his mate with the voice of the mind.

El says the witch is changed. Give her leave to help the wounded, but keep her close, Ann's thoughts reached him.

Can she not hear our plans? Our thoughts? asked Seth.

We think it unlikely. Does she seem to register that we are thinking of her? asked El.

Not a twitch, said Seth.

A puzzle, said El.

Indeed, agreed Ann and Seth, simultaneously.

The Princess turned to the commodore. "Are there any among the islanders who are well enough to speak freely to us?"

"Two of the men have injured legs, but nothing more serious, and two women are also conscious and lightly wounded. Shall I assemble these four?"

"Please do so and, if we may, we'll need your cabin for our questioning."

"Of course. Brightlamp!" The commodore called the boatswain forth and imparted his instructions. Brightlamp knuckled his forehead in the curious salute that is unique to seamen. Then Ann and El watched while the boatswain gathered a pair of men and two women, all of whom were bandaged but seemed ambulatory. Only a little time elapsed before the foursome had been helped upstairs to the quarterdeck where the commodore ushered them into his cabin.

Commodore Dell's great-cabin was surprisingly roomy and, though it was well past sundown and the large stern windows framed only the dark night, the wall of glass made the space seem even larger. The steward lit the overhead lamps and sought to linger, but a stern look from his commodore compelled the curious servant to retire.

"A crackerjack steward," Dell said when the man had departed, "but also a shameless gossip monger."

"The very last thing we need," said El and he was about to suggest to Dell that he himself retire when Ann spoke up.

"The commodore should stay," the Princess declared. "I consider him a brother officer and above reproach."

"As you wish," said El who seemed not in the mood to argue. The deity was looking tired again, Ann decided. Clearly, he was not yet well. Nevertheless, El began the interview by addressing the four islanders. "Do you recognize me?"

"You are the image of our lord, but that cannot be, for we heard he is dead," said one of the women. "My name is Sprout, sir."

"You are his twin though, I'll grant you that, sir," said the other woman. "I am called Millet."

The men were silent. Clearly the women wore the trousers on Redhackle Isle.

"Can any of you tell us what has happened on the island?"

"A fair question," said Sprout—she might have been forty or seventy—her teeth were gone. "We were at prayers—"

"Those of us who were not at the tavern," added Millet as she shot a sharp look at the men. She was younger than Sprout but not by much.

"Aye, those that remained in the tavern were burned for certain sure," agreed Sprout. "Dead and gone since that wicked den were smack in its path."

"In its path?" asked Ann.

"Of the river," explained Sprout with a tone of impatience.

"There was a flood?" asked El.

"A flood of fire there was," Sprout explained. "It come up out the ground all hissing and red like a giant snake slitherin' down the hillsides and into our town."

"My old grand-dad—El rest his soul—heard tell of such a river of fire in the old years before his time even," said Millet. "It comes from deep insides the earth they say."

"Were lava," said one of the men.

"Listen to him talk—Fredahl Cardoff—thinks he's a bloody scientist," scoffed Sprout. "*Were lava,* he tells us—and where did that cracked-brain notion spring from, I wonder?"

"I read it in a book," said the man.

"Go on," said Millet. "When did you ever have a book to read?"

"It was in the doctor's surgery. I read it as I was waitin' to have me boils lanced."

"Here—did you have that done—I—" began Millet.

"Might I ask a few more questions?" interjected El.

"Fire away," said Sprout. "At this minute, we're at liberty to chatter."

"It's not as if we had homes to go back to," said Millet.

"Dear ladies, what can you tell me about the woman who led the boatmen here?"

"The girl you mean?"

"Yes."

"Well, she's a witch ain't she? A pretty little thing—but a witch, or so she told us," Sprout declared.

"Not a bad one though—one of them good witches you hear about sometimes," added Millet.

"A looker," said one of the men.

"I'll grant you that," admitted Millet. "But not only pretty. She's kind too—good with the children—" She seemed to want to say more but stopped.

"Say," said Sprout. "We ain't all been properly introduced!"

"My name is Sprout, as I said, and this here is my sister-in-law, Millet, as she said. And that talkative bloke over there—the one that thinks he knows so much about lava—that's me brother Fredahl. And beside him is Waygo—he's the quiet one. And all you might be—?" Sprout looked expectantly at Ann.

"Well, you know the commodore, of course. My husband Seth is on deck ministering to your injured. For myself, I am Ann Stone Bride and my companion here is—"

"You don't say?" interrupted Sprout.

"Imagine that!" said Millet.

"Why, miss, you've nearly the same war name and last name as our doctor—except bein' a man he's called Andrew Stonebrook—so yours is not the same entirely but most nearly," grinned Sprout—a soft grin—not unpleasant but minus the teeth.

"A small world ain't it?" observed Millet.

Chapter 25

Island of Fire: Shadow of Doubt

The world which contains Middlemount, Redhackle Isle, Memora, and other more obscure lands, is a small one. The names "Ann" and "Andrew" are common first, or war, names. Though not one in a thousand of those called Ann or Andrew will ever go to war, the bestowing on an infant of a so-called "war name" is a centuries-old practice, handed down from father and mother to son and daughter. The parents of Ann, as well as progenitors stretching far into the past, once had a surname which is now forgotten. Yet even the royals kept to the custom of the war name. So it is that a human female child born in the town of Middlemount which sprawls at the base of the royal castle might have her umbilical cut and assume the surname of, let us say, Ompost—after her sire. That same infant may also be assigned a war name to make her Ann Ompost. Whereas high above in the castle on that self-same day, if a Wolfkind cub enters the world, she will be thereafter known as, not merely Ann, but Ann of Middlemount—the "of" being the preposition of royal prerogative.

So it was that Ann accepted as chance the fact that she shared a name similar to the island's injured and, thus-far, incoherent doctor. What the townsfolk viewed as amazing, Ann dismissed as mere coincidence. Ann and Andrew; Stone Bride and Stonebrook; it was all the same to her. And yet, the moment the island women assumed the connection, they began to talk more freely.

Thus, on account of Ann's name choice, another door, seemingly shut, was opened.

The Princess smiled, the island women smiled, and information began to flow. According to the women, Ahoo had made no attempt to conceal her identity. In fact, she had declared herself a witch and had been at church and in the process of confessing her many sins when the lava cascaded into town.

As for that, the women revealed that the eruption had not spewed from a visible cone like might be seen in southern climes where lofty volcanoes pierce the sky. Instead, Redhackle Isle seemed to be honeycombed with fissures which had previously been the source of hot springs and steaming geysers. In recent memory, the fissures had yielded curing tonics—until today when a river of fire bubbled up and ignited the wooden buildings, incinerated half the population, and flowed on until it reached the harbor, where it burned the wharf and most of the fishing boats.

The fiery river had been roiling all afternoon—burning the fields first then isolated houses—moving slowly enough at first so that sheep and other animals could be safely driven to higher ground. Unfortunately, the outlying shepherds were so busy saving themselves and their flocks that they failed to raise the alarm.

As a result, other islanders—particularly those dwelling far below the upper pastures and along the coast—were unaware of the impending disaster. The unexpected flow had picked up speed until it reached and ignited the town just before dark. Once fire surrounded the wooden buildings, it had taken less than an hour to destroy everything. *Catspaw* had apparently appeared on the horizon just in time to see the fiery finale. Sailing landward, the Middlemount ship had arrived offshore during the dying moments of the disaster when the surging flames overflowed the seawall, crawled across the beaches, and steamed to a halt in the harbor.

Many were killed. The reason those in the witch's boat and a few others still on shore had survived was prophetic. A handful of devout residents were congregated on the higher ground of the town's lone hill. Clustered in the community church, they were hearing Ahoo's heartfelt confession and lamenting the apparent absence of their deity.

Although the women spoke at length, it was nevertheless a frustrating interview.

Sprout and Millet took turns sharing infinitesimal details regarding the fiery river and their lost possessions, but they were far less forthcoming about the witch. They seemed reluctant to describe how she came to the island, being only willing to say that "the girl fell in." Moreover, they were completely silent about her conduct during the fire. They seemed to fear that they would get "the girl" in trouble if they said more. Their defense of Ahoo was strange but also touching. Whenever Ann or the commodore or El used the term "the witch," the women would instantly counter with "the girl."

As for what the women made of El, they tolerated his questions and answered him politely enough, but seemed to think the old man was touched in the head. They were willing to admit that he bore an uncanny resemblance to the household icons and public statuary of the divine El. But—inasmuch as their deity was dead—they chose to humor the poor old fellow who kept asking them questions.

After the interviews were concluded and the four survivors were shuffling out, one man lingered. Waygo stood at the cabin door and his reluctance to depart suggested to Ann that the quiet man had more to say.

"Was there something else?" the Princess prompted the taciturn man.

"Yes, ma'am, if you please."

"Commodore," said Ann. "What do you say to a spot of brandy?"

"Eh?" asked the commodore, for he was given to understand that the Princess was unfamiliar with liquor. "Oh," he added realizing Ann's intent. "Nothing could be more in keeping with my own desire. Will you join us, sir?"

Waygo smiled broadly. Evidently the tight-lipped man seemed pleased that the commodore had addressed him so courteously and even more pleased that spirits were in the offing. "I suppose it would be all right," said Waygo. "Just a wee drink—or two—if you please."

"Sit down, my friends," said the commodore with a flourish and he stomped on the cabin floor. This was apparently a pre-arranged method of signaling his steward—whose post was in the galley below—that his services were required.

Waygo, Ann, and El took seats at the commodore's broad table and Dell was still on his feet when the steward arrived.

"Sir?" he inquired.

"A bottle of brandy and—" the commodore paused to count the party. "Four cups." The steward turned to go, but the commodore called him back. "And bring Memorian cups—the finest we have—for our honored guests."

The steward raised an eyebrow and uttered, "Aye, sir," as he closed the cabin door.

The commodore remained standing and the other three sat in uncomfortable silence while they awaited the steward's return. Neither Ann nor El could intercept the commodore's thoughts, but they might have guessed what Dell was thinking as he considered his guests.

An unschooled islander, a former Princess who might have lately been a Wolfkind, and a frail deity—these were probably as stark a clash of classes and species as the commodore had ever seen assembled around his table. The group would probably make for awkward messmates and—in the commodore's experience—their diverse backgrounds probably represented a recipe for conflict. Thank El, his expression seemed to say, these landlubbers are not bound for a lengthy sea voyage together.

But neither Ann nor El could hear the commodore's thoughts, which was just as well because they were otherwise engaged in sending mental notes to one another. And the gist of their internal conversation was that—once the brandy had been served and sufficiently sampled to loosen Waygo's reluctant tongue—Ann, not El, would do the questioning.

These islanders think you're crazy, Ann told El in the voice of the mind. *That means this man will be unlikely to take your inquiries seriously. Do you agree?* El nodded his consent. *So, I'll do the talking,* the Princess thought. *And, by the way, you aren't crazy, are you?* Ann added.

"Not yet," said El aloud and the commodore, mistaking the old man's meaning, stomped impatiently on the cabin floor.

"Where is that scoundrel?" he muttered.

Three moments more passed before the steward returned bearing a tray laden with a wax-sealed bottle and five cups. He balanced the tray as he opened and closed the cabin door. Then he balanced his load again as he placed brandy on the table and distributed cups.

"You've brought one cup too many," said the commodore.

"For the lady," said the steward.

"The lady—?" began the commodore. But his question was cut short as a swathe of sheet lightning illuminated the sky outside and a silhouette appeared in the stern windows. It was a petite figure, clothed in a shirt and breeches. An outline of flowing hair suggested it was a woman who seemed to be clinging to the exterior frame of the stern windows.

Had the brandy been already served, the figure might have been dismissed as an apparition. Even so, it still might be an unsubstantial hallucination except for one thing: rather than passing through the window glass like a proper ghost, the figure made a tiny fist and tapped insistently on the glass.

"Shall I open the transom, sir?" asked the steward, as if creating a portal for the apparition was as mundane a task as opening an ordinary door.

"By all means," said the commodore. "Let's have her in."

As the steward cranked the transom open, a burst of ocean breeze filled the cabin and the figure tumbled in. The sudden gust caused the cabin lanterns to sputter, but the flames quickly regained their brightness as the occupants scrambled to their feet and the transom was closed. The moment lights were restored, all eyes were instantly drawn to the new arrival's beautiful face. It was only when she spoke that their attention left that face and focused on the pistol in her hand.

"Good evening," said Ahoo as she stood before them, her drenched clothing and saturated hair dripping on the cabin floor. "I pray you, be seated for I'm not yet accustomed to using this thing and might accidentally fire it by mistake. And in any event, I'm not liable to miss at this range."

Chapter 26

Confession

The old wives of Redhackle Isle are fond of repeating sayings they have heard from their grandmothers whether or not those sayings make sense a generation on. But one saying which has stood the test of time is a phrase which helps explain the sudden transformation of a seemingly benign person into a threat. Regarding such occurrences, the old wives would say this: "If it be a string with teeth, it be a snake."

Ahoo grinned as she pointed the pistol at each person in turn and each sat down—except for the steward who turned and locked the door.

"What is the meaning of this?" the commodore demanded.

"The meaning, sir," intoned the steward. "Is that I have taken a new position. May I offer you a cloak, miss?" The steward crossed to the commodore's wardrobe, selected a greatcoat, and draped it over the witch's wet shoulders. "Majesty," he said and stepped back with a bow.

"Thank you, Miles," Ahoo smiled. "Ah, that feels lovely especially as I feel a draft." Saying this, she swung the pistol behind her and fired at the stern windows, shattering the nearest panel into a thousand shards of leaden glass. The sound filled the cabin, and her prisoners were momentarily stunned. So disoriented were the others that, before they could rise again, Ahoo had reached into her belt and pulled and cocked a second pistol.

"One shot left," she grinned. "Who's feeling lucky?" She waggled the pistol carelessly, pointing it at each person in turn starting with Ann. "You, our mystery woman? You, our fallen deity? You, our fearless commodore? Or this cretin from the island? Or maybe I should shoot Miles to reduce my expenses? Round and round the mulberry bush...which will I choose?" She paused and brought the barrel down so that it was inches from Ann's forehead, then she suddenly shifted it to point at El. "Good night, my lord—"

El closed his eyes and seemed resigned to the ending of his life.

"Oh," sighed Ahoo as she lowered the pistol. "The look on your faces! I—I can't do it. Relax, everyone." She smiled nervously. "It was a joke, see? Ask Miles."

"Miles?" the commodore addressed his steward with an icy tone, signaling his anger.

"I—I regret to say, sir, that this young lady—well—she convinced me that you—that is to say—that—all of you would appreciate what she told me was to be a practical joke," said Miles with a nervous expression.

"A joke? Do you see anyone laughing?" the commodore growled.

"No, sir," admitted Miles.

"Have you any plausible excuse to explain your appalling behavior?"

"None, sir," Miles vacillated. "Only to say I was taken in by her enthusiasm. And by her beauty—that is—" his voice faltered.

"You are dismissed from my service! I'll deal with you later!"

"Aye, sir," said Miles, as he lowered his head and stepped back into a shadowy corner.

"Sorry," the contrite witch apologized. "Please don't be angry with Miles. It was all my doing. I'm afraid I've made a mess of things. You see, I'm new at this skylarking. I sought only to entertain. You see I—"

The witch never saw Seth coming.

Intent on her game, Ahoo was unaware that Seth had been following her. The witch hadn't expected Seth would see her climb over the ship's side. She didn't expect Seth to secure a rigging line to the railing above, grip the cord tightly, and leap over the stern. And she certainly wasn't expecting the fearless man to swing toward the cabin. So, the surprise was complete when Seth crashed through the windows behind the witch and drove his feet into her back. Seth sprawled on the floor as Ahoo careened forward. In a rapid series of mishaps, the pistol discharged as the astonished witch was propelled across the table where she collided with Ann's fist. The blow staggered Ahoo and she fell unconscious to the cabin floor.

"Love of my breath!" shouted Ann as the echoes of the second shot radiated in the cabin. "Are you injured?" she asked Seth and quickly knelt beside him.

"A few scrapes, nothing more," he assured her. "See to El."

The deity was cowering beneath the table.

"Are you hurt, my El?' Ann asked.

"My pride only," replied the old man. "I'm afraid I sought cover—out of fright—just like a common mortal."

"Is no one hurt?" the commodore asked. "Where did the ball go?"

"I have it here," stuttered Waygo.

Everyone looked at the islander who had remained seated. The shattered brandy bottle lay in pieces on the table in front of him and he was staring fixedly at the cup in his hand. The ball had passed cleanly through the bottle and then through one wall of the cup but no farther. Waygo swirled his hand so they could hear the spent pistol ball as it rolled noisily around inside the empty cup.

"A bloody miracle," Waygo blubbered.

"You can't beat the quality of Memorian clay," El observed.

At that instant, the boatswain, who had apparently been searching for the source of the shots, was calling the commodore's name, and pounding on the cabin door.

"Miles, you're back in my employ!"

"Aye, commodore."

"Unlock that damned door and send Brightlamp away. Now," said the commodore, "if everyone is quite finished admiring the crockery, would one of you mind placing this would-be assassin in a chair while I have my foolish steward call for the surgeon? Even though I am somewhat inclined to call the boatswain back and have her clapped in irons."

The witch was not moving when Seth knelt to lift her up.

"Surgeon!" shouted Miles as he unlocked the cabin door.

"The surgeon?" came the confused reply.

"Aye, you heard me! Send the surgeon to the commodore's cabin quick as you can. We have a customer here."

"Aye."

"And fetch the carpenter too. We'll need the stern windows repaired."

"Aye," said the voice uncertainly.

"You might have used the door," said the commodore to Seth as he surveyed the damage.

"No time," said Seth. "I was watching the witch on the deck above. I saw her carrying two pistols and, by the time I reached the railing, she was crawling over the side—quite the climber our little witch. Therefore, I picked up a rope and followed."

"There are no ropes on this ship," corrected the commodore.

"Perhaps then I swung here using my imagination," said Seth peevishly.

"What he means, love," explained Ann. "Is that the bit of entwined fiber which you so recently used for your dramatic entrance is not called a 'rope.' Onboard ship such devices are called 'lines.'"

"Hmm," said Seth.

"A common error which does not diminish the gallant intention of your actions," said the commodore as he bowed low to Seth. "Your wife spoke of you as an equal warrior. And having witnessed your acrobatics, I must admit I heartily agree."

The surgeon arrived.

"My patient?" asked the surgeon as he surveyed the disheveled room.

"The lady slumped in that chair," said the commodore.

"This slip of a girl?" asked the surgeon as he examined the bruise forming on Ahoo's cheek. "Which of you is responsible for this?"

The commodore blushed, "An accident I'm afraid—a sort of a joke gone wrong."

"Hmm," said the surgeon and he looked disapprovingly at each person in the room until his gaze landed on Seth, who blushed and avoided eye contact.

"I seem to have kicked her in the back," Seth mumbled.

"And she may have stumbled into my fist," Ann added.

"Hmm," the surgeon repeated. "Well, she's coming around, no thanks to any of you. I don't suppose you realize this girl is an island hero. I thought not. Are you aware she is responsible for saving those she brought to us by boat and many others besides who are still stranded on the island? Well, she is! So, let's have an end to these jokes, if you please!"

"Yes, your honor," said everyone more or less in unison, including the commodore.

"Be at ease, my dear," said the surgeon. He pointedly ignored Ahoo's attackers and turned his full attention to the witch as she began to stir. "You've had a shock, but I'm here now and it's going to be all right. I won't let them harm you."

The surgeon called for sailors to convert one of the lifeboats into a bed and he organized another detail of men to carry Ahoo there to rest. "Gently!" he shouted at the sailors who attempted to lift the groggy woman. "Handsomely, you heathen roughnecks! Don't jostle her!"

When the surgeon, the witch, and her escort had gone, the commodore sent Miles for another bottle. When the replacement arrived, the commodore poured drinks all around. "Now where were we?" he asked.

"We were about to interview this gentleman to learn the truth," said El. "Although, as things now stand, I think we can guess some of what he has to tell us."

Waygo felt the eyes of the party on him, and he asked for another drink, frowning because the hole in his cup allowed for only a modest portion. When he had downed it, he began.

"We all seen her—the girl you knocked down—two days ago fallin' from the clear sky and into the sea. We hauled her out and laid her on the beach until the doctor come. He rolled her over and looked her over and we lugged her to Wingfoot's hut where the doctor he sent some home, where me I went to the tavern. Next thing I know, my wife comes to fetch me for a crowd at the church. When I enters, here's this girl standin' at the pulpit spoutin' the wildest tales I ever heared about old man Death and old man El and the Wolfkind Princess (all of which we heard had died—not Death a'course—that would be un-possible). And more she said, about how she was attacked by invisible beasts and about her bein' stoned and her flyin' up to Velyn and her—though a witch—bein' sort'a pardoned, I think she said it was—'abso-something' she named it. And how she promised to mend her ways and—well that's when the trouble started—"

Waygo signaled for and was granted a third drink.

"Sudden, the walls of the church started shakin' and we smelt smoke and the streets was runnin' full'a fire and we was so afraid that we all froze—stiff as statues we was. But not this girl—no sir—she rousted us up and got us clear of the fire and when we was safe on the beach, she went on back into the fire—*right into it* I said—and went to the school and carried twenty children out on her back."

"Twenty at once?" asked Ann, convinced that the man was embellishing his account.

"Not at once no," said Waygo. "That'd be un-possible. No, sir, she carried 'em out two at a time—one under each arm, strong she was for such a little'un—and anyway she went back—" he paused to count on his fingers, "Eight—no ten times—back and forth in the fire in them iron boots without a pause or a yelp from her. To-and-fro she went, like the time-ticker on a clock. She pult my nieces and nephews out of that fire and many more besides—I never saw nothin' like it. It was like the fire just rolled off her. Like it was more water to her than flames. She's an angel at least and may-be a goddess—pardon me saying so, lord." he bowed in El's direction.

"No offense, my child," smiled El. "Pray continue." The deity seemed pleased that apparently Waygo believed he was genuine, even if other islanders had their doubts.

"Well," said Waygo, "that's about it really. I'd be repeatin' myself to tell you all she done—goin' back and forth into that fire savin' people—but at the last she gathered up the worse hurt and organized some rowers—me included since it was only my leg—and well—I guess you know the rest—she hauled us out to the ship and here we is."

After the islander had departed, the cabin fell silent.

"Well," said Ann, "seems like we started this journey with a witch on our trail and dreading to battle her again and now we've ended up with—"

"With an angel, it seems," said Seth. "An angel who I pounded in the back."

"And I punched," said Ann, as memories of her dearly departed garden angel caused her speech to falter and her eyes to feel moist.

Do not cry, she told herself. *Do not let the commodore see you cry.*

"I have a feeling she'll forgive you both," said El. "She's clearly a changed woman and—despite her impetuous pranks—she seems well on her way to something like sainthood."

"So, what was this business with the pistols all about?" asked Ann.

"What Waygo told us is probably true and it all sounded plausible to me," said El. "Did you see his face? He was testifying before his deity and unlikely to be lying. In any event, the notion that she rose near enough to Velyn to experience a spontaneous conversion is entirely possible. Reaching the cusp of heaven and receiving absolution would mean that she was cleansed of her wickedness and reborn to work her way through infancy, childhood, and adolescence. The latter transformation typical of what we witnessed here."

"So—the pistols—the reckless shooting—that was her play-acting like a younger, more careless, version of herself?" asked Ann.

"There you have it," the deity declared. "Consider all the trauma she has endured and in so short a time. Emerging from the shadow of Death, she is filled with the joy of rebirth, and she is a blossoming youth—brimming with compassion and altruism—capable of taking charge in a crisis, as she did at the church, and in bringing the wounded to the ship. But also devolving into silliness and irresponsible daring, as she did by barging in here moments ago with pistols at the ready. Feeling invincible, but also vulnerable, she is a typical youth, conflicted by empathy and careless mischief bordering on delinquency. A strong woman on the island, managing a crisis, but lately manifesting the persona of an impetuous girl of—I should say—about thirteen or so."

The commodore, who had been sitting silently, spoke at last, "So this *girl,* as you describe her, is—or was—a witch who is now an adolescent saint?

And this one," he pointed at Ann, "is the last Princess of the realm—except without her snout or pointed ears or tail? And this fellow," he pointed to Seth, "is her Wolfkind mate transformed into a golden-haired human? And yourself—" he apparently decided not to point at El. "Yourself—the one who chartered this cruise—is the earthly personification of our dying deity? Am I missing anyone?"

"Only me," said Esau as he padded into the cabin, placed his forepaws on the table, and looked the commodore straight in the eyes. "Only me."

Chapter 27

A New Plan

Like a Wolfkind warrior, a sea captain is unused to swooning. Commodore Alphonse Dell had never fainted in his life, and certainly he had never lost consciousness on his own ship. Not even last year when his arm was broken by a pirate cannon ball. Or five years ago on a voyage to distant southern climes when news reached him that his wife of twelve years had died in childbirth.

The commodore was surprised when the cabin seemed to spin about him and even more surprised to awaken at dawn lying supine in his bunk with the surgeon feeling his pulse.

"Hmm," the surgeon said. "He'll do." The surgeon stood and joined the others at the cabin table. "I think Ann and the girl might be allowed in now." Knowing the commodore as he did, the surgeon—who was in fact Sander Dell, the commodore's older brother—had forbade the women to enter the cabin until the commodore was quite recovered.

The women came shyly in and took seats at the table as the commodore sat up and hastily buttoned his tunic.

"Forgive me," the commodore said. Then he bowed to the surgeon. "Thank you for your service, sir, but I am quite well now—"

"They know, Alphonse," said the surgeon mildly. "They know we are brothers."

"How—?"

"My fault, I'm afraid," said Sander. "In the throes of a temporary fever, you were calling for family under the misapprehension that you were dying."

"Oh," said the commodore flatly.

"Never fear," said El. The commodore looked toward the old man, who sat at the head of the table looking robust and radiant. "We shall keep your secret. And this is your chair, I believe." The deity stood and the others stood as well. Then El strode vigorously forward, took the younger Dell's arm, and guided the commodore to his accustomed place.

"It is not entirely a secret—please," said the commodore and he motioned the others to sit as he took his chair. "The navy frowns on siblings serving on the same vessel. You know the reason I'm certain—the tragedy of The Sentinel?"

Heads nodded around the table. Everyone had heard the sad tale of the sinking of The Good Ship Sentinel. The ship went down years ago in heavy seas, a disaster which carried ninety sailors to a watery grave, including eight brothers who were serving on her.

"Someone had to keep an eye on his younger brother," smiled the surgeon.

"And someone was obliged to find a position for the black sheep of our family," the commodore noted. "But now that I'm awake I have but one question—"

"The dog?" asked El, who had remained on his feet and stood near the cabin door.

"Yes," said the commodore. "I presume my impression that the animal speaks was part of my unconscious dream."

Sander cleared his throat and cast a concerned look at his brother who, even as a boy, had exhibited a fertile imagination. Twenty minutes ago, when he'd revived his unconscious brother, the surgeon had attributed his patient's tale of magical beings, including a talking dog, to delirium brought on by fatigue. He was hoping the others would discourage rather than feed such delusions.

"Let us say that Esau is an intelligent animal who is given to mischief," El explained. "And he is most ashamed of his behavior and most concerned about your recovery and most anxious to apologize."

"Let us have him in," said the commodore.

El opened the cabin door. "Come. Come now, it is all right."

Esau peeked tentatively around the corner of the open door.

"Come in please," said the commodore. "I would stand to greet you, but I'm still feeling a bit shaky."

Esau slunk into the room, his tail between his legs, his ears down in abject humiliation and went to a far corner. He lay down and tried to look obedient. He did not speak.

Watching the animal, Sander breathed a sigh of relief.

Sometimes, the surgeon told himself, *a dog is just a dog.*

"As I counseled, brother," said Sander aloud. "Your impressions of magic were mistaken. Caused, no doubt, by your fatigue. With all due respect to these assembled, I hope they will recognize—as do I—that you need rest. My prescription for a speedy recovery is to request that you all be so good as to cut short this meeting and allow my brother to recover himself more fully. I've said all I can. I'll take my leave now. There are other patients on board in need of my attention."

When Sander had departed, the commodore sought assurance from those assembled.

"I did hear the dog speak, did I not? And tell me that my inventory of this gathering—my surmises regarding the presence of magic—my beliefs are not mistaken."

"The dog spoke," said El. "And you are not wrong."

"I'll keep my thoughts apart from my practical brother," said the commodore. "He will remain skeptical. I am the romantic in our family. He is a man of science."

"We may well have need of science," said El. "But your acceptance of magic will also prove useful to our cause. As for our Esau, he will regain his confidence shortly. He is still seeking his balance."

"As am I," said Ahoo as she stood. "My undeserved nap in the lifeboat has shamed me. I should leave this company. I have acted foolishly, and I ought not to be allowed in this party."

The commodore insisted she stay. "Your deeds on the island have been relayed to us. You are most welcome here, lady."

"Most welcome," said El as he returned to the table and placed a hand gently on the witch's shoulder. She wore a sleeveless bodice which revealed a corner of the birthmark on her back. Knowing its meaning, El did not draw attention to it. Instead, he raised his eyes toward the ceiling. "And you and the commodore have joined the ranks of our quest at a most opportune time. Listen, everyone, do you not hear it?"

The stern windows were still boarded-up—a testimony to the chaos caused by Ahoo and Seth. Thus, the group was obliged to leave the great-cabin in order to seek out the source of the noise. At first, when they emerged on deck, they thought the sound must be the cheering of the crew, undoubtedly elated to hear the news that their commodore had recovered. But as they assembled in the bright sunshine on the quarterdeck, they realized that shouts of joy filled the sea in all directions.

The blissful tumult was contagious.

Ann and Seth held hands as they whirled in a circle, then rushed to the railing taking in the scope of what they saw and heard. El clapped his hands together and danced an animated jig. Ahoo gaped in wonder as the dour Sander rushed gleefully across the deck and embraced his brother. Even Esau, who arrived last, was caught up in the revelry and he leapt about the deck barking enthusiastically.

"Sail, ho!" shouted the lookout. "Sail, ho! And ho! And ho, sir! Sails everywhere, by my sainted beard!"

"Fire a salute!" roared the commodore, his joy evident in the return of his robust sea-voice. "Fire a volley, damn your eyes!" In response, the starboard and port cannons—stripped of shot and expending powder only—poured heavy smoke over the heaving sea. From all sides, booming echoes and roiling smoke seemed to respond in a resounding series of nautical salutations.

"What is it?" shouted the witch, striving to be heard above the commotion. "What does it mean?"

"That most excellent array, my girl," laughed the commodore as he swept both arms to circle the horizon in a broad gesture, "is the Southern Fleet! Fifty ships-of-the-line! Every vessel and every man-jack aboard thought lost in a pitched battle a fortnight ago with a pirate armada! But look you! Every ship is still afloat and, by the thickness of powder smoke, armed to the teeth. With this force we shall set sail for Memora and catch the pirates with their trousers down, by thunder!"

Chapter 28

Three Wishes

The custom of a warship turning her guns toward the empty ocean and firing her arsenal to demonstrate a lack of hostile intent is a good one, so far as it goes. But, when powder and shot are in short supply, it is best to halt the ceremony well shy of the traditional twenty-one volleys. So it was that the explosive aspect of the fleet's sudden arrival at Redhackle Isle was short-lived, but that did not stop the sailors and marines cheering.

As the others celebrated the unexpected appearance of the Southern Fleet and with the hurrahs of men ringing in his ears, El walked alone to the prow and gazed skyward.

"Migral," he said aloud, "I know you are looking down on us. And I know it was you who saved the fleet—you and your faithful weather. I have been sleeping lately—tired and inattentive—but I see the miracle now. I see it clearly in my mind's eye and I marvel at your ingenuity. I thought all was lost when you died at the cave and yet you completed your mission, and you continue to further our quest. I'm sorry I doubted you. Now I see that, with your dying breath, you dispatched your rain and wind and sleet to speed southward to rescue the fleet. I see the pirate armada now—the ill-fated ships floundering in your miraculous storm while, mere inches away, the Southern Fleet sails on untouched. What a tremendous gift you have given us! Bless you always and I will be with you soon. Amen."

"Lord?" It was the witch who approached her deity on the forward deck. She'd been standing reverently apart until he had finished his prayer.

"Yes, lamb," said El.

"I wasn't listening," she stuttered.

"I understand. What brings you here, child?"

"I come to ask a favor."

"You may ask," said El. He tried not to sound suspicious.

"Well—there are two favors actually—no three—yes, three."

"Only three? Are you certain, child?" the deity smiled.

"Yes, lord," she said and, seeing El smile, she plowed on. "The first favor is for the healing of the islanders and restoration of their land. Oh—is that two already?"

"We shall count that unselfish request as one," smiled El. "But that solution is already afoot for you yourself have saved and healed the islanders and they shall soon be well enough. And as for the other—you have my word that, as soon as we depart, the blackened island will turn suddenly green as plants and trees return and the burned earth is restored to its former primitive beauty."

"And the houses?" asked Ahoo.

"It will do the survivors good to bend their grieving hearts to the task of rebuilding. Do you agree?"

"Yes. That is a fine idea," she said.

"Your other wishes?" El prompted.

"The second wish is for my step-father and for the lost sailors—the grain ship sailors—you know the ones I mean."

"These are long-dead are they not?"

"They are and I am the cause of it," said Ahoo and she buried her chin in her chest and sobbed.

El allowed the witch to cry. Then he spoke, "As for the sailors who meant to harm you, have you forgiven them?"

"In my heart, yes," said Ahoo.

"Then they are forgiven in the place which matters," El assured her. "And your father is, by you, likewise forgiven?"

"He is."

"It is well that you have made your peace with these men," said El. "But each took his own life, lamb. You know what that means."

"I know, but it was my doing, lord. Can't their souls—?" She couldn't find the words.

"That is a tall order, child," said El.

"It is my fault—my fault which imperils their souls—"

"But," El declared. "You must know that what is done for these must be done for others. Moreover, the fate of such lost souls, including the fate of your step-father, is Death's domain."

"I know this."

"What are you asking, child?" El spoke passionately, for he'd guessed her request.

"When we acquire the cup—" she began.

"*If* we acquire it," corrected El. "You must not endanger our quest by presuming the outcome."

"Very well *if* we acquire the cup," Ahoo continued. "*If* we complete the quest, Death will be enraged, and he will stop at nothing to injure all who dared defy him. For any to escape his wrath, you included, a diversion will be necessary."

"Ah, you have been studying military writings I see," smiled El.

"Yes, lord," grinned Ahoo. "I have taken—that is I have borrowed—the commodore's books and Ann's. I find that I suddenly like books," she added with a dreamy look in her eyes. "In any event, I have studied both Wolfkind tactics and the strategies of men. And there was one passage which I found of particular interest." She bit her lower lip trying to remember. "I don't recall it exactly, but it was something about sending a sparrow to do a hawk's job."

In spite of the serious nature of the conversation he was having with this earnest creature, El laughed aloud. "Forgive me, child. I think the maxim you mean is this: 'If your enemy expects a sparrow, send a hawk; if he expects a hawk, send a sparrow.'"

"That's it," said Ahoo. "And I am both the expected hawk and the secret sparrow. Death believes that I am still his ally. I will appear to him to be a hungry hawk set among the lambs while, unbeknownst to him, I have changed and will do the sparrow's work."

"Which is?" asked El, he was curious to know if the witch was planning to do the courageous thing he suspected.

"I will go with you to Deep Lake. And when—that is *if*—our quest meets with success, I will stay behind as hostage to bargain with Death while the rest escape. It is the only way."

"Go on—" prompted El.

"Death will be angry," she said. "But also bewildered. He will seize me and wish to kill me, but we know, of course, that he cannot kill a sentient being—let alone an old-world witch. But if he is not quickly appeased, he may yet unleash his flood—yes, he has told me of his deadly plans. And so, to distract him from that vengeance, I will offer him my life in exchange for the creation of a new dwelling place for those who have taken their own lives. I will bargain with him to create a balancing level between Velyn and Callus—a place not so glorious as the upper world but neither as harsh as the lower."

"The Limbo," suggested El.

"Yes."

"The scrolls speak of it," said El.

"Yes."

"And the scrolls maintain that the idea of a plane between paradise and hell was rejected," the deity observed.

"But rejected how?" she asked.

"Rejected within the old agreement betwixt myself and Death," said El and then he smiled broadly. "Ah, I see what you mean."

"Yes. Death will have me," said the witch. "And Death will lessen the agony of my step-father's soul and those souls who share his pain. Because—"

"Because Death will believe that, in granting your request to create The Limbo, he will have secretly amended our old agreement without consulting me," laughed El.

"Whereas—" the witch prompted.

"Whereas, if I agree here and now to your wish, the bargain is already amended without *his* consultation. He will agree knowing that so great a change cannot be accomplished unless I agree to it. He will agree because he will have no intention of informing me of his decision, whereas you will have maneuvered him into seconding my motion. Clever child—I like such thinking."

"Death will be appeased, my step-father's soul will rest and the troubled sailors will find a measure of peace, and I—"

"You will die surely," El frowned. "That seems a poor result."

"I do not fear dying," grinned Ahoo. "You forget that I have seen Velyn. That I have ascended to the very edge of it. Ask your bird."

"My bird?" El wondered.

"Migral," said the witch. "It was the raven who met me in the air at the border of paradise where I might have been rejected and sent to fall forever toward Callus. It was he who saved me and converted me and sent me back to the world to assist your quest. And it was he who promised that my soul will dwell there with him someday in Velyn."

"He promised you?" asked El.

"Did he not speak truth?"

"A soul in Velyn cannot lie." El said. Then he grew quiet while he weighed the import of all the witch had proposed. "Well, young woman, you seem to have thought of everything."

"Do you agree to my plan?" she asked.

"How can I refuse?"

The witch embraced him and was on the point of leaving when El drew her back and held her hand. "Was there not a third wish?"

"Ah," she laughed, "I am such a scatterbrain. I do have one last request but before I ask it, please allow me to thank you sincerely for restoring my feet."

"Your feet?"

"Yes. Have you forgotten? On the island, when I awoke in Doctor Stonebrook's care, the very first thing I did was ask directions to the church. Arriving there, I confessed my sins before the congregation, and I fell to my knees and prayed to you—to my El—to restore my feet. And they were instantly restored—so thank you."

"You're welcome," the deity responded. El did not remember receiving, let alone answering such an unusual prayer, but he surmised that the transaction must have occurred while he lay incapacitated in the bowels of the ship. "And now that I understand the details of your conversion, what is your third wish?"

"It is a selfish wish, I'm afraid," the witch hung her head.

"Speak, child," smiled El. "I have granted you two selfless wishes, surely I can satisfy something intended for yourself only."

"My third wish is foolish," she whispered.

"Let me decide," he responded.

"Very well. It concerns my iron boots."

"Yes, child?"

"They were once molded to my feet as a punishment," she said, her voice betraying strong emotion.

"That time is over," El assured her.

"Then, is it possible—that is—I wish to take them off. May I do so?"

Chapter 29

The Fleet Sails

The lightness of being which can be achieved when a heavy burden is lifted —whether that encumbrance is physical or mental—can buoy up a mortal to the point of giddiness. How much greater will be the joy when the celebrant is not mortal, but magical, and the burden lifted is not only a worldly, but a spiritual weight?

With the enthusiastic help of the ironmonger and ship's carpenter, the witch's heavy boots were summarily pried loose and cast over the side. Freed from confinement, ten pink toes wriggled and basked in the welcoming sunshine.

Moments later, the assembled crew lined the railings and sailors and marines laughed and shouted encouragement as Ahoo made a gleeful circumnavigation of *Catspaw's* main deck. She circled once, then circled again, then continued to run.

The crew celebrated her joy, and she too was laughing as she ran barefoot. Padding the restored flesh of her perfectly marvelous feet against the ship's planks, she fashioned six joyous circles—around and around until she fell, exhausted to the deck. Doctor Stonebrook, who had fully recovered from his injuries, knelt beside the giddy girl to feel her pulse.

"She'll do," he announced as the crew cheered. "Farewell, child," said the doctor and he leaned forward to kiss the girl.

"Must you go?" asked Ahoo.

"My patients need me."

"But what of me and what of your cousin?" she asked, nodding toward Ann who stood beside Commodore Dell at the quarterdeck railing.

Doctor Stonebrook followed Ahoo's gaze.

"You, young lady, will be fine. And as for that stately woman there, she seems familiar, but upon questioning her, I find she's no direct kin of mine."

"But your surnames—"

"Pshaw, child," the doctor laughed. "Both our names are common enough. And they are jumbled besides. And my given name is extremely regular and her Ann as well. I doubt that one could throw a rock here or elsewhere in the kingdom without it landing upon an Andrew or an Ann or two. But now, as for your Ahoo, there indeed is a name for the ages."

"That is not my real name," she whispered.

Doctor Stonebrook gave the girl a quizzical look. But before he could speak, she scrambled to her feet and said aloud, "I shall miss you, sir."

"And I you," said the doctor. "But apparently you and your multiple names are needed elsewhere. I will say your goodbyes to the other islanders. They'll be cross not to have seen you again and the children will weep. But it's likely they'll forgive you and remember you fondly and always. In any event, we shall be busy restoring our burnt homeland, mourning our dead, and rebuilding our homes."

"I know well that you will have assistance with the former task," said the witch. "And I too will mourn those who perished. And, as for the rebuilding, I can assure you help will arrive."

Again, the doctor regarded his recovered patient, impressed by her sincerity.

"What can I say to such optimistic prophecy?" he smiled. "Except to thank you. Your words give me hope for our future. Well, I see that my transport is alongside. Adieu, child, and all my best wishes." He held the witch's hand for some moments. Then he waved to Ann and the commodore and nodded to the sailors who assisted him over the side.

For her part, Ahoo twirled in place, then she was off circling the deck again. She continued in a broad loop, waving to the doctor's departing boat each time she came abreast of the island, until at last the boat was lost from sight. And still she ran.

"I never saw the like," the commodore grinned as he and Ann stood side-by-side like fellow officers on the quarterdeck. "That girl possesses not only boundless beauty but boundless energy as well."

"No doubt the seasoned sailors and battle-hardened marines are lusting to see her breasts bounce while she runs," observed Ann.

"At first perhaps," said the commodore. "But I know these men. They are not cheering her as a cavorting strumpet. They are captivated by the sheer joy of her girlish exuberance! It is a remarkable thing is it not, Sander?"

The surgeon joined them, and he too laughed to see the girl's energy and the crew's merriment. "The men are in high spirits indeed! And that girl—I wish she were a horse and I a betting man!"

The commodore frowned at the mention of his brother's vice—the gambling habit which had compelled him to come to sea to escape his debts.

Sander saw his brother's disapproval and demurred, "I'm joking, brother. That's all behind me now."

"Let us hope so," said the commodore. "Your report?"

"Pardon, I was forgetting," Sander snapped to attention and saluted his brother. "I beg to report, sir, that our boats have returned from running the patients ashore and they are well. As you may have noticed, the good doctor and a crew of islanders have taken one of our lifeboats which they will retain. And we towed two lifeboats shoreward last night and also left these for their use. In summary, all is as well as can be on Redhackle Isle. And I report that the ship is squared away and ready to hoist anchor and plow west to beat the ever-loving crap out of the enemy, sir."

"Very good, surgeon," the commodore grinned. "I'll have the boatswain please."

"Aye-aye, commodore," said Sander and he rushed away in search of Brightlamp who, as it happened, was already mounting the quarterdeck stairway. The boatswain nodded to the surgeon and hurried to the commodore's side.

"Your sword, sir," said Brightlamp.

"Just so," said Dell as he buckled the belt and positioned the scabbard. "I'll have the pipes, if you please."

"Pipes!" roared the boatswain.

The pipes were sounded, and the crew took up their stations as *Catspaw's* bright red and silver pennant was hoisted. For her part, the witch stopped running and rapidly climbed the stairway to stand with Ann and Commodore Dell.

"A better view from up here," said Ahoo.

"And less likely to be trampled by rushing sailors," said the Princess.

"Three cheers!" roared the boatswain as the flag unfurled.

"Hip hip hurrah! Hip hip hurrah! Hip hip hurrah!" shouted the crew.

"Hurrah!" added the witch. "Sorry," she said. "Out of sequence."

"Never mind," smiled the commodore. "Mister Brightlamp! The anchor if you please."

"Aye, sir! Ready the windlass!" Brightlamp positioned the men, but waited for the formal command to hoist anchor. "Hands at the ready, sir."

"Let's have her up," said Dell.

"And haul away, boys!" shouted the boatswain and *Catspaw* shuddered as the anchor was cranked home.

"Mainsails," the commodore ordered.

"Aloft, you barnacles!" roared Brightlamp. "Loose sail!"

A host of sailors scampered up the masts and unfurled yard after yard of billowing canvas.

"Be so good as to signal the fleet to advance in their lines," Dell said in a voice that seemed to betray his fatherly affection for his efficient young boatswain.

"Signal-man!" bellowed Brightlamp.

"Aye!" came the man's obedient reply.

"Signal all vessels to station!"

The crew cheered as *Catspaw* took the breeze and surged into the lead of the advancing fleet. Similar cheers echoed across the water as the hulls of fifty more fighting ships caught the wind and sliced through the rolling sea. And thus, with the forbidden banners of Middlemount flying defiantly atop every mainmast, the host of gallant vessels which historians would later dub "The Fleet of Deliverance" sailed westward toward the far horizon and into the annals of legend.

Chapter 30

The General

It is said that all evil stems from ignorance and ignorance can appear small until it strikes you in the eye.

By the time the advancing Fishal soldiers rediscovered the trail of the fugitives, it took the lumbering force four days to cross Middlemount's lofty Northern Range. Then they lost another day searching for a way to cross The River Smedlarge. The captain was apologetic. The general was furious.

"Someone is going to suffer for this unholy delay," sputtered the general. "And it ain't going to be me."

"The witch was supposed to guide us," offered the captain, by way of explanation.

"Shows what I've been saying all along," said the general. "Didn't I say so? That little tart is not to be trusted. It were a mistake to accept her as an ally even if she promised magic support. Some magic—damn hocus pocus claptrap bogus balderdash. Probably seen the last of her worthless bottom, I reckon, the little two-faced tart."

The two Fishal officers were meeting in the general's spacious field tent. The hour was late. With yet another rainstorm pounding down and his disgruntled men sleeping outside in sodden ditches, the general was sipping tea and eating strawberries while propped up by over-sized pillows in the four-poster feathered-bed he insisted on bringing along on every campaign. Behind his back, his soldiers called him "Feather-Butt." To his ruddy pock-marked face, they called him "General Umber."

Maps and charts and communiqués littered the general's bedspread. The ostentatious blanket was another creature comfort he insisted on dragging along into the field. It was his grandmother's quilt, one which she'd hand-stitched for him while serving her prison term for sedition. It was well and lovingly made, a miracle of the woman's craft, considering it was her grandson who had imprisoned her.

"Can't play favorites," he told his quartermaster when the subject of why he had clapped his grand-mam in irons and thrown her into the Nia Stockade came up. "Stitching a flag for the rebellion is punishable by five years and besides she didn't serve the full term." The fact that she had died in prison on the eve of her tenth month in captivity seemed to the general indisputable evidence of his clemency.

General Umber's blonde head was filled with similar notions—some were fanciful and the rest, delusional. His men—who outnumbered the old fart by three thousand to one—found their commander's delusions inconvenient. His superiors tolerated Umber's mistakes and stroked his massive ego in order to manipulate the insufferable officer into doing whatever dirty work came the army's way.

This night, General Umber was having the grandfather of all delusions. He was having a delusion for the record books, one for the ages. When the history of delusions is written, the general's delusion on that stormy night ten miles from the estuary of The River Smedlarge, will most certainly have a chapter devoted solely to it.

His delusion was this: he imagined himself to be a military genius.

"Is everything now perfectly clear to you?" he demanded the captain's agreement.

"Perfectly, sir."

"Hmm," the general placed his fat finger on the uppermost chart among the pile of maps on his bedspread. "This is the spot then?"

The captain leaned over pretending interest as he once again was compelled to examine the map for the twentieth time that evening. "Yes, sir."

"Hmm. And you say there are no more than two dozen of the blighters?"

"Our scouts report seeing twelve females and thirteen males, sir," the captain had lost count, but he was certain he'd told the general at least ten times how many Dungs the Fishal scouts had reported on the beach.

"One too many, eh?"

"Sir?"

"One too many males for them to pair up." the general said dreamily. "I wonder what that other blighter does while the couples are cupulating."

My stars! thought the captain to himself. *If this idiot says "cupulating" one more time—*

"Stands guard," said the general.

"Sir?"

"The extra male stands guard of course. Stands guard whilst the others are cupulating. I wonder you didn't figure that out yourself."

"Sir, I really should get back to the men," said the captain.

"Don't be a fool. Don't you know it's raining outside?"

"Yes, sir. I can hear the rain."

"Hear the rain? Hear the rain? That seems unlikely."

"Sir, I—"

"*Hear* the rain? What a damned-fool notion! One does not *hear* the rain—one feels it. Even the dullest schoolboy knows that."

"Sir, I only meant—"

"Hear the rain? Why, you'd have to turn your head sideways to do that. A damned-fool thing to do during a rainstorm."

"Sir—"

"The damn rainwater would go right into your ear hole! And then what? I ask you, then what?" the general demanded.

"If that will be all, sir," the captain suggested.

"No, captain! That will not be all! Do you think I ordered you here just so you could leave before I was finished with you?" the general sputtered.

"I have no idea, sir."

"No idea of what?"

"Why you ordered me here, sir," the captain said.

"You haven't? Well, you must have some notion of why I would order you here on such a foul night. Come, man, think! There must be a reason."

"Sir, I—"

"Must have something to do with all these maps, otherwise why so many and why spread them here on my lap?" When the captain did not respond, the general demanded, "Well?"

"It appears that you have called me here to discuss a strategy for dealing with the Dungs, sir."

"There you have it! Clever lad. Now, I have a plan, of course." And the general added a thought aloud, although he seemed to be speaking to himself, "Of course I have. I must have."

The captain waited.

"Now," the general vacillated, "before we hear my plan—what do you think would be best?"

"Me, sir?"

"Yes. I'm extremely curious to know what you would suggest we do to deal with the Dungs who are blocking our path."

"Shoot them, sir," the captain suggested.

"That's your plan?"

"Yes, sir."

"Not very imaginative, is it?"

"Sir?"

"I mean 'shoot them' is that your best idea?" the general sounded doubtful.

In the silence which followed, a chill wind vibrated the canvas walls of the snug field tent and the rain, which had been drizzling, hammered down with a vengeance.

"What else might you suggest?" the general prompted.

"We could use our muskets as clubs, sir, or fix bayonets."

"To what end, pray tell?"

"To club them or stab them, sir, as the case may be."

"As the case may be? As the case may be?" the general growled. "Do you think yourself in a courtroom, boy? Trying a case? What are you playing at?"

"No excuse, sir."

"I mean any fool could march my—how many men have I?"

"Two thousand and seventy-three, sir," the captain said.

"Two thousand and—here now—aren't I meant to have three thousand? The figure is here somewhere." The general scrabbled among the papers, dislodging several which floated to the floor.

"Twenty-seven died, sir."

"So many?"

"Yes, sir. Twelve died while crossing the mountains—"

"How crossing the mountains?"

"They fell, sir."

"Go on—"

"And another fifteen drowned, sir, attempting by your orders, to cross the river."

"So many?"

"Yes, sir."

"How came so many to drown?" the general asked.

"Please you, sir, they were tied together."

"Tied together?"

"With a rope, sir." The general seemed not to remember, so the captain continued. "You had them tied together, sir, three feet apart. And you ordered the front-most to walk across the river and pull the others after him."

"Did it work?"

"No, sir."

"Pity. It seemed a good plan. Did we ever get across?"

"Just barely, sir. We found the bridge, if you'll recall."

"Ah yes," said the general absently. "Now, as to the matter at hand. Your suggestions, if I have them correctly, are a) we shoot the Dungs or b) we club them or c) we stab them. Is that correct?"

"Yes, sir."

"And you're wanting me to choose, is that it?" the general prompted.

"Well, sir—" the captain began.

"I say we ought to shoot them," the general decided. "In my opinion, clubbing them would be a waste of ammunition. And as for poking them with those pointy-things—"

"The bayonets, sir," the captain added helpfully.

"Well, that would be just too gruesome. We're soldiers after all (at least I am) not brigands. So, they will be shot. And how do you propose doing that?" The general seemed genuinely interested.

"My thinking, sir, is that we wait until dawn."

"Yes."

"And march thirty men to the beach."

"Yes."

"Stop ten paces from the Dungs."

"Yes."

"Form two ranks of fifteen, have the first rank kneel and the rear rank stand."

"Yes—and then—?" the general asked.

"Well, then, we shoot," the captain concluded.

"Ah, I see. And where will I be?" asked the general.

"Nowhere, sir."

"Nowhere, you say?"

"Yes, sir."

"Why nowhere?"

"Do you wish to be present at the action, sir?"

"Do I wish to be—?" the general blustered. "Go there to the hall-tree at once and bring me my uniform jacket!"

The captain obeyed and placed the jacket in the general's hands.

"What does this say?" the general asked the captain. He was pointing at the three stars on his epaulets.

"Lieutenant General?" the captain speculated.

"Exactly! *Do I wish to be present at the action?* You're damned right I wish to be there! Now hang this back where you found it and take care—the fabric tends to bruise. Now where were we?" the general asked.

"We were shooting the Dungs, sir."

"All of them?" the general sounded skeptical.

"Yes, sir."

"Men and women both?"

"Yes, sir."

"What if we miss some?"

"We're not likely to miss at that range, sir."

"I see," the general said as he reached for a pencil and tapped the unsharpened end against his teeth. "Hmm—well, I must say, this will never do."

"Sir?"

"You propose just marching up there, stopping, kneeling, and standing, and shooting everyone in sight?"

"That is more or less the idea, sir."

"It won't do, I tell you." The general's tone was insistent, but he seemed to lose his train of thought as he dropped the pencil, pawed through the maps, then looked at the ceiling for a full minute before speaking. "Now, captain, here is what we will do—by the way are the Dungs armed?"

"The scouts report that they have stones and clubs. They may have slings as well," the captain reported.

"I see. Well, that certainly puts the matter in an entirely different light. How close did you say our men will be?"

"Ten paces, sir."

"Much too close. A random swing of a club, a well-aimed rock, an accurate sling-shot and where are you?"

"Where, sir?" the captain asked.

"Fatalities, captain! Fatalities! I'll not have my men injured! Here is what we will do—"

As the captain listened in horror, the mad general outlined his plan. He, the general, would mount his horse and lead the men out at dawn and stand *twenty* paces away from the Dungs while he pretended to negotiate their surrender. Meanwhile the thirty soldiers accompanying him would walk far up the beach then march back toward the Dungs, form up behind them, between the Dungs and the sea, and shoot them all in the back.

"In the back, sir?"

"Yes, of course, in the back," the general repeated.

"Aren't they likely to turn 'round when they see us marching back and forming up behind them?" the captain asked.

"Of course not," said the general as if explaining mathematics to a dull child. "Because I shall be holding their attention by pretending to negotiate with them. What could be simpler?"

"What indeed, sir?"

The rain had stopped by the time the captain emerged from the general's tent carrying the wadded remnants of a dozen wrinkled maps. He was met by the quartermaster who saluted and relieved him of the maps.

"What shall I do with these, sir?" asked the quartermaster.

"For all I care you can tear them into sheets and distribute them to the men to use to wipe their asses! How I need a drink!"

Thunder rumbled and it began to rain again as he and the quartermaster found shelter beneath a stand of willows. They took turns taking pulls on a bottle of whiskey.

"Mad as a goose," the captain said after he'd explained the general's insane plan to the quartermaster.

"He's gone too far this time. My cousin was in the bunch that he sent to their deaths at the river," said the quartermaster.

"Someone ought to—" began the captain, but he failed to complete the treasonous thought.

"What the crap?" asked the quartermaster who was becoming truly plastered. "What in the name of Randy's rosebush are we doing in this damn country? Whose brilliant idea was it to invade Middlemount? What the hell did they ever do to us to deserve to be invaded?"

"I wish I was home cupulating," laughed the captain and the quartermaster joined in the standing joke about General Umber's habitual inability to use the word "copulating" properly.

"I wish I was back home," chortled the quartermaster. "And old Feather-Butt was here in the rain being 'cupulated' by my old stallion."

"I'll drink to that," said the captain and then the two officers grew solemnly quiet, each thinking in his own unique way what he would like to do, or have done, to their crazy general.

The rain increased.

They opened a second bottle.

"The scouts say these Dung people are calling themselves 'The Dreamers' now," said the quartermaster. He took a drink and passed the bottle.

"Poor bastards," said the captain drinking and returning the bottle.

"Guess you'll be shooting them all tomorrow—men and women both—bang!" said the quartermaster. Then he drank and handed the bottle back.

"Poor bastards," repeated the captain taking a drink and passing the bottle.

"Here's to them," said the quartermaster. "From one sorry bunch of poor bastards to another." He passed the bottle back.

"To bastards everywhere!" said the captain and he drained the bottle.

Chapter 31

Why the Fishals Are Such Bad Shots

Know thyself and know thy enemy and see thy enemy clearly. But don't forget to look twice.

Next morning, the captain hand-picked thirty men and drew the detail aside to give them explicit instructions. The men pledged to follow his orders to the letter, and they set about loading their muskets with double-shot and making certain that, despite the sodden weather, their powder and flints were dry.

While the men prepared, the captain reported to the general's field tent.
"The men are assembled, sir."
"Very good, Captain—I say, remind me again, what is your name?"
"Cooper, sir."
"Very good, Captain Cooper, carry on."

Moments later, with the general in the lead on his magnificent white stallion, Captain Cooper and his men set out to march to the beach. As they passed the encampment, the quartermaster led the men in a cheer. Captain Cooper looked back just in time to exchange a glance with the quartermaster, who raised a bottle and mouthed the words "Hip, hip, hooray" one last time before the detail marched out of sight.

Miles away, the Dreamers waited and, while they waited, their leader Roseland was questioning Esday, the youngest Dreamer who was always getting himself into mischief.

"Why were you not at your post?" Roseland asked. Her tone was firm, but not unkind.

"I lost my way and was near their camp last night, hidden by the storm, and I heard them talking of us," said Esday.

"You were foolish to take such chances," scolded Roseland. "But since you have come back to us alive, you can at least report what they said."

"They called us 'Dungs,'" the boy said, and anger reddened his face.

"Never mind," said Roseland. "We know who we are. What else?"

"They said that they couldn't wait for tomorrow to come and that they wanted to go home."

"I know that feeling. But we'll all be home soon enough, one way or another."

Roseland looked toward the trees which lined the dunes far above the beach. The rest of the Dungs—now the Dreamers—were hiding there. They'd arrived a day ago, passing through the mountains just ahead of the slow moving Fishals and their cumbersome weapons. Four-hundred refugees—men, women, and children—had slipped across the river bridge while the Fishals floundered upstream. This multitude had arrived exhausted, only to learn that they were still in peril. The promised ships had yet to arrive and the Fishals would soon overtake them.

But Roseland had a plan. She'd detected the Fishal scouts, who were nothing if not obvious in their inefficient efforts to remain hidden. Mindful of the scouts, she kept the new arrivals concealed while she allowed the enemy to believe there were only a handful of Dreamers waiting on the beach. She would draw the Fishals out into a battle which she had no hope of winning. When she and the others on the beach were slain, the Fishals would march away, leaving the rest of her people alive to await the arrival of El's promised ships.

It will be worth the sacrifice, she told herself.

"And, pardon me, but there's something else," said Esday. The lad's additional comment pulled Roseland back to the present.

"Yes?" she prompted.

"When the rain stopped, the enemy lit a fire, and I could see their faces. They looked different without their helmets. A lot like you and me and—" The boy sniffed.

"What is it, Esday?"

"Well, some of their faces was old men, like my gram-pap—rest his soul—and some was normal men, like my papa. But most of them was just boys, no older than me and some not so old as me."

"Wars are fought by the young," said Roseland.

"They just wanted to go home," sniffed Esday.

"They're here!" shouted a sentry.

"Go stand with your papa now," said Roseland. "It'll soon be over."

The Dreamers took their places on the sand with their backs to the sea. Moments later, they saw a fat officer coming astride a white horse. The officer dismounted with the help of one of his soldiers and he walked unsteadily across the sand while the soldiers behind him suddenly veered left and double-timed down the beach. The horse, which seemed to be well-trained, stood erect, though the animal turned its head to watch the running soldiers.

"They're going the wrong way," whispered Esday.

"Never mind," whispered Roseland. "Ready your sling."

General Umber stopped several paces away from the first rank of Dreamers.

"Good morning," he said shading his eyes. "My name is General Esday Umber—"

"He has my same war name," whispered Esday.

"Steady, child," whispered Roseland.

"I bear good news," the general continued. "I am authorized by the Fishal Military Tribunal to offer you terms of surrender."

A murmur swept through the Dreamers' ranks.

"Yes, I thought that might surprise you," the general smiled. "And by the by, you sir—" He addressed one of the nearest Dreamers. "Can you tell me, please, from where you are standing, am I about twenty paces away? Twenty paces do you think? No matter, it seems about right to me. Now, as I was saying—"

The Dreamers all looked down the beach where they watched the soldiers stop and turn and begin marching back.

"Pay no attention to those men," the general stammered. "Look here. I have a document which authorizes me to—"

While the general prattled on and waved his paper about, the Dreamers formed a ragged circle, a few watching the general, some looking out to sea, but most facing the oncoming soldiers. As the soldiers continued marching, the circle tightened and the Dreamers nearest the advancing enemy raised their weapons. As if in response, the soldiers adjusted their approach a half step until they were moving steadily along a narrow strip of beach which separated the Dreamers from the surf.

"They're trying to maneuver behind us," whispered the man next to Roseland.

"Let them go, hold your ground and turn to face them," whispered Roseland.

"I say," said the general as the Dreamers broke their circle and pivoted toward the sea. "This is completely wrong. Could I have your attention please?"

The soldiers were fully behind the Dreamers now. They stopped and turned to stand ten paces away with the sea at their backs. Roseland and the others faced the soldiers, ignoring the general who continued to beg for their attention. Captain Cooper passed in front of his men until he reached the end of the file where he turned and pulled his sword from his scabbard.

"Ranks!" he shouted, and the men formed two ranks. "Front rank, kneel," the captain ordered. "Ranks, take aim!" The captain looked directly at Roseland and moved his lips. "Get down," he seemed to say.

"What?" asked Roseland.

"Dreamers get down!" the captain shouted and in the same breath he yelled "FIRE!"

The captain had been right about one thing. At that range they couldn't miss. It was a credit to the marksmanship of the men of the Sixth Fishal Company, Second Battalion, Fifteenth Regiment that all their musket balls neatly penetrated the general's portly chest.

The shooters were not only accurate but also exceedingly efficient. Seconds after the execution, while the powder smoke from their muskets still hung in the air, six soldiers unfolded their entrenching tools and rapidly dug a grave in the sand. Then they rolled the general's bloody body into the hole and shoveled the sand in after him.

As the rest of the Dreamers sat dumbfounded on the beach watching the soldiers, Captain Cooper took Roseland aside.

"What happens now?" Roseland asked. She was as stunned as her companions, but her duty as leader compelled her to try and make sense of what had happened.

"We were never here," the captain began. "Do you understand me?"

"Are you saying—?" she began.

"Half of us died in the mountains." He held the woman's gaze. "The rest of us drown in The River Smedlarge. General Umber, distraught over the tragic loss of his command, took his own life and—"

"And shot himself in the chest thirty times?" asked Roseland.

"Well, I have to say that part of my story needs work," admitted the captain. "But the rest will be believed."

"And who would believe that an officer could be so incompetent?" Roseland protested.

"Who indeed? No worries on that account. Our general's reputation will suffice to carry the tale. Now I must bid you good morning, madam. I have to return and break our camp."

"Where will you go?" she asked.

"I have no idea. We can't go home, that much is certain, and we can't stay here."

Roseland hesitated, but only for a second. "We have ships coming," she smiled. "You and your army will come with us to our new land."

Chapter 32

The Death of N'dependee

A witch's curse lingers long after it is pronounced. It follows a man to the end of the earth, ceasing only at the grave. And, if that man's heart is evil, rest assured that even death will offer no escape.

The Lord Mayor N'dependee was in a foul mood. The chancellor tried to stay out of the mayor's way, but it was difficult in the cramped cabin of the heaving pirate ship. And every time the troublesome ocean swelled, the two were thrown together like straws in a tempest.

"Get off me, you imbecile!" roared N'dependee as a particularly fearsome wave knocked the two landlubbers off their feet and sent them rolling into a corner.

"Sorry, your honor," wheedled the chancellor. "The wind."

"The wind, my sainted beard! Go on deck and tell them to turn around!"

"Turn around, my lord?"

"That's what I said!" the mayor grumbled.

"I don't think the pirates—" the chancellor began.

N'dependee kicked the hesitant underling hard. "I don't employ you to think! Go on deck, I said. Go at once and deliver my orders!"

"By your command," answered the chancellor, though he had no intention of carrying out the mayor's irrational instructions. Nevertheless, he made a show of regaining his balance—temporarily as the ship rolled again—then picking himself up off the cabin floor and moving hand-over-hand until he reached the cabin door. The door would not open. He was on the point of putting his shoulder into it when the ship lurched again, and the door opened on its own. Helpless in the grip of the tilting, the hapless chancellor was flung through the opening and onto the deck.

The door slammed shut behind him and he landed in the midst of chaos. Men stripped to the waist were running helter-skelter across the heaving deck as waves washed over the side and careened across the sodden boards from stem to stern.

Madness! thought the chancellor. *Madness to be on this ship! Madness for this ship to be on this heaving Southern Ocean! Madness for the wind to froth this ocean into frenzy! Absolute, total, and complete madness!*

The only thing madder still would be for the chancellor to pick his way across the heaving deck, locate whichever barbarian seemed to be in charge, and order him to turn the ship around.

Why turn around? Because the Lord Mayor N'dependee has issued a command? Does the pretentious bureaucrat imagine his puny edicts are sufficient to wrest their ship from the jaws of this punishing storm?

Even if the chancellor was foolish enough to deliver the mayor's ridiculous order, he doubted very much that it was possible.

Turn where? Which way is "around" on a ship which is spinning like a child's wooden top?

It was then the chancellor realized he was going to die. There was no escape from this doomed ship. He and the mayor had been compelled by the witch—may she burn in Callus—to board this wretched vessel and sail south to assume dubious posts. Enroute, they were drawn into a battle intended to destroy the Southern Fleet. Only the vaunted Southern Fleet could interfere with the Tribunal's plans to conquer both Middlemount and Memora. Why were those targets so important? Why not Mountainwing or Mistymeadows or any one of countless other "M" lands that were far more desirable conquests? The hills of Mountainwing were said to overflow with gold ore. And the merchants of Mistymeadows were so rich it was said they used bars of silver as doorstops.

Of course, no one had ever seen these other lands and they and their fabled riches may not exist but still—

"What is thy business here, little man?" A huge pirate, whose visage seemed as dark as the surrounding storm clouds, towered over the chancellor. He held a sword in one coal-black hand and a bucket in the other. "Speak, wretch, lest I cast thee into the brine!"

"Please you, sir," pleaded the chancellor. "Don't kill me with your sword!"

"My sword?" growled the pirate. "Not likely I'd soil a sword on the likes of thee. Far better and a lot less wearing on my blade to smash thy bald head with this bucket." He grinned then and dropped his bucket and leaned down to grab the terrified chancellor by his collar. He pulled the smaller man bodily off the deck, lifted the squirming chancellor up to his eye level, and laid the cold steel of the blade against the terrified man's cheek. "I need this blade sharp, see, in case I encounter a real man."

The pirate laughed and might have tossed the chancellor overboard had a wave not knocked both of them sideways. The wave surged over the pair and the pirate lost his balance and his sword as he and the chancellor tumbled across the deck. The chancellor flailed his arms as he rolled toward the starboard railing and one of his floundering hands chanced upon a line. Reaching frantically, he grabbed and desperately held on. The pirate was not so lucky—he continued sliding until he banged into the railing. He rolled back and was about to be swept overboard when he felt a hand clutching at his pigtails. The hand was small and the arm it was attached to seemed insubstantial. Nevertheless, the hand and arm seemed to hold him as the towering wave swept past.

The ship righted, the water cascaded away, and the pirate lay safe on the deck with the chancellor's fingers wrapped in his hair and the little man's other hand clutching a mast line. The chancellor's body was awkwardly twisted. His inelegant posture suggested that both of his arms had been nearly pulled from their sockets and yet, unaccountably, his outlandish grips had held.

"Father's breath," swore the pirate as he disentangled his pigtails from the chancellor's diminutive hand. "This little worm hath saved my life—what a damnable burden! Better I should have drowned!" Thunder sounded and he withdrew his last statement. "I'm joking, El!" he said. Then, not wishing to further tempt fate, the grumbling man picked up his sword which had miraculously survived the force of the wave. Using his other massive arm to lift the chancellor's limp body, he struggled across the pitching deck and plunged into the guest cabin.

Lord Mayor N'dependee looked up to see the pirate enter.

"Get out!" the mayor shouted.

The pirate blinked once, then killed the mayor with a single swipe of his powerful sword. He gently laid the unconscious chancellor into one of the hammocks. Then he kicked the mayor's headless body and the head itself through the cabin door and banged it shut.

"This ship may sink," said the pirate. "But here I'll stay. Thou hast saved my life, so I now will serve as thy protector. That is the pirate way. That is my oath." Having stated his pledge, he tore down both hammocks, rolled the moaning chancellor in one and stripped the cords from the other.

Then he rapidly threaded loose cords through the intact hammock and skillfully tied the ends to as many floor cleats as he could reach until he secured the chancellor in a make-shift web of cord. The ship continued to roll and buck, but the chancellor's cocoon of cords and cleats barely moved. Convinced that he'd done all he could to secure the man, the pirate hurriedly left the cabin.

He returned moments later with a huge axe. The resourceful pirate stood in the cabin a few seconds more, apparently making mental calculations. Then he began swinging his axe with the goal of battering a crude hole through the seaward wall. As the ocean rushed in around his feet and ankles, he directed his blows at the floorboards, striving with all his might to separate the floor from the remaining walls. He continued chopping until he felt the floor move.

"It might work," he said to himself as the surging water lifted the disengaged floor and began to draw the makeshift raft outward and onto the raging ocean. "If the damn thing holds together."

It held as the trough of the next crashing wave pulled back and sucked them away from the sinking ship and rolled the rugged craft out onto the dark open ocean. The raft spun momentarily, then coasted miraculously into sunshine and calm water.

"Father's breath!" the pirate cried as the raft bobbed languidly on gently swelling waves beneath a clear blue sky. He looked back and saw that a dark storm was still battering the pirate fleet and that the tempest was churning along a fixed line. A black roiling gale raged on one side and calm weather and placid blue water ruled the other. He was just beginning to take in this unbelievable spectacle when a Middlemount ship hove into sight and hailed him.

"Avast there, varmint!" shouted a voice from the railing. "Drop that axe and prepare to be boarded."

Seeing a forest of muskets pointed in his direction, plus a bow-chaser aimed at his testicles, and having no better plan in mind, the pirate dropped his axe and held both hands aloft in what he hoped was the universal sign for surrender. He wasn't sure however because he had never in his life been compelled to surrender. Surrendering was a foreign notion. It was something no respectable pirate would think of doing.

But he kept his hands up and thanked his lucky stars. He was thankful the little man had grabbed his hair; he was thankful the unlikely pair had escaped the storm; he was thankful he himself was alive; and he was thankful he was able to surrender without hesitation or regret for, though he was a pirate, he was especially thankful he was by no means a respectable one.

Chapter 33

The Brig

The pirate code is not infallible. It is not written down and many of its oral maxims are as intemperate as an ocean breeze. However, one dictum is absolute and that is the admonition that he who is saved from death by the act of another owes to that soul—be the savior foul or fair—man or woman—person or beast—an eternal investment of protection. It is also said that, in fulfilling this lifetime burden, more than one adhering pirate has lamented the hour he was saved and fervently wished that his foregone death had never been interrupted.

Imprisoned below decks onboard a Middlemount ship, Mastro the Large lamented his fate.

Such punishment, the disenchanted pirate told himself, *is what comes of helping others.*

The strident snoring of his cellmate had awakened the pirate for perhaps the tenth time that night. If indeed it was night. It was dark in the bowels of the enemy vessel and darker still in the airless brig. It was impossible to tell if it was midnight or sunrise or noon outside. The pirate had lost track of time since he and the little man had been plucked from the sea by this passing vessel of the Southern Fleet.

Mastro had kept his head down as Middlemount sailors seized his makeshift raft and secured his limbs with manacles and leg shackles. When they hoisted him onboard and trundled him across the warship's crowded deck, he tried to hide his face, partly because he was ashamed of having been so easily captured, but mostly to avoid recognition, for he was widely wanted for an array of crimes, including one or two that called for hanging.

Of course, there was every chance he would be recognized whether or not someone recalled his face. He was, after all, not called Mastro the Large for nothing. In a land where the average man was white and stood no taller than an ox, the dark-skinned pirate towered over beasts of burden and men.

His size was one of the reasons he'd been forced to choose the sea as an occupation. On land he was useless. No mount could carry him. His weight ruined the springs of average wagons, and he was constantly bumping into things. He destroyed the upper casements of many doorways as well as the jams on either side (for he was not only tall but also wide of body). Moreover, owing to the power of his grip, even knobs and hinges were not immune from damage caused by his unbridled muscles.

Awake in the dark brig, Mastro sighed and peered in the direction of the snoring. In the dimness, the pirate could just discern a sleeping form in a far corner. No chance for a closer look at the tiny man who had somehow prevented the pirate from being swept overboard. No way to move closer because the chains which bound the pirate to the wall constricted his movements. He was tightly encumbered, so tightly that he felt fortunate to be able to gather sufficient slack to squat awkwardly and incompletely over the honey-bucket to take a crap.

The snores grew even louder and Mastro, though he was bound by the pirate code to serve as protector to one who saved his life, decided it was time to wake the slumbering man.

"Nothing in the code prohibits a saved soul from dousing his savior in shit," Mastro said aloud. Therefore, focusing his strength, he managed to kick the honey-bucket toward the far corner.

"Dog's breath!" shouted the awakened man and Mastro knew he'd reached his target.

"Thy snoring would wake the dead," observed Mastro.

"You—you—knave!"

"Be that thy most biting insult?"

"Villain!" the man yelled.

"Better, but still lacking in venom."

"Coward!"

"That insult is hurtful and incorrect," stated the pirate, "for I am no coward, sir jackal!"

"In that case, call the argument even," came the retort. "For I am neither a sir nor a jackal." There was furious scumbling then as the target of Mastro's filth sought in vain to rid himself of the foul stench with which the careening honey bucket had polluted his garments. "It is hopeless," the wretched man said at last. "I shall never be clean!"

Silence followed this declaration, broken only by the sound of the sad man's fruitless scrubbing.

"What is thy name?" asked Mastro.

The question seemed to surprise the chancellor. "My name?"

"Aye."

"I am called The Chancellor."

"That is thy title. I am called Mastro the Large, but not merely 'the Large.' Thou must likewise have a given name."

"Why should I tell you?" the chancellor asked.

"No reason. I am only making talk to pass the time."

"The time," scoffed the chancellor. "Have you an appointment which you fear to miss?"

"Only the same appointment as thyself I'll bargain—one with the hangman."

There was silence again as both men seemed—in their own way—to contemplate the accuracy of that statement.

"My family name is Bindbuilder," said the chancellor at last. His voice seemed calm but incredibly small.
"A strong name," said the pirate.
"My given name is Percy."
"A hunter's name," the pirate observed.
"Beg pardon?"
"My old dad was named Percy—named for his sire, a gamekeeper and pheasant hunter," said Mastro. "Surely thou hast heard that Percy means *one who hides in the hedge.*"
"You're making that up," scoffed the chancellor.
"It's true."

Silence again.

"And what meaning does 'Mastro' convey?" asked the chancellor.
"It is an old-world name."
"Which means?"

Silence.

"Come-come what is the meaning of Mastro?" the chancellor demanded.
"It means *splinter*," said the pirate.
"Splinter? As in a tiny speck of wood?"
"Aye."
"Splinter," the chancellor laughed.
"Aye," Mastro grinned.
"A fine name for a specimen of your girth," the chancellor chortled.
"Is it not?" Mastro guffawed.

Then both men laughed uproariously until the latchkey struck the bars with his belaying pin. "Order!" shouted the latchkey. "Silence or I'll throw your victuals overboard!"

The prisoners grew quieter though both continued to chuckle covertly as the latchkey unlocked the brig door and used his foot to slide two bowls across the bare wooden floor. He took care to stay well clear of the pirate as he flung a skin of water into the cell and locked the door.

"Guard!" shouted the chancellor.

"What?"

"No bread?"

"Harrumph! Perhaps you'd like a napkin as well? Bread? Bread?" the latchkey's voice faded as he pulled on the stair-line, climbed out of the bilge, and yanked the stairs up after him.

The chancellor listened to the sounds of the departing guard. Then he stood and walked through the darkness toward the food and water. He was unchained for two reasons: first because the Middlemount sailors felt unthreatened by the diminutive middle-aged man and second because, in any case, the restraints were too large to remain in place on his willowy wrists and slender ankles.

"Cold," Percy said as he stuck a finger in the nearest bowl. He put his finger in his mouth for a tentative taste. "And gruel again," he sighed. Then, as he'd done for each of the six meals the pair had been served, he used his fingers to scoop the lion's share of the cereal out of his bowl and into the other vessel which he cautiously handed to Mastro. With effort, the manacled pirate grasped the bowl, positioned it awkwardly beneath his chin, and used his lips to inhale the wretched repast. As his cellmate struggled, the chancellor sat on the floor, well out of the huge pirate's reach, and ate his own meal.

"Is this supper, do you think, or breakfast," Percy asked absently.

"Noon repast is my guess," said Mastro between mouthfuls.

"As good a guess as any," said Percy. "Hmm."

"Did you find a weevil?" asked the pirate.

"No. It is these bowls. They are different, did you notice? Not carved wood today but fired clay and—" The inquisitive chancellor held the bowl up in a useless attempt to seek additional light. "If I'm not mistaken, these are Memorian craft. A strange thing."

"How strange?" asked the pirate, his tone suggesting only mild interest.

"Strange that our jailers would use such fine crockery to feed their prisoners, unless—"

"Unless this is to be our last meal," observed Mastro.

Just then the two men hushed as they seemed to hear far above the echo of cannon shot or it might be the rolling of drums.

"A battle?" asked the chancellor.

"A commotion certainly, but too brief for a sea fight," said Mastro. "A salute more likely."

Or the preamble to an execution ceremony, thought Percy.

He recalled the Lord Mayor having drummers on hand to play a tattoo as a prelude to the botched execution of the last of the Middlemounts. How many days past? Four? Eight? A dozen days? It seemed a lifetime ago. The Middlemount execution never got as far as the drummers. The thing was botched as the musicians, like the torchbearers, the axe-men, and everyone else in the town square, had to run for their lives when the pyre exploded.

Was that tower of wood really a pyre?

He and the mayor had wrangled over the term. The discussion was brief with the mayor's interpretation winning out, as usual. But the chancellor was certain he'd been right. Placing someone alive on a pile of wood and calling it a "pyre" is a misuse of the term which is rightly reserved for a funeral. No matter how one sliced it, an execution is not a funeral. Speaking of funerals, Percy wondered what had become of N'dependee. This was an abstract exercise, for he found he truly did not care. The swine had drowned no doubt and hopefully in agony, a fitting end for someone who delighted in the woes of others.

The chancellor grimaced as he thought of N'dependee and the odious things he'd been forced to do under the lord mayor's corrupt administration.

He was glad the pirate could not see his face in the darkness. N'dependee had forced Percy to watch the Middlemount execution even though the whole idea of burning and dismembering the Princess had been abhorrent to him. Burn the Princess alive and chop the corpse to bits—who thinks such things?

Why the witch, of course, Percy grimaced again as he repeated the thought. *The odious witch.*

The chancellor could still hear the sound of Ahoo's iron boots striking the cobblestones an hour before the execution, the ominous sound growing ever nearer as he and the mayor waited in the council chambers. It seemed to take forever for the witch to cross the open courtyard and climb the stone staircase. Then even longer for her to traverse the considerable stretch of hallway which separated the courtyard from the chambers where the two town officials stood nervously awaiting her arrival.

When at last Ahoo appeared, the chancellor was surprised to see a slip of a girl pushing through the broad chamber doors. She was escorted by two Fishal soldiers who, though they were of average height, seemed to dwarf the petite woman. Stories of her exploits had exaggerated her size, but the tales hadn't misrepresented her beauty. Their meeting was brief but memorable. She gave the mayor written instructions, apparently unwilling to trust his memory. As she was departing, she placed a single finger an inch from N'dependee's fat face and told him, in no uncertain terms, what would become of them if he failed in his duty.

Of course, N'dependee *had* failed, and the witch had made good on her threat.

The witch's punishment for the failed execution had been absolute and the chancellor and the mayor were swiftly banished. The vanquished bureaucrats had been ordered to board a ship and were on their way to the South Sea penal colony when a battle erupted at the same moment a sudden storm overtook them.

The pirate armada—in addition to being ordered to discover and destroy the vaunted Southern Fleet—was carrying the mayor and the chancellor to a frozen wasteland where undesirables were imprisoned. They were being shipped south ostensibly to take command of the garrison at the Newfort Gulag. But both knew their posting to the end of the world was as good as a death sentence.

No one—neither prisoners nor guards nor token administrators—ever returned from Newfort. Anyone sent there was condemned to spend the rest of his days in a primitive hut on the frozen tundra, shivering around a tiny stove, burning twigs, and eating porridge. The days were short in the far south and the nights eternally long and the air was thick with the smoke from active volcanoes whose ominous cones encircled the gulag.

The Newfort Gulag was Callus without the heat.

The chancellor shivered and then allowed himself a sad smile. It was cold in this brig, but he decided to look on the bright side, for it was certainly not as cold as Newfort. Then, while he used his fingers to scrape another portion of gruel from his bowl, the chancellor had another thought and this one was particularly sobering.

He was no longer the chancellor of anything. It had all been for nothing.

Percy had come from a well-to-do family. His gram-pap on his mother's side had been some kind of royal gamekeeper in the past and his daughters had inherited his legacy, which meant generous dowries. His father was a minor noble and the family lived comfortably in quarters near the Middlemount palace. Opportunities came his way as a boy and yet the chancellor struggled to find his place. He was a dull pupil and his endless studying for the priesthood stalled until he was passed over. The youth had gained neither a parish nor a trade. Given such failures, his father was obliged to apprentice him to a wheelwright who dismissed the hapless lad for his ineptness. Percy might have become a beggar had his marginal abilities to read and write not earned him a lowly post at the town hall.

Years of intrigues and ass-kissing and jockeying for position followed. At last, his lot improved as he rose from scribe to keeper of the flame to privy master to vermin wrangler to councilman to privet gardener to exchequer and finally to chancellor. Then, in the space of a fortnight, he endured a precipitous reversal of fortune as he tumbled downward from chancellor to banished bureaucrat to his present state as a warship's doomed prisoner.

Thinking all this, his sigh was so prolonged and heavy that Mastro took notice.

"Thou will not likely be hanged, chancellor," the pirate said with as much compassion as he could muster.

"You need not use my title," the former chancellor frowned. "I'm merely plain old Percy now—a failed priest, a disappointment to my father, too clumsy to earn a freedman's trade, too unlucky in the choice of wagons to which I hooked my star—too useless to go on living."

"That sounds like the life story of a man who would have been better off to chuck it all and go to sea," observed Mastro.

"Ha," laughed Percy. "Look around and observe what reward the act of *going to sea* has wrought me."

Silence reigned as the two men ate the last of their gruel without speaking.

"Water?" Mastro requested. "If you please, Master Percy."

"Of course," replied Percy. He uncorked the skin and held it out to the pirate.

"I can barely reach it. Would you mind?"

Percy moved nearer. Standing on tiptoe, he reached up with the skin, endeavoring to angle the spout so that the water would flow down into the pirate's mouth. He moved ever closer by degrees until the pirate seized him by the throat. Percy was too surprised to struggle. He merely went limp and closed his eyes, prepared to die.

"Sorry," said Mastro as he released the startled man. "I just had to see if it was possible to strangle the guard should he be foolish enough to come so close. It's part of my escape plan. I do apologize."

"I see," said Percy, still reeling from the shock. "You might have warned me."

"And where would be the sense in that? I certainly don't intend to warn the guard."

"You called me Master Percy?" The chancellor bent down to retrieve the water skin and was relieved to find its contents had not completely spilt while he'd been languishing in the iron grip of the scheming pirate.

"Yes. Master Percy in honor of thy schooling, which I am certain far exceeds mine own. I imagine thou canst read and write."

"Aye," said Percy. "Much good will it do me here."

"It may be of use yet. Wilt thou read something for me?" the pirate requested.

"Here? What, pray tell?" Percy sounded astonished.

"Look across there to where I can see the far wall. Dost see it also?"

"I seem to see carving of some kind—there in the wooden wall. Is that what you mean?"

"Aye."

Percy took one last drink from the skin, then walked across the narrow room and peered at the words. "The light is terrible, but it is Woolish, a language I briefly studied."

"The Wolfkind tongue? Canst read it?"

"A moment—it is an adage or perhaps a *koan*—do you know those terms?"

"Sadly, I do not."

"This is a riddle or a saying—like a small story—but I do not comprehend its meaning," the chancellor frowned.

"And what of the drawing beside it?"

"That is indeed curious, for I'm certain I have seen its like before," the chancellor moved closer, his curiosity piqued. "Give me leave to concentrate please."

"You require my silence?" Mastro asked.

"Yes please—for a moment only. It is just on the tip of my mind—"

Working intently and silently, Percy translated the words and repeated them softly to himself, but their meaning eluded him. As for the symbol, where had he seen it before? He used his fingers to trace the outline. It was a simple horizontal line and below it two lines curving in opposite directions.

"It is formed like pi," Percy mused aloud.

"What flavor?" asked Mastro, licking his lips.

"Not 'pie' that you eat. 'Pi' is a symbol I learned in mathematics: a constant number that is useful in determining the area of a circle—how large it is—how much is contained inside its dimensions—that sort of thing." It was difficult to explain these things to someone unschooled and suddenly Percy felt sorry for the many school masters who had tried so diligently to drum things into his own seemingly hollow head.

"From here the picture looks like a ship's keel with legs walking both ways," Mastro twitched his head to the right and left.

"An apt description," smiled Percy. "I marvel at your eyesight. But please, would you mind?"

"Oh," said Mastro. "Sorry I forgot to keep shut." He grew silent again.

Percy finished his analysis of the drawing. Clearly it was a symbol—a thick horizontal line and, beneath it, two spindly "legs" with feet pointing in opposite directions. Atop the horizontal line, a vertical one—a mast sticking up to continue Mastro's ship analogy—and, encircling the vertical mast, a perfect circle. A walking line with a mast and orb—where had he seen—?

"As I breathe!" Percy exclaimed.

Though tempted to ask a question, Mastro held his tongue.

The symbol, Percy told himself. *I remember seeing it that day when the witch lectured us. How long ago—my sainted stars where has the time gone?*

Thinking back, the chancellor recalled the scene in the council chambers. The witch had poked her finger in the mayor's face and was turning to go when the light from the chamber windows fell across her bare shoulders. She was wearing a sleeveless garment and her shoulders were smooth and white, but the symbol was there. It was dark brown—a burn or a tattoo or a birthmark—Percy couldn't be sure. He only caught a glimpse of it, and it seemed best at the time not to stare at a witch, whether that creature was coming or going. That day, for an instant, he considered whispering to N'dependee and calling the mayor's attention to the mark. But whispering behind a witch's back was probably also a bad idea.

As for the connection between that design seared into the witch's shoulder and this similar etching, Percy hadn't a clue. But he was satisfied that he'd remembered seeing it before, so he returned his attention to the writing. Woolish had been an elective subject intended for those priests who hoped to serve in Wolfkind households or Wolfkind halls of power. Percy had no such ambitions. However, his one friend at the seminary was taking the course and Percy had tagged along.

The chancellor twisted his head, striving to get a better view of the writing. He became engrossed in the task—so engrossed that he apparently blocked out all other stimuli. Thus, he was startled to hear the sound of Mastro's voice.

"May I speak?" the pirate asked.

"If you must," said Percy, not taking his eyes from the writing.

"We have company," said Mastro.

Percy turned to see two figures just inside the cell door standing side-by-side in the shadows. How had he not heard them entering? One of the new arrivals was tall and broad shouldered—presumably a peasant woman, based on what Percy could discern of her ordinary clothing. She wore an everyday shift, rough trousers, plain boots, and, on her head, a seaman's watch cap. The other was better dressed and wearing what appeared to be the uniform of an officer—a Middlemount officer who might be a sea commander.

"Perhaps I can help you with your studies," said the peasant. "Why don't I give you the first part of the riddle and maybe you'll be able to guess the rest?"

"No need, my good woman," said Percy with a hint of haughtiness which was fully out of keeping with the desperation of his situation. "It so happens that I have worked the entire thing out and I can state unequivocally that it makes no sense whatsoever."

"To you maybe," said Ann as she stepped forward out of the shadows. "But it is meat to me. Does not the first line suggest something to you?" Percy turned and re-read the writing while Ann continued to speak. "Do you know of any wolves that might recently have been scheduled to die?"

Percy turned and only the darkness of the cell prevented the others from seeing the terrified look of recognition as it spread across his thin face.

"And does not the phrase, 'I'm coming back' ring a bell in that bald noggin of yours, your Excellency?"

"Mercy!" shouted Percy as he fell to his knees.

Chapter 34

A Homecoming

When an evil has passed one by, there is a tendency to believe that one has dodged a surely laid bullet. Whereas, most often, one finds that he has leapt from the clutches of a certain disaster into the jaws of a larger dilemma.

Kill me!" pleaded Percy as he groveled before Ann. "But spare my mother and my sisters! They are blameless in this! They are—"

"As I breathe!" observed Ann. "Why does everyone who kneels before me presume that I kill out of vengeance? Have you not confused me with your erstwhile allies, the Fishals? Or those murderous pirates who ply the Western Sea?"

"Touch one hair on the head of that man!" bellowed Mastro. "And thou wilt answer to me!"

Commodore Dell unsheathed his sword and the latchkey, who'd been hovering behind the taller visitors, readied his pistol.

Ann turned to consider the giant who, despite his threat, remained securely chained to the prison wall. "That is indeed bold talk for one constrained by iron," she said.

"Think thou that mere chains can hold me?" roared the pirate and he strained forward though he remained far away from reaching the Princess.

"I feel certain that you would not be here if these chains had proven inadequate to bind you," Ann laughed. "And this paltry door would have offered little resistance if you had managed to free yourself—which clearly, I see you have not done. And furthermore, my blustering friend, in addressing your warning to me, you have made a grievous error."

"What error?" shouted Mastro. He continued to lean forward, though the confining chains cut cruelly into his wrists and ankles.

"Your error is this: you have instructed me not to touch a hair on this varlet's head. Whereas, we can all clearly see, even in the dim light of this cell, that this chancellor, who has fallen so low, is bald as a stone."

"Must I be mocked as well as hanged?" wheedled Percy.

"Hanged? Who said anything about a hanging?" the commodore interjected.

"Have you not come to drag us topside and stretch our necks?" asked Mastro.

"No in truth," said the commodore. "We have come hither at this girl's request. It was her desire to show us where, as a child, she was imprisoned."

"What girl?" asked Percy. Then, despite the wretchedness of his circumstances, the chancellor seemed to recover a trace of decorum as he added. "For shame! Would you bring a child hither to this vile place?"

"I've seen viler," said Ahoo as she stepped through the cell door. "Good morning, your honor." Then she turned to regard the bulk of Mastro leaning forth from the wall, but still held in check by his chains. "I wish I'd known to bring a banana for your gorilla."

"So, it be morning," said Percy unaware of how strange his comment must seem.

"Told you," Mastro said. The huge man ceased to struggle with his restraints and eased back against the wall to take a better look at the newly arrived female.

"I'd rather not stab or shoot anyone today," said Commodore Dell. "So, it will be best if you prisoners behave yourselves while we conduct our business. Move back, please." He addressed Percy. "Move back, I said!"

Percy struggled to his feet and retreated to his bunk.

"Somebody stinks," said Ahoo.

"My apologies, child," said Percy from his corner. "There has been an accident."

"I'll say," said Ahoo. "An accident of the butt." She grinned at Ann and said to her in an elaborate stage whisper, "Our chancellor, he still don't recognize me. Called me a child. Fancy that?"

"He's still in shock probably," whispered Ann. "Wait until he gets to know you as we do, my lady." She bowed stiffly.

"Charmed," said Ahoo.

"Can we get on with this?" growled the commodore. "I have other duties to attend to."

"I believe we can manage on our own," said Ann. "Not that we begrudge your company in the least, but I am certain the jailer here will be sufficient to protect us from a well-chained pirate and a weak-kneed bureaucrat."

"Aye, sir," said the latchkey as he pulled and cocked his pistol. "And I'm not liable to miss at this range."

"Where have I heard that before?" the witch laughed as she slid past Ann and crossed to examine the carved wall.

"We'll be fine," Ann assured the commodore.

"Hmm," said Dell. "As you wish, but don't linger. You'll soon be needed at the war council."

"We'll be there in good time," promised Ann and after a moment more of hesitation, the commodore departed.

"Funny how I both remember and don't remember carving this," said Ahoo as she examined the wall. For a moment, her thoughts carried her back to her childhood when she was imprisoned in this very room and then to this morning when she had dreamt of it.

A few hours ago, Ahoo had awakened from a dream with the echoes of that childhood memory lingering in her mind. She'd dressed and gone straight-way to the commodore's great-cabin and demanded entrance.

"What is the hour?" the commodore had grumbled.

"Early, sir, I beg your pardon, but I need to know something."

"Hmm," said the commodore. "What is it?"

"The ship next in line behind us, was it always a military ship?" asked the witch.

"Strange that you should ask," said Dell. "*The Snowperch* which trails in our wake is a re-fitted vessel—a captured merchant ship used to haul grain. But it is much changed from those days what with the addition of cannon and—"

"Excuse me for interrupting, sir, but what of below decks?"

"Some changed and some the same. The lower decks once served as a brig—a prison if you like—and it still meets that purpose."

"Will you show me?" the witch asked.

The commodore had raised an eyebrow, but he hesitated only a second. Strange events were accumulating. He decided it would be best to pay heed to this supposedly magical girl. "We'll need a boat crew, and shouldn't we have a chaperon?" he smiled.

"I'll get Ann!" Ahoo laughed and she rushed to the guest cabin.

Ahoo found Ann sitting in a wooden rocking chair before a mounted looking glass as she brushed her shoulder-length hair.

"Pardon me, Majesty," the witch said.

"Come in," Ann laughed. "It is well that a sister has discovered me preening. What might a man say if he were to barge in and catch El's warrior princess primping like a vain peafowl? It is well that Seth is busy touring *Catspaw's* gun deck. As it is, perhaps even you, my girl, are shocked at my vanity."

"Your attentions are logical," Ahoo said. "May I?" She held out a hand beckoning the Princess to surrender the brush.

"Of course," said Ann, though she blushed at the younger woman's request.

With tenderness and surprising expertise, Ahoo gently guided the decorative brush.

"This is ivory is it not?" she asked the Princess.

"Yes," said Ann. "And there's a matching comb."

"Beautiful," said the witch. "A gift from your mate?

"From the commodore—" Ann began, then—not wishing to foster a misunderstanding which hinted at romance—she hastily added, "A token of his late wife. The able officer assured me, with Seth's blessing, that such finery was better suited to my needs than languishing in a ship's cupboard."

"Ah," said Ahoo. "Surely that explains the commodore's attentions."

Catching Ann's eye in the smoky mirror, the witch winked and the two women shared a laugh.

"Truly," said Ann. "I like this color. Would you call it auburn or chestnut?"

"Chestnut has my affirmation," laughed the witch.

"Let it be chestnut then," said the Princess. "It is an apt description which conjures images of hearth and home. Have I mentioned that I absolutely love this shade? And the wonder is that it has grown so quickly—" She stopped there, unprepared, as yet, to reveal the details of her resurrection.

"Indeed," said Ahoo. "I wish I knew your secret of cultivating such lustrous locks in so short a span of time."

"You are skilled," said Ann. She was intent on changing the subject even as she relished the sensation of Ahoo's gentle strokes.

"My first time actually," the witch admitted.

"An inherit ability then," Ann said. "A natural."

For a time, the two were silent, Ann rocking gently while the younger woman brushed her splendid tresses which did, indeed, call to mind the earthy luster of a freshly harvested bushel of chestnuts. Soon both women, as if on cue, began to hum—singly at first and then in harmonious unison.

"A lullaby," Ann suggested, her eyes closed as she indulged an episode of nostalgic rapture. She saw herself in the garden, a busy cub, engrossed in play as she pretended to stroke the hair of her mute and ever-present garden angel.

"A lullaby," the Princess repeated.

"Perhaps," Ahoo ventured. "I seem to remember it from the deep recesses of an unhappy childhood."

"Tell me about it?"

"Another time perhaps," the witch began. "And, in fact, that other time may be fast approaching for I have nearly forgotten the reason for this early morning visit."

"Ah," said Ann. "A mystery?"

"As to that, Princess, I'll let you decide."

It had taken little persuading for the Princess to join the proposed expedition. She could see a spark in the witch's eyes. Something had roused Ahoo and, considering the witch had become an important ally in the quest of their lives, Ann thought it best to see what was afoot. As for Seth, whom they met on deck as they made their way to the commodore's waiting longboat, he was bemused that the witch had asked to "borrow" his wife. With a kiss for his bride and a nod to Ahoo, he declined to go along after extracting a promise that the impulsive witch would bring his mate back in one piece.

The commodore, the witch, and the Princess had been rowed to *Snowperch*, although "rowed" is perhaps too dignified a term. In fact, their long boat was dropped into the ocean and had merely to maintain position until the trailing ship came alongside and hauled them in. It had been an awkward transfer, but the commodore was reluctant to delay sailing progress by having the fleet heave-to in order to satisfy a girl's whim. Of course, returning to *Catspaw* would be a different matter since both ships would be required to haul in sail and flounder while the party rowed back. It remained to be seen whether that second unsavory delay would or would not be worth the time lost.

Once onboard *Snowperch*, they'd descended below decks with the commodore leading the way until the witch suddenly elbowed past. She'd sprinted ahead and seemed to be following a familiar path deeper and deeper into the lower recesses of the ship.

"We'll be at the brig next," yelled the commodore as he and Ann trailed behind with the exhausted latchkey bringing up the rear.

"I know!" shouted Ahoo and she vanished down a stairwell.

Chapter 35

New Recruits

Life is persistent. Anyone who doubts the truth of this is welcome to still her breath or stop her heart and report the result—if she can.

Having recruited Commodore Dell and the Princess to accompany her to *Snowperch* and having led them steadily down below decks to the brig, Ahoo stood next to the familiar wooden wall in the same dank room where she'd been imprisoned as a child. After studying the message she'd once inscribed there and, before anyone could stop her, she unbuttoned her shirt and exposed her shoulder.

"I've never been able to see it clearly, of course. At best, I've glimpsed a mirror image," she grinned as she lined her back up with the carving. "But it is a match is it not?"

Ann, who was growing used to the slowly maturing witch's impetuous and flirtatious behavior, was calm. Mastro and the latchkey were mesmerized by Ahoo's seductive unveiling. But it was the chancellor who cried out.

"Stars fall! We are undone!" he shrieked. Striving to press himself into a dark corner, the terrified man turned his face to the wood and clawed with his fingernails in an insane effort to escape. "The witch! The witch! The witch!" he shouted over and over again as blood began to spurt from his scrabbling fingers. "The witch," he sobbed, as he ceased his clawing and collapsed against the wall.

"Yes, the witch. Now please get dressed, child," said Ann. "These poor souls have seen enough."

"I wouldn't mind—" began Mastro, but a stern look from the Princess silenced him.

"Jailer, leave us!" ordered the Princess.

"But, madam—"

"Away, I said!"

There was something in Ann's tone—something regal—and the latchkey turned to go.

"And leave the keys," Ann added. "Because these two gentlemen are coming with us."

The man hesitated. The keys entrusted to him secured the brig and also controlled an array of manacles and leg shackles. Uncertain of the authority of this self-important woman, he was reluctant to surrender them. Tentatively, he held the tools of his jailer trade forward and the two locked eyes as each gripped the heavy ring.

"It will be alright," the Princess assured him.

"An unhappy outcome could mean my position," the latchkey said.

"I know," said Ann. "And I'll vouch for your fidelity. You may rest assured I'll take responsibility and not play you false."

"That one will bear watching," said the man as he shot a glance at the pirate.

"I'll manage," Ann said.

"I'll take you at your word," the latchkey said. Still, he maintained his grip, flexing his arm, testing the strength of Ann's hold. After a moment more, she felt the man's grasp relax until, seemingly convinced of her resolve, he opened his fingers and relinquished the keys. "There is a strong nail at the crest of the stair-well. You will find it a handy place to hang borrowed goods. And," he whispered, "betwixt ourselves, let's hope you can live up to the shipboard rumors which are swirling about the fleet."

"Let's hope so," she answered.

"Aye," he winked. "We must all have work to do and something to hope for. At present, my work seems to have led me thus: to do thy will, madam, and leave the door ajar."

Another door opened, Ann thought.

As the latchkey departed, the Princess knelt and unlocked Mastro's leg shackles. But, before freeing the prisoner's hands, she stepped back and addressed the giant. "I am told you are a pirate," she said.

"Aye, madam, that I am."

"Might I have your parole to join the Middlemount forces?"

"Thou wouldst trust my word?" asked Mastro.

"Aye," said the Princess.

"On what grounds?"

"On your honor as a gentleman," Ann smiled.

"Do I know you, madam?"

"We did battle once."

"Who won?" asked Mastro.

"Obviously, as we are both alive, it must have been a draw."

"Ah," grinned Mastro. "Thou art the Middlemount Princess, although much changed, I see."

"And I see that you are much the same—still large."

"After our long-ago duel, even though I came up short, I was given the name Mastro the Large."

"Clearly you deserve it. May I have your parole?" she asked again.

"In truth, thou hast made for me a puzzle," said the pirate.

Ann had been about to unlock the huge man's restraining manacles, but she paused.

"In what way a puzzle?" she asked.

"Well," said Mastro apologetically. "Since thou spared my life those years ago when thou might so easily have slain me, it seems that I am now—by the law of the sea—devoted to the protection of two parties, not only thou who saved me then, but also this other gentleman who saved me lately." He inclined his head toward the chancellor who remained in his dark corner and who was—against all odds—being comforted by none other than the witch.

The two former enemies sat in the corner whispering like conspiratorial school children. Ann was curious, but had not the time to contemplate their unlikely conversation, so she turned her attention to the still-chained giant.

"Surely you are large enough to do both," Ann smiled. She, of course, remembered sparing the pirate's life when the two had been locked in personal combat. It had been a near thing, her besting of this huge man. Accomplishing that arduous task had truly tested her skill and strength. So, the Princess was more than mildly curious how the diminutive chancellor might have managed to save the life of the giant pirate.

"Doing both is not my puzzle, Majesty," said Mastro. "But if thou mean to do harm to Percy, then how shall I—?"

"A moment," interrupted Ann. "Who, pray tell, is Percy?"

"Yond chancellor there in the corner," Mastro explained. "Though he no longer cares for that title."

"Your name is Percy, Excellency?" Ann asked the chancellor in a voice loud enough to reach the corner where the recently frantic man and Ahoo, his new unlikely companion, continued to linger.

"It is," said Percy, who seemed to have much recovered himself.

Isn't it amazing, thought Ann, *what affect the ministrations of a beautiful female will have on the most distressed of men?*

"Hmm," the Princess said aloud. For a moment she considered both the diminutive Percy and the gigantic pirate. "Let me set your mind at ease, friend Mastro." She unlocked one of the manacles. "Though he wronged me, I intend no harm to that man." She unlocked the other. "In fact, it strikes me that his assistance and yours will be vital to the fulfillment of our quest, for we will have need of both your strength and his cunning."

"A quest," Mastro smiled while he stretched his back and rubbed his wrists and ankles. "I love quests. My gram-pap used to read us such stories. Is there a dragon? Please say yes."

"No dragons, I'm afraid."

"A troll then?"

"Sorry."

"A damsel?" Mastro paused. "Begging your pardon, madam, but I mean a regular damsel—a distressed one?"

"Over there," said Ann nodding toward the witch. "Though I doubt she would meet your definition of distressed."

"Hmm." Mastro leaned down and whispered to the Princess. "Is yond beauty unmarried?"

"An unmarried maiden to be sure," laughed Ann. "But I'm afraid that she's much too young for you. Plus," she whispered back, "she's a witch, you know."

"Ah well," shrugged Mastro, seemingly unimpressed to have the girl's supernatural qualities verified. "So, there are no other magical or wonderful beings on this quest?"

"Does a talking dog count?"

"Absolutely!" said the pirate, his voice conveying unbridled enthusiasm.

"How about the sovereign of your fathers?" Ann ventured.

"El the Merciful is part of this quest?" the pirate asked.

"You might say he's the cause of it," the Princess confirmed.

"Very well," grinned Mastro. "I agree to join this noble quest—whatever it may be! And by the way—and this may not be a proper time to ask but I must know—what does the writing on yond wall say?"

In answer, Percy spoke.

"The wolf dies," he said, and his voice softened as he placed his hand upon his breast. The erstwhile chancellor seemed to realize that the words applied, not to the Wolfkind Princess whom he and the Lord Mayor had sought to execute, but to his own bestial iniquities. "The wolf dies," he repeated.

"And the lamb is born," added Ahoo with her hand on her own heart. Her melodic voice suggested her recognition that the mysterious words she'd carved there so very long ago were doubly prophetic. Unrecognized then, they now represented a prediction of her recent conversion from impious rascal to an unlikely, perhaps angelic, ally in her deity's desperate quest.

After speaking, both the chancellor and the witch exchanged a nod. Then the pair joined hands and fell to their knees. The dark corner where they prayed together seemed suddenly to glow with a warm and honeyed light. A light which illuminated them, though the rest of the shadowy brig remained cloaked in shuttered darkness.

Ann felt a rush of emotion as she looked at the two and understood. Since escaping death in the town square, the rescued Princess had pondered the meaning of El's cryptic expressions about a dying wolf and a newborn lamb. Those words had reached her ears moments before she changed. Her deity had required her to memorize and repeat the phrases and they had served as a password between herself and El the brigand.

The wolf dies.

The lamb is born.

It was only natural that Ann had believed the words referred to her own near death and her own miraculous transformation from Wolfkind to woman. Now she saw things differently. On that day in the town square, it was not she, but others, who were behaving savagely. It was not her Wolfkind nature, but the wolf inside the lord mayor and the chancellor which had been prophesized to die. As for the lamb—

To be certain of her new interpretation, the Princess crossed to the corner. As gently as she was able, for she was in a fever to confirm her suspicions, she interrupted Percy's prayers and pulled him to his feet. "You, sir chancellor, have mouthed the words, but do you understand their meaning? Do you declare the wolf inside you dead? Will you throw off your old savage life and pledge your obedience to our quest."

"I will, with all my heart," said Percy. "I swear it!"

"And you, lady," said Ann to the witch as she gently helped Ahoo to her feet. "I have no doubt now that you are most certainly the reborn lamb that was foretold."

For a moment, in the dim light of the cell, the Princess and the witch locked eyes. In an instant, the confining wooden planks of the ship retreated from view and Ann imagined herself a cub—an uninitiated whelp, acting out a fantasy alone among the flowers and trees of Middlemount's spacious palace grounds. Transported there, she found her younger self sharing a loving glance, not with this redeemed girl, but with her own personal garden angel. Witch eyes and angel eyes—the metallic-blue orbs were not merely similar—they were exactly and unambiguously the same. Mesmerized, Ann's lips moved and she found herself repeating a juvenile ritual she had all but forgotten. Her adult-self imagined the specter of her younger-self as a cub absorbed in play. Awake, yet also dreaming, she held both the witch and the garden angel in her unswerving gaze and, with the hopeful confidence of youth, bade the iron statue speak.

"Can you hear me? Won't you speak?" Ann asked as her childhood dream faded.

"I hear and I will indeed tell you truly that I am the foretold lamb," said the witch as her eyes filled with tears. "And, I vow with all my heart, I shall endeavor to be that good and faithful animal."

"Can you forgive us?" asked Percy.

For answer, Ann spread her arms and folded Percy and Ahoo in an all-encompassing embrace.

"Shall we pray together?" the Princess asked. The pair nodded and all three knelt on the rough planks, reciting in unison the well-remembered liturgy.

"Progenitor, sky-dweller, we call you holy. Your future reign is ruled by all you desire here below an also above. Provide us today with all we need. And absolve us according to our absolution of others. And tempt us not, but be our protection against dark forces which seek to ensnare us. Because you stand as our dominion, you are our strength, our radiance, and our ever-lasting triumph beyond the end of time. This I believe. So be it, now, and evermore. And, as for Death's dark design, may it not come to pass. Amen."

The pirate didn't join in the hugging, or the prayer. He was not a heathen. He knew the words, of course, as what human or Wolfkind, breathing or dead, did not. On his mother's knee, he'd learned the vintage prayer, though its meaning—then and now—was lost on him. He didn't share in the ritual and, in any event, he was distracted and about to burst with curiosity.

While the others prayed, Mastro the Large went exploring. Freed from his shackles, the giant crossed the cell and stood at the wall, staring at the symbol and the writing, and scratching his head. When the praying ceased, the pirate turned to regard the Princess, the chancellor, and the girl as he pointed to each in turn.

"I understand a bit now. There stands the Princess, my once opponent, who was Wolfkind and is now a woman. There stands the chancellor, a former wolf it seems. And beside him the girl, a former witch and now a present lamb. And I—" began the pirate, then he stopped and shrugged. "I have no idea of my part in all this. Maybe it would help," he addressed Ahoo, "to know what this picture," he slapped the wall, "and its twin on thy shoulder means. And remember I have not had the learning, so I shall need it put simply."

"It's an old-world symbol," said the witch.

"It's meaning is the dawning of a new day," said the chancellor.

"Now, *that* is a thing I understand," said the pirate. "A new day seems to me a fine idea. So, what say all? Are all agreed that our quest is pledged? Thou incline thy head, Great Princess, and likewise do these others nod. Good. So, a bargain is struck, and I say we should quit this foul hole straight away. To celebrate our fine new day, let's climb aloft to open sky. So, let's away. Say I."

"Well put," smiled Percy as he rushed to the wall and clasped hands with Mastro.

"So very large and yet seemingly a poet," laughed Ahoo. She skipped past everyone and headed topside shouting, "A fine new day, I say! An open sky, say I!"

"Amen," said Ann and she and the others followed the witch.

Chapter 36

Council of War

A war council often includes unexpected participants, but adversity breeds strange bedfellows.

Commodore Dell seemed to recall a saying like that.

Strange bedfellows indeed, he thought, *and none stranger than the assemblage before me this day.*

He glanced around his cabin table. Only the familiar surroundings of his great-cabin made the scene seem real. If his books and maps had not been in their proper places, the commodore might have believed he was unconscious and still dreaming.

Then, as if to dispel that particular notion, the dog sitting in the chair beside the commodore spoke.

"As you know," said Esau. "The purpose of this council and our quest is to cheat Death in order to save El and the world. Have I put the matter too plainly?" The dog turned to El who was seated beside him.

Not at all," the deity smiled. "You have gathered it in a nutshell. Has everyone studied the new plans?" he asked.

Heads nodded, including Mastro's who added, "It were read to me."

"Excellent," said El. "Is anything unclear?"

Percy stood. "I don't wish to speak for the others, but—I do not agree that Ahoo should be sacrificed."

There was silence.

"Does anyone see another way?" asked El.

Silence again.

"I thank you, my brother in this venture," said the witch as she rose to stand next to Percy. "But is there anyone here present who would not give their life to serve our deity and complete this quest?" Ahoo studied the faces of those gathered for the council—the loyal dog, Ann the risen Princess and Seth her devoted mate, the commodore, the huge pirate, and the reformed chancellor. "The birthmark on my back, etched there in the womb, marks me as the sacrificial lamb. My part in this quest is ordained and settled."

Deferring to the witch's logic, Percy nodded. The two touched hands for a moment and exchanged a smile. Then they returned to their chairs.

"Turn we now," said El in a voice as grave as his solemn message, "to the flooding of Memora."

"A heavy decision," agreed Ann.

"Better Memora than all the world," said Commodore Dell.

A sudden commotion outside his cabin drew the commodore's attention. As the clamor increased, he angrily excused himself, strode to the door, yanked it open, and was surprised to find the boatswain standing there.

"What's amiss," the commodore demanded.

"The king, sir," answered Brightlamp. "The king is alongside."

"The king? What king?"

As if in answer, an armed foursome of uniformed men shouldered the boatswain aside and filled the doorway.

"I'll have to ask you to step back, sir—begging your pardon," said the contingent's ranking officer. The unknown man's tone was polite but direct, leaving no room for objection.

Commodore Dell's face reddened but, seeing little choice, he gave way. Then the guards—for guards they were and fully armed and helmeted and dressed in uncompromising uniforms of red and black—immediately parted. A fat herald, also in red and black—yards of it by the look of him—waddled forth and filled the space between the ranks.

"All rise for His Royal Majesty, King John of Memora, Guardian of the Sacred Lakes, Nephew to the Stars, Protector of the Western Sea, Defender of—"

"Enough, you jackass!" shouted an exasperated voice. "Stand aside! This isn't a damned state visit! Give way, you bureaucratic whale!"

The herald turned sideways, and a diminutive old man squeezed past the functionary's incredible bulk. The old man blustered into the cabin wearing a tarnished crown on his bald head, a threadbare ermine cloak across his stooped shoulders, a faded red velvet tunic and matching pantaloons on his meager torso, an enormous pair of ill-fitting black boots, and an irritable expression.

"Where is she?" the King roared in a booming voice which belied his stature. His crisp blue eyes were nearly obscured by thick white eyebrows. But his gaze seemed unusually lively—the eyes of a far younger man. His ruddy complexion was a striking contrast to his eyebrows and the antithesis of his snowy beard and moustache. The King's inquisitive eyes darted from side to side as he surveyed the cabin and its inhabitants. It must have seemed to him an unlikely gathering, an odd, almost comical, menagerie of mismatched occupants—all the more incongruous because he could not see them clearly.

Having blustered in from the bright sunshine of the ship's deck, his pupils had not yet grown accustomed to the dim interior of the great-cabin, made even darker by the blocked stern windows which were still covered with a make-shift collection of lumber. The King squinted and blinked and strained forward trying to comprehend the contents of the shadowy room.

"I said where is she, damnit?" he roared.

Commodore Dell—despite the herald's instructions to stand—was the only member of the war council on his feet. As senior ship's officer, he seemed compelled to take charge of the situation. "Whom is your grace seeking?" the commodore asked.

"Whom?" The King began and then he sputtered like a pregnant ewe struggling to complete a difficult birth. "Whom indeed! I seek the squalid imposter of course! The pretentious pretender! The so-called Princess—this false Princess—who pretends to—to—"

As the King continued to seek his bearings, his wavering yet steadily improving gaze landed on Ann, who suddenly rose to her feet intending to support Commodore Dell.

"Oh, my stars!" exclaimed the King as he stared at Ann and—for the second time in as many days—another symbol of authority—first a ship's commodore and now a monarch—lost his balance, misplaced his senses, and swooned.

Only the Princess' rapid reflexes allowed her to dash forward and catch the falling sovereign before his aged head collided with the unforgiving cabin floor. As it was, the King went limp and lost his crown which clattered across the wooden planking and lodged beneath the council table. When the wayward crown wobbled to a stop, Esau leapt down to retrieve it. Like much of his behavior since his conversion, the dog's desire to snatch up the crown seemed driven by dual instincts. His reaction seemed to be a combination of a learned human deference to royalty and an automatic canine inclination to fetch.

Several moments later, the King awoke to find a circle of faces looking down on him. Some were familiar. There was Bioh, his overweight herald, and Colonel Questo, commander of the palace guard. The others were strangers to him—all save one. The King's eyes widened and overflowed with tears as he reached up and pulled Ann to him.

"My girl! My girl! My lost child! How happy! Happy am I to see you! If only your mother— But, surely you died, therefore how—how—how—?" The King seemed to lose strength and he gave way and fell back again. So baffled was Ann by the King's incoherence that the Princess let the old man drop. Luckily the surgeon, who had been summoned, was kneeling beside his new patient and caught the old man this time. Sander held the King and eased him down to lie upon blankets and pillows which had been hurriedly assembled on the hard wooden floor to create a make-shift bed.

It was an ignoble mattress and far less regal than the King was accustomed to, but that could not be helped. The monarch had fainted on the floor and there he remained while the surgeon feared to move the frail man until he was more certain of the King's condition.

Sander felt the old man's pulse then he turned to address the commodore's steward, "A draft of water," he said, "and we'll have the brandy too if you please—but wait," the surgeon asked the guard commander. "Is it permitted?"

Colonel Questo responded with a jocularity seemingly out of proportion to his King's condition.

"Oh, His Majesty will most certainly approve of that prescription," the colonel laughed. "But we have our own spirits."

The King was seen to open one eye, then quickly close it again, as the colonel sent for the royal dispenser which was in the care of the royal guard's archery sergeant.

"We keep the King's spirits safe in the royal arrow quiver," the colonel explained. "For medicinal emergencies, you understand."

The surgeon nodded and returned to monitoring his patient whose complexion seemed to reflect the returning ruddiness of a steady recovery. Moments later, a flustered archery sergeant rushed into the cabin bearing an arrow-less quiver in one hand and a long-necked silver-plated flask in the other.

"A cup if you please," requested Questo. Grasping the handiest vessel, the commodore placed the crockery into the officer's outstretched hand, whereupon the colonel examined it and grinned broadly. "A Memorian—how fitting!" The colonel knelt, gently lifted his sovereign's head, and administered the spirits.

Within seconds, the King revived. The colonel was about to stand when the King motioned for him to remain and whispered, "Another of the same, if you please."

After a second drink and a refill, the King was assisted to the commodore's chair. No sooner was he comfortably seated than Esau placed his forepaws on the table and offered the errant crown.

"A handsome animal," observed the King.

Had his mouth not been obstructed by the crown, Esau may have been tempted to acknowledge the King's compliment. As it was, the dog merely allowed the grateful monarch to accept and reseat the crown upon his bald head. When Esau resumed his seat without comment, El smiled. Apparently, the dog had learnt his lesson about speaking to humans who were as yet unaware of his magical qualities.

The King, who had retained possession of the Memorian cup, took another sip of the royal spirits. Then the much-recovered monarch set the half-full vessel aside, belched contentedly, and addressed the assemblage. "I sincerely regret my unseemly entrance and my untoward swooning. It was undignified and I apologize for such a display of unmanly passion."

The King and the dog were the only ones occupying chairs. The others inhabiting the cabin—including the members of the council, Colonel Questo, and the fawning herald—stood in a circle around the table. The King contemplated each in turn, then fixed his gaze upon Ahoo, who smiled and curtsied. The old man's gaze lingered on the witch's face. He seemed about to say something, then thought better of it, as he retrieved the cup and drank again.

"I pray thee, be seated," said the King with a magnanimous gesture. The colonel and the herald remained standing. When Ann started to take her former seat, the monarch motioned to the chair nearest his right hand, "Will you not join us here, madam?" Ann hesitated and the King added, "Please you."

Ann obeyed and sat. But she was uncomfortable. The King seemed to think she was someone else. She had no desire to delude the monarch and she was especially unwilling to mislead a grieving father.

Your thoughts do you credit, El spoke to Ann in the voice of the mind. *But only be patient and this misapprehension will presently be resolved.*

As if he had heard the thoughts of the Princess and El, the King turned to his right and placed his gnarled hand upon Ann's strong one. "You are not my daughter," the King said. "I know that now, though the resemblance is uncanny and rather alarming. Thy name, madam—no wait—let me guess. It is Ann Stone Bride is it not?"

"It is, your grace," said Ann.

"Ah," grinned the King. "And how came you by that name?"

Should I? the Princess' thoughts inquired of El.

Not yet, the deity replied and aloud he said, "I wonder if the surgeon will excuse us."

"If the King is well," said Sander politely, though his tone suggested reluctance, "I will take my leave."

"Thank you," said El. "Council business, you understand."

"Of course," said Sander as he regarded the others with stiff formality and left the cabin.

"His feelings are injured, I fear," said Seth.

"I'll speak to him anon," said the commodore. "His feelings will mend."

"Just so," said El. "But at this juncture a man of science would constitute an unwelcome distraction. Especially since I suspect our guest is about to share a revelation."

"Should the rest of us mortals also retire?" asked Percy.

Should we divide mortals and magic? Ann asked El in the voice of the mind.

Wait and see, answered El.

"It is not necessary to hide your internal thoughts," said the King turning to El. "For I too am fluent in the voice of the mind. Therefore, I have heard your thoughts, my Princess, and those of our deity and other magical voices which I cannot yet place. And I have learned, Princess, that you chose that name upon your deliverance from adversity and that you have chosen wisely, it seems."

"How is it, Your Majesty, that you can hear our thoughts?" asked Ahoo.

"Impertinence! Presumptuous child!" chastised the herald.

"Remove that whale!" shouted the King. Questo obeyed instantly and ushered the herald out. "And guard that door! Let no others enter!"

Questo unsheathed his sword, strode through the door, and pulled it shut behind him. His sturdy shadow visible at the threshold provided evidence that he remained outside, on guard.

"Pardon my foolish herald," said the King to Ahoo. "He knows not that you and I are of equal royalty."

"You flatter me, Majesty," said Ahoo.

"Not in the least," smiled the King. "It is not every day that one meets a Duchess of the Air."

"Or a legendary Island King," she smiled back.

"So," said the monarch, "forgive me, those of you who are not privy to the inner workings of magical beings. But the thoughts flying back and forth in this constricted room inform me that I have interrupted a council of war. I apologize for being able to hear the thoughts of others while concealing mine own. Think of it as my royal prerogative. Now, if you will bear with me a moment, I have no desire to—what is the word?"

"High-jack," El anticipated the King's comment.

"Yes, that is the very phrase. A word which I have compounded and which I believe is an original on my part. It is a combination of 'highwayman' and 'jack' after my humble self and the knavish one-eyed fellow whose visage appears on my illuminated deck of—" The King paused and considered his audience. "But pardon me, I am prattling—another royal prerogative and a privilege also of my advanced years. Suffice it to say, I have no intention to *high-jack*—in other words 'steal'—this council. But, if you indulge me, I will explain why—in addition to my previously stated imprudent errand to confront someone whom I thought guilty of disrespecting my late daughter's memory—I have so recently been compelled to sail from Memora."

"The floor is yours," said Commodore Dell.

The King blinked for a moment and then the old man burst into uproarious laughter. So infectious was his merriment that the others were compelled to join in. At last, after another sip of his personal spirits, the King recovered himself. "Oh, commodore, I can certainly lay a claim to the floor, having so recently been in intimate contact with it!" Again, the King laughed at his own observation and the others joined in.

When at last decorum was restored, El spoke aloud. "King John, your arrival here which appeared at first to be such an ill-timed invasion, has become instead an infusion—an infusion of much-needed good humor. Our mission is serious—and deadly so—but to go forth into battle under a cloud of woe would most certainly have doomed our quest. Tell us please the import of your journey here, for I suspect it will bear heavily on our deliberations."

"My El," said the King nodding to his deity. "I hear you, my heavenly ruler, and I obey. You are ever my sovereign and ever my strength." He looked about the room gaining eye contact with each soldier of the quest in turn beginning with Ahoo. "Duchess Ruth—you will be amazed that I know your true name—your presence here tells me that this assembly is indeed a blessed group. Will you not cast off your other unlovely name?" The witch nodded her ascent and the magical beings around the table intercepted her thought that she would henceforth prefer to be called "Ruth."

The King next engaged Mastro and Percy. "You two are well-met—two disparate mortals who have pledged your lives to this quest. I hope El will forgive me if I tell you truly that places in Velyn are already reserved for you." He then looked fondly upon Commodore Dell. "Your dear brother is presently banished from our assembly. But he will yet have a chance to put his oar in. Brotherly kinship will add the strength of fraternity to this quest. Your contributions will be invaluable and your places above are likewise assured." Seth had his head bowed and seemed to refuse to meet the King's gaze and, before the monarch could speak to him, he interrupted the royal inventory.

"Majesty," Seth mumbled without lifting his head. "If you intend to praise me and testify that my place in Velyn awaits—then I beg you do not waste your breath, for I am an aberration and not worthy to sit at a table of sentient beings and deities." With this unexpected comment, Seth suddenly stood, rushed toward the door, and flung it open, only to find his way barred by the colonel and his sword. "Must I kill this man to flee from my shame?" he asked.

Ah, thought El and the King.

Have a care, thought the Princess.

Patience, brother, thought the witch.

Be strong, thought the dog.

"Get out of my head all of you!" Seth shouted as he shoved the colonel aside and fled from the cabin.

Chapter 37

An Incident

One's internal dialogues can be overwhelming. To the constant stream of personal thoughts, add the echoes of other voices, and a mist may cloud the mind.

Out on the open deck, Seth pushed through the King's startled guards and past the working sailors. Bioh, the banished herald, approached the distressed man but was rebuffed. Disregarding all obstacles, Seth rushed onward until he reached the stern. Without a firm idea of what had compelled him hither, the confused man stood there swaying, watching the ocean roll. The waves seemed to draw him.

A bone, he told himself. *Would bone sink?*

He heard a movement behind and turned to see his mate.

"Your thoughts trouble me," said Ann. "You must believe that you are more to me than a piece of bone."

"And yet that is exactly what I am."

"You are part of me."

"Not so—I am not even a proper animal—I am nothing but a scrap—sliced and hammered by a tinker to shape a false vase. I am a counterfeit vessel—a hollow shell. Your precious Seth is nothing. He is merely—"

"Cease your lamentations!" Ann ordered. "Where is your pride? I will not listen to such nonsense!"

Embroiled in their unhappy dispute, the couple failed to notice the presence of a shadowy figure clinging to the mizzenmast. Dropping from above, the assailant lunged at Seth and sent the startled man scuttling toward the taffrail. Teetering there, Seth might have continued overboard had a vestige of his Wolfkind prowess not inspired him to grab a line—a primitive instinct which arrested his fall. Seth's swift reaction left him dangling, while the attacker tumbled, without a sound, into the churning sea.

Leaping forward, the Princess seized Seth and pulled her stranded mate to safety. As *Catspaw* sailed on, the pair watched a vague outline swirl in the wake of the ship. Seconds later, it faded to an insubstantial dot. Then it was gone.

So rapid was the encounter that only belatedly did they think to shout, "Man overboard!"

"Where away?" the lookout called.

"Astern!"

"We shan't stop!" boomed the chief of the watch. The alert sailor immediately passed word for the commodore, who instantly appeared on deck.

"Signal trailing vessel!" the commodore bellowed.

"Aye," came the reply.

Half an hour passed, during which signals reported no sighting of the attacker.

"Sound assembly," the commodore ordered. "And muster the marines. We will soon see who comes missing and put a face to this outrage."

A sweep was commenced below, including a call-up of "idlers" which roused men who, having stood their watches, were taking rest. These measures found all sailors and marines accounted for. The number of the King's company was likewise confirmed, and all members of the quest were present.

"Signal assembly on all vessels," growled the commodore. "We will ferret this out yet."

A systematic search throughout the fleet proved fruitless. Not a single jack-tar or militiaman was absent. At the commodore's request, Seth and Ann returned to the stern.

"Stand as you were," Dell requested. "Not that I doubt your reported attack, but we seem unable to locate a desperado or even a shadow to populate your recollection."

"May I examine the scene?" asked Ruth who joined the group despite being uninvited.

"As you wish," said the commodore. "It is too many for me."

Magic do you think? Ann whispered in the voice of the mind.

Nothing mortal passed this way—that much I'll wager, the witch confirmed. "Nothing," she continued aloud for the commodore's sake. "No footprints. No marks on the taffrail. And the sea has swallowed else."

"Another mystery then," Dell decided, and his exasperated tone suggested he was imagining the difficulty of entering this particular incident into the ship's log. "Regardless, we carry on," the commodore decided. "I'll take my leave. Orders must be passed to resume stations."

When the commodore was out of earshot, the witch put the question directly to her quest-mates, "And what, precisely, were you two arguing about?"

"Who said we were arguing?" Seth protested, his fiery complexion betraying a combination of ire and embarrassment.

"Tensions are running high," Ruth observed. "Heated words would be sufficient."

Ann and Seth stared at their companion who seemed to be rapidly evolving from a silly adolescent into a maturing investigator.

"Sufficient?" the Princess asked.

"To conjure a foul succubus," the witch clarified. "You must trust my knowledge of such things. That which beset you had substance only in the sense of smoke. Insufficiently corporeal to knock you bodily overboard, but undoubtedly convincing enough to compel you to take a fatal step in that direction. You were fortunate the wily menace did not trick you both over the side and into the deep."

"But how—?" Ann began.

"My fault," Seth interrupted. "Forgive me, love."

"There is nothing to forgive," said Ann.

"Yes, there is," insisted Seth. "For I was weak. I allowed my fears and my jealousies and my insecurities to take form. I surrendered to my foolish distress the moment I learned I had been formed from your rib and not from clay. Vanity ruled me and I was too weak to stop that cloying manifestation of my doubts from fomenting into the vile thing which attacked us. Forgive me please."

"Since you crave it so, I forgive you," said Ann as she took his hand. "But any one of us might have given in to our doubts."

"Not so," he smiled. "Not the Princess of Middlemount."

"With the cloying succubus overboard," said Ruth, "our rueful Seth is presently rescued from that creature's unwelcome intervention. But we must not allow his spirits to continue flagging. I have erred in not providing support. Hear me, lamb," she held Seth in her gaze. "Your depression has allowed your better nature to drift into aimless speculation. You are not nothing. You are a full-made, breathing creature—as real as any Wolfkind or human who ever lived—as necessary as the sun and rain and relevant as the bee without which the world would languish. You do yourself a great injustice to question your worth."

"You speak with the wisdom of El," said Seth.

"You honor me to say so," said the witch. "But I am a poor substitute for our deity. I beg you, my dear ones, set this dispute aside and come back to the council. Take a moment to reconcile, but a moment only. There is much to be done."

The couple watched Ruth go, then they embraced and, despite her urging, they lingered—watching the waves roll past.

"From the mouths of babes," said Seth.

"Thank Velyn that one is on our side," said Ann.

"Let us hope you are correct," her mate observed.

"I'm certain of her," the Princess declared. "And as for us—are we done with this matter?"

"My spirits are lifted," Seth said. "And I'll do my part. So—yes—let us consider this done."

"Done and done, my love," said Ann. "Come! I will race you below!"

The sailors paused in their labors to watch the handsome couple run. As Ann and Seth raced past, the pounding of their hastening feet seemed to permeate the very planks of *Catspaw*.

"These folk be most anxious to run about," said one sailor.

"Wither away one may ask," observed another.

"Waste o' breath," remarked a third. "No use to run aboard. Time enough to run when there be land under-foot."

When the joyful runners scrambled below, the men returned to their work. The breeze was stout. Sails billowed as the ship plowed onward—the entire fleet racing over the water at flank speed. Stimulated by the sturdy pace of the surging vessels, the men began to sing and would have continued singing had the wind not dropped.

In the commodore's cabin, the assemblage felt *Catspaw* shudder as the Southern Fleet ground to an abrupt halt on the still and silent sea.

Chapter 38

A Secret

Adversity is a holed cup. The liquid of solace attempts to fill and comfort the distressed, and yet it reaches only as high as the hole and slips away, never filling the cup, never soothing the hurt. So long as the open wound of the hole persists, so long does the adversity endure. Only action or the intercession of another can mend the hole.

The council unraveled. Disheartened by the lack of wind, El retired to his bed. The others likewise returned to their quarters, leaving the King and Dell to populate the council table. Then, just after ten bells, came word of a further setback when the surgeon sent news that El had experienced a relapse of his consumptive illness. Indications were that the frail deity was dying.

"It is a heavy night," the commodore sighed.

"Indeed," the King agreed. "Shall I go?"

"Stay if you will," the commodore requested.

The commodore's goal in speaking to the King alone was to try once more to convince the sovereign that flooding a portion of his home island was necessary. To overcome the formidable pirate defenses surrounding Deep Lake, artillery of the Southern Fleet must be brought into the fight. The distance from Stove Point Harbor to Deep Lake was thirty miles—nearly ten leagues and well beyond the range of even the most powerful ship's cannon.

The council's plan called for a share of *Catspaw's* power—her portable mortars—to be transported inland. To move them, the unused canals must be flooded. It seemed a difficult notion to sell to the island monarch.

Considering the commodore's logic, the old King sighed heavily. "I drained the canals for a reason," he said.

He and the commodore stood to study the island maps. It was a solemn deliberation. The absent wind continued to trouble them.

"I drained the canals for a reason which now seems unwise," the King continued. "Years ago, I went personally to Deep Lake Dam to close the outlet valves and lock them shut. Deprived of their source, the canals ran dry, and I forbade their use under the influence of my inconsolable grief."

The King paused and wiped tears from his eyes.

"I was grieving, you see, for my lost daughter—a fearless and reckless youth who had gone swimming and sadly drowned in the deep canal nearest our castle. I could not bear to—" The King paused again and looked sheepishly at the commodore. "You will think me a foolish old man."

"Not in the least, Your Majesty," said the commodore. Without another word, he walked to a nearby cabinet and returned with a bottle of whiskey and two Memorian cups.

"Your health," toasted the King as he accepted the filled cup.

"And yours," the commodore smiled and joined him at the table.

For a time, they drank in silence until the commodore spoke.

"Forgive me, Majesty. But it cannot be overstated," Dell asserted. "Unless the canal is flooded and portions of the island thoroughly inundated, the quest cannot succeed."

The irony of this desperate tactic—of flooding the island to save the world—was not lost on the King.

"Rather than fighting fire with fire," the monarch declared. "It seems we must fight the threat of Death's universal flood with a more modest deluge of our own."

The King's droll declaration seemed to settle the matter. Even the reality that his island was in the hands of unrepentant invaders might not have persuaded the King. Even the hope that his kingdom could be restored by such a bold move might not have moved him. Commodore Dell's logic was durable. But, in the end, what won the King's consent was the fact that the request came not merely from the commodore, but moreover from a war council which included in its membership El, the lord of hosts, and one Ann Stone Bride—the very image of his dead daughter.

Satisfied that he'd obtained the monarch's consent to submerge certain portions of his island kingdom, Commodore Dell was on the point of bidding goodnight when the old King elected to linger.

"Since it is just the two of us now," said the King. "I will impart to you a secret known only to myself, El, and Duchess Ruth, though I think the dog suspects and I shouldn't be surprised if Ann is aware."

"It seems, Your Majesty, that I may be the only person who does not know the details of your so-called secret."

"Indeed. Touché, commodore," the King laughed. "In any event, with El sleeping, it falls to me to impart this secret to one in whom both myself and my deity have the utmost confidence."

Despite the fact that the ship was deadly quiet in the calm and regardless of the fact that the two men seemed to be the only souls awake in the wee hours of the morning, the old King motioned for the commodore to draw his chair nearer. Then he continued, but in a low conspiratorial voice which was just barely audible.

"You know your scripture, I presume."

"All part of a nautical education," the commodore smiled.

"To be sure. But you may be unfamiliar with the tale of El and the Swan. It is in the Old Tribune—that ancient book which has fallen from favor. The tale itself is a bit long, but I will give you the main of it."

The commodore took a sip of his whiskey and leaned back in his chair with a look of complete attention on his broad honest face. The King smiled and relished a thought which he'd often had before.

Even grown people, the monarch reminded himself, *love to have a story told to them.* Casting a fatherly eye on his audience of one, the King cleared his throat and began.

"In the early days, El was intrigued with his new creations and the wonderful world he had fashioned for them. And our deity delighted in taking diverse forms so as to appear upon the earth and visit his creatures unrecognized. One day, he happened to be skimming along the waters of Deep Lake in the guise of a swan. Perhaps you will recall what happened next."

"He saw a lady," said the commodore. "And a quarrelsome person who threw a cup which belonged to her into the lake."

"Yes," encouraged the King.

"And El became a man and swam to retrieve the cup. But Death wrestled with him at the bottom of the lake and forced him into some sort of Bargain," the commodore recalled, his thoughts filled with memories of his old school days.

"And the gist of the Bargain, you will recall—" the King prompted.

The commodore thought for a moment, then responded, "The Bargain was that Death would not flood the world so long as the Wolfkind ruled. And if the Wolfkind should fall to the humans, El's life and the life of the world would be forfeit."

"Well remembered," said the King, as his tone grew grave. "And here we are on the brink of that Bargain being fulfilled. El has taken to his bed. We are becalmed short of our goal. The quest hangs in the balance. Did you ever think—when you were a callow youth memorizing the scriptures—that you would play so great a part in the prophecy?"

"Never in a thousand-thousand years," the commodore declared.

"That you should choose to express it so is prescient, for the question of time bears upon my secret. Now, tell me, my young friend," the King held the commodore's attention with a steady and significant gaze. "How old do you imagine the world to be?"

"Chronologically, I should think it to be a thousand times a thousand years old."

"Based upon?"

"The scriptures which place the beginning of our conscious history at five generations past and the beginning of the world much earlier," said the commodore feeling proud of his well-remembered lessons.

"True, our history has been around roughly 500 years by our calendar, but the world was here long before we set quill to paper," the King smiled. "And where in all this history do you place the tale of the swan?"

"Near the beginning of written history, I should imagine."

"Some five hundred years past?" the King suggested.

"Yes," said the commodore.

"Would it surprise you to know that I was there?"

The commodore blinked for a moment, looked at the dregs in his cup, and poured himself another drink. "I'm sorry," Dell stammered. "Did I hear you properly?"

"I was there at Deep Lake on the day when the swan and the maiden played out their story."

"But that's impo—" the commodore abruptly edited his comment, for his definition of what was and was not possible had been lately greatly enlarged.

"And not only El and myself," the King grinned. "But yet another member of our party." He paused, reached for the bottle, and refilled his cup—taking a moment to let the commodore consider his statement.

"You can't mean?" the commodore began.

"Can't I?"

"Let me back into this, as I might have parsed an examination question in navigation on my officers' test. Let me proceed by asking interrogatories. May I do that?" asked the commodore.

"If it helps you understand," said the King. "Of course."

For a moment, the commodore sat silently. Then he began.

"The maiden who wept for her lost cup that enormous time ago at Deep Lake—" the commodore seemed to struggle with his inquiry.

"Your interrogatory?"

"Was that maiden a Duchess?" the commodore asked.

"Indeed," said the King.

"And a witch also?"

"She was that and is."

"An old-world witch?" the commodore asked.

"That follows," the King smiled.

"That child?" the commodore downed his drink, thought about stomping on the cabin floor to order another bottle, but decided he'd better keep his wits about him. "And thou?"

"Did you not ever wonder how a common knave in that scripture story could cast a cup—even a cup as dense as a well-made Memorian—so very far to reach the center of Deep Lake?"

"*You* were that knave?"

"In a previous life, yes," said the old King.

"And Ruth, who became Ahoo, and is now Ruth again. She has led previous lives?"

"Yes."

"So, she might turn again to evil?" the commodore speculated.

"Unlikely," said the King. "I have been unable to confirm my notion with El, but do you not notice a difference between myself and Ruth, the maiden Duchess of Deep Lake?"

"You are quite opposites: man and woman, old and young, witch and king—though I wonder if those are such opposing roles, begging your pardon, sire."

"No offense taken," the King smiled. "But I will tell you that, in addition to our roles in the scripture story, Ruth and I and our diverse iterations are destined for different fates. And those fates are thus: that she will ever die young, and I will ever die old. In short, each time she is born again, she lives for a briefer time and dies younger, whereas I do the inverse. But she is very young now and therefore I sense that this time, when she is gone, her spirit will not return to this dream."

Seeing the commodore's look of confusion, the King sought to explain.

"The world which you and I know," he made a broad gesture taking in the sweep of the great-cabin. "This world around us, including also our past and our present, is our dream. We cannot see the future. The world as it was and is—this is also El's dream. Do you see how alike are our dreams and those of our deity? As with us, the future is likewise hidden from El. But Ruth's dream will be a new dream—one which neither you nor I nor even El nor any other being can imagine. Her new dream—her new morning if you will—is to us unimaginable. It will leave behind the shackles of past and present and stride into the future to encompass new worlds as yet undiscovered. Where she is bound, neither you nor I nor El can follow."

"Do you speak of a realm beyond Velyn? Why have you told me this?" the commodore implored. "I don't understand."

"Know this, my earnest friend: Soon the quest will reach Deep Lake and the contest with Death will unfold. Yes, you may count on it—the wind will soon return to bear us thither. At the moment when Ruth must die—and die she must so far as this dream is concerned. At that critical moment, I foresee that—despite her intentions—Ann may be unable to help. I am too old in this body to journey to the lake and El's mortality has advanced so that he likewise cannot go. Therefore, someone stronger must be there to support Ruth. I have given this much thought and it is the only way."

"So, Majesty, you are not here among us by chance. Though you joined the quest to pursue a false rumor about your dead daughter you were instead following your destiny," the commodore protested. "Therefore, could you not have foreseen all that has happened? Could you not have avoided being piqued by a lovers' quarrel all those years ago and not thrown the cup and not endangered El or this world and not have—" Dell's mind was beginning to reel.

"Your questions are just. But know that I am not reborn each time with full knowledge of prophecy or my destined role or even a full understanding of my powers. Like every human infant—like you yourself—I learn by stages. And moreover, as it is with every human elder, the gift of wisdom—such as it is—comes much too late."

"Youth is wasted on the young—so the poet says," the commodore seemed to remember the phrase.

"Amen," said the King. "Now I must press upon you your role at the lake. Ann's powers are daily growing more contrary and, though her heart be true, her efforts are nevertheless liable, at a crucial moment, to fall short."

"How shall I know the moment?" asked Dell.

"It will be clear to you. Be assured that you will be present when Ruth confronts Death. Your charge is a simple one: you must be guided by what the younger woman does. Support Ruth and all will be well, remember that. And now, if I have not overtaxed your powers of concentration, let us turn to the problem of the canal."

The King stood and invited the commodore to examine the uppermost map.

"I agree that the waterway must be restored," said the monarch. "Your military logic and El's web-spinning have convinced me. Our deity is indeed clever. He rescued the Princess, transformed her with a purpose, and cautioned Ann to choose a surname wisely. And faced with an array of seemingly endless possibilities, the Princess has chosen well, as El knew she would. And El guessed correctly that I would be overawed by the Princess' visage *and also* by her name."

"I have it now," Dell declared. "Your officious herald announced you as King John under the apprehension that all present knew also your surname. My nautical journeys have isolated my attention in southern climes so my knowledge of royal personages is primarily of that realm, yet I seem to recollect your lineage."

"King John of Stone Bride at your service," the monarch smiled with a wink and regal nod. "Without Ann's choice of surname, I might never have rushed to intercept *Catspaw,* much less agreed to the notion of flooding my island. The possibility of such an act would have remained for me a closed door and a locked one. Her resemblance to my dear daughter and her chosen name were, one might say, the keys to opening that door. And speaking of keys, mind now what I say—"

Using the map, the King reviewed for the commodore the details necessary to flood the canal. The commodore took notes, asked important questions, and folded the King's invaluable knowledge into the council's battle plans. They conferred for hours, but it was still dark when the King yawned.

"Suddenly I'm feeling enormously sleepy. The lack of wind was unexpected—a remanent no doubt of the aborted attempt to fling Seth overboard."

"You may not be aware of it," the commodore ventured. "But when our Middlemount party first came aboard, I challenged Seth to prove his powers."

"Ah," said the King. "Your sailors have enthralled my guards with a tall tale of this business of Seth breathing your sails to life. Assuming that miracle happened at all, I fear there'll be no repetition of that particular parlor trick—no magic wind I'm afraid. Hmm," the King paused, "that's sobering—I don't know that I've ever used those two words before in a single speech. The words *fear* and *afraid* are daunting when uttered by an everyday mortal and absolutely terrifying in the mouth of a monarch."

Another episode of silence filled the cabin until Dell hazarded a remark.

"So, there will be no miraculous wind to speed us on our journey."

"None. And, as for why the wind failed in the first place, troublesome spirits can work mischief, but—as I said before—I know these waters and I am convinced the calm will soon be resolved. So let me bid you goodnight, sir. And let's resume our planning in the morning—at nine-of-the-clock. What would that be in your sailor's time?"

"Nine bells of the morning watch," the commodore replied, knowing full-well that the island King knew how to tell time on a ship.

"Just so," said the King. "I'll see myself out."

Emerging from the great-cabin, King John encountered his herald.
"Majesty," the man bowed.
"Bioh," nodded the King. "I had in truth forgotten you. I am tardy in this. I meant to seek you out to say I regret my earlier outburst and my unkind words."

"Instantly forgotten, my liege," Bioh said.

The King regarded his subject and seemed to sense something different in the man's demeanor. "You have changed I see."

"Majesty?" Bioh asked.

"Your outfit I mean. Do my eyes deceive me? Have you exchanged your fine garments for working man's clothing? You were warned about gambling with the sailors!"

"Ah," said Bioh.

"A story perhaps?"

"Indeed."

Silence stretched between the two men.

"Must I beg to hear your tale?"

"Sorry, lord," said Bioh. "It is a matter unworthy of your attention."

"Nonsense," insisted the King. "Give forth, my loyal herald. Where is that blustery voice I love so well?"

"It is a rather ordinary tale."

"Let me judge."

"As you command—"

"Make this, rather, a request," the King clarified. "My days of commanding a kingdom seem, for the moment, to hang in the balance."

"I have every faith that Memora will be restored," said Bioh. "And I treasure and respect your authority and yet I most humbly request release from service."

"Only if you assure me this request is not provoked by my unkind behavior."

"I so assure you, lord," said the man with conviction.

"Granted then, and with regret, but with my blessing also," said the King with feeling. "May I know your intentions?"

"I will express my intentions as fully as I myself understand them," Bioh promised. "I have had what you might call a conversion brought about by that young lady." The King's former herald inclined his head in the direction of Ruth who stood amidships, her eyes fixed upon some unseen object in the distance.

"Unsurprising," said the King. "What task has our persuasive young Duchess set for thee?"

"A return," said Bioh cryptically.

"A return to—?" the King prompted.

"My former livelihood," answered Bioh. "I was once—you may remember—a carpenter by trade."

"I seem to recall your distant occupation," the King confirmed. "But that was decades ago was it not?"

"Thirty-three years since I swung the carpenter's hammer" said Bioh. "Almost to the day."

"May I ask when and how you intend to make this remarkable return to your former profession?"

"These details wait upon the disposition of the wind," said the herald turned carpenter. "I sought out that young lady to apologize for my insolent remarks. But in my attempt, I added to my earlier impertinence by interrupting her prayers. She forgave me and invited me to pray with her—the topic being the restoration of Redhackle Isle. Our subsequent conversation revealed to me that Redhackle is in strong need of builders."

"This is so," the King replied. "For I am given to understand that nearly every structure on that unfortunate island has been damaged by fire with many totally destroyed."

"Inspired by her prayers, I will go there to pledge my skills to any in need," said Bioh, his face suffused with joy which seemed to glow from some inner furnace of passion.

"Ah, yes," said the King with a knowing smile. "I understand young Ruth can be quite persuasive. Yet Redhackle surely lies in a direction which runs counter to this fleet's intended destination."

"I await only a passing galley bound for the Isle. As you know, those lively vessels regularly ply these waters, manned by freely-serving rowers whose strong backs and stout oars will be capable of bucking the fair wind, which I know will soon arrive to speed the Southern Fleet onward to liberate Memora," said Bioh. "I only regret I will not be there to savor the victory."

"Clearly your destiny will carry you elsewhere. Let us hope your threefold faith in the rowers and the weather and the fleet will be rewarded," said the King.

"I trust in my faith," said Bioh with feeling.

"I wish you well," said the King taking his former servant's hand. "Truly your vocation will do much good in restoring Redhackle. And now, I believe your counselor desires a word."

Following the King's gaze, Bioh saw that Ruth was indeed beckoning him to join her.

"Forgive me, Majesty," said Bioh.

"Tut," said the King. "Off with you. Duty calls."

As the bemused King watched his former subject rush to Ruth's side, he sent a question to the witch in the voice of the mind. *Has your beguiling magic gained yet another convert?* he asked.

There is, under the sun and stars, nothing so magical as a man following his heart, the witch assured the monarch.

"Amen," said the King aloud as he turned toward his cabin, then paused. The old man was exhausted and longing for sleep and yet he could not resist the temptation to wet a finger and hold it briefly aloft—an act of faith, to test his sense that a freshening breeze—however slight—was beginning to stir.

Chapter 39

Doldrums

A quest can manifest a life not unlike the existence of a sentient being. The world may assault and influence it. The quest—stronger for its trials—may mature and seek its fortune, only to encounter the unexpected. For a time at least, it goes to ground, licking its wounds, muted by setbacks, immobilized, and waiting. Thus, without a breeze to advance it, did the quest continue to languish.

Hours passed, but it was not yet dawn when Commodore Dell surveyed the great-cabin's unoccupied table. The group was to reassemble at nine bells, but he had not the heart to set the chairs. The overriding reality of the dead calm had disrupted the council. Last night, the King had predicted that natural forces might alter the weather. But, despite the King's optimism, the wind had disappeared altogether, with no hint of returning.

Yesterday, when the King arrived, the fleet had been eighteen hours away from reaching Memora. His royal yacht was the last vessel to leave the island kingdom and it had taken a full day for *Accipiter* to encounter the fleet. With a fair wind, it would take the fleet another hard day of sailing to reach Memora. But the wind was far from fair—as far as the blackest corner of the deepest well is from the bright promise of a midday sun.

Seeking to settle his worries, the commodore sat down and opened the King's journal. The monarch was a dedicated journalist who recorded every event—small and large—which befell his kingdom. He'd placed the document in Dell's hands, assuring him it contained information which would further the quest. The commodore had already studied its pages. With *Catspaw* becalmed, Dell sought to sooth his anxiety by re-reading the account of King John's final hours on his royal island.

The King had been forced to flee Memora in the middle of the night, escaping in his nightshirt, leaving his royal vestments behind, rushing through the dark halls of Stone Bride Castle with a handful of guards to reach the safety of the royal yacht. Onboard and seeking to discard his flimsy nightshirt, the King found in *Accipiter's* cramped cabin an old sea chest containing castoff garments and a discarded crown. These things might be his grandfather's. They would have to do.

King John's story of his desperate flight from the coast of Memora was not merely colorful, it also provided vital insights regarding the disposition of the enemy. The King reported that the pirates seemed unaware the Southern Fleet had survived, let alone did they suspect that the fleet was bound for Memora. Their ignorance seemed apparent because the invaders had failed to fortify the harbor defenses at Stove Point. Days ago, the harbor town had been assaulted by sea and completely overrun. The victorious pirates had been in the process of laying siege to Stone Bride Castle when the invaders suddenly halted their advance and turned inland.

The pirates had left a small garrison behind in Stove Point and, with the main force gone, the King decided to risk abandoning the castle. Even so, the monarch and his handful of guards had been obliged to elude armed sentinels who occupied portions of the sprawling fortress. For fear of being captured, they avoided engaging the pirates. As a result, the King and his escorts were obliged to invest a morning and afternoon of hide-and-seek before they reached the lower margins of the castle where the royal yacht was secreted. Then most of the night passed before they found an opportunity to steer the small craft past the occupied town and out to sea. At dawn, they met a merchant ship whose captain told them about some woman laying claim to the name of Ann Stone Bride. Hearing this unexpected news, the King—who had been planning to sail north to take refuge with his cousins—ordered *Accipiter* to sail east to confront the imposter.

In their haste to flee the besieged island, the King and his men had carried away some things which were trivial but also other things which were vital. The refugees had transported nonessential trinkets like the King's ancestral coat of arms, his playing cards, and his ivory chess set. Such things would have been better left behind. But happily, they had also carried with them two leather satchels containing a precise inventory of the island's many lakes and the irreplaceable Memora canal map.

The King himself had grabbed the satchels at the last moment. He took them by mistake, thinking wrongly that they contained his clothing. It is well that he did so, for the inventory and map were absolutely essential to the success of the quest. Only yesterday, the war council had been on the verge of discussing the need to flood Memora. Ann in particular had been lamenting their lack of information about the island lakes and its canal system. Moments later, the King had burst into the meeting.

With the unforeseen arrival of King John and his men, the quest had gained not only the wished-for documents but also access to their author. For the King himself had been the architect of the elaborate irrigation system which bore his family's name. The Stone Bride Canal was the engineering marvel of its time and, though the waterway had lately fallen into disuse, it might yet serve the quest. It might prove to be not only the instrument of Memora's deliverance, but also the salvation of the world.

Left alone while the others slept, Commodore Dell stayed awake. The King may feel the plan was coming together, but the commodore still had doubts. The King spoke in riddles. As for El, the old man may be the deity he claimed to be but only yesterday, while examining the map, El had cut his finger on the edge of the parchment. Should a deity bleed? Moreover, El had been ill and sleeping while the King conducted his scripture lesson. Why did a divine one need others to speak for him? Why should a deity fall ill?

Too many unanswered questions and too many negative thoughts. The commodore shook his head. He was thankful for the old King's confidence in him, but he was also thankful for the King's limitations. It was granted that the King could hear the thoughts of other magical beings. But the commodore was abundantly grateful that the monarch could not hear the thoughts of ordinary humans. If the King could detect Dell's misgivings, his faith in the commodore might dwindle.

"Schawk!" he said aloud. "A plague on my qualms. Busy yourself, man, or hazard the appearance of yet more disembodied shadows!"

Chastising himself, Commodore Dell pushed his notes and his doubts aside. He unrolled the main island map, centered it on the cabin table, and secured the parchment in place with four Memorian cups, one in each corner. Studying the map would focus him. The map told him what he needed to know. It symbolized everything he must comprehend in order to believe the council's plan would work. He hovered over the detailed document and forced himself to concentrate. He used a divider to confirm the distance from Stove Point Harbor to Deep Lake and used a pencil to record the calculation on a separate scrap of paper. The habit of treating maps with respect had been drummed into him during his midshipman days.

'Give me a map, a ship, and the stars and I am content,' his old commander used to say. Dell said the same thing to the midshipmen under his tutelage when he became a lieutenant, and to the lieutenants under his command when he rose to commodore, and to his boatswain only yesterday.

His thoughts turned to Boatswain Brightlamp. The man should be rated first mate. If they both survived, Commodore Dell would see to it. The logbook of *Catspaw* would bear out Brightlamp's sterling record. Three years of impeccable seamanship and incredible courage, a credit to his commodore and his crew. The commodore glanced at the logbook bound in loose canvas, nestled in its wooden case upon the sea desk. It had been two days since he'd found the time to pen an entry.

No, that is dishonest, he thought. *I have had the time, but I have not had the words.*

Much had happened and the commodore had used a packet envelope to jot down notes so that at least he had a record of the date, time, and latitude of events. But his shorthand: 'Middlemount landfall,' 'Late moon—the cause?' 'Our patron—a deity?' 'Redhackle—fire?' 'Redhackle—witch?' 'A yacht fleeing Memora?' 'A mad King?' and so on. The entries contained far too many questions for a proper log. How to chronicle events and people and animals who behaved—in what way? Who behaved *magically,* that was the only proper word, and yet it was an exceedingly improper word to enter in the log.

Best forget the log for the time being and concentrate on something more tangible, he convinced himself as he resumed his study of the map.

According to the map, Deep Lake was linked to Stove Point Harbor by a substantial canal which had once served as an outlet to the sea. The Deep Lake Dam marked the headwaters of the canal, and the harbor estuary marked its mouth. The distance between the two points was roughly thirty miles. Over the years, the canal had fallen into disuse. For decades, farmers and herders had usurped the fertile bed to plant crops and cultivate pastures. But the broad canal channel was still there and would still, when flooded, be navigable.

Unless the large pirate force encamped at Deep Lake was dealt with, the quest would fail. Left unchecked, the pirates would intercept and crush any effort to ply the lake in search of the fabled cup. The reconstituted canal would provide the means for the commodore to bring the fleet's firepower to bear on the inland enemy. It would be impossible to transport even one unwieldy ship's cannon overland. But a score of the fleet's squat-mouthed mortars—along with shot and wadding and powder—could be readily mounted on floating barges.

As for obtaining sufficient barges for the enterprise, the commodore had no doubt that the harbor would prove well-supplied with the utilitarian craft. Once the canal was filled with water, Stove Point's harbor barges could be poled by men and towed by oxen up the canal until they were arrayed within striking distance of Deep Lake. The mortars were unlovely weapons, but incredibly accurate. Two dozen mortars transported upstream could smother the enemy with deadly, inescapable volleys.

The entire plan—to flood the island and move the mortars—if presented to the King under normal circumstances would have fallen on deaf ears had it not been for the Princess. Perhaps El knew what he was doing after all. Maybe, as the King seemed to believe, the wind would return. On the other hand, El was fading and might soon be incoherent and the calm may not resolve in time. The commodore turned up the lamps and studied the map. There would be no harm in going over the entire order of battle once more.

"Enter," the commodore responded to a rap at his door and Brightlamp stood before him.

"Boat's away, sir," said the boatswain.

"Very good. What is the clock?"

"I make it five bells of the mid-watch, sir."

"Very good. Carry on."

"Aye, sir."

Two hours until dawn, the commodore thought, *and the boat is on its way. Now we shall see how stout our rowers are.*

Chapter 40

Two Days

The mind can absorb only what wakefulness can endure. An exhausted ox may continue to pull a wagon. But the inattentive beast is as likely to drag the cargo and his own carcass over an abyss as keep it centered on the market path. And an ox, with certain exceptions, is not a man.

Commodore Dell had fallen asleep. Hours ago, he'd removed his spectacles, intending to rest his eyes for a moment, but weariness had overtaken him. He was in his chair, bent forward at the waist, his head resting on his outstretched arm, as his upper torso sprawled uncomfortably across the Memorian map. The commodore was exhausted. Nine bells had sounded. The others had knocked. When they received no reply, they'd tiptoed in, one-by-one, and taken their chairs—moving silently, but also holding fingers to their lips like naughty school children coming late to class. When all were assembled, they sat expectantly. Moments passed until they were ready to burst with the strain of concealing their presence. At last, the commodore snorted in his sleep, turned his head, and opened his eyes.

He sat up gruffly as the others laughed aloud.

"You might have warned a fellow," he grumbled, then continued in as good-naturedly a voice as he could muster. "Princess, this is your doing no doubt."

"It was unanimous," said Ann. "We all agreed that you needed your beauty sleep."

"Harrumph!" the commodore growled. "To business." He fumbled with a confusion of maps to find his discarded spectacles which he put on and adjusted. "Let us begin."

"With all due respect to our gallant commodore," said Ann, "I am reluctant to proceed without El present."

"The old man is dying," Dell said. "I see no need to tax him further. It falls to Ann to carry the quest. I would gladly wait for the old man's return, but time is short. You must assume command, my Princess," he said with emotion.

"As you wish," Ann relented, deciding this was not the time for a religious debate. "Since the Memorian map is so neatly displayed, I suggest we pick up where we last left off. Gentlemen," the Princess acknowledged her mate, the commodore, Percy, and the pirate as these individuals left their seats to gather around the map. Then she continued with a nod to the King, Ruth, and Esau to join the standing party. "Gentle lady, Gracious King, and noble dog: the map of Memora, so lately supplied to us by His Majesty, illustrates the scope of our battle. We have but two days and much to do. At present, we have lost the wind, but in these latitudes the current will continue to carry us westward. This lack of wind cannot last, and I believe we will yet be able to recover our time. So, bear with me and I shall once more review our order of battle."

Ann paused and glanced around the table—seeking and obtaining eye contact with each member of the war council.

As she did so her thoughts returned to her first night on the deck of *Catspaw* when Seth had flaunted his powers by filling the vessel's sails with his commanding breath and she'd threatened to do the same. Where had the force of those powers gone? Earlier that morning, she'd placed herself in the stern and tried to generate sufficient breath to overcome the calm and failed. Seth too had tried and failed. Their former Wolfkind strengths seemed to be ebbing in concert with their increasing humanity and their deity's steady demise.

From the magical council members surrounding the table, Ann received assurances in the voice of the mind that, despite her changing powers, all still had faith in the Princess' abilities as a leader. From the mortals, Ann detected reassuring nods and so, buoyed by these endorsements, she confidently began her summary.

"This day, two hours before dawn, Commodore Dell dispatched a long boat under orders to row westward to gauge our distance from Memora. Ruth held a vigil on deck to keep a watchful eye on their progress through the darkness. Our resourceful Duchess of the Air might have flown there herself but bowed to the commodore's nautical expertise."

"Far better to dispatch a stealthy boat than launch a conspicuous flying witch to alarm our pirate friends," said Ruth.

"Indeed," Ann agreed. "Now that daylight has come, Boatswain Brightlamp holds the watch. The Memorian continent is, by the commodore's reckoning, some three leagues away—or nine of our land miles. A long boat with eight stout oarsmen can row a league an hour—perhaps faster going with the current and a bit slower coming back. The lack of wind will assist the speed of the scouting boat and I should not be surprised to receive their report before we adjourn."

"Can your men traverse three leagues and back so quickly?" Percy asked the commodore.

"They need not go that full distance to sight the island," said the commodore. "I sent Benjson, our six-footer, as lookout. Standing in the long boat's bow, he'll be able to spot land a league away. The moment they sight land, they have orders to return."

A rap on the commodore's door brought Brightlamp.

"And it please you, sir, the boat is back."

"How far?" asked Dell.

"The island is as you calculated, sir. Three leagues due west and with the gain from the current we're closer still."

"All we need now is a fair wind," said the commodore.

"Aye, sir."

"See to it, Brightlamp."

"Aye, sir," answered the boatswain uncertainly, suggesting he was unable to comprehend how he might execute the commodore's orders to summon the tardy wind.

"We'll have to disperse the fleet at once," said the commodore. "We're still beyond the horizon and therefore invisible to Memora, but if we drift much closer, we'll tip our hand. Signal the fleet to divide now on the current and be prepared to sail to stations the moment the wind freshens."

"Aye, sir," said the boatswain, sounding a bit more confident that he could carry out that particular order.

When the boatswain had departed, Ann resumed her summary.

"Being small," the Princess said, "the long boat will not have been detected by the enemy. Therefore, we retain our advantage. On the commodore's orders, the fleet will break into three groups. *Catspaw* will stay on this course along with two other ships. Of the remaining fleet, half will sail north and the other half south to form a blockade all along the Memorian coast. We don't expect reinforcements from either the Fishals or the pirates, but it is best to be cautious, is that not so, commodore?"

"Yes," said Dell. "When the fleet takes up stations, its presence will reassure and protect those portions of the island not yet in enemy hands. When the wind comes—and it *will* come— *Catspaw* and her sister ships will sail west and heave-to just over the horizon from the island. With fortune, we shall reach that position by noon and remain undetected until we choose to show ourselves to the enemy occupying Stove Point. And now, Your Majesty, I think it will be best for you to explain how your handsome yacht will be employed."

"The yacht, *Accipiter*, will serve as our mule," said the King. "My small swift vessel will skirt the horizon, keeping out of sight of the harbor. Gliding deftly and unseen, she'll distribute our forces to key points along the coast. *Accipiter* will first steer northward, aiming for the channel which passes beneath Stone Bride Castle. Once in the caverns beneath the castle, the yacht will deposit stout Mastro and his agile companions Percy and Esau. And these stealthy individuals will secure the keys to unlock the valves at Deep Lake. While these burglars are obtaining the keys, *Accipiter* will sail farther south to the headland here."

King John pointed to an outcropping of land south of the castle. Then he nodded to Ann to take up the narrative.

"The modest draft of the King's yacht will allow it to reach the shallows where other passengers—myself, Ruth, and a troop of guardsmen—will wade through the surf and hurry inland to obtain mounts for the ride to Deep Lake. Under our original plan we were to have taken the ship's marines on this mission. But the Memorian palace guards will be more familiar with the territory and so the marines will remain on *Catspaw* to help with securing the harbor. In any event, we riders will hasten inland, for our mounts must be obtained by dusk. The equestrian stables are not far from the beach. Having deposited the riders, *Accipiter* will instantly return to the castle, take on the three burglars, and carry them and the keys back to me at this position."

The Princess pointed to another spot along the beach south of the castle.

"By the time the burglars arrive, I and the others will have infiltrated the equestrian stables which we trust, owing to the pirates' habitual disinterest in land animals, will be unguarded. We will have secured enough horses to ride inland following the bank of the canal. If we are able to begin our ride no later than dusk, we will reach the woods which surround Deep Lake in darkness. However, the forest road is broad, so the dark will not hinder us. Beyond the woods, we will descend under cover of night into the dry bed of the canal and race toward Deep Lake Dam to unlock the tower valves. The half-moon will provide sufficient light and the way should be smooth and free of stones."

Another knock on the door of the great-cabin brought the surgeon who entered, somewhat sheepishly, and took a seat at the far edge of the council table.

"Well timed, Sander," said the commodore. "Your part in this drama will soon be revealed."

Sander nodded to his brother and seemed to visibly relax.

"The moment we riders set off," Ann continued with a nod to Sander, "the yacht will return to the fleet where Seth, Mastro, and two dozen of our most capable sailors will be waiting to be transported to the northern beaches adjacent to the island's grotto caves. Seth's group will arrive near dusk and remain hidden in the caves until full dark, at which time they will proceed to neutralize the pirates occupying the town, the harbor, and the castle."

"Neutralize them?" Percy asked.

"Our men will kill them all, one-by-one, and silently," replied Ann.

The coolness of her answer made Percy shudder.

"Commodore." the Princess motioned for Dell to continue.

"As a distraction to aid Seth and his crew in ambushing the pirates," the commodore said, "three ships—led by *Catspaw*—will approach the harbor at dusk. We will make ourselves conspicuous by forming up and tacking along a north-south line—all the while keeping well out of cannon range. At full dark, we will hang lanterns the better to be seen from shore. Our goal will be to keep the pirates' attention until the town and castle are purged of the invaders and the harbor is secured. At dawn tomorrow, with Stove Point in our hands and the canal flooded, we will transport the mortars upstream, arriving before noon to bombard the Deep Lake pirates."

"El and the commodore will arrive with the mortars," added the Princess. "During the bombardment, El and I will take advantage of the chaos to escort Ruth as far as possible until the moment when she must go alone to retrieve the cup." The Princess paused and surveyed the council. Then she asked, "Have I forgotten anything?"

As if from a deep cavern, El—though absent from the council—spoke to Ann in the voice of the mind. *My Princess, you and I were to have been Ruth's escorts, but my failing health will prevent my going.*

"I have truly forgotten that El will not be with us," Ann said aloud.

"The commodore should take El's place," the King suggested.

"Indeed, I will command *Accipiter* and ride with you to Deep Lake," said the commodore.

There was a moment of silence.

"I approve this change," said Ann. "I could ask for no better man at my side."

The group stood then and gathered around the map.

"How long for the canal to fill—until the barges can head upstream?" Ann asked the King.

"Three hours at the most," said the King. When the others looked doubtful, he added, "On my life—three hours and no more."

"And who should know better than the inventor of this miraculous hydraulic system?" asked Ann as she bowed toward the King.

"The hydraulics, another miracle," whispered Percy to Sander who was standing to his right.

"Indeed," said Sander, though his smile seemed unconvincing.

"If all goes well in securing the harbor, Brightlamp will be ready with captured barges laid alongside the fleet and armed for their voyage. This, El willing, he will accomplish by dawn of our second day," said Commodore Dell. "With fortune, my trusted boatswain will have sufficient pole-men and beasts of burden to push and tow the barges rapidly upstream. But before the barges can be obtained, our landing party must spend the night purging the town of pirates. So, Sander, please explain your design."

Sander cleared his throat. As a medical man he'd been charged by his brother with what had been characterized as the harbor surgery. He cleared his throat a second time and began.

"There is a cancerous infection in Stove Point, and it must be incised," Sander declared. "The enemy in the harbor must be removed. *Catspaw* and her sister ships could deal with them from afar. But we dare not fire on the harbor for such a bombardment would harm innocent townsfolk—if any still remain alive. Moreover, our guns would be heard inland and thus alarm the Deep Lake defenders. I am no military man," Sander said, "but I am somewhat skilled at surgery. So, we have assembled a group of our sailors who are fleetest of foot, supplied them—if you will—with scalpels, and placed them under the field leadership of one of our most skilled warriors." He bowed to Seth. "I would go with them myself, but my presence will be required onboard *Catspaw* in case there are injured to tend."

Sander sounded disappointed at having to stay behind, but he continued with his description.

"Moving under cover of darkness, Seth and his group will hunt the pirates and—as has been said—quietly neutralize them. This venture is calculating and exceedingly cold-blooded, but necessary. We do what must be done so the acquisition and provisioning of the barges may proceed unhindered."

The council stood in silence, each person staring at the map, perhaps envisioning their role in the battle plan. At last, Ann spoke.

"Amen," she said. "We ought to have a toast, I think."

The commodore was about to summon Miles to bring liquor when the ship lurched, and the unbidden steward tumbled into the cabin.

"Wind!" Miles shouted. "The wind is up and steady, sir!"

"To arms, my friends!" the commodore shouted.

The war council climbed topside, streaming past sailors who were scrambling to take advantage of the freshening wind. The burglars made their preparations. The riders and those who planned to purge the harbor rushed to secure their weapons. The commodore sent signals to confirm the fleet's dispersal and the yacht crew prepared for launch.

As the others hurried to their places, Ruth and Esau lingered and stood apart. Certain they were alone, the dog reached up with a paw and urged the witch to kneel down.

"I'm coming with you," he whispered as Ruth knelt beside him.

"Do you think I am incapable of snatching the cup?" whispered the witch.

"I trust that you will do what must be done. But you will be in peril, child, and you will not die alone," the dog promised.

Hearing this, Ruth smiled and bent down to kiss the top of Esau's splendid head.

Chapter 41

The Castle Keys

Stone Bride Castle had been erected straddling an ocean cavern. If it had not been erected just so, there would have been no secret access to obtain the keys. But it was so made. The stonemasons who labored to build the castle would have been nothing without the blacksmith, for their chisels needed constant sharpening. The blacksmith would have been hindered had not the charcoal burners constantly replenished their wooden billets to blacken briquettes needed to feed the forge. Without the work of foresters to chop bundles of billet branches, the burners would have been forced to neglect their slow-burning fires. No bundles, no fire. No fire, no charcoal. No charcoal, no blacksmith's glowing forge. No forge, no sharpened chisels. No chisels, no fashioned stones. No stones, no castle. No castle erected just so, no chance of furthering the quest. Each job had been essential. In a like manner of coordinated efforts, did the quest seek to mesh the interrelated cogs of the massive Fleet of Deliverance with the disposition of the King's diminutive yacht.

With the fleet dispersed, *Catspaw*—accompanied by *Sturgeon* and *The Hobbled Eagle*—set a course for Stove Point Harbor. Borne by blessed gales, these three ships-of-the-line sailed eastward while the remainder of the fleet separated to blockade the island at every other point of the compass. Commodore Dell, exercising a typical nautical officer's caution, wanted nothing left to chance. With the island securely blockaded, no pirate would escape, and no ship could come to the enemy's aid.

After taking guardsmen and weapons onboard, the King's yacht *Accipiter* was dispatched to fulfill the first of its mule duties by carrying the quest's burglars to a landfall north of Stove Point harbor. Mastro, Percy, and Esau were bound for the channel beneath Stone Bride Castle with orders to secure the valve keys. The keys were essential, for no amount of pounding or pressure would free the intricate valves which impounded Deep Lake. The valves could not be forced. Only by properly unlocking the mechanisms could the water be coaxed from the lake and into the canal.

The locks and keys had been the King's idea—put in place after his daughter's tragic drowning to prevent the canal from accidentally filling. For many years, the towering dam and its locked valves had held the waters of Deep Lake in check. Six small subterranean outlets relieved pressure on the dam and filled the island's aquifers to supply irrigation and household wells, but the canal itself remained empty.

That would soon change.

Percy carried with him a map of the lower regions of the castle, a detailed document drawn from memory by the King. Percy had complete confidence in the map's accuracy. What else could one do but trust a map drawn by a seventy-six-year-old man who had been born in and spent his entire life as a resident of the sprawling castle? The King knew the shortest way through the castle to reach the keys, which also turned out to be the least conspicuous route to the Room of Fasteners.

With luck and the map, the three would be in and out of the Room before the pirate guards—who were probably few enough but heavily armed—were aware they'd been burgled. By virtue of his proficiency in the leveling of doors and men, Mastro led the burglars. Percy and Esau were present in case the stout door to the castle's Room of Fasteners resisted Mastro's efforts to flatten it and it became necessary to skitter through smaller recesses to reach the keys. The King's map covered both contingencies, but Percy still had questions.

"So, sire," Percy had asked the King before they departed and after he'd examined the map in detail. "It appears that you have this particular room in the castle where all the duplicate keys and replacement locks are kept, including a single set of precious keys to unlock the water?"

"That is correct," said the King.

"And the door to this Room of Fasteners, it is locked?"

"Naturally."

"And the key to that door?"

"Inside the Room, I should imagine."

The King blinked twice, and Percy decided not to ask the obvious question. Instead, he said, "So to enter we must either batter down the door or slip past that locked obstacle by squeezing through the chinks shown here?"

"Yes," the King answered and that seemed to settle the matter.

As *Accipiter* cast off, under the command of Commodore Dell, the fleet remained in place beyond the horizon and as yet undetected. To approach the island unseen, the yacht kept well out to sea until mid-afternoon. At two-of-the-clock, many of the pirates would be at siesta—a habit which the brigands had carried with them from the swarthy climes of those strangely hot and humid lands which lay farther west. Between two and four, only a few eyes, if any, would be looking seaward and those sleepy observers might easily mistake the tiny craft for a drifting pelican. There was little enough to see. The commodore ordered the King's crew to pull down all but one sail and only a thin sliver of the yacht's pale freeboard showed above the waterline.

Fortune was with them. They were not detected as *Accipiter* glided out of the distant sea and into the watery channel which lay beneath Stone Bride Castle. Inside the cavern and far beneath the castle, the three burglars disembarked and quickly located damp stairs leading upward. By the time they disappeared at the top of the stairs, the yacht was underway to deliver the riders farther south.

As they neared the lower regions of the castle, Mastro, Percy, and the dog could hear a few distant echoes of human activity. But these sounds faded when they entered several twisting tunnels and grew fainter still as they descended to the dungeon level where the Room of Fasteners lay. They might have made better time, but Esau continued to lag behind, seeming intent on lifting his leg and taking a piss at every corner.

"Next time do your business before we set off," scolded Percy.

"Next time," the dog promised.

Percy lit a candle, and they consulted the map. They passed two more corners and arrived at the Room. It was unguarded, but the door was double-hinged and thick with iron bands. There were no accessible joints. There was no knob. Mastro strained as he tried to pry the hinges open and sought to break the bands, but it was no use.

"Have a look at the map," said Mastro as he rubbed his sore fingers and wiped his brow. "Time to try them holes."

There were five holes: two in the floor and two in the walls on either side of the immovable door, plus one in the ceiling. Percy looked up.

"Too high," he dismissed the ceiling hole. "And the wall holes are too small, even for a burglar of my stature. I'll try the floor holes. Esau, the wall is yours, with my compliments."

"See you inside," said Esau and he popped into the nearest wall hole.

Percy had been optimistic that he might fit through the floor. But he found both holes to be shallow and curved. Once inside, he could only stand in place, with no room to bend down and go farther. So, he climbed out and joined Mastro as the two humans put their ears to the main door and listened for signs of the dog. No sound reached them through the thick obstacle, but a moment later Esau popped out of the wall carrying a large ring of stout keys.

"Mud-bay-won-up-deese," the dog spoke with his mouth full, until Percy reached down and pulled the ring free. "Thanks," said Esau. "As I said, it must be one of these. I saw no other keys in that cramped room, just rows and rows and rows of hasps and locks."

"The crest," remembered Percy. He lit another candle and examined the head of each key until he found what he was looking for. "Here it is—the Stone Bride crest."

The others leaned closer to examine the crest: a golden emblem of two crossed swords with a heart on each hilt.

"That's it alright," agreed the pirate.

"Let's away," said Esau

The dog turned to go when an explosion echoed in the narrow tunnel and the smell of gunpowder filled their nostrils. The shot killed Percy instantly and, as the exiting ball clattered noisily to the cobblestone floor, Mastro could dimly perceive the assassin who stood in the shadows attempting to reload. Taking two giant strides toward the shooter, the pirate slammed the figure against the wall and the shooter's neck cracked as he crumpled to the floor.

"That shot will be heard!" shouted the dog. "Come! Our Percy is dead! We have to run!"

Mastro picked up the still-smoking pistol, stripped the powder horn and ball pouch from the dead assassin, and ran toward the sound of Esau's retreating voice. When he reached Percy's body he knelt beside his fallen friend. "Sorry," the pirate murmured. "The keys!" he roared in a voice tinged with anger and sadness.

"I have them round my neck," shouted the fleeing dog. "Come on!"

"The map?" yelled Mastro as he ran.

"Left behind!" came the dog's voice as he rounded a corner. "But I deposited plenty of traces. I'll follow my nose. You follow me!"

"Slow down damnit," panted Mastro. "I have only the two legs!"

With Esau sprinting and Mastro lumbering behind, they quickly retraced their steps. The pair pressed on, keeping well ahead of a cacophony of confused and angry voices which sounded behind them. Moments later, they reached the damp stairs and descended, praying *Accipiter* had returned from the task of delivering the riders. They need not have worried on that account. The King's crew knew the Memora waters well and the mule's timing was impeccable.

Commodore Dell helped the two burglars climb over the railing and he gave the order to cast off. The crew strained at poles and oars and soon had the yacht through the channel and out onto open water undetected. They hoisted the sail and sped south.

"Percy?" the commodore asked.

"In Velyn," sighed Mastro as he tore a strip from his shirt tail and tied it to *Accipiter's* railing as a banner of grief.

"A place in Velyn," said the commodore. He tore a strip from his sleeve and added it to the railing.

"As we speak of him, his soul ascends there," said Mastro completing the ritual benediction.

"Ah," Esau sighed. "Here's another comrade fallen, and I have no cloth to add for grieving, but I will sing if I may."

Mastro inclined his head in assent.

"Nowie, Nowie, Nowie," sang Esau and his voice filled the darkness of passing sea and sky. "Lord El almighty. Peace, we pray on all our land. Peace, we pray thy mercy."

Standing at a respectful distance, the youngest member of the yacht crew heard the song and wondered.

"That hymn seems familiar," said the youth. "Most of it at any rate. But what does 'Nowie' mean?"

"Your education is lacking, boy," said the eldest crewman. "Do you not recognize the name of the birthplace of El? The ancient village has long since vanished—swallowed it was by the sea—but that can be no reason for its memory to fade as well."

"Now I know," the lad assured him. "And I will remember."

Chapter 42

The Ride to Deep Lake

An enterprise, once set in motion, must continue to move like the clockworks of a village tower. A timepiece is an apt metaphor for a military operation. Corporeal creatures—humans especially and even animals after a fashion—may pause to mourn, but the machinations of war have not this luxury. A maneuver, once engaged, must continue forward, like relentless unswerving time, else it is likely to collapse under its own ambitious weight.

While the burglars and Commodore Dell mourned the loss of Percy, the yacht continued its rounds and sailed farther south toward a deserted beach where the purloined keys would be passed to the riders.

Accessing the stables had gone smoothly. As Ann hoped, the equestrian complex was unguarded. The only surprise was the variety of animals housed there. She had anticipated finding horses. The other creatures were unexpected. The Princess and the witch took the diverse menagerie in stride as they rode side-by-side along the broad path which led back to the beach.

I presumed you would leave the camel and the cumbersome giraffe behind. Ruth sent this thought to Ann with a broad grin.

I see you have also chosen a more traditional horse. Ann responded.

As they rode farther, they used the voice of the mind to share a secret satisfaction.

I sense that the men are not only disappointed, Ruth suggested, *but also disoriented to see our feminine countenances so compromised with tightly braided locks, pulled back, and bound with plain bands of ordinary leather.*

Let them wonder, thought Ann, *our practical plaiting is fit for warrior-work and all the better to ride and do battle.*

The Princess looked at the witch, then added a thought which had been troubling her. *I have been meaning to ask,* Ann continued. *In what way have your powers returned to you—specifically your ability to converse in the voice of the mind?*

That is a puzzlement, thought the witch. *When I awoke on Redhackle Isle, certain aspects of my former powers were unattainable. And yet lately it seems that, as El continues to fail, my powers have returned in proportion to his demise.*

A puzzlement indeed, Ann agreed, *for it seems the reverse with me. Unlike yourself, whose powers have grown while our deity weakens, I feel that my own strengths—if not lessening—are at least changing as my Wolfkind nature gives way to human traits. As my powers grow more unpredictable, I begin to wonder what my role in this quest shall be.*

Your role seems apparent, thought Ruth. *You are our strongest vessel of Wolfkind blood and Wolfkind must survive to restore El and preserve the divine world. Therefore, you must above all else do one quite basic thing: you must remain alive.*

Ann and Ruth exchanged these private thoughts as they and the others rode to rendezvous with *Accipiter* on the Memorian beach. A single rider had remained on the sand to ensure that the yacht was guided to the correct meeting spot. So precise was the timing that *Accipiter* and riders arrived at the same moment.

As the trim yacht rode at anchor, a small skiff was lowered and rowers sculled their passengers to a spot just short of the beach. Mastro and Esau joined the commodore as the three waded ashore through the shallow surf.

Watching them come, Ann and Ruth exchanged a glance. They and other riders waited in the forest shadows and remained mounted on an assortment of horses and donkeys, ready—if needed—to flee. This was, perhaps, an unneeded precaution, but all felt the weight of the quest having reached a critical juncture. Much depended on the element of surprise and, in a land crawling with enemies—not to mention informants—there were countless ways that same tactic could be turned on its head in the form of an unforeseen enemy counterattack.

The risks were real and the danger palpable. Compared to their well-supplied and numerous enemies, the allies were few in number, abroad in hostile territory, and—until the mortars could be brought into play—lightly armed. So, it was with an uneasy mixture of relief and anxiety that the riders watched the unlikely trio—a ship's officer dressed for action, a hulking pirate, and a somber dog—reach the shore and advance across the sandy beach.

With subdued caution, Ann greeted the pirate, received the keys, and tied them securely to her belt. The pirate noticed that the Princess was wearing a sword, the first real weapon Ann had carried since her transformation from Wolfkind to woman.

Having delivered the keys, Mastro relayed the news of Percy's death.

"A sad blow," said the Princess.

"He was a Bindbuilder," said Mastro. "That was his family name. He was stronger than he knew. He is in Velyn now." Eager to avenge his friend, Mastro sought to accompany Ann. He desired to ride to the shore of Deep Lake, but clearly there was no animal present which could bear him.

"Besides, Seth will have need of you to aid his work in the harbor," the Princess said. "Your knowledge of pirate ways will be invaluable to our cause at Stove Point. Join the others and you may get to smash a head or two—assuming such actions won't violate your pirate code."

"I'll smash only them what deserves it," Mastro promised. "And so, it begins. And I'll warrant you, My Lady, and you, Miss, are well-girded for battle."

An awkward moment followed as the pirate paused and seemed to be taking stock of the two women. Ann and Ruth endeavored to maintain even expressions while they exchanged a glance and a rapid succession of silent thoughts.

I wonder, Ann said in the voice of the mind, *if our pirate friend has ever seen such a sight as we two with our hair pulled back and plastered in place by unwomanly leather headbands.*

Not to mention, Ruth added. *And I'm certain Mastro won't mention it—I can't imagine his measured reaction to our borrowed tunics and vests.*

Trusting he cannot follow our thoughts, Ann smiled, *I'm certain he's familiar with those garments. If anything, I think the poor man is most nonplussed by our roomy nautical trousers which, I am given to understand, resemble shameless pantaloons.*

Indeed, Ruth agreed. *What's next for us do you think? Sailor's pigtails and tattoos? But hush, sister, our giant speaks.*

"I suppose, since I must smash them villains quietly, I'll have no need of these." The pirate handed Ann the pistol, powder horn, and shot bag he'd taken from Percy's killer. Ann thanked him and stowed the pistol and ammunition in her saddlebag, suddenly realizing that she had no idea how to use the unfamiliar weapon.

Farewells were exchanged and the party dispersed. Mastro waded back to board *Accipiter* and the crew cast off to rejoin *Catspaw*. Commodore Dell, an inexperienced horseman, went reluctantly to obtain his mount. As for Esau, though his presence was not anticipated in the battle plan, the dog remained on shore until the yacht had departed. Then he leapt up to share the saddle with Ruth.

"I can't get used to your new name," the dog grumbled. "I like saying 'Ahoo,' it tickles my tongue."

"Careful or I'll start referring to you as 'dog,'" smiled the witch. "Now we must decide upon your riding style. Would you rather straddle in front of my saddle and be borne along sideways like a newborn calf? Or would you prefer to sit with your forepaws on my shoulders and ride double behind me like a herder and her furry companion?"

A guard passed near, so they dropped their open speech. Though their sailors, marines, and guards had witnessed hints of magic, a conversation between a witch and a dog might still strike the man as strange.

"Do I have a third choice?" whispered Esau after the eavesdropping guard rode on.

"You could try a donkey."

"No thank you. I believe I'll walk as Nature intended," said Esau and he jumped down to the ground again. "I prefer a surface that doesn't wobble."

"Must we take the dog?" asked Ann as she drew even with the witch and the canine. The two then rode abreast, leaving the beach behind while Esau ran alongside with the King's guards and the commodore following.

"It fulfills a promise between us," answered Ruth with an air of mystery in her voice.

"Another prank?" asked Ann.

"Not so," she promised.

"Hmm," said the Princess.

"That word 'hmm,'" laughed the witch, "you say it often. Are you certain it means what you think it does?"

"It is a human way of saying 'now just hold on a second' or 'I really don't believe a single word you are saying.'"

Two guards drew near to ask instructions and Ann dispatched them to ride ahead as forward pickets.

Best if we switch to the voices of the mind, she cautioned Ruth.

Fine with me, the witch responded.

"Me too," added Esau.

The mind, dog, Ann repeated impatiently.

Sorry, Esau apologized, *pray continue.*

Their thoughts were interrupted as another pair of guards came near, seeking confirmation of their duties.

"Lieutenant Collin's compliments, Your Majesty," said the taller of the two guards. "And he wishes you to confirm that we should be dispatched to the rear."

"Be guided by your officer," said Ann.

"Indeed, we will," said the man, his tone suggesting relief.

"With so many royals present on this adventure," said Ann in sympathy. "It must confuse the chain of command."

"Even so," the guard agreed as he struggled to turn his mount.

Following the progress of the departing guardsmen, Ann turned in her saddle to see how Commodore Dell and Lieutenant Collin were doing. She found the guard officer holding his own while the able seafarer struggled to steer and stay atop his uncooperative plow horse.

Our commodore has his hands full. Ann smiled as she sent this thought to her companion.

Ruth looked back and smiled in turn.

Like our fearless commodore and handsome lieutenant, these palace guards are putting on a brave show, but they also appear out of their element, she laughed in the voice of the mind. *The men seem capable, but probably they did not do much guarding beyond their precious castle.*

More used to marching to-and-fro on battlements than crossing the country on horse or donkey, agreed Ann.

"Have a care!" shouted Esau. The dog had been running ahead as Ann and Ruth conversed in the voice of the mind. Now he came dashing back.

"You were cautioned not to speak aloud," said Ann irritably. "Must you—?"

"Follow!" shouted Esau and the dog instantly became invisible as the Princess and the witch topped a hill. Their horses reared and shied. Gaining control of her mount, Ann leapt from her saddle and drew her sword. Ruth also dismounted and the two stood in the gathering dusk staring downward in disbelief. Below them, scattered on the descending slope in a trampled patch of ground, lay a jumble of leather harness, military helmets, and uniform jackets—a desolate site and all which remained of the two advance guardsmen and their mules.

Chapter 43

Diversion

An infection cannot be allowed to remain entrenched, else it will spread. It must be cut away. To accomplish this, it is sometimes necessary to divert the attention of the patient.

When three ships of the Southern Fleet appeared on the horizon just before sunset, the pirates holding Stove Point Harbor were suitably alarmed. Commodore Dell had hoped that three ships would be enough to hold the pirates' attention and just the right number to cause the harbor defenders to dispatch a casual message inland to their comrades guarding Deep Lake. Three ships were, he hoped, sufficient to draw attention but not enough to pick a fight. The pirates would be curious, would probably assume the three vessels were all that was left of the vaunted Southern Fleet, and would be inclined to believe the pirate armada sent to destroy the last viable Middlemount force had done its job.

Catspaw's intrepid boatswain, Thomas Brightlamp, enthusiastically endorsed his commodore's point of view. Both Brightlamp and Dell were counting on the arrogant invaders—not only those defending the harbor but also those farther inland—to notice *Catspaw* and her two sister ships. But, so far as any military response was concerned, the two seamen expected the enemy to yawn, roll over, and go back to sleep.

Brightlamp could see a dozen Ectrican ships in the harbor, all flying the white skull banner of the western pirate kingdom. Scanning the harbor by telescope, the boatswain determined that none of the pirate ships held sufficient crews to put to sea and engage an enemy. According to intelligence reports from Memorian ships fleeing the pirate invasion, the lion's share of the pirate force had marched inland three days ago—probably grumbling with every step which took them farther away from their ships. The boatswain and his commodore had been battling pirates for a decade. So, they could confidently surmise how sea-bound brigands would react to orders to leave their ships behind and march inland like common soldiers.

As sailors, the pirates would have seldom walked farther than the length of a main deck. While on land, it is unlikely any of the old salts who made up the Ectrican pirate force would have taken more steps than were required to cover the distance between the docks and the nearest tavern.

After marching thirty miles to Deep Lake, the pirates would have undoubtedly arrived inland blistered and footsore, while cursing the unforgiving rigidity of the ground over which they'd been compelled to march. Most would never have made the trip if they hadn't been compelled to trudge so far by the Fishal troops who were rumored to be herding them along—a precaution to keep a close eye on their notoriously unreliable allies.

Upon reaching the distant lake, some pirates would probably wade in. They would be unlikely to venture deep enough to swim. Sailors were notoriously untrusting of fresh water and felt ungainly in landlocked lakes and rivers. Fresh water failed to properly buoy them up like the salty sea. Still, the brigands would likely cool their feet in any water—fresh or salt—after toiling through acres of dust, dirt, and cultivated fields.

Based on the map of Memora, the pirates' arduous journey inland would have taken them across miles of seemingly endless flatland. Then uphill, shunning a surrounding forest to follow the bank of the dry canal, until they reached Deep Lake. Their grumbling would have reached a fever pitch when the pirates were informed that the lake was to be their new and more-or-less permanent home.

For how long? The seamen would have carped.

They would have been told they were to remain at the lake for as long as it suited their leaders. Those leaders would have backed up their pronouncements. Their chief tool of enforcement was an elite troop of Fishal marksmen assigned to keep the undisciplined pirates in check. So, the unhappy brigands were stuck inland for the duration. It could be months, perhaps longer, before they could return to their ships.

Hearing this, a dozen pirates had reportedly experimented with desertion. But those twelve were soon caught and hoisted from tree branches to sway in the afternoon breeze. Informants who had escaped the inland reported the bodies dangling there, each with a firm noose severely constricting the circumference of a dead broken neck. So, the rest had apparently stayed put.

It was a notion which would account for the observations of the boatswain as he trained his telescope on each of the pirate ships in Stove Point Harbor.

"I make it no more than six men per ship," Brightlamp told the King, who sat listlessly beside him in a chair brought out from the commodore's great-cabin. El was unconscious below decks and the King too seemed to be failing. The deity was slipping away, and the old King was looking frail—his hunched body wrapped head-to-toe in blankets against the chill of sea air. "So, Your Worship, I make it seventy on ships and another fifty squatting ashore in town and in your castle—that would make less than two-hundred altogether. Do you agree?"

The King nodded.

The old man seemed distracted, so the boatswain—who was serving as acting commodore in Dell's absence—returned to his observations.

After some moments, the old monarch spoke. His voice was small, like a man with a heavy weight upon his chest striving to gather sufficient breath to be heard.

"Many townsfolk and all from the castle are dead," the King mumbled. "It is a terrible thing I have wrought."

From the testimony of survivors who had fled the island, both men knew the pirates had exacted a heavy toll on the islanders. To keep the surly shore-bound sailors entertained, their Fishal leaders had allowed those occupying Stove Point one gun per twenty men. Adding an unlimited quantity of powder, wadding, and lead, the usurpers had encouraged their irritable allies to engage in shooting contests. So, the idle pirates had amused themselves by lining local residents against walls.

The shooting had been continuous at first, day and night. After days of wanton slaughter, the few survivors who managed to flee told of horrific carnage beyond the senses to comprehend. It was a festival of death which El and the King imagined would not go unnoticed by Death himself. The dark lord, they surmised, would relish the bloodshed as he watched souls rise and fall from the comfort of his earthly throne at the bottom of Deep Lake.

Given the massacre of noncombatants, the boatswain and other members of the quest felt few qualms at the prospect of dispatching the occupying pirates. Nor, given the heavy toll exacted by the Fishals in the taking of Middlemount, would anyone lose sleep over having to deal with the usurping soldiers. And yet, the King had questions.

"When the harbor pirates send word of our ships," the King mused aloud. "Will not the Fishal soldiers come for a look?"

"My commodore considered that," said the boatswain. "But so long as we keep our distance, he suspects, and I agree, that the Fishals will remain at Deep Lake. They'll have their hands full there keeping the pirates in line. So, they're unlikely to split their force by sending soldiers our way. Commodore Dell tried to place himself in the shoes of the Fishal commander. And he decided that making too much of a fuss over the sighting of our three ships would draw unwelcome attention to the harbor and tempt the discontented Deep Lake pirates to think about abandoning their posts. My commodore believes that the invaders will ignore us, so long as we keep our present position. They'll likely think we plan a blockade and wish us luck doing so with only three ships."

Having given his lengthy answer, the boatswain turned to hear the King's response, but the old man was no longer there. Looking over his shoulder, he caught of glimpse of the King on the far side of the quarterdeck, carefully descending the ladder to reach El's cabin. Brightlamp sighed at the ignorance of landsmen. Probably the King hadn't heard a word.

Chapter 44

Death's Door

Given a choice between a lavish meal and a comfortable bowel movement, an old man might choose the latter. Also, a man of extreme years might forego an untroubled movement in favor of a stiff drink or, better yet, a visit from an old friend.

The King knocked and entered El's cabin. Sander was sitting at a writing desk jotting in a notebook. The deity seemed to be lying in the same position as the night before, eyes closed, his breathing shallow. The King and the surgeon exchanged a nod.

"Any change," inquired the King.

"No change. Still a bottomless sleep. The classic treatment is bleeding or vomiting or purging. But those drastic measures are based on the theory of 'unbalanced humors' to which I do not subscribe. For the present, he is breathing and little else."

"May I sit with him?" the King asked.

"Of course, though I doubt he'll know you're here."

The King reached for his hip flask, moved a chair near the bed, and took a drink. Then he wetted his fingers and pressed a hint of liquor to the patient's lips. Next, he held the deity's hand and spoke to El in the voice of the mind.

Can you hear me, my El?

El's thoughts came slowly and distantly, as from a deep well.

I can, El responded, *what news?*

We are lying offshore but not far enough. The wind is seaward. I can smell the stench of butchery wafting from Memora. I sense that our old enemy, Death, views the carnage at Stove Point as a fitting preamble to the world's ultimate destruction.

The King's thoughts were melancholy.

El responded in kind.

Yes, my friend, I agree that Death will consider the bloodshed at Stove Point a foretaste of the coming apocalypse. The first wave of innocent souls—animal and sentient—have filled the heavens, while the less-pure essences of the wicked join a wretched queue to populate Callus. And all this corporeal debris is accumulating, as it were, on Death's doorstep. It makes me tired.

El's thoughts seemed to tax him. He was silent for many moments. The King sat patiently and looked up to see Sander bent over his desk, apparently still intent on his writing. Looking closer, the monarch gathered the distinct impression that the surgeon was making entries in the ship's log.

Odd, the King thought, *for surely that is the commodore's task.* He felt El's hand twitch and turned his attention to his deity.

I have failed, El declared in a barely audible thought.

That outcome is not yet settled, the King assured the deity.

I have faith that the quest will prevail, El clarified. *Death hounds me, but the quest will restore me. Still, my failures haunt me and those failures are manifest.*

You judge too harshly, the King suggested.

And you are too slow to condemn, El responded. *Consider one of my most egregious failings. Centuries ago, one Dung—a single creature, mind you—defied me and I punished an entire race of innocents. Too late, I restored their dignity only to abandon them again. What will become of them?*

You made an example of a defiant race. Earthly rulers do the like every day. Such are the ways of mankind, the King declared.

Mankind, El scoffed, *such an amalgamation of saints and sinners. Warring and wailing. Cursing and blessing. Defiling the earth and restoring it. Such contradictions, such acrimony, such agony, such transitory beauty, such recurring strife.*

Complex creatures, the King mused, *and are they not fashioned in your own image?*

There, my old friend, sighed El, *there is the truth of it. I have passed to my lambs—to Wolfkind partly, to humans absolutely—my own shortcomings, my own temperaments, my own petty faults—*

And, interrupted the King, *your own wisdom, your compassion, your courage.*

This earnest exchange of thoughts between old comrades paused as shipboard sounds punctuated the night. Somewhere a cascade of bells sounded. Somewhere footfalls trod the wooden deck.

At last, El's thoughts returned to Stove Point and the matter of the quest, which compelled him to render a grim tally: *Souls fly to Velyn or fall to Callus, and flesh returns to Death—that is our old Agreement. And, as for Death's dark design, may it not come to pass. Amen.*

"Amen," said the King aloud.

Sander heard what he thought must be the end of a prayer, but still he attended to his writing. Although the King heard no more thoughts that afternoon, the monarch remained at El's bedside. In the silence which followed, the King nodded, then fell asleep.

An hour later Sander woke him.

"Sire, it is nearly dark. I must join Brightlamp on the quarterdeck. Can I get you anything before I depart?" Sander asked. The surgeon was dressed in a sea cap and greatcoat and holding his telescope.

"This bottomless sleep—is there nothing to be done?" asked the King. "El has told me Death is pulling him from us and that only the quest can prevent this disaster."

"He said as much to me before he slipped away to sleep," said Sander in a tone that suggested he thought the so-called dying deity was out of his head.

"Has he told you also of the peril which Death may visit upon the world?"

"I know the scriptures have prophesied a terrible flood," said Sander. "But do you truly believe this old man—my corporeal patient languishing here on this cot—is the sovereign of our fathers? The deity of the scriptures?"

"In a word, 'yes.' Do you find it so difficult to believe?" asked the King.

"You may not know this, Your Majesty, but I am a betting man," said Sander. "And I would say the chances that you and I are witnessing the death of a deity are long odds indeed."

"So, you believe El is dying and yet you do not believe in our quest?"

"Believe in the quest?" asked Sander. "Well, let me say that I believe in my brother. I believe Alphonse can achieve a decisive military victory here on Memora. A victory which will free your island and turn the tide in this war with the Fishals and their pirate hoard. Furthermore, I believe this can be done without the aid of a magical quest."

"And yet only yesterday I heard you and Percy speaking of miracles."

"That was yesterday," said Sander. "And I was merely humoring Percy and now Percy is dead. This is a war, Majesty. People die in war. That is reality. A war is the starkest reality imaginable. I maintain my brother is tangled up in this quest business for one reason only: because it is a way to take the fight to the pirates and their Fishal keepers. I am a man of science, sir. Do I believe that this dying relic is a deity? I do not. Do I believe that a dog can talk? I have seen that done at a carnival. Do I believe that the girl Ruth is a witch who communes with the dead—?"

"No need to answer that one," the King sighed. "I imagine you were going to tell me that 'dead is dead' or some such chestnut of folk wisdom. So, you are a man of science? I suppose we should count ourselves fortunate that—oh never mind. You will be needed on deck, no doubt. For my part, I will remain here and commune with my deity. I have no desire to stare at my unfortunate homeland and besides I'm feeling quite tired."

Sander left El's cabin. As he climbed the ladder to reach the main deck the surgeon and the King he left behind each shook his head as each marveled at the other's folly.

"Science," sighed the King aloud.

"Faith," scoffed Sander.

And, as the darkness gathered, each man in his own way wondered whether allowing the weary world to perish in a flood was, after all, such a bad idea.

Chapter 45

Eyes on Stove Point

Watching perils unfold from afar, compelled to observe, unable to assist or intervene—these limitations describe what an omniscient deity must endure. It is the price of having allowed his creatures to exercise free will. Military commanders must assume a similar role. A deity does not need a telescope nor even an ear trumpet to know when those he loves are in danger. A commander must use whatever means he can to follow distant events. A spectator's desire to intercede is seldom rewarded, and yet, neither a dispassionate divinity nor an anxious mortal has the audacity to look away.

It was nearly dark. The boatswain began to wonder where the surgeon was. In less than an hour the purging of Stove Point would commence. Brightlamp wanted Sander by his side. It would be difficult enough for two observers to follow events on shore in the dark at this distance. But it would be impossible without Sander's help. Two telescopes would be better than one.

Sander had remained behind to minister to his elderly patient and address any injuries among those assaulting Stove Point. The doctor was peeved but, for his part, the boatswain was thankful to have the commodore's brother onboard. It was bad enough having the younger Dell in harm's way. The boatswain and *Catspaw's* crew would have been beside themselves with worry if both brothers were in danger.

To succeed, Sander's surgical assault depended on the element of surprise, the silent efficiency of Seth's assassins, and the intoxication of the pirates. The invading force of idle pirates had been molded into a sprawling, brawling mass of murderous humanity by a combination of circumstances which paired the absence of activity with the presence of liquor. The harbor was filled to the brim with pirate ships. Clearly the pirates outnumbered the soldiers charged with supervising them. But the scheming Fishals kept each harbor crew small, divided, and perpetually drunk. These tactics insured the brigands would remain on the island. If not for the liquor and the watchful Fishals, the pirates—not only those at Stove Point but also those from Deep Lake—would likely abandon the island in as little time as it took them to hoist anchor.

The Fleet of Deliverance had arrived too late to save the Stove Point islanders. By sailing to blockade the remaining island harbors, the rest of the divided fleet prayed they would be at their stations in time to prevent the slaughter of other Memorians. In the fleet's sweep around the island, their cannons would sink any pirate ship they encountered. Marines would be landed to safeguard other seaside towns and harbors. If needed, the fleets' marines would march overland from multiple directions to Deep Lake to help finish off the enemy.

Dell and the boatswain hoped it wouldn't come to that. It was all well and good to speak of completing the quest. That goal was presumably a noble and essential end in itself, if one believed in fairy tales, which the boatswain did not. The seaman was not irreligious, he was simply being practical.

His thinking ran thus: even if the quest was legitimate and actually managed to restore El and thereby rescue the world, the rescued world would still be in jeopardy. Quest or no quest, there was much to do. In liberating Memora, it was essential to limit casualties among the fleet. To accomplish this, the boatswain was reluctant to rely on magic.

To liberate the present island, the pirates at Stove Point would have to be silenced by stealth and the larger force at Deep Lake would have to be engaged and annihilated the old-fashioned way. It would be the fleet's 300 sailors and marines, twenty King's guards, plus a handful of questing warriors, and a dog, against well over 2,000 pirates and as many as 500 Fishal soldiers. That was a tall order and impossible without the canal and the mortars.

The woman Ann and the others were wrapped up in their mystic quest and its goal to save El and the world. That was as it may be, but Boatswain Brightlamp was a practical military man with tangible problems. If the quest was successful and the cup secured, that might keep the world from drowning.

So be it.

If, in the process of fulfilling the quest, they not only saved the world, but also vanquished the hostile forces holding Memora, that would be well. Yet, the world's struggle would be far from over. Memora might be freed, and the world might remain un-flooded, but Middlemount would still be in the hands of the Fishals. To achieve the challenging task of freeing that captive kingdom, the fleet and the marines would need to be as much intact as possible. Quest or no, any fighter lost, and any ship sunk on their side in the fight for Memora would lessen the odds of success. El's quest may have captured the attention of some, but the boatswain considered it to be merely one battle in a much larger war.

It was a lot to think about.

How fares the ride to Deep Lake? Brightlamp wondered. Then he suppressed that thought. *We have no shortage of impossibilities. Best to tackle one impossible mission at a time,* he reminded himself as he returned his attention to the dark island.

The nighttime assault on Stove Point was not a rescue mission. There were few natives on this end of the island left alive to liberate. The goal was to exterminate the pirates. To this end, Seth, Mastro, and four dozen sailors had been carried ashore in the yacht. Their successful landfall beyond the town represented the reliable vessel's final daring afternoon run along the Memorian coast.

The boatswain swung his telescope shoreward, knowing Seth and the sailors under his command were hidden there in the grotto and waiting to advance after dark. He prayed not to see them, hoping they would remain undetected. Sander's night surgery would depend on absolute surprise.

Brightlamp sensed a motion beside him and turned to see Sander training his telescope upon the same nondescript patch of Memorian coastline.

Lowering his telescope, Sander reported that both the King and the alleged divinity were resting. It seemed that the old men had retired from the field. It would be up to the youngsters now.

"I don't know which one is loonier," said Sander. "The dithering King or the dying deity."

"They're both showing their age," said the boatswain. "What is El's prognosis?"

"Still unconscious," said Sander. "If he lives two days, I'll be very much surprised."

"Some would say two days are all we need," said the boatswain.

"Hmm," said Sander and he looked again toward the far shore.

"How will we know?" asked Brightlamp. He knew the signal as well as the surgeon. Asking the question was his way of making certain everything which could be done had been done.

"When the pirate pennants are struck and Middlemount banners hoisted in their place, we will know the plan has worked," said Sander.

"A definitive signal," said Brightlamp. "But one which will only be visible by morning light. If the pirate flags remain aloft at dawn, we shall have no choice but to sail in range and bombard the harbor."

"And if that bombardment is out of sequence with the flooding—" Sander was unwilling to complete the thought.

"Then all shall be for naught," said the boatswain and he clapped his telescope closed. Sander continued to stare toward the island, though there was little to be seen. He was reminding himself of his own words to the war council.

"The enemy in the harbor must be eliminated," the doctor had declared. "Our ships dare not fire on them lest the guns injure Memorian survivors or be heard inland by the Deep Lake defenders. I am no military man, though I am somewhat skilled at surgery. Our plan calls for sailors who are fleetest of foot, under the able field leadership of Seth Stone Bride, to dispatch the harbor pirates. With fortune, our men will confound and obliterate the pirates by the handful so that barges may be secured, armed, and launched without delay."

In making his presentation before the council, Sander found his tone surprisingly clinical for a physician sworn to "do no harm."

Such, he told himself at the time, *are the wages of war.*

To realize Sander's calculating vision, Seth and the others were to take up hidden positions in the Memorian grotto caves. Concealed there, they would wait for night to infiltrate the docks, the town, and the castle. Seth's guerillas were armed with the silent weapons of cold steel and stout leather, with short swords and knives, casting nets and garrotes. Their mission was to take the enemy down, singly and in twos and threes, without firing a shot or allowing the enemy to discharge so much as a pistol.

Concluding his recollections and his inspection of the far shore, Sander lowered his telescope. Then he and the boatswain stood in silence on the quarterdeck looking without the aid of instruments at the darkening outline of Memora Island.

"Mr. Hoy," Brightlamp shouted for the gunner.

"Aye, sir."

"We'll have the lanterns if you please.

"Aye, sir."

Chapter 46

Assassins

It is best not to think too much in a battle. Moreover, when the fight is a dishonest one which takes an enemy from behind or in his sleep, it is best not to think at all. To bombard or shoot an unseen or distant enemy from afar, these are removed actions. To creep close enough to slit a throat or garrote a victim's breath or slide a blade into the base of the neck, these things are highly personal. To commit such compulsory acts repeatedly in cold blood, in the dark, is to put one's humanity into a deep, dark pocket of rationalization and pray for the strength to fish it out again.

On Memora's rocky coast, well-hidden and awaiting total darkness, Seth looked out toward the open sea. It was cloudy with neither moon nor stars to lighten the sky. A good omen, he thought. But he also prayed that, after his mission was done, those same clouds would part to light his mate's path to Deep Lake. Was he asking too much of the weather?

Focusing on his task, he studied the dark water. He could barely detect the white sails of *Catspaw* and her sister ships standing beyond the harbor shoals, well out of cannon range. It was a ruse intended to draw the attention of the pirates offshore. Seth and the others were hunkered down inside a cave preparing to divide and conquer the murderous pirates who occupied Stove Point and Stone Bride Castle. He was under strict orders to dispatch the invaders without assistance from the fleet and as silently as possible.

Seth watched a moment more until he saw the distant ships hang lanterns—the signal to begin. He closed his small pocket telescope and placed it inside a tightly wound nest of Middlemount banners which he carried in a shoulder satchel. Having secured the instrument and flags, he moved farther into the cave. Intent on rejoining the men, he thought of the vital instructions he had earlier imparted to them.

Silence must be our watchword and stealth our maxim, he'd told them. *Our goal is to kill, not fight.*

In the growing darkness and secreted in the grotto, Seth reviewed his troops. Each man was dressed in black from head-to-toe. To perfect their camouflage, he'd directed all—excepting the dark, hulking Mastro—to use a mixture of coal tar and charcoal to completely blacken their shiny faces and hands. Then he had each man shake his torso to eliminate any bauble or loose metal that might have jangled.

"We will be the wind," Seth encouraged the men as they knelt in a dark circle around him. "We will strike quickly and quietly. We must glide forward, slaying as we go, until we have purged the town, the harbor, and the castle. One shot fired by the enemy will be one shot too many."

"Aye," the men agreed although they sounded hesitant.

"Remember, this is by no means a mission of manly toe-to-toe combat. But there is no shame in what we do. These unprincipled brigands have wantonly slain unarmed and innocent noncombatants. We are their vengeance. We are the deity's holy gleaners pulling noxious weeds. Understood?"

"Aye."

Seth glanced over his shoulder, studying the grotto entrance one last time to ensure that it was sufficiently dark to proceed.

"Disperse then in your assigned pairs. And—" he added with a sincere tone, "be careful out there. I want you all alive when this is over."

The men scattered two-by-two out of the grotto and into the inky landscape as Seth turned to Mastro.

"I have no doubt that you will try to 'be the wind,' but I fear your bulk will prove your undoing. Mastro?" he seemed to have misplaced the giant.

"Here, sir," The huge pirate's voice sounded at his elbow.

"Touché," Seth acknowledged. "Now, my enormous wind, let's go hunting."

As Sander's surgery began, Seth and the others crept forward to prey on the unsuspecting pirates. If the men were lucky, their victims would be drunk or preoccupied with thoughts of the distant ships riding just outside the harbor. If fortune favored Seth, the pirate, and the sailors, the enemy would be unfocused and not expecting a land attack.

Fortune *was* with them. As the night progressed, efficiently hunted pirates fell silently to nimble assassins. Cloaked in darkness, the quiet pairs did their work until the town, the harbor, and the castle were freed of the vermin invaders.

Just before dawn, when every shore pirate had been silenced, the attackers slipped into the placid waters of Stove Point Bay. Swimming deftly and climbing without a sound, they occupied each harbor ship. Those few pirates remaining onboard awoke to find their vessels overrun with black-clad warriors. Cornered, the brigands begged for mercy and surrendered without firing a shot.

Exhausted by their killing spree and feeling reluctant to continue the slaughter as dawn approached, the assassins clapped the surviving pirates in irons and packed them into the cargo holds of their captured ships. Upon confirming that the castle was purged as well, Seth ordered his men to strike the pirate colors and raise Middlemount banners.

The cautious assassins had done their work without losing a man and, at dawn, three friendly ships sailed landward to occupy Stove Point Harbor. It was still early in the morning when Brightlamp set crews to work rounding up barges and preparing mortars for the inland assault. Standing on the quarterdeck beside Colonel Questo, Brightlamp watched with satisfaction until the work of preparing the mortars was complete. Then he moved his gaze toward the mouth of the empty canal and seemed to be looking farther inland.

"Thinking of your commodore ashore?" asked Questo.

"He's not much of a horseman, I'm afraid," admitted Brightlamp.

"I too was thinking of my lieutenant who is also far inland. This will be the lad's first independent command and his first-ever on horseback."

"It seems our situations are exactly reversed," observed Brightlamp. "Your second and my commodore are there. And here we stand, me a naval second and you the ranking officer of King John's guards. Meantime, others are in both places. It seems to me that this war and the quest are all a-tangle."

"War makes a muddle," agreed Questo. "Let us hope our efforts will carry the day."

"Indeed, let us hope so. Because—depending on what one believes—this dawn might mark the beginning of the world's final day. Excuse me please, sir." Brightlamp leaned over the quarterdeck railing and shouted to the gunner whom he'd enlisted as his mate, "Mister Hoy! We shall have the men rest by degrees if you please. Lookouts aloft, armed marines on each pirate deck, and a guard on each barge."

"Aye, sir," said the gunner with the broad grin of a man pleased to see one of his fellows elevated to command.

Provisional Commodore Brightlamp clapped his hands behind his back. A moment later, he suggested the Colonel might go below to sleep. Then, after surveying the harbor a moment more, Brightlamp retired to his own temporary quarters. There was nothing to be done now but trust his commodore and await the flood. Thus, it came to pass that neither Questo nor Brightlamp was on duty when the pirate counterattack came.

Chapter 47

The Missed Pair

In war it is best to remember that the enemy always gets a vote.

Two brigands had been overlooked in the predawn efforts to capture and imprison the occupants of pirate ships anchored in Stove Point Harbor. A pair of Ectrican pirates, Stewprod and Zealfoot, had been drunk and napping in the stern long boats when Seth's assassins swept onboard. When the overlooked pirates woke at dawn and peeked out beneath the canvas boat cover, even their muddled minds comprehended the situation. Remaining hidden, they sat upon the keel of the long boat and conferred quietly.

"How many?" asked Stewprod.

"Too many and well-armed," answered Zealfoot.

"Surrender?" asked Stewprod.

"Not me," responded Zealfoot. "I'll die first."

"Likely we are dead either way," agreed Stewprod.

They hatched a plan to creep by degrees from the safety of the long boat to the stern magazine where they would secure pistols, powder, and shot. Then they would free their imprisoned shipmates and assemble on the poop deck. Situated there, the last vestige of the crew of the occupied pirate frigate might be fortunate enough to use the pistols and the pivoting stern-chaser cannonade to inflict casualties on the enemy. They shook hands and pledged their fortunes.

"For *Naomi*," said Zealfoot, invoking the name of their ship.

"For me mudder," said Stewprod. "Whom I never knowed, but she died a lady."

"For *Naomi* and yore sainted mudder," amended Zealfoot and he led the way.

Unaware of the plot unfolding in the stern, Sander, the King, Seth, and Mastro had boarded *Naomi* by the bow. Sander had been summoned to check on the health of a survivor who was discovered in the brig when the assassins herded the captive pirates below. The man claimed to be the Stove Point mayor being held for ransom. The King had been enlisted to identify the man and Seth and Mastro had come along to collect weapons and powder.

The visitors, having been helped aboard by the marine guards, parted company. The King and Sander followed the guards to the main cabin to interview the alleged mayor while Seth and Mastro walked sternward toward the magazine. Mastro topped the aft stairway first and saw the pirates as they aimed the stern-chaser.

"Back!" he shouted and stepped in front of Seth as the pirates fired, propelling a hail of iron in their direction. A cluster of deadly pellets struck Mastro, throwing him against Seth and knocking both men backward onto the main deck. The fleet marines onboard responded instantly and fired three vigorous volleys into the stern before the ambushing pirates could manage another shot.

When the powder smoke cleared, five pirates lay dead, and one was mortally wounded. The five were strangers, the one was intimately known. Seth knelt on the main deck. He held Mastro's bloody head and looked into the huge man's eyes as the pirate asked "Father?"

"Yes," Seth answered. "I am here."

"I tried to be good," the pirate murmured.

"You were my best good boy," Seth assured him.

Mastro smiled and closed his eyes. Seth held the fading man until the pirate breathed his last. Then he wept doubly, adding to tears shed for a lost friend the still more bitter tears of a father losing a child. Each tear became crystal and each crystal hardened into a sparkling gem. The marines gathered round and removed their caps and, though the deck was filled with a carpet of shining jewels, not a man stooped so low as to pinch a single treasure.

The marines carried Mastro to *Catspaw's* long boat and gently laid his body in the bow. Sander, the King, and the rescued mayor sat with Seth in the stern as the crew rowed across the harbor. Intent on seeing to the disposition of Mastro's body and praying his soul to Velyn, the grieving party failed to notice that Seth himself was bleeding. By the time the boat reached *Catspaw*, Seth's injury was far advanced, and the party prepared to pray for two.

Learning of the pirate's treachery, Brightlamp rowed alone to the *Naomi*, descended to the gun deck, loaded four of the ship's cannons, and nosed them downward. Packing each cannon in sail cloth to muffle the sound, he fired them in turn until the ship was thoroughly holed. Then he rowed away and left the scuttled vessel to sink—jewels, dead pirates, and all.

Chapter 48

The Flood Delayed

Mice and men may scheme. But a plan—no matter its certainty—can dissolve in a twinkling to nothing.

Far away on the inland portion of Memora Island, but still short of their goal of reaching Deep Lake, the quest faced a dilemma. Confronted by the inexplicable disappearance of two guardsmen, the women had dismounted at dusk and signaled the guards to do the same. All save Lieutenant Collin, whom the Princess had dispatched to retrieve the rear guard. That rider returned moments later, and breathless, with news that the rear guard was nowhere to be found. Hearing this sad news, the Princess ordered the mounts rounded up and placed in a willow thicket under heavy watch. Finally, Ann dispersed the men to establish a defensive parameter while she, the witch, and the commodore sought higher ground.

When Esau did not materialize, Ruth and Ann presumed the dog had been killed or captured. The missing guards and horses, coupled with the disappearance of Esau, could mean but one thing. They'd been discovered and were likely surrounded by armed pirates. To have tried maneuvering in the darkness would have been to risk total destruction. So, they sought cover and waited for sunrise.

The night passed without incident and, with the breaking dawn, came the time for a decision.

"Ideas?" Ann asked the other two.

"Too hard to evaluate our situation from this restricted vantage point," the witch replied. "The sun is up. Time now for this creature of the air to earn her title."

"A moment—will not the men be amazed to see her rising?" The Princess addressed this question to the commodore.

"I fancy they'll get used to it," said Dell.

With a wink to the commodore, Ruth launched herself effortlessly into the air without so much as squatting to obtain momentum. No musket fired and no shout rang out. If the enemy was near, they were either napping or blind. In an instant, her form was barely visible in the sky.

"Our beauty also flies I see," said Collin. The royal guards' lieutenant had crawled forward to lay supine beside the others and join them in staring at the sky.

"Like a lamb turned to hawk," said Ann absently.

"Hmm," observed the lieutenant. "Despite having magic on our side, we are at a great disadvantage here. Four men down and reduced now to thirteen."

"A baker's dozen," noted the commodore.

"And without a recipe to follow," the lieutenant frowned. His demeanor suggested he was uncertain who was in charge of their present situation. Does a deposed Princess outrank a ship's commodore on land, he seemed to wonder?

"Here comes our hawk with instructions," said Ann as Ruth's form reappeared. The resourceful witch landed heavily nearby and scurried toward them in a crouching trot. Seeing concern reflected in Ruth's face, Ann sent the lieutenant away to ready the guards. The Princess wanted the others to be prepared to sprint to their mounts and either attack or flee on her orders.

"Deep Lake is not far," Ruth said and then she paused, feeling the need to catch her breath. "Sorry—I came down a bit too precipitously—out of practice. What you need to know is this: the lake is just ahead, no pirates in sight, but between us and the lake there is a creature."

"A creature?" asked the commodore.

"It seems a dark bear, but huge and standing upright."

"Hmm," said Ann. "A Wolfkind perhaps?"

"Very like," said the witch.

Rumors of wild Wolfkind persisted in all the far-flung kingdoms. Occasionally a supposed carcass was brought forth by an intrepid explorer, only to be dismissed as the remains of a bear. A bear was similar in size and configuration to an untamed Wolfkind, but far from the thing itself.

"I'll go," said Ann as she stood up, heedless of exposure, and called the men to her.

Ought I to drop a boulder on its feral skull? offered Ruth in the voice of the mind.

An impolite greeting for one of my relations, however distant, protested the Princess, reserving her thoughts for the witch alone.

As impolite, retorted Ruth, *as snatching our men and animals?*

The guards arrived and Ann ordered them to gather the mounts. "Ruth and the commodore will lead you to the lake," she told them. As the men departed, the Princess spoke urgently to the commodore. "Take these," she said, handing the keys to Dell. "If I fail, take my place and open the locks. You know the sequence. The keys are numbered. Go ready the men. Ruth will join you shortly."

The commodore took the keys, nodded his understanding, and hurried to join the others.

Does this separation mark the beginning of my charge? he asked himself. *The King charged me to be guided by the younger woman. Does my role begin now?*

When the men were out of listening range, Ann spoke aloud to Ruth. "The Wolfkind's abductions were probably instinctual reactions," she presupposed. "With fortune, our men and animals are imprisoned, but unharmed. From your description, I presume the creature is a wild male and naturally jealous of his territory. He might even be protecting his mate and cub. Just now, when you saw him, was he stationary or circling?"

"The latter," said the witch.

"He is marking his territory then—almost certainly. He has the wind and our scent. I will part from the troop and move quickly forward. With luck, my scent will reach him first and mask the escape of you and the others." She removed her outer vest leaving only her tunic to cover her torso. "The better to sweat," she explained. "Go, Ruth, and gather the men. Instruct them not to mount, but rather to walk steadily and avoid the woods. But by no means are they to run or follow me. Understood?"

Ruth nodded but did not depart.

"What?" Ann asked impatiently.

"Only wondering this," said Ruth. "Which part of my suggestion that you stay alive did you fail to comprehend?"

"No worries," said the Princess. "I have every intention of surviving this wrinkle."

"As you wish," Ruth relented. "Just remember this particular wrinkle is about twice as large as an oxcart including the ox."

"Go," said Ann.

"Already gone," said Ruth as she left to gather the men and mounts with the goal of leading them in a wide arc to avoid the woods. Ann watched the witch go. Then, wearing a sheathed sword, she rushed toward the trees.

"El," the Princess said aloud. "I know your hearing and your vision are weakened, but I pray that you will see and hear me and give me the strength and wisdom to overcome this obstacle." She received no confirmation. She hadn't expected one. Still, she offered the prayer and began singing as she neared the dark woods. She sang aloud a warrior's battle psalm, a song of hope.

"Nowie, Nowie, Nowie, lord good almighty, into these jaws I step, into this mouth I stride, grant me strength and give me skill, to reach the other side alive."

"Amen." A booming voice added from beyond the first line of trees.

"Nastel," Ann uttered the universal Wolfkind greeting.

"Pastel," came the expected reply. "But no closer."

Ann stopped and held both hands out, the palms facing the voice, showing she held no weapon.

"Remove thy sword," the voice demanded.

"Nastel," Ann restated the greeting and unbuckled the belt. She let the sheath and sword fall to the ground. Then she took one more step.

"Stop there!" the voice commanded.

"Show yourself, brother," the Princess stopped moving but crouched, expecting an attack. Ann wondered if her fluctuating powers would be equal to a wrestling match with an untamed Wolfkind. A moment of silence followed before she heard rustling as the huge form of a dark male Wolfkind emerged from the trees to her left.

"You come from opposite my sword hand," said Ann. "That is a wise move."

"A guess merely," said the Wolfkind whose excellent speech suggested he was not entirely wild. "Most of thy hairless sorts are right-handed."

"The men you took were of the hairless sort."

"Two of these surprised me when I was on one leg and urinating. I reacted instinctively. Thou canst understand, surely."

"Yes, but they are missing nevertheless and what of my other men?"

"Captured also along with their mounts. I was done with my business when I saw that second pair and used cunning to surprise them from behind. They will not be harmed by my hand. All will be held for a time, then ransomed."

"Your intentions are noted. Be assured we will return to ransom those four. But, at present because our quest is urgent, may we pass?"

"In saying 'we,' thou attempt to mislead me," said the Wolfkind as he began to circle the Princess. "For thy troop has already skirted my woods. I saw them going with the hawk woman and the officers at their head. To safeguard thy men, that avoidance was wisely done."

"Thank you. And with your permission, I'll join them, and we'll trouble you no further."

The Wolfkind raised a single massive paw directing the Princess to remain where she was. "You spoke of a quest. What quest dost thou mean? And how art thou a human and yet thou carry the Wolfkind scent? What magic is this?"

"El's doing," stated the Princess flatly for she had no intention of wasting time to bring this creature up to date.

"Our lord? He lives?"

"Barely. Hence our quest. May I?" Ann motioned toward her fallen sword.

"Take up thy weapon," the Wolfkind said. "Art thou here to kill the pirates?"

"If we must and if their deaths serve our quest."

"Thou must needs kill them all," the Wolfkind snarled. "Kill them as they did my mate and cubs."

"It pains me to hear of your loss. We too have lost our friends."

"I am heartily sorry to hear of that pain. And I apologize for my rudeness. But I am not myself. I have been idling here in these woods, grieving my loss when I ought to have taken the fight to those barbarous invaders." The Wolfkind sat heavily down, as if pressed by the weight of a heavy load. "This grief—it is such a burden." The creature sat for a moment more with his shoulders drooping and Ann was on the point of leaving when the Wolfkind suddenly spoke. "I beg pardon, but might this be thy magic animal?" He held forth his huge paw, the hair of which seemed to be squirming of its own accord.

"That is the deity's dog you have there. And I would consider it a favor if you would release him unharmed."

"*I* release *him*?" The Wolfkind chortled despite his grief. "It is he who holds me in the iron grip of his unseen jaws."

"Esau," said Ann gently. "Let our friend go please."

The Wolfkind's paw ceased to flutter and the ground beside the creature erupted in a cloud of dust as the invisible dog dropped free.

"Tastes of chicken this beast," said Esau as his form reappeared. He left the Wolfkind's side as he shook his body and padded over to stand beside the Princess.

"The captives are nearby," the Wolfkind stated. "I will go there to release them and their mounts. I will bring them back. I would invite thee to accompany me, but those men are blindfolded, and the place is secret. I'll bring them hither, then thou may pass."

The creature rose heavily to his feet and turned toward the woods.

"Whilst at your lair," said Ann. "Why not gird for battle? Our quest has room for one such as you."

"Wouldst have me?"

"Wouldst."

"Wait here then. I'll return shortly with thy men, thy horses, and my weapon."

Within fifteen minutes, the Wolfkind returned as good as his word. Ushering the unharmed men and animals before him, he brought up the rear carrying a huge double-bladed axe.

"What is thy name?" asked the Princess after she'd dispatched the freed guards with orders to locate the troop and inform the commodore that she, the dog, and another warrior would be hurrying through the woods to join them.

"I am called Bindbuilder by my family. Although I am now the last of my kind on this island and— Why dost thou smile, is my name so comical?"

"No indeed. I apologize for my unseemly reaction. Well met, Bindbuilder," said the Princess.

As she, Esau, and their new ally rushed through the woods to join the others, Ann reached the Wolfkind with her thoughts and told of her ordeal, her transformation, the appearance of the Southern Fleet, the conversion of the witch, and as many other details as she could rightly touch on before they emerged on the other side of the trees. She included a report of her choice of surname.

"Stone Bride you say? Exactly like our dead Princess and her kingly father—that is a tale indeed," said Bindbuilder as they stood on a rise overlooking Deep Lake.

Ann was about to add to her narrative when they heard a distant rumbling. She had no way of knowing that Brightlamp had just fired cannons to scuttle the pirate ship *Naomi*.

"Thunder," said Bindbuilder. "A storm is coming."

"Consider that prescient sound our call to action!" shouted Ann as she spied the troop below and began to sprint in their direction. "Come! Make haste! We have two leagues yet to cover and our task is already overdue!"

Chapter 49

The Flood Commenced

Truth alone is strong. Truth which is shared is invincible.

While Ann led Bindbuilder and Esau down to join the others, Commodore Dell watched the unlikely trio descending the hill.

"Your keys," said the commodore when Ann and the others arrived. Then he eyed the Wolfkind and added under his breath, and just loud enough for the Princess and the lieutenant to hear, "A complication I see."

"Another volunteer to bolster our quest," said Ann.

"Hmm," said Lieutenant Collin who was, to say the least, skeptical about adding the untamed behemoth to their troop. "The men will resent one who has mishandled their fellows," he told the Princess.

"He might have done worse," suggested Ann. "And, though it stretches the truth, why not say the Wolfkind mistook our picket riders for pirates."

"The fog of war," admitted the lieutenant. "It is a far better story than to suggest the creature would have them for breakfast."

"I agree," said Ann.

While the witch and the guards scouted ahead, the rest of the troop moved quickly but carefully, skirting the edge of the woods—striving to keep themselves in dwindling cover as they approached the headwaters of the

Stone Bride Canal. The Wolfkind and the dog kept pace with the riders. As they traveled, Ann sent thoughts to Bindbuilder so that their new ally might better understand their plan.

We are nearing the Deep Lake Dam and the beginning of the blocked canal, she spoke to Bindbuilder in the voice of the mind. *The outlet runs steadily downward from the lake to Stove Point Harbor. Unlocking the valves on this end will release the lake waters and spawn the flood needed to bring up our mortars. Without the aid of those deadly weapons, our meager force will be no match for the pirates in a ground war. According to informants, at least two heavily armed battalions surround Deep Lake. Even with the help of sailors and marines from Catspaw and her sister ships, the pirates and their Fishal masters will most likely outnumber our alliance twenty to one. Only the mortars will balance the odds and only the flood can bring the mortars and only our troop can bring the flood.*

Bindbuilder absorbed this information and praised the Princess' plan. But he made an insightful suggestion. The Wolfkind warrior believed their human companions—who were also risking their lives—deserved to know the entirety of the quest. Ann agreed and rapidly repeated the complete story aloud until everyone present knew every detail, including the coincidence of the name which the Wolfkind and Percy shared.

So, there will be another Bindbuilder waiting in Velyn, if and when this unworthy vessel of mine rises to that lofty rest, the Wolfkind speculated.

And rise you will, Ann thought, *if I have anything to say in the matter.*

Moments later, Ruth and the pickets galloped back, and the troop was obliged to halt.

"We must soon descend," said the witch. "What's amiss?"

Ruth sensed a difference in the demeanor of the men and gave Ann a quizzical look.

"They know everything," said the Princess.

"So, the cat is from the bag," laughed the witch. "And that which was hidden has bubbled up to become understood in common. I presume these present men will share their newly acquired knowledge with our rear guard."

"I will inform the others," promised Collin. "Hardest to explain," he added "will be the talking dog."

"Amen," breathed Esau, his voice betraying relief at being able to speak openly.

Thinking Ruth peeved by her honesty, Ann began to apologize in the voice of the mind.

"No matter," Ruth assured her. "Let us speak openly. Our honesty may prove our most decisive weapon. The men will fight all the harder in a cause they understand."

Within half a league of the lake, the riders dismounted and led their animals down a steep stairway—a precipitous series of crude steps carved into one bank of the canal. Bindbuilder and the jabbering dog followed.

Without the King's detailed maps of the island's interior, the stairway, obscured by brambles and other cloying undergrowth, would have been impossible to locate. Reaching the bed of the canal, the troop remounted. Then, convinced that their movements in the deep channel would not be observed and anxious to make up for lost time, they threw caution aside and galloped with haste toward the dam. Their destination was the valve tower at the far terminus of the canal.

Galloping forward, they fixed their eyes on the distant tower. It was a tall and massive structure composed of sturdy brick. The tower was an imposing edifice and yet it was dwarfed by the broad earthen dam which arced around it for a thousand yards in both directions.

As the riders neared the tower and its surrounding dam, with Bindbuilder's broad strides and Esau's energetic paws keeping pace, the fine hairs on the back of Ann's neck began to prickle and stand on end. Those dormant hairs, which had previously seemed so useless, were responding to apprehension as she contemplated the danger. For it was steadily dawning on the Princess just how vulnerable was the troop.

Caught there in the spine of the canal, the men and mounts would be forfeit should the waters of Deep Lake breach the colossal barrier which stretched before them. She, the witch, the dog, and the Wolfkind would likely survive that cascade, but the mortal humans and animals at her side would not be so fortunate. Should the commodore, the lieutenant, and the others die, her increasingly human sensibilities would find it impossible to forgive herself. Her trepidation was particularly poignant since breaching the dam was precisely what she intended to do.

Reaching the base of the tower, the troop again dismounted. At Ann's insistence, the guardsmen under the joint command of Commodore Dell and Lieutenant Collin vacated the canal. Leading all mounts up the nearest staircase, the men tethered horses and mules safely above the deep channel and remained with the animals. At the same time, Ann sent Ruth, Bindbuilder, and Esau to occupy the opposite side of the canal.

When the Princess saw her divided forces arrayed on both banks of the canal and in position to watch for and warn of any pirate movements from the direction of Deep Lake, she began her part. Securing the keys to her belt and positioning her scabbard so her sheathed sword clung to her back, she climbed the tower's exterior ladder—a direct route to reach the valve locks above. Ann was thirty feet above the canal floor, clinging to the narrow ladder, when she stepped from the rungs and entered the valve tunnel.

Locating the first lock, she inserted the stout key, released the first valve, and felt the shudder of cascading water pulsating far below. Ann did not pretend to understand the principles of hydraulics she was putting into play with the release of each of the seven valve locks which lined the stone tunnel. She merely followed the King's explicit instructions as she turned each key in order. Proceeding on faith, she marveled at the noise and seismic tremors which intensified each time she unlocked a valve. Only when she had unlocked the final valve and scampered back through the tunnel and out onto the ladder did she see what her seemingly innocuous turning of seven keys in seven locks had wrought.

On either side of the ladder and barely far enough away to avoid knocking her off, massive torrents of water spewed forth from multiple points along the face of the dam. So great was the force of these cascades that Ann realized they must be escaping from solid portals within the earthen dam—otherwise the force would surely have collapsed the dam itself. And yet, this awesome display was no reckless discharge of water. It was an immense show of hydraulic power, but also a controlled event.

It took only a matter of moments for the cascading water to cover the broad channel of the canal at the base of the tower. Soon the high waterfalls, which had at first plunged far to reach the canal floor below, were spilling more gently into an ever-deepening flow. As the level in the canal continued to rise, the tumbling water—while retaining its power—seemed to reach a sort of equilibrium. Then the cascade became almost gentle and not unlike an ordinary stream of water flowing from an ordinary pitcher to fill an ordinary copper bathtub.

Watching the water, the Princess was hypnotized into inaction. Thus, she missed the urgent shouting of Ruth who yelled at her and gesticulated from the far bank.

At last, recognizing that the Princess could not hear her, the witch took flight and soared toward the ladder.

"They're coming!" Ruth shouted in the Princess' ear as she hovered next to Ann's position high on the face of the tower.

"I have nowhere to go," shouted Ann, suddenly realizing that she could climb neither up nor down.

"Put your arms around my neck," the witch shouted. "And pray I have the strength to carry both of us."

Seeing no alternative, the Princess obeyed and instantly the pair was plummeting toward the flood. Ann heard Ruth screaming and felt the witch straining to rise. Their toes skimmed the water as Ruth battled to keep them aloft. Moments later, the flying pair struggled skyward to tumble onto the far bank where Bindbuilder and Esau waited.

Righting herself, Ann looked across the canal. The commodore, the lieutenant, the guards, and all the mounts were there and safe from the flood. But the two groups stood on opposite banks. There would be no joining of forces.

"Have you enough strength to fly across?" she asked Ruth.

"Yes."

"Go then and order the commodore and the others to retreat back along the canal. With luck, they'll meet the barges coming upstream."

"Knowing what they now know, the men will prefer to stand and fight," said the witch. "Especially our commodore."

"Convince them otherwise. We need them alive."

"I'll do my best," Ruth promised as she rocketed across the canal.

"Where is the enemy?" Ann asked hurriedly as she turned to Bindbuilder and the dog.

"They are upon us," said Bindbuilder. "What orders, my Princess?"

Chapter 50

My Kingdom for a Boat

The end is most often where it is least expected and so near the beginning that it cannot be separated, let alone can it be anticipated.

From all points of the compass, armed pirates accompanied by musket-toting Fishals, crowded onto the high bank of the canal and formed a circle around the woman, the Wolfkind, and the dog.

"Hide yourself and flee," Ann ordered Esau.

"Not this time, my lady," snarled the dog as he crouched and prepared to do battle.

The encircling enemy grew nearer as the Fishals, apparently intent on saving ammunition, lowered their muskets to fix bayonets. Only the Princess' sword and the Wolfkind's axe seemed to keep the murderous mob temporarily at bay.

"Canst swim?" asked Bindbuilder.

"Yes why—?"

"Thy dog also?"

"Of course, but—"

Abruptly and without another word, Bindbuilder grasped the Princess in one meaty paw and Esau in the other and flung them both over his shoulders and into the flooding canal. The Fishals rushed forward seeking to aim muskets as the woman and the dog drifted downstream in the grip of the flow. But Bindbuilder swung his axe and mowed down the would-be shooters. He swung again in a broad arc and another rank of attackers was decapitated before the rest overwhelmed the snarling Wolfkind.

Treading water far below, Ann still held her sword, but released the cumbersome weapon as the flow threatened to sink her. Emanating from far above, she could just hear Bindbuilder's defiant howl before the cascading water swallowed the sound and propelled her downstream. The surging current pulled the Princess under for a moment and, when she next surfaced, she saw Esau paddling toward her.

"Over your shoulder, Princess!" the dog sputtered. Ann reached back with one arm and then the other as hands grappled to seize her until the guards managed to pull her ashore. Esau scrambled after her and the pair sat on the bank and watched two, then three, then a dozen pirates try to swim across the canal only to disappear in the swift current.

"Sailors make such poor swimmers," said the commodore as he offered the Princess a dry blanket and another tunic. "Shoot that one, if you please, lieutenant."

"Yes, sir," said Collin. "Sergeant Janus, if you please."

The sergeant steadied himself against a tree trunk and took aim. The musket ball rocketed across the canal and caught the floundering pirate midstream.

"That'll discourage the others," smiled the lieutenant.

"You disobeyed my orders," said Ann.

"Not so, great Princess," grinned the commodore. "We were retreating as ordered but doing so slowly."

"You did not specify the pace," added the lieutenant.

"Hmm," said the Princess.

"That word again," said Ruth as she alighted nearby.

"So, you're too virtuous to ride a horse now?" the Princess asked.

"I took a moment to fly along with the leading edge of the flood," the witch continued her report, ignoring the Princess' jibe. "The flow is moving apace and will shortly reach the harbor. Our mortar river will soon be a reality

"I imagine the pirates will have something to say about that." The Princess frowned, trying to recall if her elaborate plan had made any provision for the enemy discovering the flooding canal before the mortars were in place.

"I'll warrant you're correct about the pirates," the lieutenant agreed.

"Agreed," said the commodore. "In fact, as each moment passes, I wonder that the brigands and their foul Fishal masters haven't already come streaming along this side of the canal. It is as if they are—"

"Stuck on the other side," the Princess, the commodore, and the lieutenant said simultaneously.

"I'll have a look," said Ruth. The witch was up again, only to return moments later with her report. "Our pesky adversaries have made a mistake. Their encampment is far away, on the distant bank. They cannot easily cross the canal or bring their heavy cannon to bear since the top of the dam is too steep to reach and too narrow besides." She began laughing and nearly choked before she regained her equilibrium. "And—and being unaware of our intentions to make further use of the waterway—they are abandoning the effort to cross and breaking camp to march around the lake in order to attack us here. An honest mistake, since they presume that the distance around the lake must needs be a shorter trip than trying to march the length of the canal. But, by the time they realize the futility of their lake strategy, our mortars will be in place to greet them. Your orders, My Princess?"

"Never interrupt your enemy—" the Princess grinned.

"—when he is making a mistake," the commodore grinned also as he finished the well-known military maxim.

As Ann and the others stood apart in conversation, the marksman assigned to watch for and dispatch anyone attempting to swim the canal appeared at Lieutenant Collin's elbow.

"Sir, begging your pardon, sir," asked Sergeant Janus.

"I need you at your shooting post by the canal's edge," said his peeved lieutenant.

"That's just it, sir," the sergeant explained. "I might could stay there all day and shoot the blighters as they come, but they must have cannons. And what if they drag one of them machines up top there. My bullets are no match fer pumpkin-sized round shot. The wind of the ball alone would end my existence, begging your pardon."

"A fair assessment," said Collin. "But you're forgetting the slope."

"The slope, sir?"

"All approaches to the opposite bank are profoundly steep. No chance of the enemy dragging a cannon to any bearing point which will touch us here. Which is why the enemy is pulling up stakes and marching all the blessed way around Deep Lake. Do you see what I mean?"

"I do, sir," said the sergeant. "And I know now why those of you which went to war college have earned the chops to wear the brass and silver."

"Very good," said Collin. "To your position, please."

"With pleasure and yes, sir," said the sergeant as, following a brisk salute, the marksman returned to his post.

"Well done," Commodore Dell commended his fellow officer. "Not many superiors would have taken the trouble to explain the situation to a lower rank."

"I'm right in what I told my sergeant, ain't I?"

"You've made precisely the calculated guess I myself have made," Dell agreed. "If the enemy were able to bring cannon to bear, they'd have done so already rather than attacking with pedestrian pirates and foot soldiers."

"Let's hope it's a good guess," said the lieutenant.

"Let's pray so," suggested the commodore.

While the lieutenant and the commodore plotted strategy and organized their men, Ann pulled Ruth aside. "Our enemy's folly is our chance to enter the lake and retrieve the cup. They will be far too busy tramping around the lake to notice us."

"Should we not wait for the mortars?" the witch frowned.

"Time is our enemy. El is fading. And my powers are fading with him. We must go now," insisted the Princess.

"The lake is lower, but far from empty, so we'll need a boat to reach the deepest point," said Ruth. "Unless you intend to swim that far. I could fly there alone, but I haven't the strength or skill to carry you, let alone you and the dog."

"Esau is coming with us to retrieve the cup?" asked the Princess. "Since when?"

"Two vessels of Wolfkind blood are better than one, no?" smiled Ruth as the dog approached them. "Besides it is a pledge between us."

"There is a serviceable boat at the Wolfkind's secret cottage," said Esau. "I saw it there whilst I was invisibly dangling from the furry giant's paw."

"I love it when a plan comes together," said Ann. "First, we will pray brave Bindbuilder's soul to Velyn. And then, El forgive us, we must hurry forth to steal his boat."

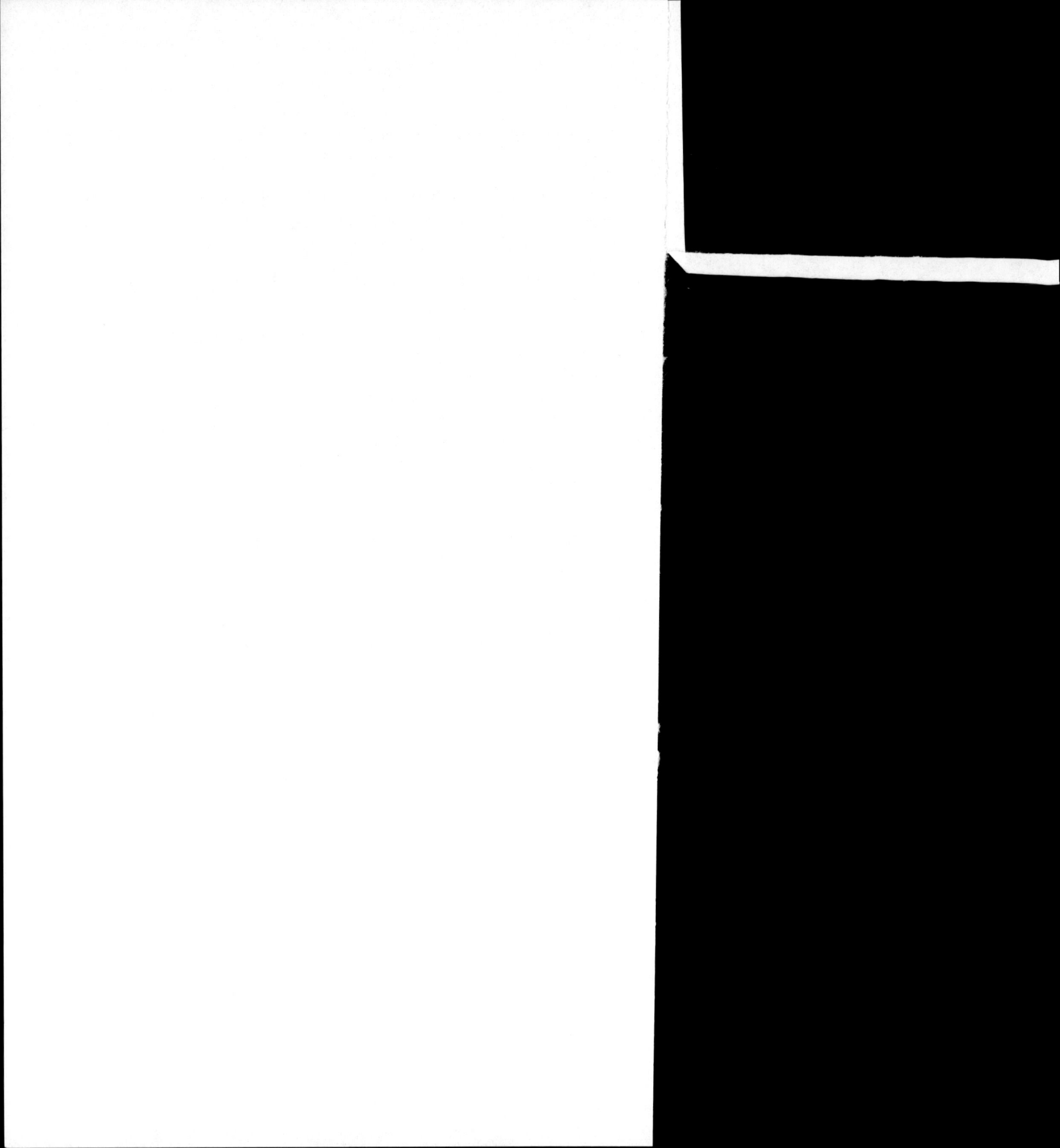

Chapter 51

Sleigh Ride

If you must separate in battle, go not alone but take with you on your right and left hand those for whom you would die and those who would die for thee. Then, having separated, continue to pray until thy force is whole again.

Three guards, including Janus, the sharp-shooting sergeant, were left under the lieutenant's command to watch the canal in case the pirates persisted in their efforts to cross the flood. The commodore and two guards were dispatched to ride to the unoccupied lakeside. Their mission was to discover the best place to launch the boat, while also keeping watch on pirate forces working their way around the far end of Deep Lake. Ruth returned aloft and sped toward the harbor to report the pirates' position and hasten the barges.

While others took up their various posts, Ann and the remaining guards rapidly returned to the woods with Esau leading them to the Wolfkind hideaway. Knowing that any boat belonging to the huge Wolfkind would itself be huge, the Princess estimated that at least eight stout men would be needed to lug the vessel from the forest to the lake. Fortunately, the hideaway was nearer the lake than Ann guessed and, more fortunate still, the place was situated at the crest of a tall grassy knoll.

Trust a Wolfkind to choose a defensible spot which overlooks the surrounding countryside, she thought. *How we shall miss his warrior skills.*

As the boat team rushed up the slope, the Princess was pleased to notice that the knoll was covered in a velvety layer of smooth grass and completely free of rocks and stones.

We will only need carry the boat to the crest of this hill, she thought. *Then from that convenient perch we can glide the entire way to Deep Lake like children sliding down a snowy mountain.*

"It will be a breeze of a descent," Esau agreed.

Joining the guards at the hideaway, the Princess and the dog discovered the Wolfkind boat was indeed huge and much larger than she imagined.

"This encumbrance, sir dog," she chided Esau. "Seems less a boat than a landlocked frigate."

"Truly, we shall break our backs getting this thing to the lake," observed one of the burly guards assigned to carry the unwieldy vessel.

The Princess was about to explain her sliding plan when the boat seemed to suddenly rise of its own volition. As everyone backed away and stood amazed, the boat turned over until its keel faced the sky. Then it hovered well above the ground and began to drift toward the hill.

"Make haste," said a familiar voice from beneath the levitating boat. "And best if thou bring along the oars or must I do all the work?"

How? Ann sent Bindbuilder the question in the voice of the mind. *We thought you dead. We have prayed you to Velyn.*

"Truly, I would have had ample time to go to Velyn and back again had I relied on thee to rescue me," shouted Bindbuilder aloud. "Hast forgotten the breadth of Wolfkind power?" he chided Ann. Then, as if to emphasize his point, the giant Wolfkind appeared in a puff of vapor. Casting off his invisibility, Bindbuilder carried the boat to the edge of the crest, flipped it over, and waited for the others to catch up.

"A neat trick," said Esau as he ran beside the Princess. "Draw the enemy in and disappear—I taught the lad all he knows."

There was room in the boat for everyone, including Bindbuilder.

"Mind those oars," he roared at the men who came straggling up out of breath. "I was weeks carving those from neighboring pines. Hold on, if you please, I have launched this craft many times, but not with such fragile cargo." He pushed off and the huge boat careened down the hill.

At first the non-Wolfkind occupants were silent. Then they uttered a few fearful noises. Eventually, they surrendered to the thrill of the ride and laughed aloud like a gaggle of excited children sledding down an endless mound of snow. For his part, Bindbuilder concentrated on navigating the speeding boat, sitting amidships, leaning right, or left, as needed to keep it on a true course.

Ruth was returning from the harbor when she looked down and saw the occupied boat streaking across the slick green grass. Taking in the scene below, the witch saw Ann laughing and cavorting with the others and was loath to descend and impart to the Princess the heavy news she bore. Instead, she trailed along, keeping the boat in sight as it rocketed toward the lake. When she saw clearly that it would reach the water, she sped ahead, landed next to the commodore, and hastily shared her news.

Seconds later, the boat and its occupants sped past Ruth and the startled commodore.

"Water, ho!" shouted the foremost guard as, without stopping, the boat skimmed neatly over the lake's sandy beach and out onto the broad surface of Deep Lake.

Chapter 52

A Farewell

Fair news travels at a leisurely pace, arriving in its own good time. Bad news falls like a blow on the ears of its unsuspecting audience.

It is a testimony to the camaraderie among men in war, or perhaps a commentary on the immaturity of men who have recently relived the childhood fantasy of sliding down a never-ending hill. Whatever the cause of their disinclination, the Princess experienced much difficulty in convincing the guards to leave the boat so the quest could proceed.

At last, the guards were put ashore, and the questing party boarded. Bindbuilder held the boat in place while the commodore, the Princess, the dog, and the witch took their places. Then the stout Wolfkind took the oars and cast off.

The men left behind were piqued at first. Then the realization of the deadly reality of the quest returned to them and they grew inconsolable. Soon each man who remained on shore fell to his knees and began to pray. They prayed for Ruth and her brave mission. They were astonished that the girl had volunteered to sacrifice herself to save her deity and distressed that the boat was bearing Ruth to her death. Unable to give voice to their grief, the guards pantomimed their affection, pretending to pull their hearts from their chests and reaching their trembling hands toward the boat.

So touched was Ruth by their sadness, she rose from the boat and flew back to the lakeside where the redeemed witch embraced each man and accepted their prayers. Then she kissed each forehead and bade the men a final farewell. While Ruth comforted the men, the tireless Bindbuilder continued rowing until he had reached such a distance that the witch was obliged to fly quite far to return to the boat. Alighting, she immediately retreated to the bow where she sat alone with her head down as the boat glided across the placid waters of Deep Lake. Much time passed before Ruth stood and returned to sit among her companions.

"Of all the difficult things I have ever done," she said aloud. "Those moments on shore among those grieving men—I—" The witch looked at Ann, but immediately dropped her gaze and suppressed her thoughts. The Princess and the others would believe that she found her moments ashore with the guards too painful to recall. In truth, Ruth had decided to withhold another matter—to repress what she'd learned when she flew to the harbor. Trusting her instincts, the witch would keep from the Princess the sad news that her wounded mate lay stricken and fighting for his life. Her concern was both emotional and practical. Not only did she desire to shield the Princess from worry, she wished also to avoid disturbing the quest at such a critical juncture. If they survived, there would be time enough to share what she knew, but for the time being Ruth found she had no words.

The party grew silent and soon the world also turned uncharacteristically quiet. The only sound was the rhythmic squeak of the oarlocks as Bindbuilder rowed steadily through the water.

"Do you sense it?" the Wolfkind asked as he rowed. "With each stroke, I feel El fading and Death growing stronger and ever nearer."

"I feel it," said Ruth.

"As do I," said Ann.

"And I," added Esau.

"I feel it also," said Commodore Dell, his voice thick with emotion.

"We are here," announced Bindbuilder and he shipped the oars.

Chapter 53

Facing Death

When far from shore, wood on water may dance like a kite on a breeze. Imperceptible tricks of wind and current conspire, stirring an otherwise inanimate boat to drift and writhe like a thing possessed.

So it was that Bindbuilder's huge boat bobbed on the surface of Deep Lake. The boat was not anchored. The lake was too deep for that. Each breeze—no matter how slight—caused the boat to pivot to starboard and back to port again. Back and forth the vessel wandered, like a waterborne metronome, as if the stern was free to meander while the prow was held in place by an unseen hand. Then the breeze ceased, and, despite the calm, it grew exceedingly cold.

"How will this proceed?" the commodore broke the silence.

"One of us must go down for the cup," Ann's tone was matter of fact, as if she were describing an everyday event—as mundane as slicing an apple or drawing water from a well.

"And bear the vexing item hither," added Ruth.

"And death will pursue the thief," said Esau.

"To retrieve the cup?" asked the commodore.

"To collect on his bargain," said Ann. "The cup is a token. With it and the end of the Wolfkind line, Death will claim El and decree a barren world."

"As it is written," a voice boomed from beneath the lake. Surges of pulsating volume agitated the water, vibrated the sky, and rolled outward to reach the world beyond the shoreline. "Here is a failed quest! So cunning to gather in this holy place all the scraps which remain of the Wolfkind race! Though I cannot kill these puny vestiges, I can hold them here until my brigand force arrives to smite them! A happy retribution! Well-played, my daughter. Well done, my loyal Ahoo."

"Master," said the witch in a voice which was exceedingly strange and seemed also to penetrate air, water, and earth. "Withhold your praise, for I have not delivered all the Wolfkind blood. The rib-man lives. Thus, I have failed."

"Not so, child," said Death. "That doomed race will end as I have foretold. As for Destin, the one whom these here-assembled call Seth, that creature will not survive the harbor—"

The dark lord's declaration pierced Ann's heart. Before Death could utter another word regarding Seth's fate, the rebellious Princess howled sharply, dove into the icy water, and swam toward the lake bottom. Defying Death, she submerged rapidly—her body slicing through the depths with powerful and angry strokes. Her loving mate was threatened so she swam madly, heedless of the consequences.

Astonished by the Princess' unexpected fury, perplexed by her unanticipated strength, Death hesitated. Before the shadowy ruler could react, Ann reached the lakebed, seized the cup, and whirled back toward the surface with the dark lord's protestations ringing in her ears.

"Blasphemy! Heresy! Sacrilege! A foul! A palpable foul!" roared Death as he churned the lake, took a watery form, and reached his icy hand toward the surfacing Princess.

Ann broke through the waves ahead of Death's tardy grasp and, with a heave of uncanny accuracy, threw the cup to Ruth. Sensing that the Princess no longer held the cup, Death passed over Ann and reached toward the witch, gripping Ruth's wrist with supernatural force.

"Traitorous harlot!" Death roared. "Would that I could slay thee!"

"A wish which I shall willingly grant," said Ruth.

Suddenly the lake, which had been writhing and foaming with Death's angst, grew calm.

"I am curious," said Death as his altered demeanor condensed his immenseness into temporary form. His chosen shape was that of a powerful giant who stood on the lake bottom and towered over the boat, but his tone sounded almost affable. "Dost propose a bargain?"

"An amazing bargain which exceeds anything found in scripture," said Ruth.

"Have a care," said Death. "Even a witch of the old-world should not make such an irreverent, not to mention preposterous claim—"

"Pardon me for interrupting such a fantastically powerful angel as yourself," began Ruth, "but I know how keenly you enjoy magic. Might I take a moment to show you a trick?"

"A trick?" asked Death in a tone which suggested sudden interest, although he did not loosen his grip on the witch's wrist. "Dost think there is a trick which I have not yet seen?"

"I would not deign to show you an ordinary trick, My Majesty."

"You have said 'My Majesty.' That is a grievous mistake on your part. Such a phrase suggests reverence. That is a dangerous error for one such as yourself who cannot die. Are you accepting my dominion over you? Or is this seeming oversight part of the trick?"

If Death can be said to physically relax and ponder, that is what Ruth had compelled Death to do as she engaged the dark angel in calculated conversation. The witch was improvising, but also confident. As she spoke—each word coming to her as needed—it was as though she was playing a well-rehearsed part. In her innermost thoughts—deep insights which she kept even from the shadowy presence who held her fast—she recognized that El must be prompting her. Her deity may be failing, but he yet guided her. Trusting El's guidance, she would faithfully play her part and pray the others would follow her lead.

While Death turned his attention fully to the witch, Ann had been treading water as she sought to govern her emotions. Mourning the possible loss of her mate, she'd been on the verge of challenging Death to personal combat—

an impetuous and foolish whim which would most certainly have hastened the demise of the Wolfkind race.

"You must stay alive," Ruth had cautioned her. A dim echo of that admonition reached the Princess.

El? Ann asked.

Stay alive, came the echo. *Trust in Ruth and stay alive. Seth may be imperiled, but the remaining threads of Wolfkind must endure. Only tenacity will prevail. A faint heart will lose the day. You must cast off the hurt and persevere. You must trust your faith.*

Shaking off her anguish, the determined Princess grew suddenly calm as she eased herself back into the boat and sent an urgent message to Bindbuilder.

We must master our anger. Ann spoke to the Wolfkind in the voice of the mind. *Your instinct and mine is to fight. But El wants us alive. To save our race and safeguard the world, we must trust Ruth and prepare our retreat.*

Bindbuilder nodded. He had shipped his oars, but—upon receiving his kinswoman's thoughts—he eased the blades back into the water. *With fortune,* the huge creature responded, *our Wolfkind seed might yet escape this trap.*

No sooner did Bindbuilder convey this thought than he and Ann ceased to move, as vigilant Death—sensing treachery—immobilized both. In enacting this paralysis, Death lost track of Esau, who had opted for invisibility. Nor did Death extend his precaution to Commodore Dell. The commodore's frail humanity presented no threat and, moreover, one glance at the motionless man convinced the dark lord that the puny mortal was already restrained.

In fact, Dell had, in the presence of Death, been at first frozen with fear. But the instant Death chose to ignore him, the commodore recovered himself. "Be guided by the younger woman," the King had instructed him.

With Esau unseen and the others incapacitated, the commodore and the witch were alone in the boat. In a twinkling, by design or happenstance, the unlikely pair inherited the mantle of the quest and became the only living creatures left to advance its mission. Dell did not shirk from the weight of his responsibility, and yet he was uncertain of his part. Sitting with his back to Death, the commodore looked to Ruth for direction.

What now? he mouthed the question.

Continuing her conversation with Death, Ruth stared hard at Dell. The commodore returned her gaze and watched intently as the nimble witch formed her free hand into a gesture which she prayed he would recognize. Her right thumb was up with the pointer finger of that hand extended, and the remainder of her digits folded into her palm. She was using her fingers to shape the image of a pistol which she pointed unambiguously at the cup in her left hand. Completing the pantomime, she gave the only mortal in their bobbing boat a significant look—part entreaty, part conspiratorial.

As Ruth held Death's attention while she prattled on about her amazing trick, she and the commodore retained eye contact. Trusting it would work, the witch attempted to address the commodore using the voice of the mind. She sent Dell her thoughts, focusing all the intensity she could muster.

My dear commodore, she began, *if ever you have sought to read another's thoughts, now is the time to exercise that ability. You are,* she told him, *unlikely to miss at this range.*

Something in Dell's expression told her he understood.

Encouraged, Ruth continued to engage Death in conversation. Their words vibrated just outside the commodore's hearing and the dialogue slipped into the background as Dell sought to play his part. Without taking his eyes from Ruth, Dell fingered the saddlebag he'd purloined from Ann's horse. With a barely perceptible motion, he slipped the inconspicuous bag off his shoulder. Easing it down, he let it descend until it rested on the keel. Then, with his eyes firmly fixed on Ruth, the commodore proceeded to do something he had done a thousand times before while wearing a blindfold. It was a game he'd played—a way to pass the time during his lonely student days—and also a personal challenge just to prove it was possible. Now, if he understood Ruth correctly, he would once more complete the blind exercise in order that his deity might live to see another sunrise.

And so, he began.

Without looking and using touch alone, Dell reached carefully down, grasped the hidden pistol, poured gunpowder into the muzzle, and rammed the powder home with the rod. Then he secured a handful of shot and rolled it in wadding, pushed the wadded ball into the muzzle, and primed and cocked the hammer. At last, using the sleeve of his long coat to obscure his motion, he brought the loaded weapon steadily up until the muzzle was level with Ruth and the cup. Catching her eye, Dell nodded, and she abruptly changed her tactic.

"Well, sir," she said aloud to Death, "here is my bargain. I will deliver myself into your hands if you consent to establish a place for my step-father and his companions to dwell."

"You speak of the Limbo?"

"I do," said Ruth.

"The Limbo which was rejected in the Old Agreement betwixt myself and El?"

"The very same," said the witch.

"Schawk, that is old news and cannot be," said Death.

"Because El rejected it?" asked Ruth.

"Because *I forbade it*," corrected Death.

"Hmm," observed Ruth. "Now that El is dying, why not amend your Agreement?"

"To make a place," the dark angel inquired, "for those who die by their own hand?"

"Yes," said the witch.

"Such an amendment would pique El," considered Death.

"Exactly."

"Ha! It will be a final insult to the imperious deity. It is done!" said Death. "Now, child, release my cup that I may drink from it and claim yourself and El as my newest residents."

"If you must," said Ruth. "But it seems to me that you have lost interest in seeing my trick, so I shall deprive you of that pleasure."

"Deprive *me*?" Death roared. "Deny me? Thou shalt not! Let us have your trick, my girl, and be quick about it! My patience is wearing thin!"

"Very well. A moment please, while I prepare." Ruth bowed her head feigning concentration while she glanced to make certain Esau had made his furry countenance properly invisible. She felt the dog climb onto her lap and take the cup's handle in his mouth. With a furtive and cautious movement, she released her own fingers from the cup while Death continued, none-the-wiser, to grip the wrist of her now-empty hand. Then she glanced to see that Dell's aim was truly laid and finally she looked up and said, "This trick is entitled *The Vanishing Vessel*. Have you heard of it?"

"Indeed, I have not," said Death with uncommon interest. But instantly, he grew suspicious. "Pray tell, how means thou the term *vessel*?"

"The term has more than one meaning?" asked Ruth, feigning innocent ignorance.

"Of course, child. Do not toy with me. Thou surely knowest that a vessel can mean either a ship at sea, or crockery, or in some cases a mortal shell. But beware! Swear now that thou dost not mean by the term 'vessel' this sacred Memorian cup *which thou hast in thy hand*. Swear that thou dost not have designs on the cup *thou holdest!* Swear it or I shall tear this boat asunder, leave its occupants to drown, and pull El to my bosom!"

"Lest you do those dreadful things, I do so swear!" said Ruth.

"Swear it fully!" demanded Death, wishing to bind the witch more firmly by compelling her to utter an irrevocable oath

Ruth smiled, for she knew that—with El's holy guidance—she had succeeded in deftly maneuvering the situation to delude Death and deliver her deity's ultimate surprise. So, she took one final look at the commodore, winked, and willingly said, "Upon my death, I swear it."

In a heartbeat, the commodore fired. Delivering a dense cluster of deadly shot, the recoiling pistol found its mark. Lethal at close range, the volley encompassed the brave witch and the troublesome cup and the invisible dog. At that instant, El was released from the Bargain.

"Row!" shouted Ann as she and Bindbuilder abruptly regained mobility in the wake of Dell's well-laid shot.

The Wolfkind boat heeled round and battled the waves in search of safety. Propelled by its powerful rower, the boat surged away from the confrontation with Death. Perhaps bridled by the sudden turn of events, the dark lord did not pursue them.

Having been fated to fire his lethal shot and burdened by a heavy heart, Dell hurled the pistol overboard. Sitting in the stern, lost in his sorrow, the grieving mortal was first to hear the distant thuds of loosed cannons. Thinking the sound signaled the arrival of the mortars and wondering that the anticipated weapons had arrived so quickly, the commodore looked skyward just as the first of a blizzard of plunging projectiles slammed into the boat.

They hadn't counted on the Fishal cannons or the horse-drawn caissons the enemy had employed to drag the big guns around the lake until their unsuspecting targets were in range. When the enemy gunners unleashed their deadly bombardment, the Wolfkind boat was reduced to splinters and brave Ann, stalwart Bindbuilder, and loyal Commodore Dell disappeared in a fury of churning destruction.

A league away from the carnage, left behind, and clinging to life, Ruth sank like a stone. Held in the icy embrace of Deep Lake, the injured witch drifted downward while fragments of the Memorian cup suspended about her. Then she felt once more the grip of Death upon her wrist.

"What are you playing at, witch?" demanded Death.

"El is not coming, lord. I have come in his stead."

"The Bargain—!" Death mouthed his protest.

"Farewell," smiled Ruth as her worldly body dissolved, leaving Death to grasp at an insubstantial swirl of empty bubbles.

"This," thundered Death, "is not the Bargain!"

Death's displeasure roiled the waters of Deep Lake, shook the shoreline, and echoed through the forest. Nature paused. The sky and the wind paused. Even the wicked pirates and the evil Fishals, even these shameless villains paused. The enemy had been celebrating their apparent victory—crowing over having vanquished the quest. But their celebration was premature, and it was also short-lived.

Onboard the nearest barge, Provisional Commodore Brightlamp and his men also felt the world suspend.

"What is it, sir?" asked the gunner's mate.

"The end I fear," said Brightlamp.

"Your orders?"

"Commence our bombardment. Fire every mortar and fire at will. Then we shall scan the killing field for flags of truce."

"And if the pirates don't surrender?"

"We'll keep firing until we run out of powder and shot."

"Or until we run out of pirates," suggested the gunner's mate.

"Until then," confirmed Brightlamp.

Epilogue

For centuries, scholars have debated whether Death might have said something at the exact moment when he realized that Ruth—whom he thought to be a raptor placed among lambs—had proven to be a treacherous sparrow. The scribes do not record Death's words. Perhaps he was speechless.

In any event, the New Chronicles are silent as to what was said. On the other hand, the writing does provide a vivid description of the actions which everyone—including bewildered Death—took at that fateful hour, on that fateful day, so long ago.

In fact, the great-great granddaughter of Ann the Bold is about to recite that very tale as she practices the ritual of her coming-of-age ceremony. Watch now as young Ann Stone Bride the Fourth arrives at the sanctuary. Not wishing to be late for her final rehearsal, she has come straight from her traditional apprenticeship at the royal iron works. Relinquishing her weighty burden, she smiles as her religious instructors struggle to take the load.

"What have you fashioned this time, child?" asks Brother Superior Clax.

"Not a craven idol, we trust," adds Brother Ashlar.

"I have cast an angel," is young Ann's reply. "For our garden."

"Hmm," says Clax. "Time is passing, child. We have much to do. This way and hurry."

Though heir to the Middlemount throne, today young Ann is merely a royal novice who, like any other adolescent neophyte, must recite her lesson. Shepherding the princess-in-training, Clax watches to make certain Ann wets her fingers at the fount. When his pupil passes behind the screen, the Brother Superior turns to see his impetuous comrade loosening the ropes which entwine Ann's latest iron sculpture. The young woman has displayed a knack at the lost-cast foundry and Ashlar cannot resist peeking beneath the canvas shroud. Clax moves swiftly to admonish his assistant, but before the pudgy man can waddle down the marbled hall, Ashar unfastens the shroud and expels an exclamation.

"Ah," Ashlar exclaims.

Enchanted, both priests gaze tenderly at the exquisite effigy of a young human girl posed in reverent prayer.

"A masterpiece," coos Clax as he admires, with an appraising eye, the smoothly rendered face with its pious mouth, curly locks, and angelic expression.

"Have you ever seen such perfection?" gushes Asher, his hand carefully fingering the work's impossibly gossamer wings.

Ensconced behind the sanctuary screen, Ann is smiling, for her keen hearing has informed her that the otherwise incorruptible priests have yielded to temptation. How could they resist an opportunity to examine her little angel? Continuing to grin as she anticipates the joy of her recitation, young Ann removes her tunic, dons the ceremonial robe, and threads the nestafil onto her bared arm. Moderating her breathing, she intones a prayer, emerges from behind the lacquered screen, and gestures broadly to set the stage.

Let us listen to her recitation, as we can be certain El is listening, even as you read these lines:

"And, as for the Memorian Cup which was coveted by Death as token of his Bargain with the Lord El, it came to pass that this self-same cup did slip on that day from the grasp of the Blessed Ruth. And it did suspend in the very air above Deep Lake, held there—unknown to Death—by the Sacred Dog

Esau. And the cup did hover within sight of Sainted Dell the Commander of Waters, who did smite the cup into a million-million pieces.

"And hear how, on that fateful day, Death did bay with rage and did carry away with him the Blessed Ruth and with her the Sacred Dog and with him the Sainted Dell. But fear not and rejoice ye, for in this brave exchange, the three heroes passed to the New Dream. And, also, was the Bargain broken and Lord El instantly restored to his health and throne. Whereupon lord El sent to rain upon the vile Fishals and their evil pirate hoards the penalty of a thousand falling stars. And thus were Memora and the island's besieged peoples delivered from their oppressors."

Young Ann the Fourth pauses now to survey her audience to make certain that both priests are listening. Their brotherly smiles are encouraging. The nestafil is tightly wound around her dark hairy forearm as she gestures to pantomime the changing of the scene.

"And it came to pass also that the Dreamers, having arrived at the Isle of Redhackle in the company of the redeemed men of Fishal, did populate and restore that once-burned island and raise fine sheep and fine horses and bring forth generations of people who taught and preached and practiced peace.

"And the islands of Memora and Redhackle having been restored, there strode forth Ann Stone Bride the Bold, the Princess of a Thousand Tomorrows, and in her company the resurrected Seth. And likewise came the forces of Brightlamp the Yeoman of Waters and his brother officer Sander the Lucky, together with the Fearsome Fleet of Deliverance. And likewise came their right-arm, Bindbuilder the Mighty, and also Good King John, the Elder of Memora. Therefore, did all this host together descend, with the wrath of El, upon the invaders of Middlemount and restore thereby the Wolfkind race and the Kingdom thereof in all its eternal and majestic glory.

"And, thus, were all prayers answered, for Death's dark design did not come to pass. Amen."

About the Author

Donald Paul Benjamin is an American novelist who specializes in cozy mysteries and high fantasy. His writing includes elements of romance and humor. He also writes about Western Colorado history. He is the author of the *The Four Corners Mystery Series*, *The Great Land Fantasy Series* and the *Surface Creek Life Series*.

In addition to his writing career, he also works as a freelance journalist, cartoonist, and photographer. A U.S. Army veteran, he served three years as a military journalist and illustrator, including a tour in Korea. Trained as a teacher of reading, he has worked with a wide variety of learners from those attending kindergarten to college students. He also holds an advanced degree in college administration. He lived in Arizona and worked in higher education for more than three decades before retiring in 2014.

He now lives in Cedaredge, a small town on the Western Slope of Colorado, where he hikes and fishes in the surrounding wilderness. He and his wife, Donna Marie, operate **Elevation Press**, a service which helps independent authors self-publish their works (see info on the following page).

Email: elevationpressbooks@gmail.com
Studio Phone: 970-856-9891
Mail: D.P. Benjamin, P.O. Box 603, Cedaredge, CO 81413
Website: https://benjaminauthor.com/
Visit the Author's Facebook Page under: D.P. Benjamin Author
Instagram: https://www.instagram.com/benjaminnovelist/

The Four Corners Mystery Series
- Book 1: *The Road to Lavender*
- Book 2: *A Lavender Wedding*
- Book 3: *Spirits of Grand Lake*
- Book 4: *The War Nickel*
- Book 5: *Rare Earth*
- Book 6: *Walking Horse Ranch*
- Book 7: *Lavender Farewell*

The Great Land Fantasy Series
- Book 1: *Stone Bride*
- Book 2: *Iron Angel*
- Book 3: *Redhackle*
- Book 4: *Bindbuilder*
- Book 5: *Nachtfalke*
- Book 6: *Isochronuous*
- Book 7: *Ruth and Esau*

Surface Creek Life Series
- Book 1: *A Surface Creek Christmas: Winter Tales 1904–1910*

In paperback or Kindle on **amazon.com** and **barnesandnoble.com**.

ELEVATION PRESS

Your One-Stop Publishing Option

Established 1976

As an independent publisher, we are actively seeking authors who desire to publish their work. For such individuals, we provide design and formatting services. Starting with an author's Microsoft Word document, we produce a book cover and interior pages which the author can submit to a traditional printer or to a print-on-demand service, such as Kindle Direct Publishing (KDP) or IngramSpark. Depending on the complexity of your book, we may also be able to convert the print PDF into a reflowable e-book.

We have successfully formatted a variety of published books including memoirs, children's books, novels, and works of non-fiction.

For more information, visit our website:

elevation-press-books.com

Made in the USA
Coppell, TX
26 October 2023